Praise for *New York Times* bestselling author
JAYNE ANN KRENTZ

Writing as Jayne Castle

"With her typical offbeat humor and flair, Castle takes a pair of power-ful, unmatchable protagonists, sets them down in her innovative, syn-ergistic world of St. Helens, and gives them a mystery to solve, villains to outwit, and a passion to explore."

—*Library Journal*

"A fun, fast frolic on another metaphysical plane! The characters are fun and sexy. . . . A romance that will link your senses to the primitive side!"

—*The Literary Times*

"Classic sharp wit and unrivaled skill for creating captivating charac-ters."

—*Booklist*

"A scintillating foray into love in another place and time [with] the heady charm of a great romance."

—*Romantic Times*

Writing as Jayne Ann Krentz

"One of the hottest writers in romance today."

—*USA Today*

"Krentz at her best . . . with the snappy dialogue that has become her trademark and a cast of characters you want to know personally."

—Sandra Brown, *New York Times* bestselling author

"The phenomenal Jayne Ann Krentz once again delivers one of her patented storytelling gems. . . . Another guaranteed top-notch read."

—*Romantic Times*

"Absolutely sizzles."

—*The Columbia (SC) State*

"The inimitable Jayne Ann Krentz [is] always a consistent delight. . . . A winner."

—*Rave Reviews*

"Krentz deftly mingles chilling danger and simmering sexual tension."
—*Booklist*

"Fast, steamy, and wildly entertaining."

—*Publishers Weekly*

"Psychic thrills and sharp wit."

—*Chicago Tribune*

"Entertaining and delightful . . . This is romantic suspense at its most enjoyable, enhanced by Krentz's trademark humor and quirky characters."
—*Library Journal*

"Spicy . . . Jayne Ann Krentz is one of the most talented authors writing romance fiction today."

—*Midwest Book Review*

"[Krentz] scores with a sexy thriller."

—*Kirkus Reviews*

"A welcome escape into art-world intrigue . . . A surprise ending caps this delightful mystery from a seasoned pro."

—*People*

"One of the feistiest, most memorable heroines . . . Jayne Ann Krentz at her very best. Pure entertainment."
—Susan Elizabeth Phillips, *New York Times* bestselling author

"A suspenseful and satisfying story that strikes a deep, human chord."
—Patricia Matthews, *New York Times* bestselling author

JAYNE
CASTLE

AMARYLLIS

Pocket Books
New York   London   Toronto   Sydney   New Delhi

Pocket Books
An Imprint of Simon & Schuster, Inc.
1230 Avenue of the Americas
New York, NY 10020

This book is a work of fiction. Any references to historical events, real people, or real places are used fictitiously. Other names, characters, places, and events are products of the author's imagination, and any resemblance to actual events or places or persons, living or dead, is entirely coincidental.

This Pocket Books paperback edition August 2021

POCKET and colophon are registered trademarks of Simon & Schuster, Inc.

For information about special discounts for bulk purchases, please contact Simon & Schuster Special Sales at 1-866-506-1949 or business@simonandschuster.com.

The Simon & Schuster Speakers Bureau can bring authors to your live event. For more information or to book an event, contact the Simon & Schuster Speakers Bureau at 1-866-248-3049 or visit our website at www.simonspeakers.com.

Interior design by Lexy Alemao

Manufactured in the United States of America

10   9   8   7   6   5   4   3   2   1

ISBN 978-1-9821-7879-6
ISBN 978-1-4516-2401-4 (ebook)

AMARYLLIS

Chapter 1

"Damn it, I don't need a conscience, Miss Lark." Lucas Trent eyed the woman seated behind the desk with grim determination. "I need a security expert."

"Our company believes that the two are not incompatible," the lady said coolly.

She was starting to irritate him already, Lucas thought. And it was unlikely that the situation would improve. Unfortunately, he needed her.

Her name was Amaryllis Lark and she worked for Psynergy, Inc. Lucas knew that, while he could do business with her, she was potentially very dangerous.

But you'd never know it to look at her, he thought.

She had green-gold eyes and hair the color of dark amber. Approximately thirty seconds after meeting her, Lucas concluded that she was the most interesting thing he had encountered since he had blundered into a cave full of mysterious relics in the Western Islands.

He was baffled by his own reaction. It was obvious that Amaryllis was, in her own way, as alien to him as the ancient artifacts. She was prim, proper, and downright prissy. She looked as if she could have modeled for a statue of one of the heroic, determined, and excruciatingly upright founders.

The expression in her green-gold eyes was perceptive, intelligent, and vaguely disapproving. The rich, thick, amber hair was bound in a prim knot at the nape of her neck. The neatly buttoned jacket of a conservative little business suit concealed whatever curves were beneath the fabric. A discreetly flared, calf-length skirt hid the rest of what appeared to be a slender figure and, judging by the trim ankles, nicely shaped legs.

Lucas had a strong suspicion that Amaryllis was stuffed to her pretty eyeballs with a host of old-fashioned, boring, and very inconvenient virtues.

Definitely not his type.

But that was not the worst of it. He was accustomed to taking challenges in his stride, after all. He might have persuaded himself to tackle this one, too, if it had not been for the fact that she worked for Psynergy, Inc.

Lucas exhaled deeply and forced himself to concentrate on the reason he was here in Amaryllis's extremely well organized, highly functional office.

He got to his feet and planted his hands on the unnaturally neat desk and leaned forward just far enough to ensure that he had the lady's full attention.

"I was told that Psynergy, Inc. was one of the best companies in the business."

"I assure you that it is, Mr. Trent." Amaryllis's feathery brows snapped together above her very straight nose. "It is also a company that maintains the highest professional standards. We do not take just any sort of case, and that is why I am obliged to ask certain questions. If you don't care to answer, that is your affair. But don't expect me to work with you without first ascertaining that you are a suitable client."

"Suitable?" Lucas set his teeth and willed his simmering irritation to stay below full boil. "I'm Lucas Trent, president of Lodestar Exploration. I've got unlimited lines of credit with every bank in New Seattle. I can call the mayor's office and get Her Honor to vouch for me. Hell, I can call the city-state governor's office for that matter. Damn it, what more do you need to know?"

"I know who you are, Mr. Trent." Something that might have been genuine excitement sparked in her eyes. "Everyone in New Seattle knows who you are." She lowered her gaze and made a small show of shuffling the forms that lay on the desk in front of her. "I'm quite satisfied that you can afford our fees."

She was blushing.

Lucas was stunned by the sight of the unmistakable tint of pink on Amaryllis's high cheekbones. The prissy little founder was actually blushing.

He looked down at his big, scarred, calloused hands, which were still flattened on the desk. He was suddenly very conscious of Amaryllis's elegant, neatly manicured fingers. The clear polish on her short nails caught his eye. He noticed that she was not wearing a wedding ring.

Lucas gave his brain a mental shake in an effort to override his basic masculine response to Amaryllis's blush. He did not date women who were endowed with her particular psychic abilities. He had enough problems.

Amaryllis was a highly trained prism. She had no true paranormal talents, as Lucas did, but she had the unique ability—and the professional training—to help people with psychic powers focus their otherwise erratic and unpredictable gifts.

It was a fact of life that even the strongest talent was helpless to utilize his or her abilities for more than a few seconds without the assistance of an equally strong prism.

The world being what it was, the economics of supply and demand pretty much guaranteed that powerful, well-trained prisms enjoyed a generous annual income.

"If you're satisfied that I can pay my bills," Lucas said, "why all the questions? I thought you folks were running a business here."

"The matter of our fees is only one of the issues with which we here at Psynergy, Inc. are concerned." The blush faded from Amaryllis's cheeks. She gave Lucas a gratingly professional smile. "It's not even the most important matter, as I'm sure you're well aware."

"Yeah. Sure." Lucas stifled a groan and straightened away from the desk. He flexed his hands as he stalked across the small office to the window. He had known this would not be easy. He came to a halt and gazed unseeingly at the busy street three floors below.

It was midmorning and the city was humming. The discordant

melody produced by traffic, dockside activity, and people bustling to and fro was a pleasant tune in Lucas's opinion. It had the lively beat of a booming economy and the exuberant lilt of a community that looked to the future with anticipation. New Seattle had not always sung such an enthusiastic song. Nor had its sister city-states, New Portland and New Vancouver.

A large percentage of the colonists who had been stranded on St. Helens shortly after the planet had been discovered two hundred years earlier had been from a region on Earth known as the Pacific Northwest. When they had found themselves alone, cut off forever from their home world, the settlers had done what colonists had always done down through the ages. They had named their new communities after the cities and towns that they would never see again. Today the city-states of New Seattle, New Portland, and New Vancouver formed a thriving, but still fragile, necklace of civilization along the edge of the western coast of St. Helens's largest continent.

The sophisticated Earth-based technology the colonists had brought with them had disintegrated within months after the newcomers had been stranded. St. Helens had welcomed the new life-forms, but it had refused to accept the alien machines they had depended upon. Rust-proof alloys had turned to dust in a matter of weeks. Plastics that were virtually indestructible on Earth had dissolved in St. Helens's otherwise hospitable atmosphere. In the end, nothing manufactured on the home world had survived. St. Helens had demanded that the newcomers adapt to the local environment or die.

The colonists had adapted, but it had not been easy. They had finally managed to get a toehold on their new world, learned to utilize native metals and materials, but the effort had cost a great deal, including the loss of several generations' worth of science and technology.

The history books informed the descendants of the founders that their modern machines and their science were both primitive by the standards of the home world. But the reality was that the ways of Earth were of academic interest at best to the current generation.

After two centuries of being on their own, no one, with the exception of the members of some obscure religious cults, expected Earth to miraculously rediscover its lost colony.

St. Helens was home and a rich, green world it was. Although a sizable portion of the planet had yet to be explored and mapped, it appeared that the descendants of the colonists constituted the only intelligent life-forms.

The artifacts Lucas had uncovered had caused a great deal of interest but no serious alarm in the academic community. It was obvious that they were very, very old. Most researchers were convinced that they were not native in origin. The consensus of scientific opinion was that the relics were the remains of some ancient spacefaring people who had briefly established an outpost on St. Helens at some point in the distant past. It was clear that whoever they were, those other settlers had long since disappeared or departed. The human population faced no competition.

"Now, then, Mr. Trent," Amaryllis said crisply. "If you still wish to hire a professional, academically trained prism to assist you, let us proceed to the next question."

Lucas grimaced at the unsubtle emphasis she gave to the words *professional* and *trained*. There were untrained, unprofessional prisms available, but it would have been dangerous for him to use one. He was already taking a risk by hiring someone from a reputable agency. Lucas would have cheerfully sold a chunk of his soul to avoid having to use a prism of any kind.

"It's not like I have a hell of a lot of choice, is it?" Lucas glanced back at her over his shoulder. He felt his jaw clench as he made a bid to keep his voice unemotional. "Ask your damn questions."

Amaryllis searched his face, her eyes sharp and altogether too probing. Lucas deliberately made his expression as unreadable as possible. He knew he was good at concealing his thoughts. He'd had a lot of practice.

"Very well." Amaryllis looked down at her notes. "You say this is a security matter?"

"Yes."

"What sort of security issue is involved?"

"Corporate security."

"I understand that, Mr. Trent," she said patiently. "I'm asking you to be more specific."

"All right. To put it bluntly, someone I trust is selling me out. Is that specific enough for you?" It was astonishing how hard it was to say the words aloud.

Lucas closed one hand into a fist at his side. He turned back to the view of the street. A deep, gnawing pain that was almost physical unfurled inside him. He had been betrayed. It was certainly not the first time, but he never seemed to grow accustomed to the cold sensation he got inside whenever it happened.

The tally was growing, he thought wearily. His wife, Dora. His partner, Jackson Rye. And now his vice president in charge of public relations, Miranda Locking.

He'd never even wanted to establish a public relations department for Lodestar. It had been Jackson Rye's idea. Jackson had had a lot of ideas for Lodestar Exploration.

"I see." Amaryllis sounded surprisingly subdued.

Lucas winced at the unmistakable hint of sympathy he thought he heard in her voice. He reminded himself that expert, full-spectrum prisms had a reputation for being unusually intuitive and perceptive. He would have to watch his step around Amaryllis.

"Someone on my staff is selling proprietary information to one of my competitors," Lucas explained.

"Did you consider contacting the police?"

"I don't want to involve the police because I don't intend to prosecute."

"I understand. A lot of our corporate clients take that approach on security matters. Few of them want the bad publicity they fear would result."

"Right. No company needs that kind of press. Makes management look stupid for not having had better safeguards in place." He already knew just how stupid he had been. He didn't need to see it spelled out in the headlines or on the evening news. Nelson Burlton, the most popular news anchor on television, would have a field day with the story.

But the bad publicity was the least of Lucas's concerns. What he craved was an answer. He needed to know why Miranda had done this to him, although the truth probably wouldn't do him any good. After all, he'd figured out why his wife and partner had betrayed him, but the answers had done nothing to lessen the chill in his gut. They had only made it worse.

If he had any sense, he'd fire Miranda and forget about finding answers.

"Rest assured that Psynergy has a policy of maintaining absolute confidentiality in all of its dealings with clients," Amaryllis said.

"It damn well better have such a policy." Lucas glanced at her again. It occurred to him that her eyes reminded him of a very special, fern-shrouded grotto pool in the islands. Serene on the surface but unfathomably deep. He reminded himself that the lively intelligence he saw in Amaryllis's vivid features was another warning to tread warily.

She cleared her throat. Her gaze slid back to the forms in front of her. "Yes, well, the first step will be to determine the identity of the culprit, won't it?"

"That won't be necessary. I already know who is selling Lodestar secrets."

Amaryllis looked up swiftly. "If you already know who is behind this, why don't you simply fire him? You just said you don't intend to prosecute."

"It's not a man. It's a woman." Lucas turned and walked back to his chair. "Her name is Miranda Locking. She's a vice president at Lodestar. I'll let her go when this is finished, but there are some things I want to know first."

"Such as?"

Lucas paused behind his chair and gripped the back of it. "I want to know if she sold me out for money, or if there was . . . some other reason."

Amaryllis's eyes went to his hands, which were clenched very tightly around the chair. "Some other reason?"

Lucas ignored her quizzical expression. He released the back of the chair and began to pace the tiny office. "There's a go-between involved, of course. A broker who buys the information from Miranda and then sells it to the highest bidder. I want to nail him, too."

"You probably won't be able to prove that this go-between, as you call him, has actually broken any laws," Amaryllis warned. "And even if you can, you've already said you don't want to go to court. If you're not willing to press charges, I don't see how you can do anything about the person who's buying the information from Miranda Locking."

Lucas paused at the far wall and examined the array of framed diplomas and certificates that hung there. "Don't worry about it. I'll deal with the broker. All I need from you is a little help picking him out of a crowd."

"I'm not sure I like the sound of this, Mr. Trent. You do realize that I can't possibly work with you if you have any intention of taking illegal action against this broker person."

"I wouldn't dream of asking you to violate your professional ethics, Miss Lark." Lucas did not take his eyes off the wall full of official papers. "And you probably have a lot of them, judging by all these fancy certificates." He leaned closer to study one of the diplomas. "I see you graduated from the University of New Seattle with a degree in Transphysical Science and Philosophy."

"Yes. I did my graduate work in Ethical Metaphysics in the Department of Focus Studies at the university."

"Impressive."

"Thank you."

"And it says here you're qualified to work with a class-ten talent."

"You did request a full-spectrum prism."

"So I did." Lucas swung around on his heel and contemplated her for a long moment. "And it appears that's exactly what I've got."

Amaryllis's brows rose. "If you choose to work with me, you will have to accept my professional ethics."

"Of course. Don't worry, I don't intend to do anything violent to this go-between, should we be lucky enough uncover his identity." Lucas kept his voice calm and reassuring as he lied through his teeth. "But if he's doing what I think he's doing, I will see to it that he is exposed."

"I don't understand. What exactly do you think he's doing? Other than buying your company's secrets, that is?"

Lucas hesitated. "I think he's a hypno-talent. I believe he may be using hypnosis to force Miranda to sell him Lodestar proprietary information."

Amaryllis stilled. She blinked once or twice and then seemed to collect herself. "Let me get this straight. You think that a hypno-talent forced Miss Locking to commit an act of corporate theft?"

"It's a possibility," Lucas muttered.

"A highly unlikely one. Look, Mr. Trent, surely you know that there are very few strong hypno-talents. It's a rare psychic power. People who do possess such skills generally go into medicine."

"Not all of them."

"Well, it's true that a few do stage acts," she admitted. "But I have never heard of a hypno-talent using his or her abilities to force someone to commit a crime. I'm not sure it's even theoretically possible."

"I don't see why it would be impossible," Lucas said.

"A hypno-talent would have to be extremely strong to force someone else to perform an act that violated the victim's own ethical code. I'd say it would require a class-nine or even a class-ten talent. You know how rare nines and tens are in any talent field."

"There are a few around."

"Less than one half of one percent of the population, according to the latest research."

"But they do exist," Lucas insisted.

"Yes, but a hypno-talent with that kind of power would be able to do very well in a legitimate profession. He or she would be working at the university or at one of the hospitals. Why would such an individual take the risk of becoming a criminal?"

"Who knows? The challenge of it all, perhaps." Lucas spread his hands. "Hell, maybe brokering the theft of corporate secrets is more exciting than a career in anesthesiology or research."

"I doubt it."

Lucas smiled slightly. "No offense, Miss Lark, but you sound a little naïve. Spend a few months in the Western Islands and you'll learn that there are a lot of people in the world who would jump at the chance to violate all your cute little notions about the ethical use of psychic talent."

Red flags appeared in her cheeks. She glared at him. "You're forgetting something, Mr. Trent. Even if a powerful, extremely unethical hypno-talent exists and happens to live right here in New Seattle, that individual could not operate alone. He or she would require an equally powerful and equally unethical prism to focus the talent."

"I know."

Amaryllis sighed. "Be reasonable, Mr. Trent. The odds are very much against such a combination getting together to form a criminal team."

"But it's possible."

She threw up her hands. "Well, yes, hypothetically speaking, I suppose it's possible. But not probable."

"I want to check it out."

Amaryllis eyed him thoughtfully. "You're clutching at straws, aren't you?"

"I'm approaching this in a rational, logical manner."

"Know what I think? I think you're looking for excuses to explain why Miranda Locking sold your secrets to your competition," Amaryllis said gently. "I understand. It's easier to believe that Miss Locking fell into the clutches of an evil class-ten hypno-talent than it is to accept the fact that she betrayed her position of trust in your firm. Isn't that right, Mr. Trent?"

She was right, but Lucas had no intention of admitting it. He reminded himself for the hundredth time in the past twenty minutes that he had known this would be unpleasant.

Hiring a professional prism to help him focus his psychic talent was something he had done his best to avoid. Utilizing the services of a trained professional in order to harness the paranormal energy of his own brain went against the grain. It was his mind, after all. He should be able to control it and use it without outside assistance.

Most talents at the lower end of the power range readily accepted the fact that their paranormal gifts were useless without the assistance of a prism. It was that way with most things here on St. Helens. Complex synergistic principles governed the natural order. It was the toughest lesson the colonists had had to learn during the past two hundred years. On St. Helens the laws of nature could be summed up with the old Earth adage, It Takes Two to Tango.

The first indications that true paranormal abilities were beginning to show up in the population had been documented less than fifty years after the colony had been stranded. It had taken another twenty years before the researchers had figured out that natural and necessary complements to the talents were also appearing.

Ten more years had passed before the experts arrived at the obvious conclusion that prisms and talents were made for each other, at least in one very crucial sense. No talent, no matter how gifted or well trained, could focus his or her paranormal powers for more than a few seconds without the aid of a prism. Most could not focus their abilities at all without assistance.

It was the general consensus that prisms were nature's way of ensuring that talents did not become dangerous or predatory. The link between prism and talent required absolute, willing cooperation from both parties if it was to endure long enough to accomplish anything useful.

The authorities who studied the phenomenon scoffed at the notion that an innocent, unsuspecting prism was at risk of being "enslaved" by a powerful, villainous talent. The scientific evidence had not stopped novelists and filmmakers from producing a host of popular tales involving mythical off-the-scale psychic vampires.

There was also a wildly successful genre of romance novels featuring implausible talent heroes who were capable of seducing beautiful, feisty female prisms and turning said prisms into love slaves.

Lucas had noticed the newest release of popular author Orchid Adams in the window of the bookshop across the street from the offices of Psynergy, Inc. The title of the novel was *Wild Talent*. He had no intention of buying it or reading it. It would only have depressed him. He was already too painfully aware of the limitations of his own abilities, psychic or otherwise, when it came to dealing with women.

In spite of all the overheated excitement generated by fictional psychic vampire talents, real-life prisms were quite safe. They had natural, built-in defense mechanisms. Prisms could simply withdraw from an unwanted focus link. If they were accidentally matched with a talent who overwhelmed their focusing capabilities, they went psychically numb.

Burnout, as the condition was called, was a short-term, temporary problem that was, nevertheless, extremely unpleasant for the prism. Those who had been through it described it as being as disturbing as losing one of their other senses such as touch, smell, or sight. It could take weeks for a prism to recover.

For that reason, responsible, reputable focus agencies such as Psynergy, Inc. requested evidence of talent classification and certification from their clients.

Lucas brought his attention back to the matter at hand. "I'm not looking for excuses. I'm looking for answers."

"Believe me, Mr. Trent, no one could be more sympathetic. I, myself, have occasionally been accused of being a trifle too obsessive about getting answers. When questions have been raised, what else can one do? However, in this instance, I feel that there are no real questions."

"If I'm deluding myself in order to avoid having to admit I screwed up by giving Miranda Locking the job with Lodestar, that's my problem. Do you want to take the contract or not?"

"If you're absolutely determined to pursue this investigation," Amaryllis began very softly.

"I am."

"And if your only goal is to identify the person to whom Miss Locking sold the information—"

"It is."

"Then that's a perfectly legal security investigation," Amaryllis concluded. "I'll work with you under the terms of the standard contract."

Lucas smiled thinly. "I thought you'd accept the arrangement. I'm a class-nine talent. That means Psynergy, Inc. can charge me a fortune for your services."

"You're free to take your business to another agency."

"We both know it won't be any cheaper elsewhere." Lucas walked back to his chair and sat down. "Let's get on with this. I haven't got all day."

"Very well." Amaryllis picked up her pen. "Now, then. You say you're a class nine?"

"Yes."

"Tested and certified, of course?"

"Of course." Lucas leaned down to unsnap the clasp of the briefcase he had set beside the chair. "I've got the usual papers to prove it." He removed the official talent classification certificate that he had been given several years earlier when he had finally, reluctantly, submitted to testing. He tossed the folder that contained the test results onto Amaryllis's desk. "All signed and sealed. If you're qualified to work with a class ten, you're safe enough with me. I only tested a nine."

"No need to be modest, Mr. Trent." Amaryllis examined the certificate with great interest. "Nines are extremely rare."

"So are full-spectrum prisms who can focus them."

"True. And that's why my firm charges so much for my services. Supply and demand, Mr. Trent. As the owner of Lodestar Exploration, I'm sure you are intimately acquainted with those basic laws of economics."

Lucas ignored that. "Well? Everything in order?"

She frowned as she flipped through the papers he had given her. "According to this, you weren't tested until the age of twenty-two. That's rather late. Most people are tested in their midteens."

"I grew up in the Western Islands," Lucas replied easily. "We don't have any fancy test facilities. There was no opportunity to get myself certified until I came to New Seattle to get my degree in Synergistic Crystal Mineralogy at the university."

"I see."

Lucas covertly studied Amaryllis's expression as she finished examining the documents. He relaxed slightly when he saw her nod to herself, evidently satisfied.

He had been forced to account for the delay in getting himself certified several times in the past. After all these years, he had his answer down to a glib spiel he could rattle off with little effort. The excuse of growing up in the Western Islands neatly sidestepped the truth, which was that he had deliberately avoided the test until he was certain that he could conceal his off-the-chart abilities.

He had aimed for a class-eight certification but his control had not been as good in those days as it was now. He had wound up with a nine.

He had opted not to go for a top-of-the-scale class ten because people tended to be wary around class tens. Most folks respected such talent, even admired it or were in awe of it, but a ten was rare enough to make them uneasy. Class tens often got treated with the same sort of cautious reserve as people who possessed great beauty or extremely high intelligence. That kind of attitude was not particularly good for business.

Amaryllis closed the folder and tapped the tip of her pen against it. "You're a detector-talent. You have the ability to sense other talents when they focus their psychic energies. That's unusual."

"And damn useless for the most part." Only a lie of omission this time, Lucas thought. He loosened his tie. "There aren't a lot of applications for that sort of psychic power."

"I realize that," she murmured sympathetically. "Most of the available job openings are in casino security."

"Yeah, I know. Personally, I've never been attracted to that line of work." Lucas was well aware that detector-talents were often employed to ensure that talents who had a gift for analyzing the laws of chance did not cheat at cards or dice. "My interest in gambling is limited to business decisions."

"I suppose you plan to utilize your ability to detect a working talent to determine whether or not Miss Locking has been hypnotized?"

"Right." Lucas leaned forward, braced his elbows on his thighs, and clasped his hands loosely between his knees. "When I realized that someone was selling Lodestar information, I conducted a preliminary internal investigation. I kept Miranda under surveillance for a few weeks. Fed her false data to see where it went."

"What did you learn?"

"That she makes regular contact with a man named Merrick Beech. I think he's the broker. I want to confirm it, and I also want to find out if he's been working with a prism to hypnotize Miranda."

"In order to do that, you'd need to catch Beech in the act of actually focusing with an intent to hypnotize. Do you have any idea of how difficult that would be?"

Lucas narrowed his eyes. "I think I'll have a chance to do just that on Thursday evening."

"Thursday?"

"Miranda and Beech are both scheduled to attend the reception that will follow the dedication ceremony at the New Seattle Museum."

Amaryllis's eyes lit with sudden enthusiasm. "They're opening the new wing of the museum on Thursday night, aren't they? The gallery where the Western Island relics will be on display."

"Yeah." Lucas frowned. "Even a strong hypno-talent would be forced to regularly renew whatever hypnotic suggestion he's giving his victim, right?"

"Yes. Especially if it's a suggestion intended to make her act against her basic inclinations."

"And he'll have to use a prism to focus that suggestion."

"Yes, but as I've already told you, it's almost impossible—"

"My guess is that Beech will use the opportunity Thursday night to work on Miranda. I want to catch him in the act."

Amaryllis bit her lip. "You want to employ me to help you focus your detector-talent the night of the reception?"

"That's it." Lucas smiled grimly. "Simple, straightforward, and perfectly legal. Not to mention entirely ethical."

Amaryllis drummed her short, neat nails on the desk. "The reception will be an exclusive affair. I'm sure that only VIPs and major contributors will get invitations. I'm afraid I don't move in those circles."

"I think I can pretty much guarantee that getting an invitation for you will not be a problem," Lucas said dryly.

Amaryllis blushed again. "Yes, of course. You're the person who found the relics, aren't you? I expect that the Museum Guild authorities would give you anything you wanted."

"Let's just say, they're grateful."

"I'm sure that's putting it mildly," Amaryllis murmured.

Lucas shrugged. Everyone knew that the museum considered the Western Islands relics to be the most significant contribution ever made to its collections. The artifacts were expected to draw huge crowds, not to mention extremely healthy donations.

Amaryllis regarded Lucas with somber consideration. "I have to tell you that in my professional opinion, I believe you will be wasting your time on this investigation, Mr. Trent. It's almost inconceivable that someone has actually been able to use hypnotic suggestion on Miss Locking unless—"

"Unless what?"

Amaryllis sighed. "Unless she was a willing subject. In which case she's simply a dishonest, mercenary, untrustworthy employee. Not a victim of a criminally inclined hypno-talent."

"I thought she was more than just another employee," Lucas said quietly.

"The two of you have a personal relationship?"

"Not in the way you probably mean. But, yes, we have a relationship. Three years ago Miranda was engaged to marry my partner, Jackson Rye. I gave her the VP job in public relations after Rye was killed in the Western Islands Action. I knew she needed the work. And I felt the company owed her something."

Amaryllis was silent for a long time. "Very well, Mr. Trent. I'll sign a contract with you." She picked up her pen and started to write her name at the bottom of an official-looking form.

"Thanks."

"By the way, have you thought of a cover story to explain my presence at the reception? I'll need to be quite close to you at all times, you know. Perhaps I could masquerade as a member of the catering staff. Of course, that would mean you'd have to clear it with the company that is handling the food service for the museum."

"Your cover won't be a problem." Lucas studied the tiny round earrings she wore. "I'm going to take you along as my marriage agency date for the evening."

Amaryllis's pen jolted to an abrupt halt midway through her signature.

"I beg your pardon?" She stared at him with widening eyes.

"It's no secret that I'm in the process of registering with a match-making agency. Everyone, including Miranda, knows I'm in the market for a wife. I'll just tell anyone who asks that you're a candidate for the job."

Chapter 2

Lucas Trent, the Iceman himself. He had been right here in her office.

Amaryllis managed to wait until the door had closed firmly behind her new client before she succumbed to the amazed wonder that she had barely been able to conceal during their conversation.

Lucas Trent. He had been sitting there on the other side of her desk. She had signed a contract to focus for him.

Amaryllis sagged weakly in her chair. She still could not believe it.

The man they called the Iceman had been haunting her for months. It had been a gentle haunting, to be sure, nevertheless she had been intimately aware of his existence in a way she could not explain.

A year ago a single news photo of him had transfixed her attention. She had picked up the paper one morning and found herself riveted. It wasn't his business success, or the tales of his exploits during the Western Islands Action that had captured her interest. It was not even the discovery of the artifacts that had intrigued her so much.

She thought it was something about his eyes.

It was not as if she had been obsessive about it, she assured herself. In the months since he had appeared on television and in the papers, her awareness of him had quietly receded to the back of her mind. She'd had more important things to do than dwell on Lucas Trent and she had done them.

She led a busy life, and the past few months had been especially full. What with ending her relationship with Gifford, quitting her job at the university, joining Psynergy, Inc., and preparing to register with a marriage agency, she'd had very little time to think about the Iceman.

His name had actually been familiar long before his discovery of the relics. Everyone had become aware of Lucas Trent three years ago when pirates had attempted a takeover of the Western Islands.

The pirates, a motley coalition of outlaws, career criminals, and assorted riffraff from the three city-states, had united under a leader to try to take control of the rich resources of the Western Islands.

Amaryllis had been busy with her research and teaching at the university during the Western Islands Action, but she had heard some of the details. She knew, for instance, that Lucas's wife and his partner had been killed during the initial pirate raid.

In the chaotic days that followed the raid, Lucas had put together a hastily deputized police force from among the miners, technicians, traders, cooks, sailors, and shopkeepers who had found themselves stranded in the islands when the fighting broke out.

It was during the Western Islands Action that Nelson Burlton had dubbed Lucas the Iceman. Burlton and the other correspondents who had covered the story had marveled at the effectiveness of Lucas's strategy and tactics. The pirates had been driven from the islands in complete disarray in less than two weeks.

But it wasn't Lucas's success as a commander three years ago that had caught Amaryllis's attention. In truth, she had been too occupied with final exams to notice him. It was his discovery of the relics that had made her so intensely aware of him.

She would never forget the photo of him that had been snapped soon after he had emerged from the jungle with the artifacts in his hands. The harsh landscape of his face had been indelibly imprinted on her mind.

Today she had been shaken to realize that, if anything, the news photos and film clips had understated the reality of Lucas's features. His face was not exactly a thing of beauty. It was a graphic rendering of masculine strength and determination. His bold cheekbones, aggressive nose, and strong jaw were as exotic, compelling, and mysterious to Amaryllis as the alien artifacts themselves.

She knew now that the news photos had failed utterly to capture the bleak, icy gray of his eyes. Nothing could have prepared her for her first in-person glimpse into those veiled depths. The chill of a fierce self-control swirled there. Amaryllis decided that Lucas's nickname suited him far better than Nelson Burlton could possibly have guessed.

The bad news, so far as she was concerned, was that whatever it was about Lucas that had tugged at her senses through the medium of film and photograph was a thousand times stronger in real life. His laconic, Western Islands drawl ruffled the tiny, sensitive hairs on the nape of her neck. The sight of his big, competent, jungle-roughened hands had done strange things to the pit of her stomach.

She was no closer to a logical explanation for her reaction to him now than she had been a year ago.

She was relieved when the door to her office slammed open.

"Well?" Clementine Malone, owner and sole proprietor of Psynergy, Inc., strode into the room. Her shrewd, dark eyes gleamed as brightly as the metal studs on her black leather jacket and pants. Her short, stark white hair, cut to resemble a stiff brush, seemed to actually bristle with anticipation. "Did you get Trent's signature on a contract?"

"Right here." Amaryllis waved the signed forms. "I'll be working with him on Thursday night. But I think I'd better explain something, Clementine. There are some problems with this job."

"We can handle 'em." Clementine plucked the contract from Amaryllis's fingers and scanned the signatures. "Nice going. Very nice, indeed."

"Thanks." Amaryllis watched her boss flip through the short contract. The knowledge that Clementine was pleased should have given her a good deal of satisfaction. Lucas Trent was, after all, the most important client Amaryllis had signed up since she had come to work for Psynergy, Inc. six months ago. She knew it was not only an important step in her new career as a professional prism, it was also a coup for the firm.

Clementine glanced up from the contract. "I knew you could do it. I was just saying to Smyth-Jones that this contract will put Psynergy, Inc. into the big leagues. Proud Focus can eat our exhaust."

Proud Focus was Psynergy, Inc.'s chief competitor. There were a number of firms that offered psychic focus services in New Seattle, but the rivalry between Proud Focus and Psynergy, Inc. had a personal twist. Proud Focus was owned and operated by Clementine's personal permanent partner, Gracie Proud. Amaryllis knew that although the two women had been living together in a blissfully happy union for some fifteen years' duration, they were enthusiastic rivals when it came to business.

"Sorry, Clementine." Amaryllis reached across the desk to take back the contract. "I'm afraid you won't be able to brag about this deal too loudly. Mr. Trent wants it kept quiet. Security work, you know."

"Sure, sure." Clementine winked as she propped one leather-sheathed hip on the edge of the desk. The steel hoop rings in her ears swung gently. "But word has a way of getting around in Trent's circles. If he's pleased with our services, he'll recommend us to others. And the next thing you know, we'll be the most exclusive agency in town."

"We already are the most exclusive agency in town," Byron Smyth-Jones, Psynergy's Inc.'s combination receptionist and secretary, said from the doorway. "How many times do I have to tell you that, Clementine? You have to think big in order to be big. Attitude is everything. Vision precedes reality."

Clementine eyed Byron with mild disgust. "What in the name of the five hells ever possessed me to send you to that positive synergy management seminar last week?"

"You sent me because you know I'm destined for the top." Byron gave her a complacent grin.

He was in his early twenties, lean, good-looking in a youthful way, and painfully trendy, in Amaryllis's opinion. His long blond hair was pulled back and tied with a black leather cord. He wore khaki trousers and a matching shirt. Both garments were festooned with countless epaulets, buckles, snaps, and pockets. An artificially weathered leather belt and deliberately scuffed boots completed his ensemble. He could have served as a model for an ad featuring the Western Islands look.

The style had exploded onto the fashion scene a year earlier when popular news anchor Nelson Burlton had gone on location to the Western Islands to cover the discovery of the artifacts. For nearly a week, Burlton, looking attractively rugged in Western Islands gear, had appeared nightly on the evening news. He had not only focused public interest on the alien relics, he had done wonders for the khaki manufacturers.

The young males of the three city-states had gone wild for what had come to be known as the Western Islands look. To date, the fad showed no signs of waning. A new wave of public excitement generated by the impending opening of the relics gallery at the museum had only served to fuel the rage for the style.

"Destiny is a function of synergy and can be easily altered," Clementine intoned.

Byron made a face. Then he grinned at Amaryllis. "Don't you just hate it when she starts quoting some old dippy philosopher?"

"She's quoting Patricia Thorncroft North," Amaryllis said, automatically slipping into her academic persona. "North was not some old dippy philosopher. She was one of the discoverers of the Three Principles of Synergy. If it had not been for North and her work, you might not have your present cushy job with Psynergy, Inc."

Clementine gave a snort of muffled laughter.

Byron groaned and put a hand to his forehead as though he had suddenly taken ill. "Please, not another lecture, Amaryllis, I beg you. I'm still recovering from the one you gave me yesterday."

"But she's so good at them," Clementine murmured.

Amaryllis flushed. She was still not accustomed to the phenomenon of office humor. There were too many occasions when she could not tell the difference between good-natured teasing and more serious remarks. Things had been different at the university, she reflected. Sometimes she missed the sober, serious-minded atmosphere of the Department of Focus Studies. But only sometimes.

"The point here," Byron continued in the painstakingly exaggerated tone one used to explain basic synergy to a child, "is that you have landed one very big fish for good old Psynergy, Inc., Amaryllis. I'd ask for a raise right now if I were you. Timing is everything in business, you know."

Amaryllis smiled wryly. "I appreciate the advice, Byron. But I think I'd better hold off asking for a raise. I have a feeling Mr. Trent is not going to be a happy, satisfied client when this job is finished."

Clementine's eyes widened in alarm. "What the hell are you talking about? Why shouldn't he be a satisfied customer? I know he's a nine, but you can handle him. Hell, you're a full-spectrum prism. You're certified for tens."

"It's not that." Amaryllis studied the contract unhappily. "There won't be any problem focusing his talent. But he's looking for answers, and I don't think he's going to get the ones he wants."

"So?" Byron frowned. "He has to pay the same fee, whether he gets his answers or not."

"Yes, but he probably won't go away happy," Amaryllis said. "You know how it is with high-class talents. They tend to be arrogant and difficult. When they don't get the results they want, they usually blame the prism who worked with them. They claim the focus was of poor quality or not strong enough to handle their psychic energy."

Clementine's gaze sharpened. "You said it was a security job. What's Trent looking for?"

Amaryllis sighed. "Brace yourself, because you're not going to believe this. He thinks a strong hypno-talent has used psychic suggestion to force one of his executives to steal proprietary information from Lodestar Exploration."

"A hypno-talent?" Byron's eyes widened. "Are you serious?"

"That's ridiculous." Clementine scowled. "That kind of thing never happens except in films or an Orchid Adams novel."

"Psychic vampire," Byron whispered in a voice laced with theatrical dread. "Able to seduce innocent lady prisms and turn them into love slaves."

Clementine grimaced. "Sounds like Trent may have spent a little too much time out in the jungle."

Amaryllis regarded the contract with morose foreboding. "I tried to talk him out of it."

"What?" Clementine nearly fell off her perch on the corner of the desk. "You tried to talk him out of the contract? Are you crazy? He's the most important client we've ever had."

"I'm afraid he's going to be the most dissatisfied client we've ever had," Amaryllis said. "That's not going to be good for business, Clementine."

"Damn." Clementine pursed her lips, obviously weighing the pros and cons of the situation.

An air of gloom settled on the small office.

"Hey, look on the bright side," Byron said after a moment. "They call Trent the Iceman. He's a living legend. He didn't become one by being stupid. He must know the hypnosis thing is very improbable. Maybe he just wants to check out all possibilities before he makes his move. A superstrong hypno-talent who could force someone to act against his or her will is at least a theoretical possibility, isn't it?"

Clementine grimaced. "Sure. And it's theoretically possible that the Return cult kooks are right when they say that the curtain will re-open one of these days and we'll all go back to Earth."

"Get serious, Clementine. Trent's not crazy the way the cultists are." Byron turned back to Amaryllis. "I know he's a class nine. He told me that much when he made the appointment. But what kind of talent is he?"

"He's a detector," Amaryllis said. "He can sense when other talents are working."

"Is that all?" Byron was clearly disappointed.

"According to his certification papers." Amaryllis straightened the forms on her desk. "A class-nine detector."

"Class nine." Clementine whistled in awe. "What a waste. All that psychic power and no useful talent to go with it. Sort of like putting a hot engine in a big, souped-up ice-cycle and then putting it up on blocks."

"Bad synergy, all right." Byron shook his head. "Just imagine what it would be like to know that you had a high-grade talent, but the only thing you could do with it was detect other people when they used their talents."

"Must be frustrating for him," Clementine agreed. "No wonder the news reports have never said much about his psychic abilities. He probably doesn't like to talk about them."

"You know"—Byron pursed his lips—"I thought for sure he'd have some really interesting talent."

Amaryllis glanced at him. "Such as?"

"Well, they call him the Iceman because he's so good at finding jelly-ice, right? I thought maybe he'd at least have a talent for locating valuable ore and mineral deposits or something."

"Apparently he did his prospecting the old-fashioned way," Amaryllis said. "Detailed research and a lot of grueling fieldwork. He has a degree in Synergistic Crystal Mineralogy."

Amaryllis did not know much about the complex process involved in the search for jelly-ice, but she knew it was difficult, sometimes dangerous work. It was also vital, high-paying work.

Jelly-ice was slang for the substance known in technical circles as semiliquid full-spectrum crystal quartz. Jelly-ice had a multitude of strange properties, including a weird, jellylike consistency when it was in its natural state. But the most important fact about the stuff was that it could be made to produce energy. Clean, efficient, inexpensive energy.

Lucas Trent had made his fortune by locating several extremely rich deposits of jelly-ice in the Western Islands. The company he had founded, Lodestar Exploration, was one of the most successful in the business.

"I don't give a damn how he goes about finding jelly-ice," Clementine said. "All I care about is that it's made him a very important person here in the city." She leveled a finger laden with several steel rings at Amaryllis. "I'm counting on you to convince him that even if there's no psychic vampire hypno-talent involved in this case, he got exactly what he paid for from Psynergy, Inc."

"Right, boss."

Clementine stood and planted her hands on her hips. "Trent is contracting for a professional, highly skilled prism, and that's just what we'll give him. Whatever answers he gets when he links with you are his problem."

"I trust you'll remember that when it's time to hand out the yearly bonuses," Amaryllis said politely.

Clementine gave a crack of laughter. "Don't worry, you've already earned your bonus. Hell, I couldn't lure a class-nine talent through the door until you came to work for me. Nines are snobs to the bone. They insist that any prism they work with must have a string of diplomas and degrees. Even eights are awful damn fussy."

Byron made a face. "Too bad Trent's talent is such a boring one, huh, Amaryllis? The job might have been kind of exciting under other circumstances. I mean, this is real security work. We don't get a lot of that."

"Mr. Trent's particular talent may not sound thrilling, especially since we're highly unlikely to uncover a real, live hypno-talent at work," Amaryllis admitted. "But I think the job will be quite interesting in its own way. At least it will be a change of pace for me. This will be the first time I've gone undercover."

Byron brightened at that news. "Where will you be working?"

"I'm going to hold a focus for Trent on Thursday night at the reception that the New Seattle Museum is hosting to celebrate the opening of the relics wing."

"What's this about working undercover?" Clementine frowned. "I thought this was just a straight security check gig. No one said anything about undercover work."

"It's no big deal," Amaryllis assured her.

Byron refused to be discouraged. "I'll bet Trent has arranged for Amaryllis to masquerade as a member of the catering staff at the reception. That way she'll have an excuse for being nearby when he wants to link."

Clementine's brows rose. "I can see her now in a snazzy little black-and-white server's outfit carrying a tray of hors d'oeuvres. Let's be sure to get a photo before she leaves for the assignment. We can frame it and hang it in the reception lobby. Put a little slogan under it. You know, something along the lines of We Go All Out to Serve Our Clients."

Amaryllis drew herself up very straight in her chair. "For your information, I won't be serving canapés or champagne on Thursday night."

"No?" Clementine eyed her with grave interest. "Is Trent going to get you into the reception as a journalist or as a member of the museum staff?"

"Not exactly." Amaryllis tried to look calm and composed. "I'm posing as his marriage agency date for the evening."

The effect was immediate and not especially gratifying, in Amaryllis's opinion.

"You're going to the reception as a marriage agency candidate for Lucas Trent?" Byron looked stunned. "I don't believe it."

Clementine whistled soundlessly. "Hot synergy. Who'd have thought of that?"

"What's so strange about it?" Amaryllis angled her chin. "Mr. Trent happens to be in the process of registering at a matchmaking agency. He told me so himself."

Clementine's eyes danced. "Talk about life's little ironies, huh? What would your aunt and uncle say?"

"Aunt Hannah and Uncle Oscar don't know about this, and I have no intention of telling them." Amaryllis fixed Clementine and Byron with a warning glare. Her aunt and uncle, together with most of the rest of her family, lived an hour's drive from the city in the rural farm town of Lower Bellevue. There was no reason for any of her relatives to ever learn about Thursday night's activities. "Furthermore, if either of you blabs, I will personally exact a terrible vengeance."

Byron held up both hands, palms out. "Don't worry, Clementine and I won't breathe a word."

"We won't have to," Clementine said dryly. "The museum reception will be heavily covered by the media. You can bet that a lot of the out-of-town papers will carry the story. Nelson Burlton himself will probably be there. Trust me, Amaryllis, on Friday morning your aunt and uncle will open the *Lower Bellevue Journal* and see a lovely picture of their precious niece clinging to the arm of one of the richest men in the city."

"Oh lord." Amaryllis dropped her head into her hands. "I forgot about the press."

Byron's eyes danced with mischief. "This assignment is starting to sound more interesting by the minute."

Amaryllis glowered. "That's enough out of you, Smyth-Jones."

Clementine held up one hand for silence. "That's enough, boys and girls. We're trying to run a business around here. Save the squabbling for later. Amaryllis, you'd better take the rest of the afternoon off."

"Why?"

"Because in about forty-eight hours you'll be attending the major social event of the season in the company of one of the most important businessmen in the city. Something tells me that you haven't got a thing to wear."

Panic assailed Amaryllis. "Good heavens. I've got to go shopping."

Byron eyed her with critical appraisal. "Try one of the new flutter dresses. Green would be good on you."

"He's right, Amaryllis." Clementine paused in the doorway. "Try that boutique on Fifth Avenue. That's where Gracie does a lot of her shopping. Tell the store to send the bill to Psynergy, Inc." She winked. "The dress will definitely be a business expense."

"The best part," Byron said with unconcealed envy, "is that you'll get to ride in his car."

"What's so special about that?" Amaryllis asked.

"It's an Icer. I saw it parked outside. What a beauty."

<hr />

With any luck, she would finally exorcise Lucas Trent from her mind tonight.

Amaryllis slipped the new flutter dress over her head and watched in the mirror as it floated into place. Experimentally, she took a few steps, watching her reflection. The green, jewel-toned scarves that comprised the cleverly designed gown wafted gently with every move. The silky material seemed to be in constant motion. When she turned slightly, it clung briefly at hip and thigh. When she walked, it drifted around her legs and danced on the air.

She took two quick steps, pirouetted, and whirled around to peer at her image in the mirror. The scarves settled demurely into place. She touched the neckline, wondering if it was just a bit too low, and then reminded herself that this was an evening affair. Many of the gowns would be cut much lower than hers. She checked closely to be certain that the straps of her white bra did not show.

It was a sensible, functional, well-made bra, designed for long wear and many trips through the washing machine. She had bought it during the semiannual underwear and foundation sale at a major downtown department store. It was a practical, serviceable piece of clothing. She had half a dozen others just like it in the top drawer of her dresser. But she knew that it was not the sort of bra that one wore under a flutter dress. She wished she had a silky little scrap of lingerie to go with the gown. Something in black lace, perhaps.

On the other hand, she would probably never have an opportunity to wear the flutter dress again, so it was just as well that she had not invested in a fancy designer bra to go with it. It would have been a waste of money.

Pleased with the dress and with the fact that she was ready ten minutes before Lucas was scheduled to arrive, Amaryllis walked out of her bedroom. She felt calm and collected, just the way a good prism was supposed to feel before an intensive focus session.

Then the reality of what was about to happen hit her again. She was going to spend the evening with Lucas Trent.

She clasped her hands very tightly together and took several deep breaths. She was annoyed to note that her palms were damp. She had tried to ignore the nervous anticipation that had been building within her, but things were getting worse. It was ridiculous. She had to get a grip, she told herself.

She came to a halt in the middle of her small living room and gave herself a stern lecture. To focus effectively for a high-class talent, a prism had to be composed and in command. A prism who could not control herself could not control a strong talent. She had to do a good job tonight, if not for herself, then for the sake of Psynergy, Inc.

As usual, thoughts of duty and responsibility had a wonderfully calming effect on Amaryllis's nerves. She was relieved to feel her pulse slow. The cool mantle of professionalism descended upon her.

Much better. Almost normal. This was a working evening, she reminded herself. She was under contract. This was not a social event.

The fact that she had been anxious for the past two days must not be allowed to affect her performance.

The fact that she was going to focus for the Iceman was irrelevant.

The doorbell chimed.

Lucas had arrived.

She would walk, not run, to the door, Amaryllis told herself.

The bell chimed again as she went down the short hall. Somehow the usually mellow tones seemed to have been infused with an imperious note. High-class talents were an impatient lot, Amaryllis thought. They were difficult, demanding, and arrogant. That was the principal reason why they rarely got along well with full-spectrum prisms.

For some reason, although she had taken her time getting to the door, she felt a little flushed when she finally opened it. Lucas stood on the front step.

"You're early," Amaryllis said.

Lucas frowned. He glanced at his black wrist watch. "It's exactly seven o'clock."

"Is it? Imagine that." Amaryllis summoned up a smile. "Sorry. Guess my clock is slow."

Lucas was dressed in conservative, formal evening black. Black shirt, black jacket, black trousers, and black tie. Not a hint of khaki in sight, Amaryllis noticed. She wondered what he thought of the current fad for Western Islands gear. Not much, judging from the fact that his dark hair was cut short and brushed back in a crisp, no-nonsense style.

Lucas surveyed her from head to toe. "Something wrong?"

Good grief, she was staring. "No, of course not." Amaryllis hurriedly stepped back into the hall. "Come on in. I'll just be a minute. I have to get my purse."

"There's no rush." He walked through the door. "I allowed plenty of time."

The implication that he had expected her to keep him waiting annoyed Amaryllis. "Wait here. I'll be right back."

She went into the bedroom and snatched her purse off the dresser. When she returned to the outer room she found Lucas examining the contents of her bookcase. He had a copy of Orchid Adams's newest release, *Wild Talent*, in his big hands. He glanced at Amaryllis with an odd expression.

"Don't tell me you like these psychic vampire romance novels," Lucas said. He sounded wary, not derisive.

"As a matter of fact, I enjoy them very much."

"But you don't really believe there are off-the-scale talents who can take over helpless prisms, do you?"

"Of course not. That's why they call it fiction, Mr. Trent."

"I don't read much fiction. I prefer nonfiction."

"I'm not surprised that we have different tastes." Amaryllis gave him a grim little smile. "There's an old saying that high-class talents and full-spectrum prisms generally have nothing in common except the ability to hold a focus."

"True." His eyes moved over her as if he were assessing all the various ways in which they differed. "Shall we go?"

"Certainly."

The phone rang just as Amaryllis turned to lead the way toward the door. She ignored it.

"Feel free to answer it," Lucas said easily. "We're in no hurry."

"You're sure?"

"Believe me, I'm not in a rush to spend the evening sipping green wine punch and eating soggy hors d'oeuvres."

Amaryllis went to the phone and lifted the receiver. "Hello?"

"Oh, hello, dear." Hannah Lark's voice sounded warm and cheerful, as it always did. She was a doctor, and her bedside manner stemmed from a genuinely caring nature. "I'm glad I caught you."

"Well, actually, Aunt Hannah, I'm just on my way out the door." Amaryllis slid a quick glance at Lucas, who was now studying her collection of music discs. "Can it wait?"

"This will only take a moment," Hannah assured her. "I'm filling out the marriage agency forms for you, as we agreed, and there are one or two questions I thought I'd bounce off you."

"Not now, Aunt Hannah, please."

"Do you have any strong preferences when it comes to physical appearance?"

"Uh, not really."

"Height? Weight? Eye color?"

"No, Aunt Hannah. It doesn't matter."

"You're sure, dear?"

"I'm positive."

"Good, that makes things much simpler. Now, then, intelligence and education are critical, of course. I've already made a note of that. What about mutual interests? How picky do you intend to be in that area?"

"Very picky. Compatibility is a must. Listen, Aunt Hannah, someone's waiting for me. We'll have to do this some other time."

"Who's waiting?" Hannah's voice sharpened with interest. "A man?"

"Well, yes, as a matter of fact."

"Someone from work?"

"Sort of. I'll tell you all about it later."

"You're avoiding me, Amaryllis." Hannah sighed. "This happens every time I try to get your attention long enough to complete this form. You can't make excuses forever. The Synergistic Connections agency is the best matchmaking service in the city-state. They only handle a certain number of select clients. Their list was already filled for the next six months. It wasn't easy convincing them to make room for you. I had to pull a few strings."

"I know I'm lucky that you were able to get me registered with Synergistic Connections. I promise I'll call you tomorrow so that we can fill out the form together, but I can't do it now. I really have to run."

"All right, we'll do it first thing in the morning. There's no excuse for waiting any longer. By the way, where are you going tonight?"

"The reception at the museum."

Hannah gave a delighted gasp. "Are you serious?"

"Very. Talk to you later, Aunt Hannah. Good night." Amaryllis dropped the phone back into the cradle before her aunt could recover from her shock. She looked at Lucas. "Let's go before she calls back."

Lucas's gaze was unreadable as he followed her to the door. "You're registered with Synergistic Connections?"

"My aunt insisted." Amaryllis grimaced. "She says it's the agency that matched her and my uncle Oscar."

A glimpse of genuine understanding appeared in Lucas's eyes. For one brief, shining moment, Amaryllis felt an unexpected sense of mutual empathy flash between them. She and the Iceman might be polar opposites in some ways, but when it came to the business of marriage, they comprehended each other very well.

Marriage was a serious matter. It had been since the founders, faced with the task of creating a colony that could survive the rigors of being stranded on an alien world, had deliberately set out to promote a strong family structure. Their historical and psychological research had convinced them that only a society founded on the firm support of rock-solid families could meet the challenges that lay ahead.

The institution of marriage was regarded as a permanent commitment. It bound not only two people but two extended families. Under the guidance of the founders, the monumental weight of social pressure and the enormous power of the law had been brought to bear in order to enforce the unwritten as well as the written rules that governed the social order.

Amaryllis knew those rules only too well. Her parents had not been married. She had not only lost both her mother and her father when she was less than a year old, she had paid the price of their indiscretion.

One of the most unpleasant fates that could befall a child in such a family-oriented society was to be born out of wedlock. The shame and the humiliation cast shadows for years, especially in small towns such as the one where Amaryllis had been raised. She was well aware that she had been very fortunate, under the circumstances. Many bastard children did not fare so well.

Hannah and Oscar Lark had taken her into their home after her mother's death. From birth, Amaryllis had been surrounded by a host of loving relatives. There was little the Larks could do about the cruelty of her classmates or the whispered gossip of adults, however. Nor could anyone make up for the fact that her father's family, the wealthy and influential Baileys, chose to ignore Amaryllis.

For her part, Amaryllis had vowed early on never to embarrass her aunt and uncle or any of the rest of her mother's relatives. She knew her duty and her responsibilities. High on the list was the necessity of contracting a proper, agency-sanctioned marriage when the time came.

She had put off the inevitable as long as possible. She had finally run out of excuses.

Sooner or later, almost everyone, gay or straight or in-between, got married. Same-sex alliances, known as permanent partnerships, were as binding as heterosexual unions and had equal status as well as equal responsibilities to the community. Divorce was virtually impossible.

Given the legal ramifications, the expectations of families, the pressures of society, and the permanence of marriage, very few people attempted to find their own mates. It was understood that judgments made in the heat of passion were not to be trusted, which was not to say that passion was forbidden. On the contrary, affairs were quite common before marriage and were known to occur after the event as well. Discretion was expected from everyone involved.

The guiding principle behind the actions of responsible people was Don't Embarrass the Family.

The founders had been far more concerned with the stability of the social structure than with individual happiness. Nevertheless, for the sake of the institutions they valued so much, they had tried to ensure a high percentage of reasonably contented couples.

To that end, they had established marriage agencies staffed with trained synergistic psychologists to help individuals choose mates wisely and well. Although marital alliances based on such ancient considerations as property and family connections occasionally took place among the very wealthy, most people registered with matchmaking agencies when the time came to get serious.

It was considered remarkably stupid to even consider contracting such a formal and terribly permanent alliance without the assistance of a good counselor and a respected agency.

Lucas followed Amaryllis out the front door. "I'm registered with Synergistic Connections myself."

"I'm not surprised." Amaryllis paused to activate the jelly-ice lock on her door. "It's not as though either of us has a lot of choice, is it? There are only a couple of agencies in New Seattle that handle high-class talents and full-spectrum prisms."

Lucas slanted her an enigmatic glance as he guided her to the sleek sports car parked at the curb. "No one will suspect you're a full-spectrum prism tonight. After all, I'm a class nine, and everyone knows that no agency would match a nine with a strong prism."

Amaryllis smiled very sweetly as she got into the car. "High-class talents are notoriously difficult to match with anyone, prism or non-prism. They tend to be arrogant and overbearing."

"It's common knowledge that full-spectrum prisms aren't any easier to match," Lucas said. "Too damn picky."

Chapter 3

Lucas stood with Amaryllis at the far end of the museum hall and tried to keep his attention on Miranda Locking and Merrick Beech. It wasn't easy tracking their progress through the crowded room. The task was turning out to be ten times more complicated than it should have been because Amaryllis's dress kept moving. She looked as if she were enveloped in a cloud of brilliant butterflies. Every move she made distracted him from his mission.

The fluttering dress annoyed Lucas. He had contracted to pay an outrageous sum for a trained, experienced prism. In his considered opinion, Amaryllis was anything but professional this evening. She looked provocative, enticing, and, on top of everything else, she smelled good.

"Have you spotted Miss Locking?" Amaryllis asked as she bent to examine the artifacts in one of the display cases.

"They're on opposite sides of the room, but they're making their way toward each other."

She peered at one of the strangely shaped objects in the case. It was made of a silvery green metal. Shaped something like a flashlight, it had no obvious light source. "Let me know when you're ready to link. In the meantime I'm going to get a good look at these relics. I can't believe I'm lucky enough to be among the first people to see the exhibition. I thought I'd have to wait months to get tickets."

"I'm glad one of us is having a good time," Lucas muttered.

"Once in a while my job brings a few really terrific fringe benefits," she said cheerfully. "This is definitely one of those occasions."

"Nice to meet someone who enjoys her work."

"Oh, I do. When I left my position at the university six months ago, I wasn't at all certain that I would ever be happy in business. No offense, but I assumed that the commercial world would be rather uninspiring."

"It has its moments."

She glanced at him, her eyes wide and unexpectedly intent. "It certainly has had a few interesting moments for you. You've led a very exciting life, Mr. Trent."

"Lucas."

She smiled. "Call me Amaryllis."

"Amaryllis. Don't tell me, let me guess. Your parents got caught up in the craze for old Earth flower names, right?"

To his surprise, the glow of interest in her eyes faded. It was replaced by an expression of cool politeness. "My aunt once told me that my mother chose Amaryllis because she wanted a name that would be exotic enough to make me dream my own dreams."

"And have you dreamed your own dreams?"

Amaryllis lifted a shoulder in a small shrug. "Sometimes one has to pay for other people's dreams."

"I'm not big on cryptic statements. What in the five hells does that mean?"

"Nothing." She gave him a bracing smile. "Sorry. Didn't mean to get deep and mysterious. Maybe these relics are having an effect on my mood."

Lucas frowned. "Why did you leave the university?"

"You know how it is." She turned back to the display case. "People change. I felt it was time to try a new direction in my career."

Lucas was the first to acknowledge that he had no great gift for intuition, but he had a strong suspicion that there was a lot more to the story than Amaryllis implied. He wondered if a man had been involved. Then he wondered why he should care if the answer was yes.

Wrong place, wrong time, wrong woman.

"What is Miss Locking doing now?" Amaryllis asked.

Lucas scanned the crowd and spotted Miranda. "She just stopped to shake Madison Sheffield's hand."

The professional detachment vanished from Amaryllis's gaze in a heartbeat. "Madison Sheffield is here tonight?"

"Just one thrill after another when you focus for me."

She ignored the sarcasm. "Where is he?"

"Who? Sheffield? Over there by the buffet table." Lucas gave her a sidelong glance. The keen interest in her face irritated him. Everything about her was beginning to bother him, he concluded. The sooner this evening was over, the better. "You can't miss him. He looks like he's trying to sell used cars."

"Don't be rude." Amaryllis stood on tiptoe in an effort to see over the heads of the crowd. "Madison Sheffield will very likely be our next governor."

"Probably won't be any worse than the present governor," Lucas said philosophically.

He was well aware of who Madison Sheffield was. His secretary had instructions to toss the unending stream of solicitation letters from the ambitious city-state senator's office. It was nothing personal. She also had orders to chuck the campaign fund requests from the incumbent, Tyler Wingate. Lucas was not particularly interested in politics or politicians.

But he was not surprised to learn that Amaryllis was excited by the sight of Madison Sheffield. It figured, he told himself. Sheffield was just the sort of politician who would attract the vote of an upright, prissy little prism who was overly concerned with ethics and other vague academic matters.

Sheffield was making a bid for the governor's seat on the Founders' Values ticket. He was running on a platform that emphasized a return to the supposedly sterling virtues of the First Generation colonists. People were responding to the Sheffield campaign in droves. The man had charisma.

"He's even more impressive in person than he is on television," Amaryllis declared.

Lucas eyed the senator. It was fair to say that Sheffield was tall, lean, and possessed of a nose and brow that would have done credit to any founder. His aquiline features gave the impression of a man who was ascetic in his habits. His expensively styled brown hair was tinged with just enough silver to add a distinguished touch.

Sheffield's tailor had taken care of the rest.

Amaryllis's dress fluttered again. Bored with the sight of Sheffield shaking hands, Lucas found himself distracted by the movement. The rational, intellectual side of his nature considered the perplexing question of how the gown could both reveal and conceal at the same time. It was a frustrating problem, one which only served to heighten his irritation.

Apparently having lost sight of Madison Sheffield, Amaryllis came down off her toes and turned back to the array of artifacts in the display case.

"These are incredible," she said. "Whatever the metal is, it survived, which is saying something. The alloys and high-tech materials that the founders brought with them from Earth rotted away within months. They had to learn to use native materials. I wonder why these didn't disintegrate."

Lucas forced himself to stop watching the drifting scarves long enough to glance down at the silvery relics. "The researchers don't have a clue."

"Do you really think they're alien in origin?"

"That's the consensus of opinion."

She glanced up. "How can the experts be certain? There's so much of this world that we haven't yet explored. Perhaps it's an alloy composed of some metals that are found on the other side of the planet or in the oceans."

"Theoretically, it's remotely possible that those items are made of some rare St. Helens materials," Lucas said. "But it's highly unlikely. Trust me, the lab folks subjected the artifacts to every test they could imagine. All of the results indicated that they did not originate on St. Helens."

Amaryllis gazed thoughtfully at the relics. "I wonder what happened to the people who made them."

"Probably the same thing that almost happened to the First Generation founders. They didn't make it to the Second Generation. Maybe they never discovered the basic Three Principles of Synergy. Or maybe they refused to accept the fact that the only way to survive was to learn to utilize native materials. When their technology went down, they went down with it."

"But their technology didn't disintegrate. It's right here in front of us."

Lucas smiled wryly. "Their tools survived, but they wouldn't have done the owners any good if they lacked a power source. I'll bet that whoever left these items behind never discovered jelly-ice."

"Do you suppose the people who invented these artifacts came through the curtain, the way the founders did?"

"Who knows?" Lucas watched a wispy green scarf settle lovingly around Amaryllis's hip.

"Perhaps they got trapped here, too, when it closed."

"Could be. Or perhaps they returned to their home world before the curtain came down. Maybe these things are just so much garbage they left behind."

The story of the curtain was familiar to every schoolchild. It marked the major turning point in human history on St. Helens. The drifting web of raw energy had materialized in space near Earth two hundred and fifty years ago. It had lasted just long enough for scientists and researchers to discover it, study it, and eventually to take it for granted. The curtain was assumed to be a permanent feature of the solar system.

To the people of Earth, who had not yet found a practical means of voyaging beyond the nearest home-system planets, it had been an astounding discovery.

The curtain had had several bizarre properties, the most intriguing of which had been its ability to warp the fabric of time and space. It had functioned as an energy gate to the distant star system that contained St. Helens.

Forty-five years after the discovery of the curtain, the first colonists had shipped out for the new world that had seemed so Earth-like and which, because of the energy gate, was now so comfortably close to home. Supplies could be transported easily, which was invaluable because technology kept breaking down on the new planet. Visits to friends and relatives on either world were possible. Earth-based corporations opened branch offices on St. Helens.

Five years later, just as the founders had settled in, the energy curtain had closed without any warning. It had never reopened.

"Perhaps the curtain was a gateway between many different worlds," Amaryllis said. "Not just between Earth and St. Helens." The scarves of her dress fluttered gently, as though responding to a tiny shiver that had gone through her. "It's a weird thought, isn't it? The people who made these artifacts might have been here when the founders arrived."

"I doubt it."

"What makes you say that?"

"Several reputable psychometric talents have studied them." Lucas took a sip of his weak green wine punch. It was nasty stuff. "These things are old. Very old."

Amaryllis nodded. "Well, it will give the researchers something to study for years."

"Yeah. Keep 'em busy." Maybe it wasn't just the damn flutter dress, Lucas thought. Maybe it was his own hormones. They had been vegetating for longer than he cared to contemplate.

Several months ago, without conscious motivation, he had lapsed into an extended period of self-imposed celibacy. It was as if something inside him had finally balked at the prospect of going through the ritual of beginning and ending another extended affair.

Perhaps the decision to register with a marriage agency had roused his dormant physical needs, he thought. He certainly seemed to have sex on the brain tonight.

"Evening, Trent. Good crowd, eh?"

Lucas stilled at the sound of the familiar voice. He nodded politely to the silver-haired man and the elegant, middle-aged woman who stood with him. Jackson Rye's parents. Just what he needed to make this evening complete.

"Good evening, Calvin," Lucas said. "Beatrice."

Beatrice Rye inclined her head in a gesture that obviously required extraordinary willpower. "Hello, Lucas. How nice to see you." Her hostility burned just beneath the surface of her blue eyes.

Lucas relaxed slightly when he saw the young man who had accompanied the Ryes. "How's it going, Dillon? Congratulations on graduating from UNS."

Dillon, the only member of the Rye family who seemed to have any fondness left in his heart for Lucas, smiled his irrepressible grin. "Thanks. Thought I'd never get out of the university. Now all I have to do is find a job."

"That shouldn't be too difficult." Lucas took Amaryllis's arm. "Amaryllis, I'd like you to meet the Ryes. Calvin, Beatrice, and their son Dillon. Amaryllis Lark."

"How do you do." Amaryllis gave the three a gracious smile.

"Miss Lark." Calvin tipped his silver-maned head in a patrician gesture. His voice was crisp and formal.

"A pleasure," Beatrice murmured. Several generations of good breeding hid most but not all of the cool reserve in her voice.

"Nice to meet you, Miss Lark," Dillon said cheerfully. "Aren't these artifacts like totally synergistic? Leave it to Lucas to find them in the middle of a jungle. Dad says Lucas has the luck of the devil."

"They're incredible." Amaryllis seemed oblivious to the undercurrents that were flowing back and forth between Lucas and the older Ryes. "Absolutely fascinating."

"You must excuse us." Calvin grasped Beatrice's elbow. "I want to have a word with Senator Sheffield."

"Of course," Amaryllis said. "Nice to meet you."

Beatrice favored Lucas with a measure of silent condemnation before she moved off into the crowd with her husband.

Dillon hung back. He waited until his parents were out of earshot before he took a step closer to Lucas. "Can I stop by your office next week? I need to talk to you. It's really important."

"Sure." Lucas glanced at the retreating Ryes. A whisper of the old sense of loss flickered through him. He squelched it with ruthless will.

There had been a time when he had been welcomed into the Rye household. He had valued the tenuous ties of quasi-adopted kinship far more than the Ryes had ever realized. Intellectually, he had acknowledged that Calvin and Beatrice's acceptance of him was prompted by pragmatic business considerations, not true affection. Nevertheless, they had been warm and cordial. Lucas had settled for the reasonable facsimile of a family that the Ryes had provided.

He had tried to be realistic about the situation. He knew that they had all been bound together by the brilliantly successful partnership between Jackson and himself.

But three years ago, Jackson Rye had been murdered by the pirates who had invaded the Western Islands. His mother had made it clear that the Ryes held Lucas morally responsible. After all, Lucas had been the one with experience in the islands. He had been raised amid their dangers.

Dillon leaned closer with an air of urgency. "Listen, Lucas, do me a favor and don't mention this to Mom and Dad, okay? I don't want them to know that you and I are going to talk business. I want to handle this on my own."

Lucas raised his brows. "What kind of business are we going to talk about?"

"I'll explain later." Dillon lifted a hand in a quick, casual farewell. "See you around, Miss Lark." He hurried off into the crowd.

Amaryllis glanced at Lucas. "Rye. Wasn't that the name of your partner?"

"Jackson Rye. He was Calvin and Beatrice's oldest son. Dillon is their youngest."

Amaryllis frowned. "Jackson Rye was killed at the start of the Western Islands Action, wasn't he? The news accounts called him a hero."

"Yes."

"Did the family inherit their son's share of Lodestar Exploration?"

"The Ryes are no longer involved with the company," Lucas said bluntly. "I bought them out eight months after Jackson was killed."

"I see."

The Ryes had wanted nothing from Lodestar except money after Jackson was killed, Lucas reflected. They certainly hadn't wanted their quasi-adopted relative. Lucas had politely unadopted himself.

Two more people emerged from the crowd. They homed in on Lucas with the skill of experts. Several heads turned to follow the handsome, sleekly coiffed man. The extremely thin blonde at his side carried a camera.

Amaryllis made a tiny, excited sound. "Is that Nelson Burlton?"

"Yeah. Try to contain yourself."

"Trent." Nelson came to a halt. "Knew you'd be around here somewhere. Hell of a crowd, huh?" He waved a manicured hand at his companion. "Elaine Crew. Friend of mine. Photographer with the *New Seattle Times*. Here on assignment. Me, I'm not working tonight."

"Amaryllis Lark, friend of mine," Lucas said.

Nelson Burlton turned the full power of his famous smile on Amaryllis. He held out his hand. "Miss Lark. A pleasure."

"It's wonderful to meet you in person. I feel as if I already know you." Amaryllis blushed furiously. "I suppose everyone tells you that, don't they?"

Nelson winked. "Hey, comes with the territory." He turned back to Lucas. "I told Elaine here that I'd talk you into letting her get a shot of you standing next to the display case. What d'ye say?"

Elaine smiled. "I'd really appreciate it, Mr. Trent. My editor at the *Times* will be grateful."

Finding himself cornered by reporters and photographers did not usually fill Lucas with delight, but tonight he was almost relieved by the interruption. He needed something to force his thoughts back to the business of the evening.

"Why not?" Lucas said. He set the glass of watery punch down on a nearby table and waited with stoic patience while Elaine unsheathed her camera.

Just as she was about to snap the picture, Amaryllis slipped gracefully out of range.

"No, wait, I want you in the shot, too, Miss Lark." Elaine lowered her camera and motioned Amaryllis back to stand beside Lucas. "Please."

Amaryllis shook her head politely but firmly. "I don't think that would be right. Mr. Trent is the one who found these wonderful relics. I had nothing to do with it."

"But you're with Trent, aren't you?" Nelson gave Lucas a speculative glance. "Someone said that you had recently registered with a marriage agency. I assumed that Miss Lark was a date."

"She is," Lucas said.

"But this is just an initial, get-acquainted date," Amaryllis interjected hastily. "Lucas and I hardly know each other." She gave Lucas a meaningful look. "Isn't that right?"

Her determination not to be photographed standing next to him exacerbated Lucas's simmering irritation. She was happy to gush over Madison Sheffield and Nelson Burlton, he thought, but she didn't want to appear in the newspapers with the man who had brought her to the party.

He gave her a deliberate smile. "I'm sure we'll be much better acquainted before the evening is over. After all, our agency claims to hit a perfect match on the first date ninety-four point six percent of the time. That's one of the reasons I registered with them."

Nelson uttered his famous, well-modulated chuckle. "After covering Trent all these years, I can assure you that he doesn't believe in wasting time. The Iceman is a man of action, Miss Lark."

Amaryllis turned a vivid shade of pink. She did not exactly breathe fire, but Lucas was almost positive he could see the flames in her spectacular green eyes. For some reason, her glare did wonders for his mood.

"So the rumors are true, Mr. Trent?" Elaine asked. "You are registered?"

"It's time," Lucas said. "I'm not getting any younger."

Nelson nodded. "I know what you mean. I'll be registering myself one of these days. Will you be staying here in New Seattle after you get married, or will you return to the Western Islands?"

"I intend to run my business from the city." Lucas watched Amaryllis. "It's time for Lodestar Exploration to diversify and expand its scope beyond the search for jelly-ice. I'll need to be here at company headquarters to oversee that change in direction."

"Sounds like new horizons for Lodestar." Nelson gave Lucas a speculative look. "Any chance that one of those new ventures might be a shot at politics? Your name has come up as a possible candidate for city-state senator. Any interest?"

"None whatsoever," Lucas said. "If you want to talk politics, I suggest you corner Sheffield."

"I spoke to him earlier." Nelson winked. "He's on an agency date, too. I have a hunch he'll be announcing his engagement soon."

"Not much of a surprise there," Elaine muttered as she made an adjustment on her camera. "Everyone knows that the voters will never go for an unmarried governor. Especially not one who's so big on founders' values." She gave Amaryllis a determined smile. "Now, then, Miss Lark, if you'll just step a little closer to Mr. Trent, I'll get this shot, and then Nelson and I will stop pestering you."

Amaryllis made one last bid to avoid the inevitable. "I really don't think—"

"Don't be shy, Amaryllis." Lucas reached out to catch hold of her before she realized his intention. He felt her flinch in surprise as he carefully wrapped his fingers around the fine bones of her wrist. He smiled at her as he drew her gently but inexorably to his side. "As I said, we're going to be intimately acquainted before this evening is finished."

Amaryllis opened her mouth with the obvious intent of making a scathing retort, but before she could say anything the camera flash went off. She blinked several times and closed her mouth.

"Got it." Elaine lowered the camera and gave her victims a breezy smile. "Thanks. And best of luck to you both."

Nelson nodded. "Appreciate the info on Lodestar's new direction, Mr. Trent. Okay if I give your office a call later this week to get some details?"

"Sure," Lucas said. "My secretary will put you in touch with the right people." He kept his grip on Amaryllis as Nelson and Elaine plunged back into the crowd in search of new victims.

"That was unnecessary," Amaryllis hissed.

"It was unavoidable. We agreed on the cover story for this evening. The press was bound to want photos."

"A shot of you would have been fine. There was no need to let that photographer take a picture of us together. It'll probably be in the paper tomorrow."

"Probably. And there will undoubtedly be several more photos taken before the evening is finished." Lucas glanced down at her. "What of it?"

Amaryllis sighed. "My aunt may see one of them."

"So?"

"You don't know my aunt." Amaryllis's mouth tightened. "Never mind. Let's get on with our business, shall we? Where are Miss Locking and Mr. Beech?"

Lucas surveyed the crowd and spotted Miranda on the other side of the room. She was not alone. Beech was next to her, his head bent attentively. They were obviously involved in an intense conversation.

"They're over there, near the large display case at the far end of the hall. They're alone together, and Beech looks serious. Something's going on right now. Ready?"

Amaryllis glanced at him in surprise. "You're strong enough to detect a talent from here?"

"I can handle this room." Lucas tightened his hold on her wrist.

"But where is Beech's prism?" Amaryllis tried to peer over the heads of the crowd. "I don't see anyone close to him except Miss Locking."

"Who knows? It could be any one of the people within a radius of ten feet of where Beech is standing." Lucas was impatient to get into the link. "That waiter with the champagne tray, for example. He's close enough to link."

Amaryllis looked doubtful. "Beech would have to be awfully strong to impose a hypnotic suggestion using a prism who's standing that far away. Something tells me this isn't going to be very useful, Lucas."

"That's my problem, not yours."

"Remember that when it comes time to pay the bill."

"I will." Lucas hesitated, feeling unexpectedly awkward now that the moment was at hand. "Look, I haven't had a whole lot of experience with this kind of thing. There aren't a lot of trained prisms out in the islands. I'll probably be clumsy by your standards."

"Don't worry about it," she said softly. "I've worked with a lot of amateurs."

Lucas gritted his teeth. "Thanks."

"I didn't mean to offend you."

"Forget it." He could feel the heat in his face, but he forced himself to ignore his own embarrassment. There was no way to explain to Amaryllis just why he had so little finesse. It wasn't easy focusing a portion of his talent through a prism while he simultaneously exerted a tremendous effort to conceal the full extent of his abilities from the person who held the focus.

Slowly, carefully, Lucas eased into the link. He braced himself for the short moment of disorientation that always preceded the connection. He opened his mind cautiously, a little at a time, groping for the focus.

And suddenly it was there on the psychic plane, a glittering crystal prism. Strong and clear and ready for him. It bore almost no resemblance at all to the weak, cloudy prisms he had used in the past.

It was beautiful. Incredibly, indescribably beautiful. It was perfect.

Before he could fully admire the prism, he almost staggered beneath a wholly unexpected wave of deep sexual desire. *He wanted Amaryllis*. He needed her as he had never needed anything before in his life. He was shatteringly aware of her in a psychic sense. It seemed to Lucas that he was drowning in the very essence of Amaryllis's femininity.

Something was very, very wrong.

He was getting an erection. Shocked, Lucas released the link as though it were made of fire. Out on the psychic plane, the wonderful prism winked out of existence.

It wasn't supposed to be like this. True, he had only used prisms in

a limited manner in the past, but he had read a lot about the phenomenon. He knew that his previous experiences were typical, even if he
had been clumsy and even if he had only worked with weaker prisms.

The link between a talent and a prism was by nature an impersonal
one. He had never heard of a case in which there were sexual over-
tones in the act of holding a focus. People said if you blindfolded a
talent, it was impossible for the talent to tell if he or she was working
with a man or a woman.

"Lucas?" Amaryllis sounded breathless. "Is anything wrong?"

"No." He wondered if she had felt anything. Maybe it was just
him. Damned hormones.

Lucas fought for control. He was the Iceman. He exhaled halfway
and fumbled again with the delicate link. Slowly, carefully, he took
hold of it.

It was as though he used his big, calloused hands to grapple with
a strand of silk spun from fine crystal. He was terrified of ripping the
fragile thread to shreds.

"It's okay," Amaryllis murmured at his side. "I won't break."

Gingerly, Lucas tightened his grip on the link. He felt the power
vibrating in it, a natural complement to his own strength. She could
handle him, or at least as much of him as he intended to use. Lucas
relaxed slightly.

An unwarranted exhilaration rushed through him. It felt so good.
So right. The sensation of intense intimacy returned. In that moment
he felt closer to Amaryllis than he had ever felt to any other human
being in his life.

He longed to know if Amaryllis was feeling the same surge of sexual desire that was soaring through him. He did not dare look at her.

He ordered himself to concentrate. This was business. Amaryllis
probably didn't feel a thing. She was a pro. This weird stuff was probably only happening on his end of the link.

He eased raw energy through the unbelievably clear prism.

Out on the psychic plane, the normally chaotic, unpredictable talent flowed into the prism and emerged in the form of strong, sharply
delineated bands of colored light. Almost a full spectrum. Lucas

damped down the power level. He was supposed to be a nine, he reminded himself. He had to be careful.

But he allowed himself another few seconds to savor the experience. While it flowed through the prism, the rush of talent was steady and sure. He could use it just as he used his other senses. Pleasure and deep satisfaction welled up inside him.

This was how it was meant to feel, he thought. Natural. Powerful. It paid to work with a professional.

With gathering confidence, Lucas concentrated on the task at hand. His goal was to detect Merrick Beech in the act of using a hypno-talent.

The hum of music and conversation faded around him. Another kind of noise filled his head. He recognized it immediately. It was the echo of a strong talent at work somewhere nearby.

"I've got him," Lucas muttered.

"You've got someone." Amaryllis's voice held a new note of tension. "But it doesn't feel like a hypno-talent. I've focused for hypnos in the past, and they didn't feel anything like this."

"Damn." She was right. Lucas realized that while she was holding the focus, she felt and experienced everything he did. He did not want to dwell on all the ramifications right now. "What's going on?"

"I can't tell." Amaryllis paused. "But because you're a high-class detector, you're picking up the prism's energy, too. There's something familiar about the way he or she is working."

"Familiar?"

"A prism's technique usually reflects his or her training. There are nuances of style that vary from prism to prism—" Amaryllis broke off, apparently concentrating.

"Can you tell if the prism is a man or a woman?" Lucas asked.

"No more than you can tell if the talent is male or female."

He was in no doubt about the gender of the prism he was using, Lucas thought grimly. But she was right. He could not tell the sex of the other talent or prism in the hall.

"What sort of talent is it, Lucas?"

"I'm not sure. I'll try to get a handle on it." Lucas retuned the bands of light, searching for one that would clarify the other's talent.

He caught it, held it, analyzed it. "What the five hells is he doing?"

"Lucas?"

The strange talent snapped off abruptly.

Lucas reluctantly released the psychic link with Amaryllis. She looked at him with mute question in her eyes.

"He stopped focusing," Lucas said. "Shut down as though someone had thrown a switch."

"He?"

"Yeah, I'm pretty sure there's only one person in this room who would be using that kind of talent."

Amaryllis's fine mouth tightened into a disapproving line. "Whoever it was, he burned out his prism."

"You think so?"

"Yes, I do. He was too strong. They were obviously not properly matched by his focus agency. Obviously, he wasn't a Psynergy, Inc. client. We would never make a mistake of that sort."

"Of course not," Lucas murmured.

"That poor prism. Won't be able to work for at least a week, maybe longer. I understand the feeling of losing your ability to hold a focus is extremely unpleasant."

"It's not painful, is it?"

"No. Not exactly. But most people who've been through it describe it as a sense of something missing. As if they've lost a part of themselves. They say it feels very unnatural. There is no excuse for that sort of mismatch between prism and talent."

"Uh huh." Lucas listened to the lecture with only a portion of his attention as he searched for Miranda in the crowd.

"You said you knew who the talent is?"

"What? Oh, yeah, I think so. I'm guessing that because of the sort of talent he was using and the power level he employed, it was probably—hold on a second." Lucas broke off as Miranda Locking abruptly turned away from Merrick Beech and went down a darkened hall. "There she goes. Wonder what she's up to now."

"Who? Miss Locking?" Amaryllis followed his gaze. She frowned when she caught sight of Miranda. "She looks very upset."

"Maybe Beech isn't willing to pay her what she thinks Lodestar information is worth," Lucas muttered. "This whole thing has been a waste of time and money. I shouldn't have bothered to figure out why she was doing it. I should have just fired her and been done with it."

"She's headed toward the corridor that leads to the ladies' room." Amaryllis set down her glass. "I've got an idea. I'm going to follow her."

"What the hell do you think you're doing?"

"Miss Locking appears to be extremely anxious about something. I'm a prism, remember? That means I'm intuitive by nature."

"I've always felt that the theory that prisms are naturally more intuitive than other people was a myth," Lucas said dryly.

"Well, it's not. I'll follow Miss Locking into the restroom."

"Why?"

"In her present condition she might want to talk to another woman."

"You think she'll bare her soul to you? Forget it. That's the dumbest idea I've heard in a month."

Amaryllis met his eyes. "You want answers, don't you? I might be able to get them for you if I move quickly enough."

"Damn it, I don't want you getting involved in this."

"I already am involved. And I'm the only one who can follow Miss Locking into the restroom." Amaryllis whirled about and hurried off through the throng.

"Just a damn minute. Come back here. I'm in charge of this fiasco." Lucas realized that he was talking to himself. Never a good sign.

He swore silently as he watched Amaryllis make her way along the fringes of the crowd.

He had known it would be a mistake to work with a full-spectrum prism. Amaryllis was probably trying to prove how clever she was. Overcompensating for her lack of real talent, no doubt.

Typical prism. Headstrong, difficult, and unpredictable.

Unable to think of anything else to do, Lucas went after her.

Chapter 4

Amaryllis's hands were still trembling with reaction. She could not believe what had happened. She was a professional. True, she had only been working as a commercial prism for a few months, but she'd had years of experience in the academic world. She had a wall papered with degrees and certificates.

But she had been totally unprepared for the effects of the link with Lucas. Nothing in her experience had led her to anticipate such a shockingly intimate sensation.

The few seconds of disorientation and the accompanying sense of vulnerability that preceded the actual link had not disturbed her. She was accustomed to that feeling. Every prism experienced a moment of blind, groping awareness. It passed as soon as the psychic link between talent and prism took hold.

The focus link itself was a remarkably uncomplicated, emotionally neutral matter. It was as natural as using one's eyes or ears or taste buds. The only way it differed from any of the other human senses was that it required two minds in order to function in a reliable fashion.

But what she had experienced during those few moments when she had held the focus with Lucas could definitely not be described as uncomplicated or emotionally neutral. What she had felt was pure, scorching sexual desire.

It was impossible, Amaryllis thought as she wove a path through the crowded hall. Nothing in the exhaustive research and testing done on the nature of the connection between talents and prisms had ever indicated that a sense of sexual intimacy was involved. She herself had worked with countless talents in and out of the lab. She had never felt anything that could have been described as even mildly arousing.

It seemed to Amaryllis that she could still smell the smoke from the fires of searing desire that had been lit during the link with Lucas. Now that she was free of the psychic connection, the deep longing was receding. But she had an unpleasant suspicion that the aftereffects were going to last for several hours.

It had been a struggle to conceal her reaction from Lucas. She hoped he hadn't noticed just how stunned she had been. At least she had managed to hold the focus in a reasonably professional manner.

Amaryllis took comfort from the knowledge that she had done her job properly, even under such adverse circumstances.

She would think about the problem later, she told herself as she followed Miranda Locking from a discreet distance. There had to be a logical explanation for the phenomenon.

At the moment she had other problems. Her client *wanted* answers. She would try to get them for him. This kind of thing was not in her job description, but Amaryllis believed in going the extra mile, regardless of the task. She knew what it felt like to need answers.

Miranda Locking did not pause at the door of the restroom. She went straight past it, moving swiftly down the hall toward the shadowed regions of an office corridor. Her high-heeled evening shoes made a loud tapping on the hardwood floor.

Surprised, Amaryllis grabbed a fistful of fluttering scarves and quickened her pace. Miranda's blond hair gleamed briefly in the hallway light, and then she turned a corner and disappeared.

Amaryllis broke into a run. Scarves flying, she rounded the corner.

And collided with Miranda Locking and Merrick Beech.

"What the hell?" Beech, a soft-featured man with a noticeable paunch, grunted heavily. He stumbled back against the wall, lost his balance completely, and sat down hard.

Miranda shrieked as Amaryllis plowed into her. "What do you think you're doing?" She staggered. Her high heels shot out from under her and she fell to the floor. Her large purse flew from her hand.

"Oomph." Amaryllis landed on top of her in a tangle of wildly fluttering scarves. "Sorry."

"Get off me, you idiot." Miranda struggled to a sitting position. "Who are you, anyway?" Her eyes narrowed with sudden suspicion. "Did you follow me?"

"Sort of." Amaryllis scrambled to her knees.

Out of the corner of her eye she saw Miranda's purse lying on the carpet. It had come open. A sheaf of papers had fallen out and scattered across the rug. Amaryllis saw the familiar green-and-gold Lodestar logo at the top of one of the pages. She could also see the red "Confidential" stamp.

"Damn." Merrick Beech apparently noticed the papers at the same moment that Amaryllis did. "The bid numbers." He started to heave himself to his feet.

A large foot sheathed in polished black leather came down on top of the incriminating papers.

"Five hells," Beech muttered. "Should have known you'd show up sooner or later, Trent."

Without a word, Lucas bent down to retrieve the papers that had fallen from Miranda's purse. He glanced at them briefly as he straightened.

"How much did you pay her, Beech?" he asked very softly.

"I don't know what you're talking about." Beech stood and brushed meticulously at his clothing. "Miranda and I are close friends. We were just having a quiet conversation here when this odd woman interrupted us."

Amaryllis glared at him as she got to her feet.

"I know who you are, Beech, and I know what you are," Lucas said. "I'll deal with you later. Get out of my sight."

Beech bridled. "Don't give me orders. You can't prove I did anything illegal, and even if you could, you wouldn't press charges. We're all adults here. We know the facts of corporate life."

"I said, I will deal with you later, Beech."

At that moment Amaryllis could have sworn that she felt a cold wind move through the hall, but the scarves of her gown did not move.

She shivered and automatically glanced around to see if there was an open window in the vicinity. She did not see one.

Beech's eyes widened and then narrowed quickly. His face turned an unpleasant shade of red. "You can't intimidate me."

Lucas just looked at him. He said nothing.

"Bastard," Beech snarled. "I'll go to the police."

Amaryllis was outraged. "Really, Mr. Beech, you have no call to act as if you are the offended party here. I think it's obvious to everyone present that you have been involved in some sort of unethical and very probably illegal activity. You should be ashamed of yourself. My personal opinion is that Mr. Trent should prosecute."

"Oh, shut up," Beech muttered. "There isn't a damn thing Trent can do to me."

"What about your own conscience, Mr. Beech?" Amaryllis demanded. "How will you justify your activities to yourself?"

Icy amusement glittered in Lucas's eyes. "Yeah, Beech. What about your conscience? Maybe it needs a little prodding."

Beech sputtered in helpless fury. "Don't threaten me."

"I'm not threatening you. I'm going to give you some advice. It's time for a lateral career move, Beech. Get out of New Seattle and stay out."

"You can't do this to me." Beech started to edge his way along the corridor wall. "You know you can't."

Lucas gazed at him thoughtfully. Another whisper of cold wind wafted through the hall. Amaryllis's dress did not flutter, but she realized she had goose bumps on her arms.

Beech's mouth worked. Then, with an inarticulate exclamation, he turned and fled.

Amaryllis exhaled deeply, releasing the breath she had not been aware of holding.

Miranda lifted her chin and stared at Lucas with seething, defiant eyes. "He didn't have to pay for the information, Lucas. I gave it to him for free."

Lucas studied her with an unreadable expression. "Mind telling me why?"

"You fool. You really don't know, do you? In three long years, you've never once figured it out."

"Enlighten me."

Miranda raised her head with fierce pride. "I did it to avenge Jackson."

"Jackson?" Lucas stared at her.

"He was your partner and you killed him, you murdering bastard. I knew I'd never be able to prove it, so I found another way to get revenge."

"What are you talking about?"

Miranda shoved a wing of pale hair back out of her eyes. Tears shimmered on her cheeks. "You know damn well what I'm talking about. You wanted to get rid of Jackson because you had no further use for him."

"Miranda—" Lucas broke off abruptly, as if he had no more words.

"You used him to set up your business contacts here in the city because his family had the connections you needed. Then you got rid of him."

Shocked, Amaryllis took a step toward Miranda, her hand outstretched. "That's not true. It can't be true."

"What would you know about it?" Miranda pulled quickly back out of Amaryllis's reach. "You weren't there. Lucas set him up to be killed by those pirates. I know he did. It's the only explanation. There's no other reason why it happened the way it did. No reason why Jackson would have been at that cabin with *her* that day."

"Miss Locking, listen to me." Amaryllis took another step closer.

"Don't come near me," Miranda hissed. "Lucas knew what would happen when he sent Jackson to that abandoned base camp. He sent Jackson into the jungle to die." She spun around and ran off down the hall. The echo of her footsteps rang in the corridor for a long time.

"Three years." Lucas eased the Icer to a stop in front of Amaryllis's small house. "She blamed me for Jackson's death for three years. Plotted against me all that time. And I never knew what was going on."

Amaryllis gave a small start at the sound of his voice. It was the first time Lucas had spoken since the scene with Miranda and Beech in the museum corridor. It was not just the surprise of hearing the heavy silence broken at last that made her flinch. It was the disbelief and pain embedded in the words.

She glanced uneasily at Lucas's grim profile. He sat, one big hand resting on the steering bar, and gazed out into the night. The light from Chelan and Yakima, St. Helens's two moons, etched his face in cold silver and bleak shadows.

"I'm sorry." Amaryllis decided that this was not the time to mention that she would put his bill in the mail first thing in the morning.

"I trusted her."

Amaryllis did not know what to say to that. "Don't blame yourself. It's common knowledge that high-class talents are not usually very intuitive."

"I wanted to do something for her." Lucas clenched the steering bar so tightly that the moonlight gleamed white on his knuckles. "I knew that Rye's death had hit her hard. The company had an obligation to take care of her. She had been engaged to Jackson. They were due to be married in the spring of that year. Lodestar looks after its own."

"I understand. These things are difficult." Amaryllis groped for the door handle.

"She was smart and well educated." Lucas sounded as if he was unaware that he had a listener in the car with him. "Good family background. I had no reason not to trust her."

"Of course you didn't. How could you have known?"

"I thought we had both gone through all five hells together. That we shared some kind of bond because of what had happened. I never told her that Rye had betrayed us both."

Amaryllis thought she had heard incorrectly. "Your partner betrayed you?"

"There was no point telling Miranda the whole damn story. She was already hurting. I tried to bury the truth as deep as I could for everyone's sake."

It was time to end the evening, Amaryllis thought. The assignment was finished. If she had any sense, she would get out of the car and bid Lucas good night. He had his answers. As Clementine had said, it was up to the client to deal with the results of a focus session.

"Would you like to come in for a cup of coff-tea?" she heard herself ask.

He turned his head to look at her. His eyes glittered in the moonlight. She knew that he was somewhere else, sunk deep in his memories.

"Coff-tea?" Lucas repeated blankly.

Amaryllis panicked. Stupid, she thought. Very stupid. Lucas was hurting, but there was nothing she could do for him. "Never mind." She gave him a quick smile and shoved open the car door. "It's late. I'll be in my office at nine if you have any further questions concerning the results of your security problem. But I think it's been wrapped up. It was obviously a personal situation."

"Yeah." He watched her face in the moonlight. "Personal."

"The case was unpleasant for all concerned, but at least it was relatively straightforward." Amaryllis summoned up what she hoped was a breezy smile. "No psychic vampire hypno-talents involved."

"No psychic vampires."

Amaryllis scrambled out of the Icer and bent down to look at him. "Good night, Mr. Trent."

"I'll come in for coff-tea."

"Uh, well—"

He opened the door on the driver's side and climbed out of the car. Amaryllis watched him walk around the front of the sleek vehicle. She realized her mouth was still open.

Lucas went past her up the path to the front door.

"Wait a second." Amaryllis hurried after him.

He came to a halt on the top step and waited patiently for her to unlock the door.

Unable to think of anything more clever to do, Amaryllis deactivated the jelly-ice lock. The door opened.

With the air of a man walking in his sleep, Lucas moved into the darkened hall.

"This way," Amaryllis said very brightly. What was she doing, she berated herself. This was not a good idea. Definitely bad synergy, as Byron would say.

She dropped her purse on a small table and led the way into the kitchen. The Iceman was here in her house. Again. For the second time. Amaryllis felt an oppressive sense of impending danger mingled with great excitement. Her breathing quickened.

She must stay calm and in control. She was a professional.

She walked into the kitchen, aware of Lucas following close behind her. The orderly pattern of the pristine black-and-white tiles that marched across the floor and up the walls calmed her immediately.

She took a deep breath. Here, amid the neat, the functional, and the familiar, she regained her sense of self-possession.

Lucas glanced curiously around the black-and-white kitchen as he shrugged out of his jacket. "This house fits you, doesn't it?"

"What do you mean?"

"Very neat. Very clean. A certain air of the fastidious, which I suppose suits a full-spectrum prism. A place for everything and everything in its place."

She was too neat for him. That was a first. "A little bit of clutter goes a long way in a small house like this."

"Personally, I don't worry a whole lot about clutter." Lucas tossed the jacket carelessly across a nearby stool. He sat down at the white tiled counter. "Growing up on the edge of a jungle teaches you to tolerate a low standard of housekeeping. You can never get rid of all the bugs, and there's always something green growing on the shower wall."

"I see." They really were complete opposites, Amaryllis thought. Amazing. Just as all the syn-psychs who studied powerful prisms and talents claimed.

"Does this happen a lot?" Lucas watched her with faintly narrowed eyes.

"What do you mean?" Amaryllis busied herself with her new coff-tea machine. She was very proud of the gleaming black appliance, which was trimmed with a great many impressive red buttons. It had been one of the first purchases she had made after taking the high-paying job at Psynergy, Inc.

"Do you invite all the losers in for coff-tea and pity?"

She looked up from the act of spooning the fragrant ground coff-tea into the machine. "I have no idea what you're talking about, Mr. Trent."

His expression darkened. "I don't need your damned sympathy, you know."

"Okay. Right. No problem. You won't get any sympathy out of me. Still want the coff-tea?"

He scowled. "Yeah."

"How do you want it?"

"Make it a triple. Straight up. No cream, no sugar, no spice."

"Triple strength?" Amaryllis raised her brows. "You don't have to prove anything to me. I know you're the big, tough Iceman."

He had the grace to flush. "I learned to drink my coff-tea in the Western Islands. We like it on the strong side."

"You got it. Strong it shall be." Amaryllis adjusted the buttons on the machine. The comforting aroma of the brewing coff-tea filled the cozy room.

"I don't have this kind of problem a lot, you know," Lucas said. "I'm usually careful. But when I screw up, I generally do a hell of a job of it."

"Are we talking about coff-tea or personal relationships?"

"I'm careful who I trust."

Amaryllis nodded. "Personal relationships. Got it. Who says a full-spectrum prism can't carry on a meaningful conversation with a high-class talent? You mustn't blame yourself, Lucas. We all make occasional mistakes when it comes to trusting the right people."

"All these years Miranda has believed that I deliberately set Jackson up to be killed because I wanted to get rid of him." Lucas shook his head. "I knew the Ryes held me responsible in a way for Jackson's death, but even they never accused me of arranging for him to be murdered."

Amaryllis removed the pot of freshly made coff-tea and poured the golden brown brew into two mugs. "The news accounts called Jackson Rye a hero. They said he was killed at the beginning of the invasion."

"I was away on one of the neighboring islands when it happened. Jackson told people at company headquarters in Port LeConner that he wanted to take a break. He said he was going up into the mountains with a friend."

Amaryllis put a mug on the counter in front of him. "What about the pirates?"

"No one knew the bastards were on the island at that point. Jackson and—" Lucas hesitated a beat, as if searching for the right word. "Jackson and his companion went to an abandoned company camp. They planned to stay in one of the old cabins and do some fishing. And a few other things."

"What happened?"

"When I got back to headquarters, I realized something was wrong. I went up to the old mountain camp to look for Jackson and his, ah, friend. I found the bodies." Lucas pulled the mug closer and gazed into the murky depths of the coff-tea. "At first it appeared that the pirates had happened onto the camp by chance, discovered Jackson and his companion, and killed both of them so that they couldn't give a warning."

Amaryllis shuddered. "How ghastly."

"Later I learned that the situation was somewhat different."

"What happened?"

Lucas looked up, his eyes bleak. "The leader of the raiders was reasonably well organized. When it was all over, I searched his ship's cabin. He had extensive files. All sorts of records, notes, and plans. I discovered that it wasn't just bad luck that Jackson had gone to that old camp on that particular day. He was in league with the pirates."

Amaryllis nearly spilled her coff-tea. She stared at Lucas from the other side of the counter. "He was working with them?"

Lucas wrapped both hands around his mug. "Anyone who wants to take control of the Western Islands has to deal with Lodestar Exploration."

"Yes, of course." Amaryllis frowned. "It's no secret that Lodestar virtually runs the Western Islands."

"The company doesn't have much choice. The amenities of civilization are a little short out there. The only reason anyone even lives in the islands is because of the jelly-ice."

"I know."

"Lodestar is the chief employer in the islands. The company provides all the basic services and ensures reliable supply lines. Taking control of Lodestar means taking control of the islands and vice versa." Lucas paused. "I didn't want to get rid of Jackson Rye. He wanted to get rid of me. He knew he needed help, at least at the beginning, because my employees, on the whole, are loyal. And I have a lot of friends out there. He required manpower so he did a deal with the pirates."

Amaryllis hesitated. "He wanted sole control of Lodestar?"

"The idea was that when the gang took control of the islands, I would be among the victims. I was supposed to be the dead hero. With me out of the picture, Jackson would take control. He planned to run Lodestar single-handedly."

"But what about his deal with the raiders?"

"You'd have to have known Jackson to understand. He expected to win at everything. He was from a world in which Ryes always came out on top. He thought he could handle the pirates after he was in charge of Lodestar."

"My God."

Lucas met her eyes. "Truth is, it wasn't a bad plan. He probably could have gotten rid of his so-called allies once he was in control. The pirates were loosely organized and undisciplined. They had few supplies. They couldn't have lasted long without Lodestar assistance."

"So Jackson Rye planned for the pirates to do his dirty work for him. Then he intended to turn on them once you were safely out of the picture."

"That pretty well sums it up," Lucas said wearily. "But the leader of the raiders had already figured out that Jackson was potentially dangerous. He never had any intention of allowing Rye to remain alive. He just used Jackson and then killed him."

"The story was in the papers for weeks," Amaryllis said slowly.

"But I never heard that your partner had betrayed the company and all those people."

"You didn't hear about it because I kept it out of the news reports." Lucas's smile was cold. "Figured it wouldn't do the company image any good."

Amaryllis watched him. "Is that the real reason you hushed up the facts?"

"I'm a businessman at heart. I always do what's best for the bottom line."

"Mr. Expediency, is that it?" Amaryllis took a sip of coff-tea. "Know what I think? I think that there were a few other reasons why you decided to bury the truth."

"What other reasons?"

"The Ryes and Miranda Locking. You didn't want any of them to learn the awful truth about Jackson, did you? You tried to protect them all."

Lucas's expression was unreadable. "Like I said, it wouldn't have been good for the company image."

"I think it was very noble of you to protect his name and reputation," Amaryllis said.

He gave her a derisive smile. "If you really believe that, you're not nearly as smart as full-spectrum prisms are supposed to be. What I did wasn't noble. It was pragmatic."

"No." She shook her head. "Definitely noble. But I must admit, I'm amazed you were so successful at concealing the facts."

"As president and sole surviving owner of the company, I was in charge. I also had a couple of friends who helped me handle the situation. The reporters got the news I wanted them to get."

"I see."

Lucas swallowed the last of the coff-tea. "And if you still believe that I kept things quiet because I was so damn noble, there's one other fact you should consider."

"What's that?"

"I mentioned that Jackson Rye took a companion with him the day he rendezvoused with the pirates."

"Yes. You said he was killed, too."

"That companion wasn't a man. It was my wife."

Amaryllis's eyes misted. "I'm so sorry, Lucas. I recall reading that your wife also died during the initial raid. How terrible that she happened to be with Jackson that day at the camp."

Lucas's mouth curved in a bleak smile. "Are you always this naïve or do you have to practice?"

"I beg your pardon?"

"Dora and Jackson were having an affair. Now do you understand? She didn't just happen to be with him that day. They went to the camp because she was sleeping with him, because they often disappeared together, and because she knew all about Rye's deal with the pirates."

This time coff-tea did splash over the edge of Amaryllis's mug. She ignored it. Unable to think of anything to say, she reached out to touch Lucas's hand with what was meant to be a fleeting gesture of silent sympathy.

Lucas caught her fingers before she could withdraw. He squeezed gently, just enough to convey a warning. "I don't know why I told you the story. I've never told anyone else. I expect you to keep it confidential."

"Of course."

"Absolutely confidential," he emphasized. "I don't even want your boss to know. Understood?"

"Yes." Amaryllis could have sworn that she felt another whisper of the cold wind she had sensed earlier in the museum corridor. "Understood. You have my word on it."

"The word of a professional prism." Lucas turned her hand over, exposing the inside of her wrist. He studied the veins that ran just beneath the skin as if they were lines on a map that led to some unknown destination. "If you tell anyone else what I told you tonight, I can make life difficult for you."

Amaryllis looked into his eyes. In that moment she knew that the chill that filled the kitchen emanated from him. A dark fog seemed to be gathering beneath her kitchen cupboards. She was afraid to turn her head and look.

Lucas was doing this, she thought. She did not know how, but she knew that he was responsible. Anger blossomed inside her.

"Don't you dare threaten me, Lucas Trent. I gave you my word of honor."

"Sorry." Lucas released her hand abruptly. "I'm in a lousy mood, and you're catching the brunt of it. That's not right. None of this is your fault."

"No, it isn't." Surreptitiously, she waggled her fingers to make sure they all still functioned properly. The sensation of a cold wind blowing disappeared. She glanced at her kitchen cupboards and saw nothing but clean black-and-white tiles. "And I don't appreciate being intimidated."

"Something tells me there's not much that could do that."

And I'll bet it would take a heck of a lot to intimidate you, too, she thought. "Look, don't be too hard on yourself just because you put your trust in the wrong people. It happens to everyone. Even prisms make mistakes like that."

"Even prisms, huh?" Amusement flickered in his gaze. "That certainly makes me feel a lot better. You ever make that kind of mistake?"

She reflected fleetingly on her relationship with Gifford Osterley. "Even me. Being a prism doesn't guarantee perfect intuition, you know."

"Amazing. I would never have guessed." Lucas's lashes lowered slightly, just enough to veil his eyes. "Who was he?"

Amaryllis was so irritated by his undisguised condescension that she considered showing him the door right then and there. But she felt a niggling sense of guilt at the thought of throwing him out. He had, after all, just spilled his guts to her. That couldn't have been easy or simple for a man like him. He obviously regretted the indiscretion already.

It occurred to her that telling Lucas one of her own small secrets might make him feel that the scales had been balanced. Perhaps that would put him in a better mood when he received the bill in a few days. One of Clementine's many axioms rang in Amaryllis's head: *A happy client is a repeat client*.

"His name was Gifford Osterley," Amaryllis said quietly. "We worked together at the university until I left six months ago. He's a full professor. Next in line to become head of the Department of Focus Studies."

"Prism, I take it?"

"Oh, yes. Very strong. Practically a full spectrum."

"Not quite as strong as you, then?"

A trickle of unease went through Amaryllis. "I *am* a full spectrum, after all."

"How could I forget?"

She cleared her throat. "At any rate, Gifford and I were involved, if you know what I mean."

"I think I can figure it out."

She frowned. "It was serious. We talked about marriage."

"A nonagency marriage?" Lucas gave her mockingly scandalized look. "You? I don't believe it."

"Don't be ridiculous." Amaryllis set her teeth. This was what came of trying to be sympathetic and kind to Lucas Trent. He had no ability to appreciate her generosity of spirit. "We would have registered with an agency when the time came, but we both expected that the counselors would have declared us a good match."

"Do I hear a touch of prism arrogance here?"

"I suppose you could say we were a little arrogant," Amaryllis admitted grudgingly. "We are both very highly trained prisms, you know. We thought we knew what we were doing."

"Yeah, I saw all your fancy degrees."

"Gifford has even more than I do."

"Hooray for him. So what happened with you and Osterley?"

"I discovered that Gifford had a relationship with an attractive talent who worked as his research assistant."

"He was sleeping with her?"

Amaryllis looked down at her unfinished coff-tea. "Yes."

"How did you find out?"

"The hard way." Amaryllis swallowed. If there had been a mirror in the kitchen, she knew she would have seen her face go from pink to red. "I blundered into a focus session in one of the labs and discovered Gifford and his research assistant together."

"Focusing on something other than academically important psychic matters, I take it?"

Anger, pain, and embarrassment fused within Amaryllis. The image still burned in her mind whenever she recalled that traumatic afternoon. "They were having sex on Gifford's desk, if you must know."

Lucas's eyes glinted. "His desk, huh?"

"Yes." Amaryllis raised her chin, the better to look down her nose at him. "I would have thought it would have been extremely uncomfortable, but they appeared to enjoy it."

"I take it you've never done it on a desk?"

The last remnants of Amaryllis's charitable inclinations dissolved. "I'm glad you find it amusing. I certainly didn't."

Lucas's expression relaxed. "I'll give you the same advice you just gave me. Don't beat yourself up about it. It wasn't your fault that you fell for the wrong guy."

"I felt like such a fool," she whispered.

"Well, at least you weren't downright stupid about it." Lucas paused. "Unlike me, you didn't think you were so smart you could just skip a marriage agency altogether."

Amaryllis stared at him. "You mean you didn't use an agency when you got married the first time?"

"Hell, no." His mouth curved faintly. "I was an islander. I knew how to take care of myself. I'd been running a successful company since I was twenty-four. I could find jelly-ice in the heart of the jungle. I was rich and getting richer. I figured I could choose my own wife without any help from the experts."

"What happened?"

Lucas looked away for a brief moment. When his eyes met hers again they were unreadable. "The same thing the experts say usually happens when people choose their own spouses. I screwed up big time."

"That is so sad. Were you very much in love?"

"Sure." Lucas gave her a laconic look. "People who run off to get married always think they're in love, don't they? Why else would they run off?"

"I don't know." Amaryllis looked down at her hands. "My parents ran off together shortly after I was born. But they didn't get married. They couldn't. My father already had a wife."

Understanding lit Lucas's eyes. "I see."

"They were both killed in a storm on the way to the Western Islands. I was with my aunt at the time. Everyone thinks my parents intended to start over under a new name and send for me when they found work."

"I'm sorry." Lucas hesitated. "So you were left . . . alone?"

She smiled wanly. "You may as well use the right word. I was illegitimate. One of the things that attracted me to Gifford was that he didn't seem to care about the fact that I was a bastard. Some people do, you know."

"Yeah. I know."

"But to answer your question, no, I wasn't alone. My mother's people took me in."

"Your aunt and uncle?"

"Yes. And the rest of the Larks, too. They were all kind and loving. I couldn't have asked for a better family."

"What about your father's people?"

Amaryllis poured herself another cup of coff-tea. "They prefer to pretend that I don't exist."

"Figures."

A short silence descended. It lasted just long enough for Amaryllis to again regret having invited Lucas in for coff-tea. What on St. Helens had gotten into her, she wondered. She had just told a virtual stranger some of her most deeply held secrets. Not all of them, but more than enough. She had turned into a blathering idiot. And all because she'd felt sorry for a client.

It was time she went back to behaving in a more professional manner. She glanced pointedly at the clock. "It's getting late."

"So it is." Lucas got to his feet with a surprising show of reluctance. "I'll be on my way. Thanks for the coff-tea."

"You're welcome."

He smiled wryly. "And the sympathy."

Amaryllis softened. "I know it must have been a difficult evening for you."

"I've had worse." He scooped his jacket off the stool and started for the door.

Amaryllis trailed after him. "Lucas, there's something I wanted to ask you."

He turned around with unexpected swiftness. "Yeah?"

"That other talent you detected tonight," she began slowly.

Something that could have been disappointment flashed in his eyes. The next instant it was gone. "What about him?"

"When I sensed him through you, I realized that he was very powerful. But I couldn't identify the type of talent he was focusing. I've never come in contact with any psychic energy of that nature. It was very subtle but very strong."

"He was good," Lucas agreed without much interest.

"Well, you're the great detector," she challenged. "Could you tell what sort of psychic power the person was focusing?"

Lucas looked amused. "You didn't realize who the talent was?"

"No."

"I can't be absolutely certain, but given the situation, I'd stake next year's profits that it was Madison Sheffield."

"Sheffield." Amaryllis was astounded. "Senator Sheffield?"

"The next governor of our fair city-state, or so everyone claims. I guess you could say he was working the room."

"Are you serious?"

Lucas eyed her thoughtfully. "You really didn't understand what was going on, did you?"

"No, I did not. When I work with a talent, I can sense what he or she senses. You have the ability to detect other talents, so naturally I picked up the other talent in the room at the same time you did. As I told you, I also picked up the echoes of the other prism."

"You said the prism's style of working felt familiar."

"It was. I would swear that whoever it was trained at the same place I did, the Department of Focus Studies at the university. I could feel Professor Landreth's influence."

"Who is Landreth?"

"He was the head of the department for years."

"The name sounds familiar."

"Probably because of the newspaper articles that were written about him after he was killed in a hiking accident last month. It was a terrible tragedy."

Lucas nodded. "I remember something about it now."

"He was a brilliant man." Amaryllis spoke forcefully because Lucas did not seem overly impressed with just who and what Professor Jonathan Landreth had been. "He contributed enormously to our understanding of the focus link and how it works. More importantly, he wrote the Code of Focus Ethics. His death was a great loss to the profession and to research."

"Uh huh."

"It was a great personal loss for me, as well." Amaryllis's teeth clamped together again. "He was my mentor. I admired him enormously. I miss him."

"I'm sorry." Lucas looked as if he didn't know what else to say. "Well, I should be on my way."

"Wait, you didn't tell me what sort of talent Senator Sheffield was focusing."

"From what little I got before he burned out his prism, I'd say that he was generating pure bat-snake oil and charm. In other words, charisma."

"Charisma?" Amaryllis repeated, uncomprehending.

"It's a politician's stock-in-trade."

"But charisma is not a psychic power."

"What would you call it?"

"I don't know." Amaryllis waved one hand in a small, vague gesture. "A personality trait or something, I suppose. But not a psychic talent."

"Power is power." A smile came and went at the edge of Lucas's mouth. "Regardless of whether or not it's been documented and studied by the experts."

Amaryllis pursed her lips. "I'm not sure about this. I don't think that it would be ethical to focus charisma, assuming it's a form of psychic energy. Especially if the talent was a politician."

"Don't worry about it. It's not your problem. So what if the guy was focusing with an intent to convince people to vote for him and to donate to his campaign fund? That's what politics is all about."

Amaryllis was not mollified. "But if charisma can be focused for those purposes, it would be an act of deliberate misrepresentation or fraud or something."

Lucas looked amused. "Welcome to the real world, lady."

She scowled. "Doesn't it bother you that a very high-class talent in Sheffield's position is using his abilities to con people?"

"He's a politician, Amaryllis."

"But he was using an academically trained prism to focus."

"So what? I used one tonight, too."

"But Sheffield's prism should know better than to become involved in an unethical use of talent. Professor Landreth drilled the Code of Focus Ethics into all his students."

"No kidding."

"There are standards in my profession," Amaryllis snapped. "And the prism who was working with Sheffield tonight may have violated them."

Lucas propped one shoulder against the wall and studied her with an expression of reluctant fascination. "I have some advice for you, Amaryllis. Nobody likes a self-appointed conscience."

"Spoken like a talent with a classic case of prism envy." Amaryllis reached past him to yank open the door. "Good night, Mr. Trent. Rest assured, your bill will be in the mail first thing in the morning."

Lucas didn't move and the door stayed closed. "You asked me a professional question. Mind if I ask you one?"

Amaryllis watched him with deep suspicion. "What is it?"

"Was it good for you, too?"

"What?" she whispered.

He appeared to be satisfied with her stunned expression. "So, it wasn't all happening on my end. I wondered about that. I told you, I haven't had a lot of experience with the focus link, and I didn't know if getting sexually aroused was a common side effect or if it was relatively rare."

Amaryllis was nearly speechless. She knew she was blushing from the top of her head straight down to the soles of her feet. "I assure you, I have no idea what you're talking about."

"Just tell me how long I can expect the effects to last."

"Effects?" she repeated weakly.

"Yeah. Effects. How long will this overpowering urge to take you to bed last?"

"Mr. Trent, please."

"Will it disappear by morning? It's kind of distracting."

Amaryllis swallowed and then took refuge once more beneath the mantle of professionalism. "I don't know how long the feeling lasts. I have never heard of any link producing sensations of the sort you're complaining about. Furthermore—"

"I'm not exactly complaining."

"Well, that's what it sounds like to me."

"Maybe kissing you would work off a few of the side effects." Lucas tossed aside his jacket and reached for her.

"Mr. Trent. You're a client."

"Yeah, I know." He wrapped her in his arms and pulled her against his chest. "Don't worry, I always pay my bills."

"That's not the point."

Amaryllis flattened her palms against his broad shoulders. She barely had time to notice that his gleaming gray eyes were as impenetrable as the dark fog that she had imagined coalescing beneath her kitchen cabinets.

His mouth came down on hers.

Chapter 5

Lucas knew that kissing Amaryllis was the act of a desperate man. He had told himself that taking her into his arms would be the quickest way to shatter the illusion of sexual desire that had held him in thrall all evening. He knew more about the nature of illusions than most people, he had assured himself. Hell, he was an expert. He knew one when he saw it.

But the reality of Amaryllis's sweet, warm, incredibly sexy mouth did not have the therapeutic effect he had anticipated. Her lips actually trembled. A shiver went through her, sending shock waves through him.

The evidence of her response sent Lucas straight over the edge. He had a mental image of a jungle canyon full of exotic flowers, and then he was falling straight into the mass of petals. The hot, heady fragrance of desire inundated his senses.

"Lucas." Amaryllis gave a soft, delicious cry and threw her arms around his neck. *"Lucas."*

She wanted him. The knowledge was dazzling. She wanted him just as badly as he wanted her. At least this was a case of mutual sexual synergy. The link had definitely worked both ways.

He tightened his grip on her slender body until he could feel her high, firm breasts crushed against his chest. The weightless scarves of the flutter dress were no barrier to his hands. He groaned as he traced the graceful line of her spine down to the curve of her elegantly rounded buttocks.

Amaryllis shivered in his grasp. She clung to him.

Lucas tore his mouth free from hers. "So much for working off the side effects." He scooped her up in his arms and started toward the closed door of what had to be a bedroom.

Amaryllis clutched at his shoulders as he carried her down the hall. She looked up at him from beneath half-closed lashes. Her eyes were so deep he was sure he would drown.

Somehow he got the door open without dropping her. Two more strides through the shadows brought him to the bed. Moonlight from the window revealed a prim, white bedspread.

Lucas turned and fell backward across the bed. He pulled Amaryllis down on top of him. She sprawled on his chest amid a flurry of silken scarves.

"I've never heard of anything like this happening," Amaryllis gasped. "Honestly."

"It's okay, it's okay." He caught her face between his hands and kissed her heavily. "Don't worry about it."

"Yes, but—" She broke off and began to kiss him wildly. His mouth, his jaw, his ear. Her fingers dug fiercely into his shoulders.

Euphoria roared through Lucas. No woman had ever attacked him with such gratifying enthusiasm. He rolled Amaryllis onto her back. The pins fell from her hair. Lucas wrapped one fist in the soft tresses. It was too dark to see the color of Amaryllis's eyes, but there was no mistaking the sheen of excitement in them.

He wedged one leg between her knees. The heat of her thighs threatened to burn through the fabric of his trousers. He covered her mouth with his own and fumbled with the scarves of the dress.

It took forever to get one breast free, but the feel of Amaryllis's tight nipple more than compensated for the effort. Lucas scraped his palm lightly over the delicate bud and then hesitated, afraid to bruise her with his big, calloused hands.

"It's all right." She gripped the fabric of his shirt. "I won't break."

Lucas uttered a thick, hoarse sound that was half groan and half laughter. It was the second time that evening that she had assured him that she wouldn't break under his touch.

"That's good to know," he said.

He bent his head and reverently took her nipple into his mouth. Amaryllis made a soft, wordless sound and clenched her fingers in his hair.

He slid his knee higher between her legs. The scarves fluttered anxiously for a moment and then parted with only token protest. He reached down and cupped the heated center of her warm body. His hand closed over panties that were already damp.

Amaryllis went rigid beneath him. Her eyes widened in the moonlight.

"You're as ready as I am," he breathed, awed by her response. He inhaled deeply, entranced by the searingly erotic, utterly feminine fragrance that drifted through the shadowed room. "It's definitely not an illusion."

"Illusion?"

"I figured that whatever it was that got me into this condition during the focus link was some kind of artificial stimulation," he confided. "An illusion. But when I realized that you had felt it, too, I decided it didn't much matter what had caused it. I don't know about you, but this is real enough for me."

"Wait a second. You're making love to me because you were sexually aroused by the link?"

"I don't think the reason matters much now." He began to probe beneath the edge of her underwear.

"Wait. Stop." She released her grip on his hair and grabbed his arms. "Stop it right now. This has gone far enough."

"What are you talking about?" He kissed the curve of her throat.

"You heard me." She shoved imperiously at his shoulders.

Lucas blinked, dazed by the sudden turn of events. He realized that she was trying to push him aside. "Amaryllis, what's wrong?"

"Get off me."

It dawned on him that mentioning the link had been a serious mistake. "Take it easy. I didn't mean that I was making love to you just because of what happened this evening. Amaryllis, listen to me."

"Off."

Reluctantly, he eased himself onto one elbow, freeing her. "Just listen for a moment, will you? I'm sorry if I offended you."

"I'm the one who should apologize," she said crisply. "I don't know what got into me."

"You?"

"I'm the professional here." She crawled to the edge of the bed, slid her legs over the side, and stood. "You're just the client."

"Just the client." Lucas propped his head on his hand and watched her in the shadows.

"As a qualified and certified professional prism, it's my duty to adhere to the Code of Focus Ethics. I should never have allowed you to kiss me. It was completely out of line. You're a *client*, for heaven's sake."

"Actually, I think of myself more as a man than as a client."

"Well, it's my responsibility to think of you as a client, nothing more and nothing less. It was obvious that you experienced some unfortunate side effects from tonight's link."

"I wouldn't call the side effects unfortunate. Just a little unusual."

"As a trained professional, I ought to have made allowances for the fact that the focus did not proceed in the normal manner." Amaryllis buried her face in her hands. "I can't believe that I allowed you to carry me in here and . . . and . . ." She dropped her hands to her sides. "I behaved in a thoroughly unprofessional manner."

"Must be tough trying to live up to your professional code of ethics all the time."

"It has never been particularly difficult until tonight."

"I'll try to take some comfort from that." Lucas exhaled slowly and sat up on the edge of the bed.

Amaryllis scurried to the bedroom door. She dithered a moment. Lucas realized that she was trying to decide whether or not to turn on the light. She apparently concluded it would not be a good move. She edged out into the hall and turned to wait for him.

"Please hurry." Amaryllis folded her arms beneath her breasts. "It's quite late. I have to go into work early tomorrow morning."

"Yeah, sure." Frustrated desire clawed at his insides as he watched the way the hall light made her amber hair glow. "You want to get my bill in the mail."

"Lucas—"

"I'm going, I'm going."

He made his way down the hall with stoic determination. His jacket was lying on the floor, right where he had dropped it a short while earlier. He scooped it up and slung it over his shoulder.

Amaryllis hurried after him. "I really do apologize for my unprofessional and ethically questionable behavior, Lucas. I don't know how I could have been so irresponsible."

It was too much. Lucas swung around at the door and put his hand across her mouth, effectively silencing her. He gazed down into her huge green eyes. "If you apologize for your lack of professionalism one more time, I will not be responsible for my actions. Clear?"

Her eyes widened above the edge of his hand. She nodded quickly.

"Good night, Miss Lark." He took his palm away from her mouth and opened the front door. "Go back to bed and cuddle up with your professional code of ethics. Personally, I'm going to go home and take a cold shower."

He walked out into the night and closed the door very deliberately behind himself. He paused on the front step to take a reviving breath of chilled air, and then he went down the steps to his car. His body was tense and heavy. A deep restlessness swirled in his gut. And in his head.

The former he could deal with. But the latter did not bode well.

This was what came of dealing with prissy little prisms. He opened the car door and slid behind the steering bar. He tossed his jacket onto the seat.

For some reason he recalled the novel he had noticed earlier on Amaryllis's bookshelf. *Wild Talent*, by Orchid Adams. A psychic vampire romance.

Lucas wondered what Amaryllis would say if she realized that she had come within a hairbreadth of making love with an off-the-scale talent whom most people would say fully qualified as a genuine, real-life psychic vampire.

He thought she was a prissy, sanctimonious little prig. Amaryllis sat hunched over her morning cup of coff-tea and bleakly contemplated the disastrous evening. It was not an edifying endeavor.

It had been a very long night. A glance in the bathroom mirror earlier had sent a shudder through her. The dark circles under her eyes were not especially flattering.

She had relived the farewell scene at her front door countless times, and it never got any better. She could still see the derision in Lucas's expression as he made his exit. He thought she was a prim, stiff-necked prism who couldn't unbend long enough to enjoy a night of mutual sexual synergy.

Amaryllis groaned. Better Lucas thought her a narrow-minded, strait-laced prig than that he learn the real truth, which was that she was an idiot.

It was the only logical explanation.

Surely only an idiot would have turned down the chance to make love with the only man who had ever made her feel such passion.

What had stopped her, Amaryllis wondered. It certainly wasn't the Code of Focus Ethics. She had fibbed when she had told Lucas that sleeping with a client was against the code.

The truth was, the code had nothing to say on the subject of personal relationships between prisms and talents. In reality, it was not considered a problem for most people. It was only in psychic vampire romance novels that full-spectrum prisms got passionately involved with powerful talents.

The phone rang just as Amaryllis started to pour herself a second cup of coff-tea. She knew who was on the other end even before she heard her aunt's cheery, determined voice.

"Amaryllis, dear, your picture is in the paper this morning. Have you seen it?"

"No, Aunt Hannah, I haven't."

"Your uncle and I are so excited. I called everyone in the family right after breakfast."

Amaryllis closed her eyes in despair. "Wonderful."

"You didn't tell me that you were going to attend that museum reception with Lucas Trent," Hannah Lark said. "He's the president of Lodestar Exploration."

"I know. I was focusing for him, Aunt Hannah. I was there on assignment."

"You did say something about the evening being work related. But, dear, he's not just any client. He's the man who commanded the defense of the Western Islands a few years ago. He's a hero."

Amaryllis remembered the bleak expression in Lucas's eyes when he described how he had buried the truth about Jackson Rye's betrayal. She didn't care what he said, she knew he hadn't done it for the sake of the firm. He had done it to protect all of the people who would have been hurt. "More than you'll ever know, Aunt Hannah."

"And he found those weird relics, too. It says here that he's looking for a wife. The implication is that you're an agency date, but, of course, we know that's impossible."

"Right. Impossible."

"You aren't even registered yet."

"I was working undercover, Aunt Hannah. It was a security job. The agency date stuff was the story we used to explain my presence at the reception."

"Security work, you say." Hannah's voice sharpened. "Was it dangerous?"

"Not in the least." Amaryllis pulled the morning paper across the counter and studied the photo of herself standing next to Lucas in front of a display case. She winced when she noticed that her mouth was hanging open. "It was a very straightforward assignment."

"Well? Don't leave me hanging. I promised your uncle that I'd find out everything I could about Lucas Trent."

"What do you want to know?" Amaryllis asked warily.

"Well, under the circumstances, I think that the most important thing is to find out which matchmaking agency he's registered with."

Horror shot through Amaryllis. "Aunt Hannah, don't go getting any ideas. He's listed with Synergistic Connections, but he's a serious talent. Class nine."

"What a pity." Some of the enthusiasm drained out of Hannah's voice. "Are you certain?"

"I saw his certification papers. I worked with him last night. Yes, I'm certain." Amaryllis frowned at the recollection of that first surge of power through the prism. Definitely a full class nine. If she hadn't seen his papers, she would have guessed that he was higher than a nine. But his certificate had been very specific. Lucas was a class nine stuck with the almost useless ability to detect other talents at work.

"Oh, well. It was just a thought," Hannah murmured. "You know, I've heard that there have been one or two rare instances in which an agency matched a full-spectrum prism and a strong talent."

"The instances are so rare as to be in the realm of legend," Amaryllis said dryly. "I repeat, don't start thinking of Lucas Trent as a possible match for me. It's not in the cards."

"It really is a shame," Hannah said regretfully. "I wonder if Mr. Trent would have been a possibility if he weren't a class nine. Just speculating, you understand."

"Don't bother," Amaryllis muttered. "Even without the talent-prism problem, I can promise you that no reputable agency would have matched us. Trent is not just my polar opposite psychically, he's also my opposite when it comes to temperament, personality, and personal philosophy of life."

"Oh, well, all the more reason for finishing the forms from Synergistic Connections. I promised your counselor, Mrs. Reeton, that I would turn them in this week."

"Why don't you just send the questionnaire to me, Aunt Hannah? I'll fill it out in my spare time."

"No, you won't. You'll put it aside and never get around to it. You've been dragging your feet about this long enough. I blame your poor attitude on that unfortunate affair with Gifford Osterley. Sometimes I think he actually broke your heart."

"He didn't break my heart. Or, if he did, I've recovered."

"I'm not so sure about that. You've been running scared of men ever since."

"Not true." Amaryllis fiddled with her coff-tea mug. "I've just been cautious." *Except for last night*, she thought.

"Too cautious, if you ask me. When I was your age, I was out almost every night until I met Oscar. No offense, dear, but you're a bit of a stick-in-the-mud when it comes to your personal life."

"A prissy little prig, would you say?"

"No, of course not. Just a bit shy, I think. Well, Synergistic Connections will find you some compatible dates. Now, then, let's see, where did we leave off on this questionnaire?"

"I don't remember."

Hannah ignored that. "Ah, here we go. Physical characteristics desired in mate. We're almost finished with this section. You told me that you didn't have any strong preferences."

"Gray eyes," Amaryllis heard herself say.

"I beg your pardon?"

Amaryllis toyed with the phone cord. "I want him to have gray eyes."

"You're going to get choosy about eye color?" Hannah demanded in disbelief. "Why in the world would you care about something so inconsequential?"

"I don't know." Amaryllis felt suddenly, inexplicably inclined to be stubborn. "But since this is my registration questionnaire, I'm going to be picky about eye color."

"That's ridiculous. Dear, are you feeling well? You sound a little strange this morning."

"Long night. Listen, Aunt Hannah, I've got to run. I'll be late for work."

"What about the questionnaire?"

"I'll give you a call this evening."

"See that you do," Hannah said. "I'll be waiting. We have to complete this quickly. Mrs. Reeton wants to schedule the personal interview."

Raw panic nearly overwhelmed Amaryllis. Filling out the agency questionnaire was one thing. The personal interview with her assigned syn-psych counselor was another. This was getting serious. Reality hit

Amaryllis with the force of lightning. She was on the verge of getting herself married.

"Bye, Aunt Hannah. I'll call you later, I promise." Amaryllis slammed down the phone. Her fingers were trembling.

She regarded her shaking hand with disgust. It was too much. She was turning into a nervous wreck, and all because of Lucas Trent. She had to get a grip. She needed to get her mind off her personal problems.

She gave herself another minute to calm down and then she lifted the receiver again. She dialed the number of her office.

Byron answered on the first ring. "Psynergy, Inc. We make it happen. How can I help you?"

"Byron, it's me, Amaryllis. Put Clementine on the phone, will you?"

"You sound terrible."

"Gosh, thanks. And a cheery good day to you, too. Get Clementine, please."

"Didn't things go well with your hot date last night? What happened? Wasn't he straight?"

"Get Clementine," Amaryllis said grimly.

"Okay, okay. Here you go. Great shot of you in the morning papers, by the way. You look like you're about to deliver a lecture to the photographer."

"Give me Clementine."

"You got 'er."

Clementine's deep, no-nonsense voice came on the line a few seconds later. "Amaryllis? How did it go last night?"

"It went very smoothly. No problems. Case closed."

"No mysterious off-the-chart hypno-talent at work, I take it?"

"Of course not. The motivation for the corporate theft was personal. A little old-fashioned revenge. It's over. I'll send Trent the bill as soon as I get to the office."

"Get to the good stuff," Clementine urged. "What happened after the reception? Was Trent any good in bed?"

Amaryllis gritted her teeth. "We kept the relationship on a strictly professional footing."

"Boring."

"Clementine, I want to ask you something."

"Shoot."

"Have you ever heard of a politician, or anyone else, for that matter, using a prism to focus something like charisma?"

"Charisma?" Clementine sounded surprised. "That's not a talent. It's like charm or a cheerful disposition or something. Some people have it, some don't. It's a personality trait, not a psychic power."

"Last night when I focused for Lucas Trent, I . . . we . . . stumbled into another strong talent and prism team working in the same room."

"So? There are a lot of strong talents and prisms running around. Chances are good that there were a few in that room last night."

"But the talent felt very odd. I'd like to get another professional opinion on it."

"What the hell is wrong with my opinion?"

"Nothing," Amaryllis said hastily. "But I'd like to talk with someone in the academic world. Call it professional curiosity. I think I'll go out to the university today."

"Hang on. That art dealer from Cascade Galleries called for an appointment. You know the one, the class-six talent with the nifty ability to detect forgeries. She needs a prism to help her look at some paintings that have been offered for sale."

"Have Zinnia Spring handle it."

"You know Zinnia only works nights. Damn it, Amaryllis, I'm trying to run a business here. I'm not paying you to satisfy your professional curiosity. Besides, it's none of your business what that other team was focusing. Stay out of it."

"Please. My intuition tells me this may be important. I want to check it out."

Clementine sighed. "All right, but get back here as soon as possible."

"Thanks."

Amaryllis hung up the phone and sat gazing glumly at it for a long while. Clementine was right. Whatever had happened with the other talent and prism team at the reception was none of her business. But she couldn't shake the urge to check into it. Things had felt wrong.

Maybe she was, indeed, turning into a sanctimonious little prig, a busybody who thought it was up to her to make sure everyone else stayed on the straight and narrow.

She wondered if Synergistic Connections would match her with a man who was just like her.

It was not a thrilling thought.

———

The carved relief that covered the entire south wall of the university library depicted the First Generation settlers in their finest hour. Amaryllis paused on the broad steps to gaze at the massive figures hewn from stone. As always, the sight elicited a quiver of admiration and pride in her.

The scene showed the stranded colonists fifteen years after the closing of the curtain. The last of their Earthbound machines had long since failed, forcing them back to a technological level that had been the rough equivalent of the seventeenth century on Earth. They had been forced to find ways to work with native materials.

The artist had created a memorial that had inspired students for nearly a hundred years. The stoic, determined faces of the men carved into the stone were turned resolutely toward the future as they drove primitive plows pulled by big, shaggy six-legged ox-mules through the mud. The women cradled infants to their breasts as they sowed grain from heavy sacks slung across their backs.

The young children were depicted sitting under trees, poring over heavy, handmade books while teachers supervised their instruction. The books were a very significant part of the scene. The cumbersome, handcrafted books had been the salvation of the First Generation.

When the settlers had realized how swiftly their sophisticated technology was failing, they had launched a prodigious effort to save as much of the contents of their computerized library database as possible.

It had been a harrowing race against time. The colonists had set up a scriptorium that had functioned around the clock for months. Information from the disintegrating computers had been painstakingly transcribed by hand onto thick paper made from native St. Helens plants.

There had not been time to salvage everything. The founders had soon realized that only a fraction of the database could be saved before the computers fell apart. Priorities had to be set.

The desperate colonists had concentrated primarily on the basic information they knew they would need to survive. The dazzling technology of Earth was of no use to them. They ignored it in favor of more pragmatic data related to farming, medicine, and survival skills. They had also copied information relating to the social structures that would support a stable community.

A hard, realistic lot, they had not allowed themselves to dwell on what had been lost. But their heritage was built into their language. It showed in many ways, including the whimsical tendency to name the exotic new flora and fauna of this world after the plants and animals that had been left behind. There were no real physical similarities between the life-forms of St. Helens and those of Old Earth, but that had not stopped the colonists from choosing names that held memories.

The library that housed all the precious home-world knowledge turned to dust along with the computers that had housed it. But the founders had salvaged enough to enable them to gain a toehold on St. Helens. The history texts they had copied so laboriously had taught them how to build plows, how to sow and reap and spin and weave. They had learned to make clocks and boats and sewage systems.

Their hand-copied library had saved the founders, and they had made certain that future generations never forgot the lesson.

Amaryllis dashed a small tear from the corner of her eye and continued on up the steps of the library. She walked past it, turned left, and went through the impressive arched doorway of the Department of Focus Studies.

Old memories came back in a rush as she walked along the corridor. Her office had been the second one on the right. She felt a small pang of wistfulness when she noticed the new name on the door. She reminded herself that she had made the right decision when she had left the academic world six months earlier. It had taken her a while to realize it, but now she knew that she belonged in the business sector. Even if she was a professional snob at heart.

"Amaryllis. Long time no see. What are you doing here?"

Amaryllis smiled at the woman who had just rounded the corner. "Hello, Sarah. This is just a social call. How are things going with you?"

"Great." Sarah Marsh tossed a swath of long dark hair over her shoulder and grinned. "Got a paper coming out in the summer issue of *Focus Studies*."

"Very impressive. Congratulations." Another jolt of wistful regret. No one in the business world cared much about the acclaimed papers Amaryllis had published in the professional journals.

"With any luck, it will ensure that I get promoted to assistant professor in the spring." Sarah shrugged. "But who knows? Things have been a little chaotic around here since Professor Landreth died."

"It's hard to imagine the department without him. We all knew that he was getting on in years, but somehow it seemed as if he'd be here forever."

"Uh huh. Running the department with his iron fist," Sarah concluded dryly.

"Iron fist?" Amaryllis hesitated. "I certainly never thought of him as a dictator."

"Oh, come on, Amaryllis. Landreth was one of the best scholars in the three city-states, but there was no getting around the fact that he was a martinet. Seemed like he was always lecturing staff and students alike about the importance of professional ethics and standards. Let's be honest. The man was a stiff-necked prig."

Amaryllis flushed. "He was very dedicated to the profession."

Sarah chuckled. "True, but he was also rigid, obsessive, and narrow-minded. He's only been gone a month, but there's a new wind blowing through the department and I, for one, welcome it."

Amaryllis decided it was time to change the subject. "I assume Gifford will be taking over as head of the department?"

"Gifford?" Sarah's dark eyes widened in surprise. "He's not here anymore. Didn't you know?"

"No. I haven't, uh, spoken to him recently."

"He left the department two months ago. Opened his own focus agency. Took Natalie Elwick with him to run his office. Remember Natalie?"

"She was Irene Dunley's assistant."

"Right." Sarah made a face. "Guess Natalie figured she'd never be anything more than a junior secretary as long as Irene Dunley was here, so she took Gifford up on his offer."

"It's hard to believe that Gifford has gone out into the commercial sphere."

"I hear his new agency is very exclusive. Employs only full-spectrum prisms and accepts only VIP talents."

"I see."

"Is that why you're here today? Did you come to see Gifford?"

"No. I came to see Effie Yamamoto."

"You'll be glad to know that she's the new acting head of the department. Everyone expects her to be permanently appointed to the position sometime within the next few months."

"Effie will do a fine job." Amaryllis made to step past Sarah. "Is she still in her old office?"

"No, she's moved into Landreth's office." Sarah lifted a hand in farewell. "See you around."

Amaryllis hurried off down the corridor. A moment later she came to a halt in front of a familiar office. The door was open. Irene Dunley, a tall, sturdily built woman in the middle of her life, was seated behind an immaculately neat desk. The only paper on the polished surface was the one she was working on at that moment. Everything else, except for the telephone and a single pen, was stored out of sight. Irene had always been a model of organization and efficiency.

Amaryllis smiled at the sight of Irene. The woman was almost as much of a legend in the department as Landreth himself. The professor had often claimed that he could not have run the place without her.

Irene's hair was cut in a crisp, efficient style. Her firm, matronly body was encased in a serviceable blue suit. She looked up at Amaryllis's light knock.

"Miss Lark. This is a surprise."

"Hello, Irene. I haven't seen you since Professor Landreth's funeral. How are things going?"

"As well as can be expected under the circumstances. There's been an unnecessary amount of disruption and confusion, what with the suddenness of the transition, but I expect to have things under complete control very soon."

Amaryllis glanced around. "It looks like everything's already under control. That doesn't surprise me. Professor Landreth always used to say that if there was such a thing as a talent for organization, you possessed it."

Irene smiled sadly. "Professor Landreth had such a dry sense of humor. Very few people appreciated it."

"What are all those boxes doing there in the corner?"

Irene glanced at the stack. "Those are Professor Landreth's personal effects. I packed them up myself the day after he died. I notified the authorities, but so far no one has come forth to claim them. Is there something I can do for you, Miss Lark?"

Irene did not waste time during office hours, Amaryllis reminded herself. "I came to see Professor Yamamoto."

"I'll let her know you're here." Irene pressed the button on the intercom. "Miss Amaryllis Lark to see you, Professor Yamamoto."

"Oh, really? What wonderful news! Send her in."

Amaryllis nodded at Irene and then walked through the door of the inner office. "Hi, Effie."

"Amaryllis." Effie rose from behind her desk and held out her hand. "Good to see you. Come on in."

Amaryllis closed the door, went forward to shake hands, and then sat down. She grinned at her old friend. "Looks like you've come up in the world. Congratulations. About time."

Effie laughed. "Things have changed around here. Coff-tea?"

"Thanks."

Effie was several years older than Amaryllis, a distinguished scholar in her late thirties. Her dark eyes gleamed with intelligence. She had an innate sense of style that Amaryllis had always admired. Her black hair was in a sleek, chin-length bob that swung elegantly whenever she turned her head. Her trim, expertly tailored suit somehow managed to appear both professional and extremely fashionable. Amaryllis wondered if she should redo her own wardrobe now that she was making a handsome salary. One night in a flutter dress and a person's taste underwent a drastic change.

"Saw your picture in the paper." Effie winked. "Looks like your social life has improved considerably."

Amaryllis felt her cheeks grow warm. "It was a business thing."

"Ah, yes. Business. Very interesting business from what I saw. So what's the Iceman like in person?"

"He's a class nine, Effie."

"Oh. Well, so much for any long-term hopes there, hmm?" Effie handed Amaryllis a mug and sat back down behind the wide desk. "Still, that leaves open some short-term possibilities."

"I don't think so," Amaryllis said austerely.

"I assume this is not strictly a social call?"

"To be honest, no. I wanted to ask your opinion on something."

Effie spread her hands. "Ask away."

"I'll come straight to the point. Have you ever heard of a prism working with a talent for the purpose of focusing charisma?"

"Charisma's not a talent. It's just a natural part of some people's personality."

"But what if it were a talent?" Amaryllis insisted.

"Well? What of it?"

"A politician could use it to con people into supporting him."

"Politicians are in the business of conning people into doing just that." Effie grimaced. "Even if a particular candidate with a high-class talent was able to use a prism to augment an aura of charisma, it wouldn't be illegal."

"No, I suppose not. But it would definitely be unethical."

"Since when has politics ever been a model of an ethical profession?"

Amaryllis smiled ruefully. "I know what you mean." Now that she was actually sitting here with Effie, she was no longer certain quite what to say. She was not sure how to explain the sense of wrongness that she had felt when Lucas had briefly picked up Senator Sheffield's talent. "What if I told you that I think I witnessed a prism assisting a politician to focus charisma?"

Effie gave an eloquent shrug. "I'd say there wasn't much anyone could do about it."

"What if I told you that I'm almost certain that the prism was trained by Professor Landreth?"

Effie eyed her thoughtfully. "Assuming it can be done at all, a prism would have to be very powerful in order to focus something as vague as a personality trait."

"This prism was powerful."

Effie chuckled. "You know as well as I do that Landreth would never have approved of one of his students focusing for deceitful purposes. He would have made a fuss about it if he had discovered what was happening. But that would have been highly unlikely."

"Because it wouldn't be easily detected?"

"Exactly. How could anyone distinguish between a real personality characteristic and an augmented one?"

"If psychic energy was involved, a strong detector-talent could pick it up," Amaryllis said cautiously.

"Perhaps, but again, not likely. It would take a strong one. Class-nine or class-ten detectors are extremely rare."

"But they do exist."

Effie tilted her head slightly to one side. "You're convinced you encountered a prism working with a politician in an unethical manner, aren't you?"

"Yes."

"My advice is to forget about it. It would be unethical, but not illegal. Only some anal-retentive type such as Professor Landreth would make a stink about it."

Amaryllis managed not to wince, but it wasn't easy. "Professor

Landreth would have been very upset if he thought one of his prisms had violated the Code of Focus Ethics."

Effie leaned back in her chair. "Just between you and me and ninety-nine point nine percent of the faculty, Landreth was a brilliant man, but he was a fussy old codger."

"He had very high standards," Amaryllis said quietly.

"His standards, as you call them, drove the rest of us nuts. Gifford Osterley left the faculty because of him, you know."

"No, I didn't realize that."

"Landreth and Gifford got into a major row over changes in the curriculum." Effie shook her head. Her beautifully cut hair swung in a perfect wave. "Gifford never stood a chance, of course. Landreth outranked him. When the smoke cleared, Gifford handed in his resignation."

"I see."

"It may have been for the best. Gifford has his own firm, probably making double what he used to make here. He always was ambitious."

"The pay is definitely better in the commercial world," Amaryllis agreed. She got to her feet. "Good-bye, Effie. It was great to see you again. Good luck with the new position."

"Thanks." Effie surveyed her office with satisfaction. "I can tell you one thing, things are going to be a different around here."

"I believe you." Amaryllis turned and walked into the outer office.

Irene looked up as she went past the desk. "Oh, Miss Lark, there's something I wanted to tell you."

"What was that?"

Irene cleared her throat discreetly and lowered her voice. "Professor Landreth was always so proud of you. He used to tell me that you were the most talented prism he had ever trained."

Amaryllis took a step closer to the desk, aware of a little twinge of warmth deep inside. "Did he really say that?"

"Yes." Irene's eyes abruptly glistened with unshed tears. "Everyone around here seems to be glad that he's gone. They all talk about how things are going to change now that the old coot, as they call him, is out of the picture. But I miss him, Amaryllis."

"Oh, Irene." Amaryllis went behind the desk and put her arms around the older woman. "I miss him, too."

Irene turned reverent eyes toward the portrait of Jonathan Landreth that hung on the far wall. "I went to work for him after my husband died, and I was with him for twenty-five years. He was good to me, Miss Lark. He was a little gruff on the outside, but he contributed so much to this department. And he always told me that I was invaluable to him. Invaluable. That was his exact word. He needed me, Miss Lark."

Amaryllis hugged the older woman's broad shoulders for a few seconds. She felt tears well in her own eyes. "I think we may be the only people who miss him."

Irene stared at the portrait. "I'm afraid so."

The phone call came late that afternoon. Byron had already left the office for the day, and Amaryllis was almost out the door. She glanced at the shrilly ringing instrument and debated the wisdom of answering it. It couldn't be Lucas. She was crazy to think that he might call. He had made his opinion of her very clear last night. He wasn't the sort of man who would be attracted to a prissy little prig.

The phone rang again. It was no doubt a business call. Amaryllis's sense of responsibility overcame her odd reluctance to pick up the receiver. She reached for it.

"Psynergy, Inc. Amaryllis Lark speaking."

There was silence on the other end of the line, but Amaryllis could hear someone breathing.

"Hello? You've reached the offices of Psynergy, Inc. Can I help you?"

"You were a friend of Landreth's." The words sounded muffled, as though the caller spoke through a thick cloth. It was impossible to tell if the voice belonged to a man or a woman.

"Who is this?" Amaryllis asked sharply.

"If you want to learn the truth about Jonathan Landreth, talk to the woman called Vivien of the Veils."

Amaryllis gripped the phone very tightly. "Tell me who you are."

"She's a syn-sex stripper. Works at a nightclub called SynCity. Ask her about Jonathan Landreth if you want to know the truth."

"Wait. Please, tell me what this is all about."

The line went dead. The caller had cut the connection.

Chapter 6

"Good morning, Mr. Trent. Hobart Batt from Synergistic Connections here. Just thought I'd check in to see if you were having any trouble filling out the registration forms. We had rather expected to have it back by now."

Lucas tightened his fingers around the phone. He told himself not to lose his temper with the syn-psych counselor. It was unfortunate that Batt's chiding tone set his teeth on edge, but it did not take much to do that this morning.

It was Monday, three whole days since the fiasco in Amaryllis's bedroom. Lucas knew that he ought to be glad that Hobart Batt had called. It was definitely time to get moving on the task of finding a suitable wife. But for some reason it was the last subject he wanted to discuss.

"I haven't had a chance to finish the questionnaire," Lucas lied.

"No problem," Hobart assured him. "A lot of clients get bogged down in the middle of the questionnaire. It's somewhat lengthy, but that's only because we here at Synergistic Connections pride ourselves on being thorough."

"Yeah, sure. Thorough." Lucas opened a drawer and slowly withdrew the thick questionnaire. He gazed at it with a sense of deep foreboding.

"A properly filled out questionnaire gives us a good basis to begin the matchmaking process," Hobart continued briskly. "The results will, of course, be supplemented by the extensive personal interview. At that time we'll also administer a revised MPPI."

"MPPI?"

"The Multipsychic Paranormal Personality Inventory. The standard syn-psych test used with high-class talents such as yourself."

"Do you use it with strong prisms, too?"

"Certainly," Hobart said. "We're all accustomed to thinking of prisms and talents as being quite different from each other, but technically speaking, the ability to focus a talent through a psychically generated prism is itself a talent."

Lucas cleared his throat. "Do you ever match full-spectrum prisms and high-class talents? I mean, I know it must be a very rare occurrence, but I just wondered if it happens once in a while."

"Almost never. Everyone knows that full spectrums are rarely compatible with very strong talents," Hobart said.

"Because the prisms are so damn picky?"

Hobart chuckled. "Well, yes, in a sense. They prefer to think of themselves as extremely selective. But, then, so are powerful talents. Once in a great while we get a match, though. As I recall, the last one that we did at this firm was some five years ago. Why?"

"Just asking."

"How far into the questionnaire are you, Mr. Trent?"

Lucas flipped open the first page and gazed moodily at the array of questions. "I'm still on the first section."

"Preferred physical characteristics?" Hobart made a tut-tutting sound. Distinct disapproval this time. "My, we aren't making much progress, are we?"

"We?"

Hobart coughed slightly. "Say, what if I drop by your office this morning and give you a hand."

"Never mind, I can do this myself."

"Exactly which question are you stuck on, Mr. Trent?" Hobart asked suspiciously.

Lucas scanned the list. "Eye color. I'm doing eye color even as we speak."

"You haven't gotten past eye color?"

"I had to do some thinking on the subject, but I've reached a conclusion. Whoever she is, she'll have to have green eyes." Lucas picked up a pen and circled the word *green* on the questionnaire.

"Green eyes? I thought you told me when you came to the office that you weren't too particular about physical characteristics. You said you wanted to emphasize compatibility, intelligence, and temperament."

"Call me shallow, but I've decided I want a woman who is compatible, intelligent, good-tempered, and who also has green eyes. Is there a problem with that, Batt? Because if so, I can always go to another agency."

"No, no, it's not a problem, Mr. Trent," Hobart assured him quickly. "I just hadn't realized that you were so particular about that sort of thing. Now, then, if you need any help with the questionnaire, please remember that, as your personal syn-psych counselor, I'm available for consultation at any time."

"Given the size of the fee that Synergistic Connections charges, I think that goes without saying," Lucas muttered. "You'll have to excuse me, Batt. I've got an appointment."

"Certainly, certainly. I'll call you in a couple of days to see how you're getting along."

Lucas hung up the phone. The sense of doom thickened. Registering with an agency was the smart thing to do, he reminded himself. No doubt about it. Five years ago he had proven beyond a shadow of a doubt that, while he was very good at finding jelly-ice, he was remarkably incompetent when it came to the business of finding a life mate.

He had been searching for something besides jelly-ice for years. It was only recently that he had finally put the need into words. He was tired of being alone. He longed for what most people took for granted, a family of his own. He wanted to feel connected. He wanted to look in his children's eyes and see the future.

He had no clear memories of his parents. He only knew that, like so many others who did not fit into the conventional routine of life in the city-states, they had ended up in the Western Islands. The frontier attracted the drifters, the loners, those with shadowed pasts, and those without family ties the way honey-syrup attracted bee-flies.

In the islands a man or a woman could start a new life with no questions asked. Lucas sometimes wondered if it was the burden of an off-the-scale talent that had driven his father to the edge of civilization. Psychic power was an inherited characteristic.

His parents had not survived long enough for Lucas to ask them why they had moved to the islands. Both Jeremy and Beth Trent had been killed in a violent windstorm when their son was three.

There had been no relatives to take Lucas in and raise him. That task had been shouldered by a dour old jelly-ice prospector named Icy Claxby.

Claxby had been as alone in the world as Lucas. In addition to teaching his young charge everything he knew about finding jelly-ice and survival in the jungle, Icy had taught him how to get by without the cushioning network of an extended family.

But the one thing that Icy Claxby had not been able to teach Lucas was how to control the unpredictable flashes of the powerful talent that had made its first appearance shortly after Lucas hit puberty. Icy, an untrained prism, had done the next best thing. He had given Lucas some important advice.

"If you ever get yourself tested, boy, you're gonna go right off the scale," Claxby said. "That ain't good. It ain't good at all."

"Why not?" Lucas asked. He was only thirteen, and he was still having fun with the process of discovering his erratic psychic abilities. "I thought you said high-class talents are respected in the city-states. They get good jobs and stuff 'cause they're usually smart."

"A powerful talent gets respect, but too much talent scares folks. I'm just a medium-spectrum prism, kid, untrained to boot, but I can tell you that you've got more talent than those fancy lab techs will be able to measure. If they figure out that you don't fit into their notion of what's normal, they'll get spooked. Word will get out, and you'll have nothin' but trouble."

"I wouldn't mind throwing a scare into Kevin Flemming," Lucas said, thinking of the bully who was making life miserable for him and his classmates at the small school in Fort LeConner.

Icy's alarm was immediate and plain. "Five hells, boy, you ain't *tryin' to use your talent at school, are you? Damn it, I warned you not to ever fool around with it in front of anyone except me."*

"No, sir," Lucas said. "I haven't tried to use it at school."

Icy's expression relaxed slightly. "There's other ways of dealin' with a bully. Find one."

"Yes, sir."

Icy gripped Lucas's shoulder with hands that bore the scars of a lifetime spent on a harsh frontier. His faded eyes glittered beneath his shaggy brows. "Listen, boy, I'm serious about this. If folks find out that you've got a powerful talent, there'll be hell to pay."

"Like what?"

"People will call you a psychic vampire."

"So?" The possibility held distinct appeal.

"So you'll have problems gettin' a job, for starters. Men won't want to hire you. Others will refuse to work with you or for you. Lots of ice miners are superstitious, you know that."

"Yes, but—"

"You won't be able to date any decent females 'cause their parents will think you're a freak. You been talkin' lately about havin' a real family of your own someday. Well, you'll never find a wife because no matchmaking agency will register you. See what I'm sayin'?"

"Yeah," Lucas said. Being a psychic vampire was apparently not as exciting or as useful as it sounded. It could prevent him from having a family of his own. Bad synergy. "I see."

Lucas had found another way to deal with Kevin Flemming, a method that had involved a large bucket of garbage and a pair of small, harmless twin-snakes.

Dealing with the erratic bursts of talent had proved to be much more complicated. Icy Claxby was an untrained prism. He could provide only limited guidance.

Psychic power made its own demands on a growing boy, just as all the other natural human needs and abilities did. The inborn urge to use the talent, to control it, and to understand it drove Lucas to seek solitude for extended periods of time. Icy Claxby had always been a loner himself. He didn't ask many questions about Lucas's absences.

With increasing frequency, Lucas took refuge in a small, hidden grotto he had discovered deep in the jungle. There, secure in the knowledge that no one could come upon him without warning, Lucas had spent endless hours teaching himself to deal with the strong spikes of psychic energy that his mind produced. The realization that he might never be able to work with a prism who could focus his full spectrum of talent had made him struggle all the harder to learn to control it himself.

He'd had some limited success, much to Icy's surprise. Lucas taught himself enough to conceal the extent of his talent from others, including prisms and synergistic psychologists. If he concentrated, he could force his psychic energy to obey his will for a few seconds at a time without using a prism. The hard-won skill had saved his life and the lives of others on more than one occasion during the Western Islands Action.

It was in the course of cleaning out the pirates that Lucas had discovered there were other powerful talents with secrets living in the islands. The knowledge that he was not the only freak in the world had reassured him. But Rafe Stonebraker and Nick Chastain valued their privacy as much as he valued his. The three men became friends and allies, but they rarely discussed the subject of their off-the-chart talents.

Icy Claxby died the year Lucas turned eighteen. Work, study, and the search for jelly-ice had filled the void for a time, but in the end a cold, dark well of loneliness had opened up somewhere deep inside Lucas. He spent long hours in his hidden grotto, gazing into the fathomless jungle pool. His dream of having a family of his own returned to haunt him.

Eventually he had formed a partnership with Jackson Rye, and for a time the fantasy of belonging to the Rye clan had kept the old dreams at bay, but Lucas had never lost sight of his goal to have his own family.

Five years ago he had met Dora. She had been as alone in the world as he. It seemed to him that they had a lot in common.

The runaway marriage had been a disaster, just as everyone had predicted. It took Lucas less than six weeks to realize that he had been married for his money. Family law being what it was, divorce was not a possibility, so Lucas spent the next eighteen months hoping that his beautiful, sexy, vivacious wife would learn to be happy with him. There were times when he thought he was making progress.

But one day, in a low moment, he had made the mistake of telling Dora about his talent. Whatever affection she might have had for him evaporated in an instant.

"Five hells," Dora whispered, horrified. "You're some kind of psychic vampire."

"It's not like that," Lucas said desperately. "It's harmless."

"You're a freak, that's what you are. A damned freak. You should have told me before I agreed to marry you."

Lucas looked into her eyes and knew that he had just destroyed any hope of having the relationship he had yearned for. He should have listened to Icy Claxby.

"You can skip the outraged horror act." Lucas smiled humorlessly. "We both know you would never have turned down the chance to be the wife of the owner of Lodestar Exploration, even if you had known that he was a freak."

"You aren't the only owner of Lodestar," she reminded him.

In the end Lucas had learned the true meaning of being alone when he found himself sharing a home with a woman who wanted another man.

He pushed aside the old memories with the same ruthless control that he used to conceal his talent. He focused on the Synergistic Connections questionnaire.

Hair color. Did he really give a damn about hair color? What did it matter, anyway. A woman could dye her hair any color she chose.

A rich shade of amber brown would be nice, though.

He frowned when he noticed that the word *amber* did not appear on the list of hair colors. Light brown, dark brown, and reddish brown were offered, but not amber. Lucas picked up a pen and wrote in his selection.

Then he realized what he'd done.

"Damn." Lucas flipped the questionnaire closed and shoved it back in the drawer. He reached for the phone and dialed swiftly, before he could give himself time to reconsider.

A plumy masculine voice answered. "Psynergy, Inc. We make it happen. How can I help you?"

"I'd like to speak to Amaryllis Lark, please."

"One moment."

There was a pause and then Amaryllis came on the line. "This is Amaryllis Lark."

Lucas frowned at the tension in her voice. "Something wrong?" He thought he heard her breath catch. He didn't know if that was a good sign or a bad one. Life was complicated for the intuitionally impaired.

"Is that you, Mr. Trent?"

"I'm not a client any longer. You can call me Lucas."

"Is there a problem with your bill?"

"I haven't seen it yet." Lucas lounged back in his chair. "It's probably sitting in my secretary's In basket." For some reason he began to feel a little more in control of the situation. "I'm calling to ask if you'd like to go out with me."

"Out?"

"Yes, out. You know, like on a date."

"A date?"

She was floundering badly. He could tell that much. Lucas wondered if it was an indication that she was trying to think of a way to turn him down or if she was so excited by the prospect of seeing him again that she could hardly speak. He suspected it was the former, not the latter.

"As I just pointed out," he said, "I'm no longer a client. That being the case, I wondered if maybe your professional code of ethics would allow you to see me socially. Now that you've sent the bill and all."

"You're registered at a marriage agency."

"So are you. What has that got to do with anything? There's nothing in the agency contract that says we can't date whoever we want while we're waiting for them to find Mr. and Mrs. Right for us."

"You're serious, aren't you?"

"Do I sound like a stand-up comedian?"

"No."

"Good. Would you like to go out to dinner tonight?" He realized he was holding his breath.

"As it happens, I have plans for this evening," she said slowly.

"I see." He exhaled deeply. It was probably better this way. No point getting involved in an affair that was limited by its very nature. He would go back to saving himself for his future wife.

Amaryllis hesitated. "You're welcome to join me."

On the other hand, his future wife was highly unlikely to be saving herself for him, Lucas thought. He straightened in the chair. "Yeah, sure. I'll join you. Where are we going?"

"It's sort of a business matter, not a social thing," she said hesitantly. "I have to see someone at a club down in Founders Square. Someplace called SynCity."

Lucas opened his mouth. Nothing coherent emerged. Just something that sounded like "Huh?"

"SynCity. Have you heard of it?"

"Uh—"

"Lucas, is something wrong?"

"Uh—"

"Look, if this is a problem for you, feel free to decline," Amaryllis said crisply. "I realize it's probably not what you had in mind for the evening."

"No," Lucas managed. "No, it's not, but it's not a problem." Fortunately he was sitting down, he thought. Otherwise he would very likely have hurt himself. "Can I ask what sort of business you have with someone at the SynCity Club?"

"I don't have time to explain it now. I've got an appointment in a minute. I'll tell you all about it this evening. I'll pick you up around eight."

"That's not necessary," he managed. "I'll pick you up."

"That's very nice of you. And, Lucas?"

"Yes?"

"Thanks," Amaryllis said in a soft, urgent rush. "I've never been to any of the clubs in Founders Square. I appreciate the company."

"Sure. My pleasure. I think. See you at eight." Lucas very carefully replaced the phone.

He sat staring blankly out the window for a long while. He tried hard, but he could not think of a single reason why prim, straitlaced Amaryllis Lark would want to spend the evening at one of the raunchiest syn-sex strip clubs in town.

Dillon Rye sauntered into Lucas's office shortly before five o'clock. He was dressed in some designer's razzle-dazzle version of traditional Western Islands gear. Lucas hid a grin. The tough, no-nonsense denizens of the islands would have laughed themselves silly at the sight of the multitude of shiny snaps, zippered pockets, useless epaulets, and innumerable flaps that decorated Dillon's khaki shirt and trousers.

"Hi, Lucas." Dillon threw himself down into the nearest chair. "Saw your picture in the paper. How're things going with Miss Lark? Did the agency date work out?"

Lucas folded his arms on the desk. He saw no reason to correct the impression that he had met Amaryllis through an agency. "We're going out again tonight, as a matter of fact."

"Struck lucky on the first match, huh? Totally synergistic, man. I hear it often happens that way. Those agency syn-shrinks know what they're doing. Do I hear wedding bells?"

"No," Lucas said. "You do not. Amaryllis and I are still in the initial stage of getting to know each other."

"Oh. Well, it sounds hopeful, at least. The time has come, as they say. You're at that age where responsible men are supposed to get married. You can't put it off much longer, can you?" Dillon spoke with the serene complacency of a young man who would not have to concern himself with society's expectations for several more years.

Lucas decided to change the subject. "What did you want to talk about?"

Dillon sobered instantly. His blue eyes, so reminiscent of Jackson, turned uncharacteristically serious. "I need a loan. A big one."

Lucas eyed him thoughtfully. "Why?"

"For the investment opportunity of a lifetime."

"Ah. One of those."

"Lucas, I'm serious about this. It's my big chance. If I get in on the ground floor, I'll be worth a fortune in three years."

"What sort of investment are we discussing?"

Dillon leaned forward in his chair. His expression lit with the fires of youthful enthusiasm. "A guy I know who is putting together his own exploration company. Sort of like Lodestar. But instead of jelly-ice, he's going to search for deposits of fire crystal."

"Fire crystal? Dillon, use your head. Fire crystal is almost as scarce as First Generation artifacts."

The spectacularly beautiful, bloodred gemstone known as fire crystal was the by-product of a synergistic reaction that occasionally took place between seawater and a rare plant known as crimson moss. The moss grew on shoreline rocks in certain remote coastal locations. During the formation process, chemicals from the seawater and the moss combined to alter the basic structure of the rocks. Fire crystal was the result.

The gemstone did not form every time seawater and crimson moss came in contact. If that had been the case, it would have been relatively simple to duplicate the process in a controlled fashion. But for some as yet undiscovered reason, the making of fire crystal was unpredictable. The synergistic reaction took place only rarely. One theory was that the red crystal was formed only when the seawater was infused with the excretions of some unidentified species of fish during its spawning process.

"Come on, you're exaggerating," Dillon said. "Fire crystal's not that scarce. The fact that it's rare is what makes it so valuable."

Lucas shook his head. "Trust me, Dillon, this has all the hallmarks of a scam."

"I'm telling you, this guy I know has developed an instrument that can locate deposits of the stuff."

"If a commercially viable gadget had been invented to find fire crystal, it would be front-page news."

"He's keeping it a secret until he can get the patent."

"Is that what he told you? You're being taken, Dillon."

"That's not true. This guy is on the level."

"Is he affiliated with a reputable firm?"

"Not exactly," Dillon admitted. "At least, he was with a big company but he quit when he got the idea for this instrument. If he'd stayed with the company, the firm would have tried to retain the rights to the device."

"What company was he with before he came up with his idea? Seastar Mining? Bancroft Exploration? Gemsearch?"

Dillon's features compressed into stubborn lines. "He can't risk telling anyone where he worked. You know how it is with big corporations. They might take him to court in order to get their hands on his invention."

"I'm sorry, Dillon, but this guy you know sounds like a con artist. My advice is to stay clear of him."

"Five hells," Dillon exploded, "you sound just like Dad. I thought you'd be different. I thought maybe you'd understand."

"You asked your father for a loan?"

"He told me I was an idiot." Dillon's mouth twisted bitterly. "I'm twenty-three years old but everyone treats me as if I were still a kid. Mom and Dad want me to choose between going on to grad school or finding a job in a corporation. But I want to do something interesting with my life."

"Interesting?"

"Something with potential. Something exciting. Jackson was out in the Western Islands looking for jelly-ice when he was my age. So were you, for that matter."

"Dillon—"

"If Mom and Dad have their way, I won't even get out of New Seattle. Sometimes I feel like I'm going to suffocate. They've got my future all mapped out for me, and it's so boring and predictable, it makes me sick."

"Boring?"

"I can see it all now." Dillon fanned his hands out as if revealing a vision. "First a nice, safe, nine-to-five job with a nice, safe, dull company. A few years of quietly going crazy as I work up through endless layers of do-nothing management. A few piddling little raises along the way. The next thing you know I'll be in my thirties. I'll be registering with a marriage agency and getting ready to start my own family."

"What's so bad about starting your own family?"

"Nothing. When the time is right. But I want to live first. Right now my whole future is going down the drain and all because I can't get a simple loan."

Lucas hesitated and then decided to go with his instincts. "Do you want to come to work for Lodestar?"

"Are you crazy?" Dillon's eyes blazed. "I'd give my right arm to go out to the islands to work for Lodestar. But you know how Mom and Dad have been since Jackson got killed. They'd never let me go to work in the islands."

"You don't need your parents' permission to apply for a job," Lucas said quietly.

"Easy for you to say. You don't know what it's like having a family breathing down your neck." Dillon broke off, flushing. "Sorry. Didn't mean to insult you."

"Forget it. You're right. I don't know what it's like to have a family breathing down my neck."

"After Jackson died, Mom and Dad changed." Dillon's gaze slid awkwardly away for a few seconds. Then he slammed a bunched fist down onto the arm of his chair. "Damn it, I loved my brother, but I've spent my whole life in his shadow. He was always the star. Athletics, business, women, you name it, he was a success. He even died a hero."

"I know, Dillon."

"I want to prove to my folks that I'm as smart and savvy as Jackson was. I guess I want to prove to myself that I'm as good as he was."

"Listen to me, Dillon," Lucas said. "You don't have to prove a damn thing to anyone. Live your own life, not your brother's."

"You don't understand." Dillon surged to his feet and stalked toward the door. "No one understands."

Founders Square was the oldest neighborhood of New Seattle. The twelve-block district near the waterfront marked the location of the colonists' first permanent settlement.

None of the buildings in the area actually dated from the first years of colonization because the original structures had all been built of Earth-based materials. They had quickly disintegrated along with virtually everything else that had been made on Earth.

The stranded settlers had rebuilt using native materials. Many of those buildings still stood, as grim and determined-looking in their way as the people who had built them. These sturdy, stalwart structures were not what anyone could call striking architectural statements, but they were important. They represented the beginning of history on St. Helens.

Lucas had a hunch that the founders would have been shocked to the core of their sturdy, upright souls if they could have foreseen what would become of the neighborhood.

Founders Square was now home to the city's most popular nightclubs and casinos. After dark an aura of decadent glamour enveloped the old district. The garish lights of the main strip were bright enough to make visitors ignore the warren of grubby alleys and narrow side streets that angled away from the main thoroughfare.

The flashy casinos promised high-stakes gambling and exotic entertainment. Smaller clubs offered dancing, syn-sex shows, and cheap green wine.

It took Lucas some time to find a parking space. He finally managed to squeeze the Icer into a tiny slot on a skinny side street two blocks off the main strip. A small, blinking sign advertising a grungy syn-sex club glowed coldly above the entrance to a very dark, very narrow lane.

A man would have to be desperate for sex to risk going down that dark alley, Lucas thought.

He glanced at Amaryllis as he deactivated the Icer's engine. She was eyeing the flashing syn-sex sign with distaste. She looked as thoroughly disapproving as any founder.

"So, do you come down here often?" Lucas asked neutrally.

Amaryllis started nervously. "No. I told you, I've never been in the square after dark."

"Are you ready to explain to me why we're celebrating our first date here?"

"I'll explain it on the way to the SynCity Club." She opened the door and got out.

Lucas looked at his watch as he climbed out of the car. He had picked up Amaryllis less than twenty minutes ago. They hadn't been together a full half hour yet, and already his mood was starting to deteriorate.

So why was he here, Lucas wondered. But as soon as he took Amaryllis's elbow he had his answer. Just touching her caused every muscle in his body to tighten with sexual anticipation. He could tolerate five hells' worth of irritation for the sake of this sensation even if he did end the evening under a cold shower.

With Amaryllis's arm tucked into his own, Lucas started toward the bright lights of the strip two blocks away.

"I know I've been acting very mysteriously, Lucas, but there's a reason."

"I'm listening." Lucas kept an eye on the yawning mouth of an alley that was crammed with darkness. It was a reflex on his part, the result of having grown up on the edge of a jungle. The predators that hunted in the city walked on two feet instead of the four, six, or eight appendages common to much of the wildlife of the Western Islands, but they were just as dangerous.

Amaryllis shoved her hands into the pockets of her coat. "I got a strange call Friday afternoon as I was leaving work. I spent the weekend thinking about what to do next."

Lucas absently tracked two shadowy figures who hovered in a darkened doorway. "How strange was this phone call?"

"The person on the other end of the line would not identify himself. I was told that if I wanted to know the truth about Professor Landreth, I should talk to a woman who works at the SynCity Club."

"What the hell are you talking about?" Lucas came to an abrupt halt and spun her around to face him. "What's Landreth got to do with our date?"

"Calm down, Lucas. There's no need to get emotional."

"I'm not emotional, I'm pissed off. There's a difference. What do you think you're doing?"

"The caller said that someone named Vivien who worked at the SynCity Club could give me information."

"About Landreth?"

"Yes."

"That's crazy."

Amaryllis lifted her chin. "That's why I'm here tonight, Lucas. I want to talk to her. I told you it was business. If you'd rather not accompany me, I'll understand."

Lucas gripped the lapels of her coat. "I don't believe this. Don't tell me that our little security job the other night at the museum gave you visions of becoming an amateur detective?"

"I admired and respected Professor Landreth more than anyone else on the faculty at the university."

"So what?"

"Questions have been raised, Lucas. I feel that, in honor of his memory, I must pursue the answers. You, of all people, must know what if feels like to need answers."

"What questions have been raised?" Lucas asked very carefully.

"Well, first, there is the matter of a Landreth-trained prism engaging in unethical focusing."

"Not that nonsense again. What's it got to do with this?"

"Don't you see? One thing leads to another. The more I wondered why a properly trained prism would get involved in unethical activities, the more I began to ask other questions."

"Such as?"

"Such as, what if Professor Landreth knew about the prism's unethical behavior? What if someone didn't want him to know?"

"Five hells," Lucas muttered. "I think I see where this is going."

"And then I got that phone call implying that there was a mystery connected to Professor Landreth. Lucas, if there is even the slightest possibility that his death was not an accident, I'm going to insist upon a full investigation."

"Fine. Go to the police and tell them that some anonymous caller told you that a syn-sex stripper may have information about Landreth. Let the cops take it from there."

"The case is closed as far as the police are concerned. You know as well as I do that they're hardly likely to reopen an accident investigation just because I got an anonymous phone call."

The light was poor on the side street, but Lucas had no difficulty seeing the determination in Amaryllis's face. It alarmed him as nothing else had done in a long, long time. "Amaryllis, listen to me, this is not a good idea."

"I just want to talk to Vivien to see if she really knows anything, that's all. You don't have to stick around if you'd rather not get involved."

"You're not listening, Miss Lark. I'd rather *you* didn't get involved."

"I thought you would have some empathy for my feelings."

"Because I know what it feels like to want answers? Amaryllis, bear in mind that I didn't particularly like the ones I got."

Her soft mouth firmed in a small but significant gesture that Lucas was beginning to recognize. Amaryllis had dug in her heels.

"I'm committed to this," she said austerely. "Look, I told you that I was coming down here on business tonight. If you would prefer to spend the evening somewhere else—"

"Anywhere else."

"Then feel free to get back in your car and go home."

"Do you really think I'm going to leave you all by yourself down here?"

Something in his voice must have gotten through to her because Amaryllis's expression turned wary. "Probably not."

"Probably not is right." Lucas released her lapels, seized her arm, and started toward the bright lights that marked the strip. "Let's go."

She quickened her pace to keep up with him. "I appreciate this, Lucas. I didn't want to come down here alone, but I hope you don't feel that I used you. You did volunteer."

"Yeah, sure. There's just one thing, Amaryllis."

"Yes?"

"When this is over, you owe me a real date. I intend to collect."

When the club door opened, the sensual, driving rhythms of heavy ice rock spilled over Amaryllis in a wave. Drunken laughter and the din of voices pitched above the level of the music created a wall of noise. Flashes of arcing light zipped back and forth through the shadows, creating just enough illumination to reveal the club's customers seated at small, round tables.

Amaryllis came to a halt just inside the door and gazed around in dismay. "We'll never find a place to sit."

"What?" Lucas asked.

She cupped a hand to her mouth. "I said, we'll never find a table."

"We should be so lucky. Come on, unfortunately I think I see one over there near the wall."

Amaryllis slanted him a sidelong glance as he guided her through the darkened club. Lucas was not in a good mood. It had been a mistake to bring him with her, she thought. On the other hand, she was very glad he was here.

A waiter materialized out of the darkness the moment Amaryllis sat down.

"What'll it be?" he asked in a bored voice. "Two-drink minimum."

Amaryllis looked up at the young man who was standing impatiently in front of her. He was very handsome, very blond, and for an instant she feared that he was very naked. Then she noticed the tiny, tautly stretched leather thong that barely covered the critical regions of his anatomy. Actually, it was difficult not to notice the garment. It was at roughly eye level.

In an effort to conceal her shock, she hastily averted her eyes and gazed fixedly at Lucas. "Wine." The word came out in a squeak. She cleared her throat. "I'll have a glass of wine, please."

"Green, white, or blue?" The waiter demanded.

"Green, please," she said quickly, opting for the weakest of the three.

The waiter glanced at Lucas. "And you, sir?"

"What kind of beer do you have on tap?"

"Jungle Fever, Twin Moons, and Five Hells."

"Five Hells."

"Got it. Be right back."

Amaryllis could not resist another glance at the waiter as he wheeled and disappeared into the crowd. She was curious, in spite of herself, to see where he stashed the small notepad he used to jot down drink orders. There did not appear to be any pockets in the leather thong that she could see.

Lucas leaned across the table. "Not quite what you expected?"

"I didn't know what to expect." Blushing furiously, Amaryllis jerked her attention away from the waiter's muscular flanks. "I've got to figure out a way to talk to this Vivien person."

Lucas shrugged. "Ask our server when he gets back."

"Good idea."

A drumroll silenced the music and the crowd. On stage the arcing jelly-lights began to pulse in rapidly shifting patterns between floor and ceiling. A murmur of anticipation rose from the onlookers.

A man dressed in formal evening wear stepped out from behind the heavy blue-and-gold curtains. He had a microphone in his hand.

"Ladies and gentlemen." The announcer paused to make certain he had the full attention of the crowd. "Welcome to SynCity, where your most erotic dreams come true. Tonight's performance is about to begin. For those of you who have never experienced synergistically augmented sexual entertainment, allow me to present the two people who will thrill you tonight. York and Yolanda."

The crowd roared its approval as the outer layer of the curtain rose. A man and a woman stood revealed in the flashing lights. Both wore skintight garments fashioned of a glittering, silvery material. Their hair had been dyed a matching shade of silver white. Long silver gloves covered their hands and arms.

The music swelled as York and Yolanda bowed to the audience. It took the announcer several minutes to regain the attention of the crowd. When he had it, he gave a leering smile and winked broadly.

"York is a class-eight talent, ladies and gentlemen. He is a syn-sex generator. One of those rare individuals gifted with the ability to pick up strong sexual sensations, heighten those sensations, and project them toward those of you who are lucky enough to be sitting in our audience tonight. Yolanda is the powerful prism who will assist him. Let's hear it again for York and Yolanda."

The crowd broke into eager applause. Shouts of encouragement went up around the room. Amaryllis frowned at Lucas.

"There is no such thing as a . . . a syn-sex generator," she hissed across the table. "And even if there were, he couldn't possibly project the sensations of sexual activity to a room full of people."

Lucas glanced around. "Tell that to this crowd. The first rule of good theater is that the audience wants to believe. And this crowd definitely wants to believe."

The announcer raised his hand for silence and got it. "Ladies and gentlemen, prepare to enjoy a truly unique sexual experience. You are about to discover new levels of erotic stimulation. I give you Vivien of the Veils."

The inner curtain rose. A woman appeared in the spotlight. She was shrouded from neck to toe in flowing purple. Her head was bowed. Purple hair cascaded down her back to her waist. Massive purple crystals sparkled on her wrists and decorated the gold circlet that bound her hair.

Amaryllis stared. "Do you think that's the Vivien we came to meet?"

"Wouldn't be surprised. Probably not a lot of Viviens around here. At least not a lot who wear veils."

The music fell into a low, throbbing beat. York and Yolanda took up positions at the edge of the stage. They clasped hands and closed their eyes as if in intense concentration.

The thonged waiter returned just as Vivien lifted her head and began a series of sultry, sinuous movements. Amaryllis picked up her glass and sipped cautiously at the weak green wine. She watched, first in amazement and then with increasing embarrassment, as the dancer's veils shimmered and swirled. Glimpses of Vivien's buttocks and breasts created a ripple of excitement in the audience.

"Reminds me of that dress you wore to the museum reception," Lucas murmured.

Amaryllis was outraged. "That's not true. My dress was perfectly decent."

"Whatever you say."

The men in the crowd hooted and applauded as the first of Vivien's veils fell away. The women in the audience cheered a moment later when a man emerged from the shadows and strode onto the stage. He wore a pair of thigh-high leather boots and a thong that was even smaller than the waiter's.

The male dancer reached out to snatch one of Vivien's veils. It came free, baring the dancer's breasts, which were supported by a purple harness that emphasized purple rouged nipples. Amaryllis decided that she and Vivien did not shop at the same semiannual underwear and foundation sales.

Vivien circled her partner in a series of unmistakably erotic movements. The man responded with strong pelvic thrusts, which Amaryllis knew could not have been good for his lower back.

The music quickly grew more intense. The beat became relentless. At the edge of the stage, York and Yolanda were bathed in a sheen of sweat.

The male dancer lowered himself onto a purple velvet rug. Vivien, now almost completely nude, straddled his hips.

Embarrassed, Amaryllis turned her attention to the audience. The heavy breathing in the immediate vicinity was quite audible. A few people began to pant and moan. A shrieking cry of ecstasy emanated from a dark corner of the room. A man's husky groan sounded from a neighboring table.

On stage, York and Yolanda strained mightily as Vivien and her companion ground away at each other.

"I don't believe this for one minute." Amaryllis glowered at Lucas. "It's all an act."

Lucas smiled. "Want to prove that York and Yolanda aren't doing a damn thing except sweating up there on the stage?"

Amaryllis understood immediately. "You want to link? Here? Now?"

"I'm a detector, remember? If York is using any talent, I'll pick it up."

Amaryllis's cheeks burned at the memory of the sensual sensations that had flooded through her the last time she and Lucas had linked.

"I don't think that's such a good idea." She almost winced at the prim tone in her voice. "I'm supposed to be here on business."

Lucas grinned. "You're scared."

"That's not true."

"Don't worry, you're a professional, remember? You can handle it."

He was goading her. Amaryllis knew it but she couldn't seem to rise above it.

"All right," she muttered. "But just for a moment."

Lucas's eyes gleamed in the darkness. He reached across the table and took her hand.

The link happened quickly. A few seconds of seeking, the brief sensation of vulnerability, and then Amaryllis went to work. The prism took shape on the psychic plane.

"You know, professionally speaking, Miss Lark, you're good," Lucas drawled softly. "Very good."

Talent pulsed through the prism.

The noise of the music and the crowd faded. To her dismay, Amaryllis became acutely aware of the warmth in her lower body. She had been doing a reasonably good job of suppressing her reaction to Lucas all evening, but something about the link loosened those inner controls. His fingers tightened around hers.

"I'm not picking up anything from York," Lucas whispered. "The guy's a complete fake."

"I knew it." Amaryllis hastily broke the link. The prism winked out of existence.

A woman's shriek sliced through the dark room. A man gave a muffled groan. The couple sitting at the neighboring table began to kiss passionately.

"Want to leave?" Lucas asked gently.

"I have to talk to Vivien."

"We can wait outside until the performance is over and then go to her dressing room."

Amaryllis felt absurdly grateful for the suggestion. "Excellent idea." She leaped to her feet.

Lucas put down his unfinished beer, stood, threw some money down, and took her hand. He forged a path through the maze of tiny tables. The cries and moans of people who appeared to be in the throes of sexual climax rose and fell.

"I can't believe that all these people have actually convinced themselves that they're being sexually stimulated by York and Yolanda." Amaryllis said. "This is nothing more than self-induced mass hysteria."

"I guess it works for them," Lucas said.

Chapter 7

"Hold it." Amaryllis held up an imperious hand as Lucas reached for his wallet. "What do you think you're doing?"

Lucas glanced at the expectant expression on the face of the massive man who blocked the stage door entrance. The guard looked as if he had once been severely overmuscled. He was now seriously overweight. He created a formidable barrier.

Lucas assessed the situation and looked at Amaryllis's disapproving frown. "What do you think I'm doing? I'm going to bribe him to let us in so that you can meet Vivien of the Veils. That's what we're here for, isn't it?"

"We shouldn't have to give this person a bribe just to get in the door. It's not right."

The heavyset guard eyed Amaryllis with kindly indulgence. "You must be new in town."

She took a step toward him. "I am not new in town. And even if I were, I'd still know that bribery is wrong."

The big man looked at Lucas. "No offense, but I'd suggest you get yourself another lady friend. Don't think you two have much in common."

"You'd be surprised." Lucas shoved three bills into the guard's massive fist. "Can we go inside now? We're in a hurry."

"Be my guest. Viv's door is the third one on the left." The guard heaved his bulk off a stool and indicated the entrance with a surprisingly gracious wave of his broad hand.

Amaryllis favored the big man with one last reproving frown as she went past. "You should be ashamed of yourself, you know."

"Oh, I am, I am." The guard beamed.

Lucas took Amaryllis's arm before she could continue the lecture. "Let's go."

The corridor inside the entrance was cramped and narrow. Lucas could have easily touched the low ceiling. The throbbing music from the stage created a dull background roar. The walls vibrated.

The sign on the first door indicated that it was a storage closet. The second door was labeled "Wardrobe." A large purple star glowed on the third door.

"Something tells me this is Vivien's." Lucas halted in front of the star and knocked twice.

"Come on in, it ain't locked," a woman called out loudly enough to be heard over the music.

Out of the corner of his eye, Lucas saw Amaryllis's hand clench around her purse strap. She looked anxious but resolved. *Real founder material*, he thought as he opened the door to reveal a dingy dressing room decorated entirely in purple.

Vivien, garbed in a purple dressing gown, was seated in front of the mirror. She paused in the act of wiping off some purple makeup. Her eyes moved over Lucas with businesslike speculation. Without the elaborate makeup, her features were far less exotic than they had appeared on stage. The hard lines around her eyes and mouth bespoke a wealth of streetwise experience. But the smile she gave Lucas was polite, almost indulgent.

"Sorry. I don't do unscheduled private acts. You gotta make an appointment."

"I'll keep that in mind," Lucas said.

Amaryllis stepped out from behind Lucas. "Hello. My name is Amaryllis Lark."

Vivien switched her appraising glance to Amaryllis. "New in town? Not a bad stage name. If you're looking for a job, you'll have to try somewhere else. Me and York and Yolanda have a long-term contract here."

Amaryllis blinked. "A job?" Understanding lit her eyes. She turned pink. "Oh, I see what you mean. No, I'm not looking for work. I just wanted to ask you a few questions."

"Questions, huh?" Vivien's gaze sharpened. "You two cops?"

"No, of course not," Amaryllis said quickly. "This is a personal matter."

"Personal." Vivien turned back to the mirror and began to smear cream into her purple eye shadow. "That'll cost you."

Lucas reached for his wallet a second time. Ignoring Amaryllis's obvious disapproval, he dug out a few more bills and handed them to the stripper.

Vivien made the money disappear into the front of her purple gown. She met Amaryllis's eyes in the mirror. "Ask away, honey."

Amaryllis clasped her hands in front of her. "Well, I suppose what I want to know is, were you acquainted with Professor Jonathan Landreth?"

"Sure, I knew Jonny." Vivien expertly massaged more cream into the skin above her eyes. "Funny little guy. Always acted as if his underwear was a couple of sizes too small, but other than that, he was okay. Real reliable. Never missed an appointment."

Amaryllis cleared her throat. "You called him Jonny?"

"Sure. What else?" Vivien sighed. "I was real sorry to hear about his accident last month. Poor old Jonny was definitely wound a little too tight, but he was a perfect gentleman. And he always paid up front."

Amaryllis's brows came together in obvious bewilderment. "What did he pay for?"

"Paid to watch me dance, naturally. Private performances only. Jonny never wanted to sit out front with the audience. Kind of shy, I guess. He wanted to watch me perform for him alone." Vivien chuckled. "Said he didn't need York and Yolanda to get him hot."

Amaryllis threw Lucas an uneasy glance. "I see."

"How come you're so curious about Jonny now that he's dead?" Vivien asked.

Amaryllis hesitated. "Someone suggested that you might be able to tell me something about him."

"Like what?"

"I was told that you knew the truth about him." Amaryllis shrugged. "I wondered if that meant that you knew something about his death."

"Jonny's death?" Alarm flashed in Vivien's face. "I don't know a damn thing about it. Look here, if you've got any idea of involving me in that, you can think again. Get out of here right now or I'll call Titus."

Lucas figured Titus was the mountain who stood guard at the door. "It's okay," he said. "We're not trying to tie you to Landreth's death. We know it was an accident."

Vivien's gaze flicked back and forth between Lucas and Amaryllis. "That's what it said in the papers. He fell off a cliff or something, right?"

"Right," Lucas agreed. He gave Amaryllis a warning look.

She pursed her lips, apparently not certain how to proceed. "When did you last see Professor Landreth?"

Vivien shrugged. "Night before he died. His regular appointment."

"No offense," Amaryllis said, "but it's hard to envision Professor Landreth having a standing appointment with you."

"Well, believe it. I danced privately for Jonny one night a week for two years. He was as regular as clockwork."

"I see." Amaryllis said. "Did Jonny, I mean, did Professor Landreth seem anxious or preoccupied the last time you saw him?"

"What d'you mean?" Vivien still looked suspicious.

"I'm not sure," Amaryllis admitted. "I suppose I'm asking if he seemed different that night. Distracted, perhaps?"

A shrewd light gleamed in the stripper's eyes. "You're with an insurance company, aren't you? That's what this is all about. I'll bet you're trying to get out of paying off on Jonny's policy. Well, you won't get no help from me."

"I'm not working for an insurance company," Amaryllis said hastily. "I just want to settle a few outstanding questions, that's all. Professor Landreth was a friend of mine."

"Friend, huh?" Vivien reached for a brush.

"He was my mentor at the university."

Vivien softened somewhat. "I guess you could say that Jonny was a little more tense than usual that last night. But it was hard to tell with him on account of he was always on the rigid side, if you know what I mean. Actually, he'd been fussing for a couple of months, now that I think of it."

"What did he fuss about?" Amaryllis asked.

Vivien looked expectantly at Lucas. With one shoulder propped against a purple wall, Lucas stoically dug his wallet out of his pocket once more. Silently he removed some cash and handed it to Vivien. She gave him a radiant smile and turned back to Amaryllis with a confidential air.

"In the past few weeks Jonny talked more than usual about how there was still a lot the experts didn't know about the synergy of psychic talent. He rambled on a bit about how no one had documented all the different types of power yet. About how some talent might be dangerous."

"Dangerous?" Amaryllis repeated.

Vivien used a tissue to remove several more layers of makeup. "You have to understand, Jonny was always carrying on about his research. I tuned him out most of the time. My job was to relax him."

"Did he mention any names?" Amaryllis asked cautiously.

"No." Vivien tossed the tissue aside. "Hell, I wouldn't have remembered if he had. None of my business. Excuse me. Gotta use the facilities."

Vivien rose from her purple cushioned stool. The dressing gown billowed out behind her as she crossed the threadbare carpet to open a narrow door at the rear of the room.

Lucas averted his eyes quickly, but not before he caught a glimpse of a familiar, silver-haired figure seated inside the small bathroom. Yolanda did not look up from the magazine she was reading.

"Be out in a minute, Viv."

"Sorry, Yo, dear. Didn't hear you in there." Vivien slammed the door and heaved a deep sigh of resignation. "Yolanda and me gotta share the crapper. Her dressing room is right next door. The jerk who owns this joint is too damn cheap to give his star dancer her own bathroom. Can you believe it? I swear I'm gonna quit one of these days. There's better clubs on the strip."

"I can't believe it," Amaryllis said.

"Can't believe that Vivien and Yolanda have to share a restroom?" Lucas took Amaryllis's hand as they walked out of the alley behind the SynCity Club. "Hey, being a syn-sex stripper's a tough way to make a living."

"Don't be ridiculous. I'm not talking about the dressing room facilities. I'm referring to the fact that Professor Landreth had a standing appointment with Vivien."

"As perversions go, I'd say Landreth's was fairly innocuous."

"But it was so unlike him. I knew him for years, and I never had an inkling that he, well, you know."

"Someone sure as hell had a more realistic view of the sainted professor." Lucas guided her through the crowd toward the side street that led back to where the Icer was parked.

"What do you mean?" She glanced at him with a searching frown. "Oh, I get it. The person who sent me to see Vivien obviously knew about the appointments."

"Yeah."

One block off the main strip, the number of people on the sidewalk dwindled swiftly. The music, noise, and laughter that blared from the open doors of the clubs receded into the distance. Lucas tightened his grip on Amaryllis's arm, keenly aware of the sound of her footsteps ringing lightly on the stone pavement. He began watching alley entrances and dark doorways.

"Vivien wasn't very helpful, was she?" Amaryllis said after a while.

"She didn't have anything to tell you because nothing out of the ordinary occurred the night before Landreth's death," Lucas said deliberately. "You heard her say that the professor was always tense."

"Yes, but she did imply that the night before he died, he had been more tense than usual. In fact, she said he'd been that way for several weeks."

"She's a performer. She probably felt obliged to give you something for your money."

"You mean for your money," Amaryllis muttered. "I still don't approve of bribery."

"I don't know how in five hells you've managed to get this far in life without learning a few of the fine points of pragmatism. The future belongs to the expedient."

"Nonsense. You don't really believe that."

"We'd still be trying to get through the stage door entrance if I hadn't bribed the guard," Lucas said. "But given the fact that you and I are never going to see eye to eye when it comes to personal philosophies, let's move on."

"To what?"

"I'll grant you that this evening has had its interesting moments, but things have gone far enough. Think about it logically, Amaryllis. If there had been anything strange about the circumstances of Landreth's accident, the police would have pursued an investigation."

"Talking to Vivien has given me an idea, Lucas." Amaryllis sounded as if she had not heard a word he'd said. "It might not be a bad idea to talk to a few other people who saw the professor just before he was killed."

"I was afraid of this. What is it with you? Looking for answers is one thing. Getting obsessive about them is another." Lucas sensed the movement in the deep shadows of the alley before he saw the two men. "Damn. Just what I needed to make this evening perfect."

"What are you doing?"

He didn't respond. Lucas used his grip on Amaryllis's arm to shove her behind him as he pivoted to face the gaping mouth of the alley. There was a clattering noise as she fetched up against a heavy metal garbage can.

"Oh, dear," Amaryllis said in a very small voice.

A rustling sound announced the indignant departure of some small animal that had been dining on the contents of the overflowing trash container.

"Lucas?"

Lucas heard her quick, sharp intake of breath. "Stay between me and the wall. Understand?"

"Yes," she whispered.

The first man emerged from the alley. He moved with the sinuous glide of a practiced street predator. He was followed by a slightly shorter man who approached with a crablike gait. In the weak light of the streetlamps Lucas saw that both men were dressed in Western Islands gear. Each wore his long, greasy hair tied with a leather thong. The first man wore the designer version of the fashion look. He was covered with an array of zippers, pockets, epaulets, and gadget loops.

But the smaller man wore the real thing.

Lucas glanced at the knives in the men's hands, and then he concentrated on watching their eyes.

"Nice outfits," Lucas offered politely.

"Ain't they, though?" The tall man in the fancy gear snaked closer. "Me and Dancer pride ourselves on being stylish, don't we, Dancer?"

"Yeah, Rand, stylish. That's us." Dancer's teeth glinted in a savage grin.

"Something we can do for you two fashionable gentlemen?" Lucas asked.

"Well, now that you mention it, there surely is." Rand motioned with the knife. "You can start by handin' over your wallet."

"And then you can hand over the lady." Dancer licked his lips. "Been a long time since I had a chance to crawl between the legs of a pretty little thing like her."

"What a disgusting little creep you are," Amaryllis said loudly.

"Quiet, Amaryllis." Lucas did not take his eyes off the approaching men.

Dancer spit on the sidewalk. "Don't worry, I like 'em feisty. More fun that way."

"You are both a disgrace to the clothes you wear," Amaryllis informed Dancer and Rand.

"Huh?" Dancer's face screwed up into a tight frown.

"You're wearing Western Islands frontier gear, but it's obvious that neither of you has ever been anywhere near the islands. I suspect you wouldn't last five minutes in a real jungle. You lack the fortitude to live on the frontier."

Rand scowled at Lucas. "You better shut her up real fast."

Lucas shrugged. "That's easier said than done."

"You're frauds, both of you," Amaryllis declared. "A couple of city street punks playing at being real brave frontiersmen."

"Stop her right now." Dancer's voice rose with alarming suddenness. In the blink of an eye he was losing whatever control he possessed. "Hear me? Make her be quiet."

Rand cast an uneasy sidelong glance at his companion. Then he grimaced. "Better do as he says," he advised Lucas.

"Sorry," Lucas said briefly. "I've got better things to do."

He knew that this was the best chance he was going to get. He summoned energy and poured it into the illusion.

He had no way to focus, so he could not generate a solid, substantial image, just a ghostly apparition. Without a prism he could not make it last for more than a few seconds. But after all the years of practice, he had enough control and enough power to create a brief distraction. With any luck, that was all he and Amaryllis would need.

Lucas readied himself. He felt the stirring of a cold wind. It was a familiar sensation. It often preceded his use of talent, especially when he was attempting to control it without the assistance of a prism.

"What the hell?" Rand swung toward the figure of a policeman that had coalesced in the shadows near a gate. "Where did he come from?"

"What are you talkin' about?" Dancer shifted his attention toward the figure in the shadows. "I don't see nothin'."

The policeman winked out of existence. Lucas moved at the same instant that he lost the ghostly image. He lashed out with his foot and connected with Rand's knife hand. Bone cracked.

Rand grunted with pain and dropped his weapon. He clutched at his injured wrist and stared at Lucas, eyes slitted with fury. "Get him, Dancer. Get the bastard. Hurry. We got money ridin' on this."

Dancer was already moving forward with his peculiar gait. His knife wove an intricate pattern in the air. Lucas recognized the fighting style. And the talent.

"You were wrong, Amaryllis," he said softly. "Dancer has spent some time in the islands. Long enough to pick up the Knife Dance. Isn't that right, Dancer?"

"Damn right. I was there three years ago." Dancer's eyes glinted. "Nearly took the islands, we did. If it hadn't been for you, Trent, me and the others would've been runnin' the whole show by now."

"He knows who you are," Amaryllis whispered.

"Stop talkin' and rip him open," Rand screamed. "We won't get paid if we don't finish this."

"With pleasure. *Link*." Dancer leaped at Lucas. The knife darted about in dazzling, almost hypnotic movements.

Lucas estimated that Dancer was a class-five or perhaps a six talent. He was more than just a skilled knife dancer. He had a gift for hand-to-hand fighting techniques. Rand was obviously working as his prism tonight.

"Dear God." Amaryllis had apparently just realized that they were facing a talent-prism fighting team.

"Run," Lucas ordered. He kept his full attention on Dancer. "Get out of here, Amaryllis. Head for the strip."

The trick to dealing with a knife dancer was to ignore the blade. The movements were calculated to be simultaneously terrifying and entrancing. The snakelike motions held the attention of the victim until the dancer was ready to slash.

Lucas edged back a few steps. He switched his gaze to Dancer's feet in order to avoid the entrancing movements of the knife. He groped for and found the metal lid of the garbage can.

Lucas swept the can lid around in a wide arc just as Dancer leaped. The knife blade clashed dissonantly against the makeshift metal shield.

Dancer hissed and tried to scramble back out of reach. Lucas gave him no chance to recover his balance. He went in low and fast, using the lid as both armor and weapon.

"Bastard. I'm gonna kill you, Trent." Dancer tried and failed to sidestep the garbage can lid. It caught him on the shoulder with enough force to cause him to stumble.

Lucas discarded the lid and seized Dancer's knife arm. He twisted hard. Something cracked.

Dancer screamed in pain. The knife clattered to the pavement. Lucas slammed a fist into Dancer's jaw. The knife dancer crumpled.

"Lucas," Amaryllis called. "Behind you."

A roar of rage made Lucas spin around. He saw Rand bearing down on him. The irrational glitter in the man's eyes was visible even in the weak light. Rand's face was contorted into a grotesque mask. He had another knife in his fist. *Must have grabbed it from his boot,* Lucas thought.

Lucas braced himself, but at that moment Amaryllis took a step forward, away from the brick wall. She raised a large object that she had apparently retrieved from the garbage can. It looked like a small wooden packing crate.

She waited until Rand's maddened charge had carried him one step past where she stood. She raised the packing crate on high and then brought it down hard against the back of Rand's skull.

Rand lost his footing and sprawled forward. His face made forceful contact with the sidewalk. He twitched but did not move.

Lucas glanced at Rand, aware of the adrenaline flowing through his veins. He remembered the sensation all too well. He looked at Amaryllis and grinned. "We make a good team."

Amaryllis ignored him. Her gaze was riveted at a point just beyond Lucas's shoulder. *"Lucas."*

Lucas heard them. He turned his head to glance briefly at the three figures who were sauntering cautiously out of the shadows of a doorway. The noise of the skirmish had drawn would-be opportunists in the same way that the struggles of a wounded animal drew hopeful scavengers.

Lucas grabbed Amaryllis's hand. "Time to leave."

"Definitely."

She ran with him toward the car, which Lucas judged to be closer than the safety of the main strip.

He risked another glance over his shoulder as they pounded down the street. The new arrivals were still milling about, apparently trying to decide upon a course of action. He hoped that they would opt to go through Rand's and Dancer's pockets rather than try to run down the escaping prey. A tough decision, but someone had to make it.

He spotted the two men lounging against the fender of the Icer when he and Amaryllis were still half a block away.

"Five hells." This whole thing was starting to look a little too organized for his peace of mind. The tactics were not unlike the ones the pirates had used in the islands. He wondered how many of the riffraff had escaped after the main force had been routed.

"This way." He yanked Amaryllis around the corner of a building.

"There they go." One of the men leaning against the Icer straightened. "Shit, they're getting away. After 'em."

Lucas drew Amaryllis past several darkened doorways. She was breathing quickly, but she was keeping up with him. They bred them for endurance in the country, he reflected. He would have been dragging a city-born lady along the sidewalk by now.

He spotted the deep darkness of a nearby alley. He hesitated briefly, but when he heard the sound of pounding footsteps closing in swiftly from behind, he knew he had to evaluate the limited options. He wasn't president of a major corporation for nothing. He knew how to make executive decisions.

He pulled Amaryllis into the alley. It took approximately three seconds for him to realize that there was no opening at the far end. By then it was too late. The footfalls of their pursuers were too close.

Then again, Jackson had always told him that he wasn't executive material.

"We're trapped," Amaryllis breathed.

Lucas pressed her back against the nearest brick wall. "I hope you're as good as you keep telling me you are."

"What are you talking about?"

"*Link.*" Lucas grabbed her hand. He needed all the power he could get.

"What good will that do? I hate to be a wet blanket, but your ability to detect other talents, impressive as it is, isn't going to be of much use here, Lucas."

"Don't move, don't say a word, don't even breathe if you can help it. Just give me a clear prism so that I can focus."

Amaryllis did not hesitate. A few seconds of blind seeking, a slight sense of disorientation, and then a crystal-clear prism formed out on the psychic plane.

He sent the raw energy of his talent through it and watched with a sense of satisfaction as it separated itself into colored beams. He chose the darkest band.

And then he went to work crafting a solid brick wall across the entrance of the alley.

He heard Amaryllis draw in her breath when she saw what he was doing. He knew she must have been shocked, but her concentration did not waver.

The wall materialized out of the dark night. It matched the walls of the buildings on either side.

The running footsteps were very close now.

Lucas was torn between the necessity to work quickly and the equally urgent need to work carefully. The danger was that he could easily overwhelm Amaryllis's ability to focus if he used too much of his talent. She was full spectrum, but he was off the chart.

He was already pushing her harder than he had ever pushed a prism. But she did not waver. He used a little more talent. He knew he was going beyond the range of a class ten now.

The focus stayed steady.

Lucas took a chance and eased more power through the prism. The illusion of a brick wall became increasingly solid. It blocked the entire entrance of the alley. Lucas could no longer see the street, which meant that their pursuers could not see the alley.

The nature of an illusion was such that even a good one could not completely block out direct light. The effect was that, viewed from the alley side, the wall glowed because of the light from the streetlamps. But since there was no light from the alley to pass through the illusion, the wall would appear solid when seen from the sidewalk.

At least, Lucas hoped that it appeared solid.

The other potential problem with the effect was that the "wall" had no substance. If someone tried to lean against it, he would tumble straight through and find himself in the alley with Lucas and Amaryllis.

Lucas felt sweat trickle down his back. At any second he might overpower Amaryllis. If that happened, things were going to get nasty. But even in that dire moment, a part of him took a surging pleasure in being able to use the full range of his talent for an extended period of time. The experience was intense and incredibly satisfying. Lucas reveled in it.

Footsteps came to a halt on the other side of the illusory brick wall.

"Where the hell did they go?" a man growled.

"Must have ducked into a doorway or somethin'."

"They gotta be around here somewhere. I saw 'em turn down this street."

Lucas realized that some of the bricks at the top of his wall were partially transparent.

Amaryllis gave his hand a reassuring squeeze. She said nothing, but he sensed that she was trying to tell him that she was all right. He remembered what she had said when they had linked the night of the reception. *I won't break.*

Lucas eased a smidgen more talent through the prism, just enough to solidify the upper layer of bricks.

"These doors are all locked or boarded up," someone said on the other side of the illusion. "So are the windows. They didn't have time to pick any locks or bust any glass. Where are they?"

"Looks like they got away," a second voice declared in disgust. "I told you we shouldn't have tried to work with knife-happy Dancer and his pal. Guy's never been the same since the Western Islands Action."

"Not like we had a lotta choice. Wasn't time to hire reliable talent. The client's pissed off. Somethin' to do with gettin' even because Trent threw him outa the city. He wanted the Iceman taken out at the first opportunity. This was it."

"Yeah, well, I guess your client's gonna have to stay out of the city awhile longer. Dancer and Rand really screwed this one up. Come on, let's get outa here before someone calls the cops."

Lucas listened to the receding footsteps. He held the brick wall illusion in place until he was certain that the men were gone. When he was satisfied that he and Amaryllis were alone on the street, he cut the flow of energy.

The wall vanished. The empty sidewalk and street in front of the alley reappeared.

He heard Amaryllis exhale slowly and deeply. She did not say a word. The glorious satisfaction that he had experienced a moment ago vanished along with the illusion of the wall. Reality returned with a thud.

Now she knows, Lucas thought. A cold chill settled in his gut. Amaryllis was the first person to learn the truth about him since Dora had died.

Psychic vampire.

"Let's go," Lucas said wearily. "We need to find a cop. A real one."

———

Dancer and Rand were still lying on the street where Lucas and Amaryllis had left them. Their pockets were empty and they were not in a cheerful mood. They were more than willing to blame their companions who had been assigned to wait near the Icer.

"We'll pick the rest of them up soon," one of the officers assured Lucas. "We know most of these guys. Any idea of why they targeted you tonight?"

Lucas rubbed the back of his neck. "I think a guy named Beech can answer that question."

"Is that a fact?" The officer gave Lucas a speculative look. "You must've pissed him off."

"I sometimes have that effect on people."

———

Amaryllis remained silent during the drive back to her little house. Lucas couldn't tell if she was angry, shocked, or horrified. He felt the cold feeling grow inside him.

This was the end. Well, he had known from the start that this would not be a long-term relationship.

A bleak desperation seized him when he found himself walking Amaryllis to her front door. He tried to tell himself that the feeling of impending loss was crazy. After all, it was not as though he and Amaryllis had ever had much of a future. A short-term affair was the most he could have expected. Perhaps even that prospect had been as much of an illusion as the brick wall that he had built tonight.

"I'm sorry." He stood on the step and massaged the back of his neck as Amaryllis deactivated the door lock. "I should have told you, but I've never told anyone except Icy Claxby and my wife, Dora."

Amaryllis stepped into the hall and turned to face him. "Who's Icy Claxby?"

Lucas stopped rubbing his neck. He was not going to get rid of the tension that easily. He braced one hand against the doorjamb. "Icy raised me after my parents were killed. He was an untrained prism. He recognized what I was. Warned me not to tell anyone. Said people would call me a vampire."

"Psychic vampire."

He closed his eyes briefly and steeled himself against the pain. "Yeah."

"But you were tested." She searched his face. "You're certified as a class nine."

"I didn't take the test until I knew I could control the talent."

"You've got more than one talent. You're not just a detector. You're also an illusionist."

"Yes."

"It's extremely rare to have two types of psychic power." She sounded curiously detached, as if she were giving an academic talk on the subject.

"Amaryllis, I realize that this has come as a shock."

"Yes, it has."

"I know that professional prisms are always careful not to work with strong talents who might burn them out. And God knows I've heard all the urban legends about off-the-scale talents. But you worked with me tonight. Nothing happened to you. I didn't take over your mind or anything."

"No, you didn't."

"Which proves that the myths are garbage. Nothing more than horror stories designed to give people a few cheap thrills."

"Is that right?"

"Of course it is." Why was he struggling against the inevitable, Lucas wondered. There was no point trying to convince her to ignore what had happened. He was wasting his time. "Besides, we're not likely to get into a situation like that again. I don't see why we need to let it get in the way of a relationship."

She contemplated him for a moment. Her eyes were wide and deep in the glow of the door lamp. "I've always known that I was a strong prism."

"For which we can both be grateful," Lucas muttered.

"But I've never thought of myself as a freak."

He frowned. "You're no freak. What the hell are you talking about?"

"Don't you see, Lucas? I was able to hold the focus for you tonight. You must have been operating at what would be the equivalent of a class eleven or maybe even a twelve."

"Look, I know how you must have felt, but—"

"If you're some kind of psychic vampire, what does that make me?"

He stared at her. "What did you say?"

"My power is as strong as your own," she said very quietly. "Technically speaking, when it comes to psychic energy, power is power, regardless of whether one is a talent or a prism."

Wispy remnants of the deep satisfaction Lucas had experienced during the link drifted through him. "I hadn't thought about it in quite those terms."

Amaryllis walked back out onto the front step, stood on tiptoe, and put her arms around his neck. "It seems to me that you and I have a few more things in common than we originally thought." She brushed her mouth lightly against his. "You don't know what a relief it is to realize that I'm not the only one around with more psychic energy than the lab techs can measure."

Lucas wondered if he had stepped into the center of one of his own illusions. In the next instant he concluded that this was no time to question the nature of reality. He was a pragmatic man by nature, not a philosopher.

He crushed Amaryllis against his chest, lifted her off her feet, and carried her back through the front door.

Chapter 8

Amaryllis heard the front door slam shut and realized that Lucas had kicked it closed. He did not bother to hunt for the small panel on the wall to switch on the lights. Instead, he carried her through the moonlight and shadows into the living room.

The urgency in him threatened to steal her breath. His undisguised sexual desire was as potent as the power of his talent. It swirled around her as if it were a cloak, enveloping her completely. Amaryllis felt the heated rush of passion flowing through her, driving out the tension and fear that had gripped her during the encounter with the street thugs.

With wholly uncharacteristic recklessness, she cast aside her questions and her common sense. The future could take care of itself. The only thing that mattered was this moment and the possibilities inherent in it. She had waited so long for the man of her dreams.

"Lucas." She tightened her arms around his neck.

"I'm here," he whispered. "I couldn't leave now for all the jelly-ice in the Western Islands."

He lowered her onto the couch and sprawled heavily on top of her. His mouth closed over hers as he pulled the remaining pins from her hair. He inhaled deeply.

"It reminds me of the jungle flowers," he said.

She felt his strong hands on the buttons of her blouse. His fingers trembled as he opened the garment. He broke off the kiss to gaze down at her breasts. "So beautiful." He touched one nipple wonderingly and then bent his head to take it into his mouth.

Another wave of excitement flashed through Amaryllis. She lifted herself against Lucas and felt the hard, thickened evidence of his desire. She struggled with his clothing until she got his shirt undone, and then she touched him with shy eagerness. He groaned.

She stroked him more daringly, relishing the taut contours of his chest. When her fingers brushed against his rib cage she felt a long, unnatural furrow of toughened skin.

"You were hurt," she whispered.

"Accident." He dismissed the incident with a drugging kiss. "Long time ago. You want me, don't you? You really want me. I can feel it."

"I've never wanted anything more in my life," Amaryllis said simply.

It was true. A joyous abandon swamped her senses. She was powerful, more so than she had dreamed. She had discovered the truth about herself with a man who could share that power with her. The knowledge was dazzling.

A lifetime of self-restraint went up in smoke. Amaryllis felt wild and eager and free. She hovered on the brink of great discovery, and she could scarcely contain herself. Questions awaited answers.

Lucas rained kisses on her bare shoulders and nibbled at her ear. There was a desperate, straining impatience in his every touch.

He reached down to seize a fistful of her skirt and haul it up to her waist. The feel of his calloused hand on her thigh was so intensely intimate that she cried out with pleasure.

"Are you all right?" He lifted his head to search her face.

"Yes, yes, of course I'm all right." She shoved her fingers into his hair and dragged his mouth back down to hers.

He gave a soft, husky laugh that dissolved into another aching groan. She heard something tear and realized it was the crotch of her panties.

"Damn," Lucas muttered. "I didn't mean to do that."

"Don't worry about it. There are a lot more where those came from. I buy them by the dozen on sale." She raised one knee and pressed it urgently against his muscled thigh.

Lucas cupped her gently and buried his face in the curve of her throat. "Remind me to buy the next dozen for you."

He lifted himself away from her, just far enough to allow him to unbuckle his belt. He got his trousers unfastened and then he eased himself back down between her legs.

He stroked her, his hand vibrating with his own urgency. Amaryllis trembled. She was intensely aware of her own dampness, and she knew that Lucas was breathing in the scent of her body. She was grateful for the shadows.

She felt him part her with his fingers, and then she felt the broad head of his shaft. There was moisture on it. Uncertainty flared for the first time. She had not expected him to be quite so large.

Lucas started to ease himself into her. He paused.

"You're tight," he whispered. "Small and tight."

"No, I'm not. I'm perfectly normal. The problem is that you're too big." She smiled and touched the side of his face. "But don't worry about it. I won't break."

He made a hoarse sound deep in his throat, and then he surged into her, filling her with a suddenness that sent shock waves through every nerve in her body.

Amaryllis gasped and stiffened. She dug her nails into Lucas's back. She had expected some pain, but not quite this much. She inhaled quickly, trying to breathe her way through the moment.

"Amaryllis."

She almost laughed in spite of the discomfort she was experiencing. The stunned shock in Lucas's voice was a thousand times greater than her own.

"Don't worry." She framed his face between her palms and kissed him fiercely. "I won't—"

"I know, I know, you won't break." He returned the kiss with great tenderness. "Why didn't you tell me?"

"Because it wasn't important."

"The hell it wasn't." Lucas started to ease himself back out of her.

"No." Amaryllis clutched at him. "Don't stop. Not now. I want this. I want you."

"Not half as much as I want you. But I never expected that you would be a virgin."

"I told you, it doesn't make any difference. I'm old enough to make my own choices."

"Yes, you are, aren't you?" Lucas's eyes glittered in the shadows. "Link."

She did not understand at first. "What?"

"Link with me."

She obeyed. She was already too disoriented to notice the vulnerable sensation that always preceded the focus link. Her mind looked out on the psychic plane. Instinctively, she created a prism.

"Beautiful." Lucas thrust deeply into her body at the same instant that he poured sparkling waves of energy through the prism.

He made no effort to focus the raw talent. Instead, he let the waves of light splash and froth in a waterfall that cascaded into a brilliant, swirling pool.

The result was a swirl of sensations and an almost unbearable sense of intimacy.

He was her true mate. The one for whom she had waited.

Talent and prism bound by their own shared power.

Amaryllis wanted to scream as the pleasure stormed through her, but she could hardly catch her breath. She was being tumbled about in a fountain of light, color, and energy. Excitement, euphoria, and laughter exploded within her.

She was dimly aware that the pain was still present, but it had blended with all of the other sensations. She could no longer distinguish it, let alone identify it.

"Unbelievable," Lucas muttered against her ear. He began to move rhythmically within her. Simultaneously, he reached down to touch the small bundle of nerve endings hidden between her legs.

Amaryllis stopped breathing for an instant. A delicious tension seized her insides.

"Hold me." Lucas pushed himself deeper into her. "Don't let go." He withdrew slowly and then eased forward once more. "Don't. Let. Go."

"Never." She clung to him.

Wild power crashed through the prism.

It was too much. The tightness in her lower body came undone with no warning. Amaryllis fell headfirst into the whirlpool of sensation. The focus link fractured and disintegrated as she lost what was left of her concentration, but it didn't seem to make any difference. The waves of pleasure continued to wash over her.

She was vaguely aware of Lucas thrusting into her one last time. He went rigid. Then he gave a shout of exultant satisfaction and fell heavily on top of her.

"Have you ever done that before?" Amaryllis asked a long time later.

"Never." He cradled her face between his hands and looked down into her fathomless eyes. "I knew that I was hurting you. I hoped that if you concentrated on holding a focus, you might be distracted from the pain long enough to let yourself get used to the feeling of having me inside you."

"That was very clever of you."

"Thanks. Considering that I was pretty distracted myself at the time, I thought it was fast thinking on my part."

She did not respond to his small attempt at lightness, but she continued to fix him with a steady, thoughtful expression. "Lucas, exactly what did you feel when we linked?"

"I felt very, very good," he said. "I still do."

"But something happens between us when we link. Something that isn't normal."

"It may not be normal, but it feels good, so why worry about it?"

"But, Lucas—"

He put his fingers over her mouth. The last thing he wanted tonight was for her to question the attraction between them. "We both know that it's uncommon for strong talents and prisms to be attracted to each other, but maybe when it does happen, some of the sexual attraction spills over into the link. Does that sound so strange?"

"Yes."

"I vote we don't sweat it."

"There hasn't been much research done on talents and prisms who are physically attracted to each other," she said.

"Probably because it happens so rarely. Look, I don't know about you, but I'm not volunteering for any lab analysis. If you want to conduct some more private experiments, on the other hand, that's okay by me." He wrapped his fingers in her hair and pulled her head down a few inches so that he could kiss her.

She came to him willingly, her mouth warm and soft. Lucas could smell the scent of himself on her. Satisfaction flared deep within him.

But when she lifted her head a moment later, her gaze was still troubled.

"What's wrong?" Lucas asked.

"Nothing."

A chill of fear uncoiled within him. He was the first to acknowledge that he knew very little about the workings of the female mind, but he wasn't stupid. He knew that whenever a woman said that nothing was wrong, there was trouble ahead.

Amaryllis had waited a long time to take a lover. Perhaps she had been disappointed with her first taste of passion. Maybe she was already having regrets.

He couldn't let her go now. Not yet. He had only just found her. He fought back the sense of impending loss and asked the question that was threatening to drive him mad. "Amaryllis, you waited a lot longer than most people do to take a lover. Why me?"

"You know what they say about prisms. Picky, picky, picky."

A long while later Amaryllis roused herself again from the languid aftermath of passion.

"Lucas?"

"Yeah?" He was sprawled beneath her on the couch this time. He looked and sounded as though he was on the edge of sleep.

"Do you really think that Merrick Beech hired those thugs to kill you?"

He yawned. "I'd say it's a safe bet."

"What are we going to do if the police can't find Beech?"

"They'll find him. He doesn't have the brains to hide for long."

"You're sure?"

"I'm sure." He reached for her.

The enticing aroma of hot coff-tea woke Lucas the next morning. He stretched slowly, savoring the fact that he was in Amaryllis's bed. He could hear her moving about in the kitchen, but the fragrance of her body still clung lightly to the rumpled sheets. He inhaled deeply.

He could live on that scent, he decided. He wouldn't need air or food, just the sweet, incredibly alluring fragrance of Amaryllis and the knowledge that she responded to him.

The memories of the night poured through him like raw psychic energy through a prism. Lucas was aware of his body's instant response. He groaned when he realized that he was as hard now as he had been last night.

He shoved aside the covers and sat up resolutely on the edge of the bed. He contemplated the day that stretched before him. He had some appointments at the office, and Amaryllis undoubtedly had to go to work. But the promise of the evening that lay beyond shimmered tantalizingly in his mind.

He surveyed Amaryllis's neat bedroom with great interest as he made his way to the adjoining bath. Everything was black and white in here, just as it was throughout the rest of the little house. Very clean and orderly looking. Functional.

He opened a closet and concluded that there would be room for him to keep a change of clothes in it. He peeked into a dresser drawer and grinned when he saw two neat piles of carefully folded underwear. All in white.

Whistling softly, he went on into the black-and-white tiled bath.

The sight of his beard-shadowed face in the mirror brought him to a halt. He winced as he rubbed the dark stubble. He'd have to remember to pack a razor the next time he went out with Amaryllis. No problem. He would make it a point to put one in the glove compartment of the Icer today.

He planted his hands on the edge of the wash basin and leaned closer to the mirror. He knew he'd never been handsome, but he hadn't realized until this morning just how grim his face had begun to look lately. Talk about psychic vampires. He squinted thoughtfully at the bright lights alongside the mirror. The glare made his eyes appear to be sunk in deep shadows.

And where the hell had that gray in his hair come from? He knew he was no more than six or seven years older than Amaryllis. He'd heard that some women actually preferred older men.

And some preferred their lovers to be younger.

For some inexplicable reason, he found himself wondering what age Amaryllis had selected on her agency questionnaire as the preferred age in a spouse. Not that it mattered, he told himself swiftly. Marriage had nothing to do with this relationship.

His gaze went to the sight of the thick scar tissue that stretched across his ribs. The line marked the passage of a pirate's bullet. He scratched the old wound absently and then paused when he noticed how well the bathroom lights illuminated the ugly fan-shaped mark on his shoulder. It was a souvenir of an encounter with a large bat-snake.

There was no getting around the fact that he did not present an inspiring sight in strong light. All in all, he looked like a man who had spent too much time in the jungle, Lucas thought. Not a pretty picture. He eyed his unprepossessing reflection in the mirror with misgivings. It might be a good idea to make it a point to make love to Amaryllis only in the dark.

On the other hand, if the knowledge that he was an off-the-chart talent had not frightened her, maybe she wouldn't freak out because of a few scars.

In any event, he was feeling far too ebullient to allow his own image to depress him for long. He stepped into the white tiled shower and immediately devoted himself to formulating plans for the evening ahead. Dinner at a really good fish house. Founders Grill, maybe. A good bottle of wine. A rich, robust blue vintage, not the weak green stuff. He would insist on a table in a secluded corner where he and Amaryllis could discuss their future.

Bad idea.

Lucas winced as he soaped his chest. Talents and prisms didn't have long-term futures together. They had short-term affairs, if they had anything at all.

Besides, other than psychic power, he and Amaryllis didn't have a lot in common, anyway.

Okay, so they would sit in the secluded corner and discuss their affair.

And then they would go home. His place this time. He would make love to her all night long. Just to be on the safe side, he would turn out the lights.

Fifteen minutes later Lucas sauntered out into the kitchen. Amaryllis was puttering around behind the counter. She was dressed for work in a conservative business suit. Her hair was pinned into a neat knot on top of her head. Small, tasteful drops of gold gleamed in her earlobes.

Lucas smiled. In spite of her sober, serious attire, she looked fresh and bright in the morning sunlight that streamed through the windows. A fresh shock of wonder hit him with enough force to make him nearly double over. She was his, at least for a little while.

Amaryllis turned her head and saw him. A delicate blush stained her cheeks, but her eyes were brilliant and deep.

"Good morning." She turned away quickly to busy herself at the counter. "Coff-tea?"

"Yes." Lucas forced himself to move forward. "Please."

"I've got some fresh pear-berries."

"Sounds good." Lucas eased himself down onto the nearest stool, spun around once just for the hell of it, and then gripped the edge of the tiled counter. He thought of the plans he had made in the shower.

"About tonight," he began.

"Strange you should mention that." Amaryllis poured the coff-tea into a mug. "I was just about to bring up the subject."

"You were?"

"Yes. I had an inspiration this morning, Lucas."

He was suddenly, inexplicably cautious. "What sort of inspiration?"

Amaryllis put down the pot and turned to regard him with brimming enthusiasm. "About how to find out more about what Professor Landreth did on the day he died."

Lucas chilled. "I thought we had agreed to let the matter drop."

"Oh, no." Her eyes widened innocently. "Whatever gave you that idea?"

"Forget it. Just a false hope."

"The thing is, this morning I suddenly recalled the boxes stacked in Professor Landreth's old office."

"Boxes?"

"His things," Amaryllis explained. "All his books and records and files. His secretary, Irene Dunley, said she packed them up shortly after the professor died. His personal effects from the office are all sitting there in boxes waiting to be picked up by his next of kin."

"So what?"

"Lucas, think about it. Professor Landreth's appointment calendar is probably buried in one of those boxes."

"I know I'm going to hate myself for asking this," Lucas said slowly, "but what do you plan to do with Landreth's calendar?"

Amaryllis gave him a triumphant smile. "I plan to use it to learn who he saw and where he went on the last day of his life."

"I thought he went up into the mountains. He had a weekend cabin, you said."

"Yes, but he never left the office before five o'clock, even on Fridays. Professor Landreth had a very sound work ethic."

"Figures."

"We may very well find some useful clues in his calendar."

He was getting irritated again. Happened every damn time. "You're doing all this just because you happened to discover that a prism who may or may not have been trained by Landreth got a job focusing for Madison Sheffield?"

She stiffened. "That's what aroused my interest, yes. But the deeper I get into this case, the more questions I have. Doesn't the fact that Sheffield's campaign began to take off in a big way only a couple of months ago bother you?"

"Not particularly."

She let that pass. "I'll bet that it started building fast after he began using a university-trained prism to focus his charm or charisma or whatever he's doing."

"So?"

"So what if Professor Landreth found out what was happening? What if he tried to interfere?"

"Amaryllis, what the hell are you implying?"

"I don't know," she admitted. "But the deeper I get into this thing, the more questions I have. I'm going to ask Irene Dunley if I can go through the boxes stored in her office. With any luck, I'll find the professor's calendar. I'll want to see if anything unusual jumps out at me. Tonight I can assess the situation and maybe make some plans."

Lucas brooded over his coff-tea. "Are you telling me that you intend to spend the evening pursuing this damn investigation?"

She looked hurt. "I thought you'd want to be involved in this, Lucas. You seemed interested in helping me last night. But if you've got other plans for the evening, I'll understand."

"What makes you think I had other plans for the evening? I can't conceive of anything I'd rather do than go through Landreth's desk calendar with you. Hell, I don't know why I didn't think of it myself."

Amaryllis stood quietly in the center of O'Rourke's Antiques and held the focus while her client, Marilyn O'Rourke, turned a cracked earthenware plate in her hands.

"Definitely Second Generation," Marilyn murmured. "A fine example of the early pottery techniques used by the founders. What a lovely discovery. Picked it up at an estate sale last week."

Amaryllis smiled. "Your intuition was sound, as usual, Marilyn. I don't think you really need me."

The antiques dealer beamed happily. She was a short, fashionably dressed woman with a keen eye and an impeccable clientele. She had a standing account with Psynergy, Inc. A class-five talent with an ability to sense the age and genuineness of almost any antique she touched, she was a natural success in her chosen career.

"I always like to be certain." Marilyn set the old plate down with great care and picked up a crudely painted bowl. "Besides, it reassures the customers to know that I've authenticated everything in my shop with the assistance of a prism from a reputable firm. So many charlatans around in this business, you know."

Working with Marilyn required very little effort. Amaryllis barely had to concentrate in order to create a prism and hold the focus. It occurred to her that the difference between handling the dealer's psychic energy and focusing Lucas's raw power was like the difference between moonlight and sunlight. The first gave off only a pale glow. The second created a dazzling glare so hot and intense that it left afterimages on the psychic plane.

Amaryllis examined her link with Marilyn while the dealer went about testing the new items in the shop. It was perfectly normal. There was absolutely no sense of intimacy. Neither she nor Marilyn felt as if their personal spaces had been invaded in any way. They shared psychic energy in a synergistic fashion that allowed them to work together, but neither could sense the other's emotions, nor were their own emotions affected. They simply cooperated in a natural fashion to make use of a tool that required two people to operate.

No big deal.

According to all of the research data Amaryllis had ever seen, it was always like this when talents and prisms worked together.

Except when she worked with Lucas.

"I think that does it for this lot." Marilyn smiled with professional satisfaction as she dusted off her hands. "I'll call some of my Second Generation collectors and let them know I've got some very nice pieces in the shop."

Amaryllis broke the link. The prism vanished. "Will there be anything else, Marilyn?"

"Not today."

"Would you mind if I used your phone?" Amaryllis glanced at her watch. "I've been trying to get hold of someone all morning. She hasn't been at her desk. It's almost lunchtime. I'm afraid that if I wait until I get back to the office, I'll miss her again."

"Help yourself." Marilyn waved toward the phone on the counter.

"Thanks." Amaryllis went behind the counter and picked up the receiver. She dialed Irene Dunley's office number and waited impatiently for a response.

To Amaryllis's enormous relief, the phone was answered on the third ring.

"Department of Focus Studies. Professor Yamamoto's office," Irene said in firm, authoritative accents.

"Irene, this is Amaryllis Lark. I've been trying to get hold of you all morning."

"I'm sorry, Miss Lark. I had a dental appointment, and since Professor Yamamoto was out of the office today, I turned the phones over to a student assistant. You know how that goes. What can I do for you?"

"I've got a favor to ask."

"What is it?"

"I'd like to drop by the office after work today and take a quick look inside those boxes you packed. The ones that contain Professor Landreth's effects. I know it sounds a little weird, but I can explain."

There was a short pause on the other end of the line. "You want to examine the contents of the boxes?"

"Yes."

"Oh, dear."

An unpleasant chill of apprehension went down Amaryllis's spine. "Is something wrong? I realize it's an unusual request, but I really do have a very good reason."

"I'm sure you do, Miss Lark. That's not the problem. The thing is, when I got back to the office a few minutes ago, I found a note from the student who handled the phones while I was out this morning. Apparently he did manage to answer them once or twice."

"A note?"

"It says that a member of the family finally called about the professor's effects. They'll be picked up first thing in the morning."

Amaryllis sat down hard on the nearest chair, a large stuffed leather bag affair that dated from the Early Explorations Period. "I see. But the boxes are still there in your office?"

"Well, yes." Irene cleared her throat. "But I'm afraid I can't allow you to go into them this afternoon, Miss Lark. Now that a member of the family has finally come forward to claim them, I don't feel that I have the right to let anyone else touch the contents. You'll have to get the owner's permission."

"Yes, of course." Amaryllis tried to think.

"May I ask why you wished to get into the boxes?"

Amaryllis hesitated. There was no point alarming Irene by bringing up suspicions that could not yet be substantiated. "I was just curious about some of Professor Landreth's old notes regarding lab test procedures. Nothing important. Thanks, Irene."

"Good-bye, Miss Lark."

Lucas answered his private line on the second ring. He did not look up from the latest field report that had just arrived. "Trent here."

"Lucas? It's Amaryllis. I'm afraid I'm going to have to cancel our date tonight."

His stomach clenched. "Why?"

"It's a little difficult to explain on the phone. Something's come up. I have to go out this evening."

"Alone?"

"Yes. Please, Lucas, don't ask me any more questions. It's better if you don't know the details."

A curious mixture of relief and foreboding washed through him. It didn't sound as though she had plans to meet another man, Lucas thought. That was the good news.

That left the bad news.

"Listen to me very carefully, Amaryllis. I will meet you at your place right after work. Don't leave home without me."

Chapter 9

"This is the second date that you've managed to ruin." Lucas stood next to Amaryllis in the deep shadows of the towering university library and studied the darkened entrance of the building that housed the Department of Focus Studies. "Don't think I'm not keeping a running score."

"Stop whining," Amaryllis whispered. "I warned you that you wouldn't want to come along."

"Yeah, you did. Funny, I never would have guessed that you had a hobby like this."

"Like what?"

"Breaking and entering."

Amaryllis pulled the collar of her jacket up around her neck with an uneasy motion. The light from the twin moons lined her delicate profile. Her expression was serious and profoundly resolute. One glance told Lucas that he didn't stand a chance of talking her out of this crazy plan.

"I'm not going to steal anything," she said. "I just want to get a quick look at Professor Landreth's calendar."

Lucas heard the thread of apprehension beneath the bravado and felt a twinge of sympathy. "Do you think they'll drum you out of the Corps of Upright Ethical Prisms if anyone finds out about this?"

"I should think that you'd be more concerned with being laughed out of the Western Islands Adventurers' Club for failing to strike the right note of devil-may-care recklessness."

"There is no Western Islands Adventurers' Club. I dissolved their charter in a fit of pique years ago."

"There's no Corps of Upright Ethical Prisms, either. I think it was disbanded due to lack of interest." Amaryllis glanced around. "Come on, let's go. The sooner we get into the building, the sooner we can get out."

Lucas swallowed another remark, which Amaryllis would no doubt have deemed negative, and followed her across the brick walkway. To his great relief, she did not head toward the front steps of the Focus Studies building. Instead, she led him along a shrub-shrouded path and around a corner to the rear of the department.

A moment later she came to a halt at what was clearly a service entrance. She studied the jelly-ice lock.

"With any luck, no one's changed the code since I left," she whispered.

It would all be so simple if she were unable to open the door, he thought. "Your idea of luck and mine are two different things."

"Keep watch," she hissed.

Lucas morosely did as he was told while Amaryllis punched in a series of numbers. Fortunately or unfortunately, depending on your point of view, campus security was lax in the extreme. He had seen no sign of a guard since they had arrived, and there was no one around now to witness Amaryllis's debut as a B&E artist.

"Ah hah."

Her soft exclamation told him that the door had opened. She stepped into the dark hall and turned to beckon him.

"Hurry," she said.

"Don't worry, I'm right behind you." Lucas moved into the hall. He pulled the door closed behind him, cutting off the weak shaft of moonlight.

The darkness in the hallway thickened abruptly. Lucas heard a soft thud.

"Ouch," Amaryllis muttered.

"What happened?"

"I forgot about the coatrack back here."

Lucas dug out a pencil-thin flashlight and switched on the narrow beam. He aimed it at the floor. "Better?"

"Much. Very clever of you to think of bringing that flashlight along with us."

"As a professional sidekick, I try to make myself useful."

Amaryllis started forward. "Professor Landreth's old office is down this hall. I hope that no one's changed the code on that door, either."

"Given the general state of security around here, I think you can count on it."

"There's never been much of a problem with crime on campus." Amaryllis paused in front of a door that had a frosted glass panel.

Lucas played the light over the name scrolled in black on the front. Euphemia Yamamoto.

Amaryllis punched in another code. The jelly-ice lock dissolved without protest. The office door opened easily when the knob was turned. Lucas saw the orderly stack of boxes against the far wall when he followed Amaryllis into the room.

"Five hells," he muttered. "There's a dozen of them. It will take hours to go through each box."

"Mrs. Dunley is a very methodical person." Amaryllis crossed the room to where the boxes were stacked against the far wall. "I know her. She'll have organized everything very precisely. All I have to do is find the one that contains the items taken directly from the top of his desk."

Lucas aimed the flashlight at the labels on the boxes. They were all clearly dated and labeled in excruciating detail. "Landreth: Private Files—Focus Studies Research Reports." "Landreth: Private Files—Case Histories of Class-Two Talents and Associated Prisms."

Lucas moved the light beam to another row of boxes and discovered more helpful labels. "Landreth: Personal Effects—Desk Drawer Number One." "Landreth: Personal Effects—Desk Drawer Number Two."

"I see what you mean," Lucas said. "Talk about a clerical mentality."

"Be grateful." Amaryllis shoved a box aside to gain access to the one behind it. "Professor Landreth always said that Mrs. Dunley had a talent for organization. It was one of the reasons they worked so well together."

Lucas flicked the light upward to get a closer look at the portrait on the wall. "Is that the great man himself?"

Amaryllis glanced at the picture. Her face softened. "Yes."

"Vivien was right. He looks like a guy whose underwear is two sizes too small."

"Don't be disrespectful."

"Yes, ma'am."

Amaryllis tugged another box forward. "Here we go. This looks like a good candidate."

Lucas moved closer to get a look at the label on the box she had uncovered. "Landreth: Miscellaneous Items from Desk."

Amaryllis started to lift the lid and suddenly hesitated. Lucas glanced at her. There was just enough light to see that she was nibbling uneasily on her lower lip.

"If you're going to search that box, then do it fast," he said roughly. "If not, let's get out of here. I don't like this situation one damn bit."

Without a word, Amaryllis gingerly removed the lid and set it aside. Lucas raised the light and aimed the beam into the open box. Neatly bundled pens, pencils, and desktop accoutrements were packed inside. A large, handsome desk calendar bound in what appeared to be very expensive Green Specter snakeskin lay on the bottom.

"Looks like being head of the Department of Focus Studies paid well," Lucas observed as Amaryllis removed the calendar. "Green Specter snakeskin doesn't come cheap."

"We took up a collection and gave him this calendar a few months before I left." Amaryllis touched the bronze-green snakeskin with reverential fingers. "It was in honor of his thirtieth year in the department. I picked this out myself. Professor Landreth was quite pleased."

Something in her voice sent a jolt of alarm through Lucas. "You're not going to cry, are you? Amaryllis, we don't have time for that. Save it."

"I'm not crying." She sniffed and wiped her eyes with the back of her hand as she carried the calendar to the desk. "Hold the flashlight so that I can see what I'm reading."

Guilt trickled through Lucas. He had to keep reminding himself that Amaryllis had actually been fond of Jonathan Landreth. "Sorry."

"Never mind." Amaryllis smiled wryly as she opened the calendar and started to flip the pages. "Mrs. Dunley and I seem to be the only ones who had any real affection for poor Professor Landreth. I hadn't realized until lately that most of the people in the department considered him a prissy, rigid martinet."

"I guess they just didn't understand him the way you did."

"He was brilliant, Lucas. He devoted his life to furthering the study of the principles of psychic synergism. He always said that there was so much more to learn, that the swift evolution of psychic talent in humans on St. Helens was unprecedented."

"Uh huh."

"What little information we have suggests that on Earth psychic abilities were either nonexistent or so undeveloped that they were frequently dismissed as manifestations of pure fantasy by most experts."

"Yeah, right." Lucas motioned with the light. "Could you save the lecture until some other time? I don't want to hang around any longer than absolutely necessary."

"Yes, of course. Sorry." Amaryllis concentrated on the calendar. "This section covers the last few days of his life. Let's see, he was killed on the thirteenth of the month. That was a Friday."

"Figures."

She turned another page. "Here we go. These are the entries for the thirteenth. I wonder if I should take a look at the whole last week, just in case."

Lucas glanced at the entries on the pages. They had all been penned in a painstakingly precise hand. "Why don't you just take the entire calendar home with you?" He was aware of a stirring sensation on the nape of his neck. "You can study it at your leisure."

Amaryllis gave him a shocked look. "I couldn't possibly remove the calendar. That would be theft."

"Excuse me, but I'd like to point out that you're already walking a pretty fine line just being in here tonight."

Her fingers clenched around the calendar. "I'm well aware of that. But I couldn't think of anything else to do. I told you that I had to act quickly because Mrs. Dunley said that one of Professor Landreth's relatives is going to collect the boxes first thing in the morning."

"Yeah."

"It was not an easy decision to come here tonight. But I finally decided that it was a question of priorities. I felt that the importance of the investigation of the professor's death outweighed—"

"Could you save that speech for later, too?"

"Lucas, is something wrong?"

"Other than the obvious?" Lucas let his senses float, widening his awareness the way he did when he was in the jungle. "Maybe. I don't have a good feeling about this."

"You're nervous. I knew I shouldn't have involved you." Amaryllis bent over the last entries in the calendar. "Most of these notes were made by Professor Landreth himself. I recognize his handwriting. He paid close attention to his schedule."

"Hooray for him. I let my secretary handle my calendar." He followed her fingertip as she read off the entries.

"Nine o'clock, Test Results Meeting." Amaryllis frowned. "That was a regular weekly event here in the department. Nothing out of the ordinary. Eleven o'clock, departmental budget review. Noon, lunch with Professor Wagner. Wagner is with the history department. An old friend. Three o'clock—"

Lucas glanced at the name that had brought Amaryllis to a screeching halt. Gifford Osterley. Before he could comment, a jolt of warning flashed through him. He switched off the light.

"Lucas?"

"Quiet. I think I heard someone. Security guard, probably." He took her arm and edged away from the desk.

Amaryllis did not argue. He heard her close the calendar very quietly. He plucked it from her hand and used his sense of touch to return it to the open box. Then, guided mostly by feel, he found the lid and replaced it.

He had good night vision, but even for him the secretary's office was as black as the inside of a cave. A light appeared through the frosted pane of glass in the door. Someone with a flashlight was coming down the hall. Whoever it was, he moved with the brisk, confident pace of a person who had every right to be where he was.

University security had finally put in an appearance.

With one hand wrapped around Amaryllis's arm, Lucas relied on his jungle-honed sense of orientation to guide him to the solid paneled door of the inner office. He had noted its location earlier, just as he had automatically made a mental map of the position of everything else in the room. After a lifetime in the Western Islands, a man got very good at that kind of thing.

A soft, scraping footstep sounded in the outside hallway. Lucas felt Amaryllis flinch. He drew her into the second office and gently closed the door.

There were windows in this room. A pale swath of moonlight slanted across the desk. Keeping his grip on Amaryllis's arm, Lucas urged her across the office. He set his teeth as he eased open one of the windows.

There was no squeak.

"Out," he whispered. "Hurry."

He bundled her through the window. She scrambled awkwardly but silently over the sill. He heard her land softly on the ground.

The door of the outer office opened. The beam of light appeared beneath the door of the inner office. Lucas put one leg over the sill. If the guard was the meticulous type, he would check the second office, too. Lucas figured he had about three seconds.

He slipped through the window.

Amaryllis grabbed his hand. Together they crossed the lawn, hugging the shadows of a tall hedge. Then they hurried to the safety of the Icer, which Lucas had parked behind a large storage facility.

"Whew." Amaryllis collapsed into the passenger seat as Lucas got in beside her and activated the engine. "That was a close one. I didn't know that university security checked inside the buildings. I assumed that the guards just patrolled the grounds."

"You want a professional tip?" Lucas did not turn on the Icer's headlights as he drove past the library. "Never assume anything when you plan a fun-filled evening like this."

Amaryllis didn't surface from the depths of her uneasy thoughts until Lucas drove through a set of elaborately designed gates. He guided the Icer slowly down a narrow drive. It took her a moment to realize that he had not taken her home. She gazed around in wonder as the car wended its way through the heart of a strange garden.

Unfamiliar trees with massive leaves loomed on either side of the drive. They formed a thick canopy that blocked out most of the moonlight. The headlights revealed glimpses of exotic foliage that looked dense enough to serve as a wall. Plants with broad leaves edged with what looked like golden fringe dipped and swayed. Here and there flowers glowing with surreal colors appeared and disappeared in the lights.

"I've never seen anything like this," Amaryllis whispered. "It looks like a giant's garden. Everything is oversized. It doesn't look real."

"The last owner of the house was a class-seven horticultural talent. He used the gardens for his botanical experiments. I bought the place because it reminds me of the islands."

A colonnade of massive fern-trees ended in front of a house that was as bizarre as the gardens. Amaryllis studied it with open-mouthed amazement. Moonlight gleamed on delicate spires, fluted columns, and tall towers. The style was unmistakable. The mansion dated from the Early Explorations Period, which made it nearly a hundred years old.

The first long-distance voyages through St. Helens's uncharted seas had been undertaken during that era. Enthusiasm, optimism, and expectations had run high, and the mood of the times had been reflected in the soaring architectural styles.

Amaryllis eyed the elaborate waterfall of steps that led to the heavily carved front doors. This was Lucas's home. She had never envisioned him living in such a fantastical creation. And yet, in some strange manner, it suited him. He was a man apart, and his residence was definitely apart from the ordinary, too.

"How do you find the time to take care of this place?" Amaryllis asked.

He smiled fleetingly. "I don't. I pay people to do it. A team of gardeners handles the outside, and I have a staff of housekeepers who come in during the day."

Amaryllis blushed at her naïveté. "I keep forgetting you're rich." She cleared her throat. "I'm surprised someone hasn't tried to get you to open the house and grounds for guided tours."

"The Preservation Society made a stab at it. You know what those folks are like. Anything over fifty years old is an historical monument to them. I told them that if the bottom ever fell out of the jelly-ice business, I'd contact them and we'd talk about paid tours then."

Silence fell.

"I should go home," Amaryllis finally said. "I have to do some thinking."

"About Gifford Osterley?"

She froze. "You saw his name on the calendar?"

"I grew up in a jungle, remember?" His smile held little humor. In the shadows his eyes gleamed with watchful speculation. "I was trained to be observant at an early age."

"Naturally." She couldn't think of anything to say.

Lucas opened the Icer's door. "Come inside, Amaryllis. I think we'd better talk."

"I don't know why his name was on Professor Landreth's calendar." Amaryllis paced back and forth across the high-ceilinged, old-fashioned living room. "I can't even come up with a likely explanation. According to my friends in the department, Gifford and Landreth had a major confrontation a couple of months ago. Gifford handed in his resignation because of it. Lucas, there are so many questions."

"Here." Lucas thrust a small glass into her hand. "Drink this."

Amaryllis frowned at the dark, intensely aromatic liqueur. "What is it?"

"Moontree brandy."

She hastily clutched the glass with both hands. "Good heavens, that must have cost a fortune."

Lucas's mouth curved faintly. "Don't worry, I save it for special occasions."

"Oh." She sniffed cautiously at the exotic brandy. "Well, thank you. You really shouldn't have."

Moontree brandy was a near-legendary liqueur, so far as Amaryllis was concerned. Certainly no one back home in Lower Bellevue ever had a bottle of it stashed in a cupboard. The production of the brandy was extremely limited because the tree produced fruit only on the rare occasions when both Chelan and Yakima were in total eclipse.

The botanists had not yet been able to explain the exact nature of the synergistic reaction between the eclipsed moons and the tree. All attempts to grow the moontree under controlled conditions had failed.

"Sip slowly," Lucas advised. "The stuff has a kick."

"So I've heard." Amaryllis took a tiny taste—and promptly gasped for breath as a fierce rush of heat filled her mouth. The heady warmth was immediately followed by an equally luscious sweetness.

Lucas leaned back against a table and crossed one ankle over the other. "Like it?"

"It's . . . interesting." Amaryllis resumed her pacing.

"You're going to talk to Osterley, aren't you?"

Amaryllis stopped in front of the window. She looked out into the eerie garden. "Yes."

"I don't suppose it will do any good to tell you that I don't think that's a real bright idea."

"I have to talk to him, Lucas."

"Why?"

"Because he may have been the last person Professor Landreth spoke with before he died."

There was a clink as Lucas set his brandy glass down on the table.

He crossed the room and came to stand behind Amaryllis. "This has gone far enough. Stay out of it. It's not your job to investigate Landreth's death."

"I can't stop now," she whispered. "Ever since I sensed that prism working with Sheffield, I've had a nasty feeling about this whole situation. Call it prism intuition."

"I prefer to call it a lack of common sense. I've said it once, and I know it probably won't do any good, but I'll say it again. Talk to the cops if you really believe that Landreth's accident needs more investigation."

"I can't go to the police until I have something substantial to give them."

He put his hands on her shoulders and turned her around to face him. "Are you sure there isn't another reason why you don't want to talk to the authorities?"

"What are you implying?"

"I think you want answers. But I'm beginning to wonder if you're afraid of what you'll discover. Are you worried that someone you know might be involved in this?"

"Do you really think that I'd avoid going to the authorities in order to protect someone?"

"If you cared about that person, yes." Lucas framed her face with his hands. His thumbs moved along the line of her jaw. "I think your sense of loyalty is even stronger than your sense of professional responsibility."

"This is not your problem, Lucas."

"The hell it isn't." He covered her mouth with his own before she could protest.

The following morning Amaryllis was ushered into Gifford's plush offices. At the sight of her, he rose politely from behind his desk.

"Hello, Amaryllis. This is a pleasant surprise. What brings you to Unique Prisms? Looking for a job?"

"No. This is a private matter."

"Interesting." Gifford motioned toward a chair. "Please, sit down."

"Thank you." Amaryllis studied him covertly as she took the chair.

She had always considered Gifford a handsome man, and nothing had changed in his physical appearance during the past six months. But for some reason, he no longer seemed nearly as attractive as he once had. There was an aura of weakness about his well-chiseled features, a languid, self-indulgent quality that she had not been conscious of when she worked at the university.

Perhaps she had been too much in awe of his research accomplishments in the old days, she reflected. Next to Professor Landreth, Gifford had been the most esteemed scholar in the entire department. No one could dispute his academic abilities.

His eyes were a riveting shade of blue. He had taken to wearing his light brown hair in the Western Islands style. It was tied at the nape of his neck with a strip of black ribbon. Amaryllis was beginning to think that Lucas was the only man in New Seattle who didn't wear his hair in the new fashion.

She had to admit that Gifford was in excellent shape, perhaps even leaner than when she had last seen him. She wondered if he still played golf-tennis on a regular basis. She glanced at his well-manicured hands and noticed that they also appeared soft. The only calluses Gifford had ever known were the ones he got from his golf-tennis racket.

My, she was getting picky these days, she thought wryly. There was a time when she would have found his hands attractive.

The biggest difference in his appearance was his attire. Gone were the slouchy jacket, the denim trousers, and the running shoes that were de rigueur among faculty members at the university. Today Gifford was a model of executive style in a silver gray suit and a pale gray shirt. A red bow tie added just the right note of whimsical, rakish elegance.

Amaryllis smiled. "You're dressing better these days, Gifford."

"I can afford it."

Amaryllis glanced around at her surroundings. The office complemented the man. A pale gray carpet and sleek black furnishings comprised a suitable backdrop to the power suit. Red flowers in a red vase provided an exclamation point to the room. The dramatic effect was not unlike that of the red bow tie on Gifford's silver gray suit.

"Congratulations." Amaryllis settled into the expensive office chair. "I take it business is good?"

"Very good." Gifford chuckled as he resumed his seat. "I don't miss academia, that's for sure. Should have left the faculty years ago. Don't know why I waited so long. What can I do for you, Amaryllis?"

"I'll come straight to the point. Did you see Professor Landreth the day of his death?"

Gifford blinked, clearly startled, then his expression grew thoughtful. "That's an odd question. Why do you want to know?"

"Last Friday night I got a phone call. Anonymous. The caller implied that there was some mystery surrounding Professor Landreth. I decided to look into the matter."

"Since when do you do security work? That sounds like a job for the cops."

"Their investigation turned up no indication of foul play."

"Most likely because there wasn't any foul play," Gifford muttered. "The only one who might think there was something suspicious about Landreth's death was his secretary. Irene Dunley had a crush on him for years. She's probably having a tough time accepting the fact that he's gone."

It was Amaryllis's turn to blink. "I know Mrs. Dunley was very loyal to Professor Landreth. Fond of him, even. But what makes you think that she was in love with him?"

Gifford grimaced. "I walked into her office one day right after you left the faculty. She was in tears. She had just learned that Landreth had some kind of standing appointment with a sleazy syn-sex stripper who works in a club in Founders Square. I think she had found a note about one of his appointments and had been curious enough to call the number. You know what they say about curiosity."

Amaryllis was speechless.

Gifford was amused. "What's the matter? Can't imagine old Landreth with a syn-sex stripper? Don't you know that the prudish, straitlaced types always turn out to have the most interesting tastes when it comes to sex?" His mouth twisted. "Present company excepted, of course."

Amaryllis kept her shoulders very straight. She would not allow herself to be embarrassed by Gifford. He was the one who should have been ashamed of himself. "Will you please answer my question? Did you see Professor Landreth that day?"

"It's none of your business, but the answer is no, I did not see him."

"According to his calendar, he had an appointment with you for three o'clock."

"Did Mrs. Dunley tell you that?"

"No. I saw the calendar entry myself. Your name was written in Professor Landreth's own hand."

"Was it? I can't imagine why. He and I had absolutely nothing to say to each other. In case you didn't hear about it, the two of us nearly came to blows a couple of months ago. I resigned my position in the department because of that old bastard."

"Why did you dislike him so much?"

"Are you kidding?" Gifford raised his eyes toward the ceiling. "Let me count the ways. Landreth may have been a good researcher at one time, but he had been past his prime for years. He refused to move with the times. His methods were antiquated, to say the least. He wouldn't allow even minor changes in the way things were done in the department. And he was obsessed with his damned professional standards."

"He had every right to be obsessed with standards," Amaryllis retorted. "Professor Landreth virtually wrote the Code of Focus Ethics. He was almost single-handedly responsible for raising our profession to its present high regard. Why, if it hadn't been for him, you probably wouldn't be sitting behind that desk in this plush office."

Gifford shook his head. "You haven't changed a bit, have you. Pity. I would have thought that six months in the real world would have polished off some of the prissy naïveté."

Amaryllis clutched her purse tightly and stood. "You're certain you didn't see Professor Landreth the day he died?"

"Positive. Believe me, I would have gone out of my way to avoid a meeting with the old coot. He was the last man on St. Helens I wanted to see."

The world seemed to be full of people who had never cared for Jonathan Landreth. Amaryllis turned without a word and strode to the door.

"Amaryllis?"

She paused, one hand on the knob. "Yes?"

"I saw your picture in the paper. You were with Lucas Trent at the museum reception last Thursday night."

"What about it?"

Gifford gave her a knowing look. "I'm assuming it wasn't an agency date, although that was the implication. You and Trent aren't a very likely pair. So it must have been business. Were you focusing for him that night?"

"I don't discuss clients."

"So it was business." Gifford nodded, apparently satisfied. "I thought as much. Word has it that Trent is a class nine, but the poor guy's just a detector. What was it, some kind of security matter?"

"I said, I don't discuss business."

Gifford gave her a goading smile. "Did he suspect that some arch criminal talent was plotting to steal those artifacts he discovered? Or was it closer to home? I hear one of his vice presidents just left the company with no notice. Someone named Miranda Locking."

No one had ever said that Gifford was stupid, Amaryllis reminded herself. "You're awfully well informed."

"I make it a point to be informed," Gifford said softly. "It's good for business."

"Excuse me. I've got another appointment." Amaryllis opened the door.

"One more thing, Amaryllis. If you ever decide that you want to make some real money in the focus game, you're welcome to apply for a position here at Unique Prisms. I pay top dollar. You can make as much money in six months working for me as you'll make with Clementine Malone in a year."

Logic and intuition came together in a flash of understanding. "It was one of your people who was working with Senator Sheffield the night of the reception, wasn't it?"

"How did you know about Sheffield?" Gifford's eyes narrowed. "Did Trent use his talent to spy on him?"

"I learned about Senator Sheffield's talent quite by accident." She could be cool and obscure, too, Amaryllis thought. "He's strong, isn't he? A class ten?"

"Who knows? He refuses to be tested." Gifford's smile came and went. "Claims it's an invasion of privacy. Says the founders would never have tolerated such a blatant intrusion on the rights of the individual."

"So, it was one of your people holding the focus for him that night. That explains a few things."

"What are you talking about?"

"I knew I recognized the prism's style and technique," Amaryllis said. "I thought at first that it must have been someone Professor Landreth had trained, but it could just as well have been someone you trained. Your techniques would have a signature very similar to Landreth's because Landreth trained you."

"You know, Amaryllis, you really should consider my offer of a job. We run a very exclusive service here at Unique Prisms. We're highly selective when it comes to our clients."

"Selective?" Amaryllis asked coldly. "Or unethical?"

Gifford gave her an inquiring look. "Are you accusing me of not upholding the code, my dear Amaryllis? I'm deeply wounded."

"One of your prisms helped Sheffield focus charisma the other night."

"Everyone knows that charisma is not a psychic talent. Just a personality trait." Gifford spread his hands. "What can I say? Sheffield has terrific voter appeal."

"You can call it anything you like. All I know is that Sheffield is a powerful talent. He may very well have been using that talent to get campaign contributions."

"So? That's what politicians do."

"He burned out his prism, Gifford. Doesn't that bother you at all?"

"There are risks in every business. Prism burnout is a short-term problem."

"Focusing a talent with the intent to defraud is not just unethical, it's illegal."

Gifford's smile did not reach his eyes. "I repeat, charisma is not a talent. It's not listed in any professional directory of talents. It has never been documented as a psychic ability. It's just a personality trait. Rather like your prissy views on sex and prism ethics."

Amaryllis flushed. "I think I understand why you and Professor Landreth never got along very well, Gifford. Professor Landreth, after all, was a gentleman."

"Such a gentleman that he kept a weekly standing appointment with a syn-sex stripper?"

Amaryllis went out the door and closed it quietly behind herself.

Chapter 10

"Well, dear," Hannah said on the other end of the phone, "I think that wraps up the personal characteristics section of the questionnaire. I must say, you've become terribly specific about what you want in a husband."

Amaryllis fiddled with her desk pen and studied the notes she had made on a sheet of paper. "The more I thought about it, the more I realized I had some definite preferences, Aunt Hannah."

"Let me see if I've got it all right. Dark hair, gray eyes, mid-thirties, successful entrepreneur, small-town or rural background, university degree. You want a man with some knowledge of hand-to-hand fighting skills. Someone who is not afraid to take a few chances." Hannah paused. "Oh, yes, one who is a conservative dresser."

"I think that about sums it up, Aunt Hannah."

"Picky, picky, picky," Hannah muttered. "Very well, I've filled out the rest of the questionnaire for you, so we're finished with the initial phase of the process. Your great-aunt Sophy gave me a hand with some of it."

A small degree of relief went through Amaryllis at that news. "Great-Aunt Sophy knows me well."

"She's the one who told me not to worry too much about how choosy you've suddenly become," Hannah said dryly. "She said it was a positive sign. She thinks it means that you're starting to take a more active interest in this whole process."

Amaryllis smiled in spite of her mood. Great-Aunt Sophy could always be counted upon to throw a different light on the subject. A memory flickered in the back of her mind. It dated from her seventh year.

It had been a hot summer day. Lower Bellevue had been baking in relentless sunshine for nearly a month. Sophy had taken Amaryllis and a young companion named Linda into town. The girls had gone into the ice cream parlor to purchase cones while Sophy had done some banking next door.

When the two children had emerged, dripping cones in their hands, Linda had pointed to a striking woman who was getting out of an expensive car.

"Know who that is?" Linda gave Amaryllis a sly look. "That's your grandma."

Amaryllis studied the elegant, dark-haired woman. "She's not my grandmother. My grandmother has blond hair and she's not as tall."

"Everyone has two grandmothers, dummy. That lady was your daddy's mother. Her name is Mrs. Bailey. That makes her your other grandmother. My mom told me so."

"Don't believe you."

"Go ask her," Linda urged.

"Okay, I will." Amaryllis went forward with determination. A question had been raised. It would be answered. She would prove Linda was dumb, and that would be the end of the matter.

The closer Amaryllis got to the stranger, the more impressed she was. With her expensive clothes, imperious stature, and aristocratic air, Elizabeth Bailey was a vision on the streets of Lower Bellevue.

Elizabeth did not see Amaryllis until she felt the tug on her skirt. She turned her head and glanced down. A strange look appeared in her green eyes.

"Let go of my skirt," Elizabeth said very quietly. "Do not touch me."

"Excuse me," Amaryllis said. "You're beautiful. My friend says you're my grandmother. Are you really my grandmother?"

Elizabeth's face tightened. "Of course I'm not your grandmother. You have no grandmother. You're a bastard." She turned and walked away without another word.

Amaryllis stood staring after her, ice cream dripping on the sidewalk, until Sophy emerged from the bank. Other children had called Amaryllis a bastard. But this was the first time an adult had done so to her face. When an adult said something, you had to take it seriously.

Sophy had taken one look at the car parked at the curb and another at Amaryllis's face. She had put two and two together instantly. Heedless of the melting ice cream, she had pulled Amaryllis into her arms.

"Don't take any notice of Elizabeth Bailey, dear."

"Is she really my grandmother?"

"Yes, but she doesn't want to admit it because she feels guilty."

"Why?"

"It's a long story, sweetie, and this is neither the time nor the place to tell it."

"She hates me. And I hate her."

"Someday you'll understand."

"What will I understand?" Amaryllis demanded with the stubborn determination to learn the answers that was to become a lifelong trait.

"Someday you'll know why Elizabeth did what she did," Sophy said, "and why she can't forgive herself or anyone else."

"But what did she do?"

Sophy sighed. "She's the one who forced your daddy to marry the wrong woman. Elizabeth knew from the beginning that it was a bad match, but all she could see was money and land and status. She thought those things would make your father happy, but they didn't. All he wanted was your mother, but he was too young to fight Elizabeth."

"I hate her," Amaryllis said. She whirled around and flung her ice cream cone at Elizabeth Bailey's expensive car. The contents of the cone spattered across the windshield.

Sophy contemplated the mess with a curious expression. "Couldn't have said it better myself."

The ice cream cone incident was the last time she had ever done something so blatantly outrageous, so reckless, so out of control, Amaryllis reflected. Until she had met Lucas Trent.

"This is so exciting, isn't it?" Hannah said on the other end of the phone.

"Thrilling."

"I'll mail this form off to your counselor, Mrs. Reeton, this afternoon. You should be hearing from her soon. She'll want to schedule an appointment for the two of you to get together for the formal interview."

"Can't wait," Amaryllis said. "If you're through with the questionnaire, I should get back to work, Aunt Hannah."

"Of course, dear." Hannah cleared her throat discreetly. "How is your social life?"

"My social life?"

"Are you still seeing Mr. Trent?"

Amaryllis's mouth went dry. "Occasionally."

"What a pity he's a strong talent. Now that I think about it, he meets some of the criteria that you listed on the questionnaire, doesn't he? Dark-haired, successful entrepreneur—"

"It's purely a superficial resemblance, Aunt Hannah. I really have to go. Give my love to Uncle Oscar and the rest of the family."

"I will. Oh, by the way, Oscar and I will be in the city the day after tomorrow. We'll spend the night at that little hotel near your place since you don't have an extra bedroom."

"Great. I'll look forward to it. See you soon."

"And you're still planning on coming home to Lower Bellevue for Sophy's birthday party week after next, of course."

"Wouldn't miss it for the world, you know that. Good-bye, Aunt Hannah."

"Good-bye, dear. See you on Friday."

Amaryllis dropped the phone into its cradle and went back to the notes she had been making when Hannah had interrupted her. None of the points she had listed connected with anything in any way that formed a pattern or inspired a flash of intuition, but she could feel the storm clouds of wrongness gathering. A growing restlessness pervaded her entire being. She needed answers.

She studied what she had written on the pad.

1. Prism using Landreth's techniques and style focuses for Madison Sheffield. Unethical, but not illegal, use of

Sheffield's talent. Prism most likely trained by Gifford, not Landreth. Same techniques account for similarities in focus style. Landreth would not have approved.

2. Phone call indicating that there was something mysterious about Landreth and that Vivien of the Veils might have info. Gifford suggests that call was possibly made by Irene Dunley because Irene secretly loved Landreth. Irene knew about Vivien of the Veils. But what did she think Vivien might know?

3. Note on Landreth's calendar made the day of his death indicates a three o'clock appointment with Gifford. Gifford claims to know nothing about it. Says he would never have met with Landreth in any event. Serious animosity between Landreth and Gifford.

4. Landreth died at approximately seven o'clock in the evening, according to newspaper accounts. Fall from path along cliff near his weekend cabin. No sign of foul play. Did he cancel his three o'clock appointment with Gifford? Did he change his mind? Did something else come up?

5. Few people mourned the passing of Jonathan Landreth. He was respected, but he was not well liked except by me and Irene Dunley. Did he have some actual enemies? Did anyone else dislike him as much as Gifford?

Amaryllis put down her pen and pondered. Her intuition was churning, but perhaps she was overreacting to the scanty evidence. After all, a lot was going on in her life these days.

Mentally, she composed another list. This one included all her recent stress factors.

1. Involved in a passionate affair with an unsuitable talent.

2. First visit to a syn-sex club. Meeting with stripper. Attacked in Founders Square. Learned that Lucas was an off-the-chart talent. Made love. Big night, all things considered.

3. In the midst of registering with a marriage agency.
4. Engaged in act of breaking and entering.

No doubt about it, her stress level was high, Amaryllis concluded. And the list of stress factors was lengthening with each passing hour.

But the questions would not go away.

The door slammed open. Clementine charged into the office as if she sat astride her high-powered ice-cycle. She throbbed with outrage.

"What in the five hells is going on, Lark?" Clementine planted her hands on Amaryllis's desk and thrust out her strong chin. "If you're not happy here at Psynergy, Inc., tell me about it. Don't go looking for another job behind my back. You want a raise? Is that it? You've only been here six months, but you did bring in a major client. I'm willing to negotiate."

Amaryllis had been working for Clementine long enough to become accustomed to her volatile boss's moods. "Calm down. I'm not looking for another job. Whatever gave you that idea?"

Clementine's steel rings glittered as she drummed all ten fingers on Amaryllis's desk. "I just got back from having lunch with Gracie. She says that gossip has it you were seen coming out of the offices of Unique Prisms this morning."

Understanding dawned. Amaryllis smiled ruefully. "Gossip has it right. I went to talk to Gifford Osterley. He and I go back a long way together. We knew each other when we both worked at the university."

"I'm aware of that." Clementine straightened and scowled down at Amaryllis. "I thought that whatever was going on between the two of you was over."

"It is. I went to see him about a business matter."

"What kind of business takes you to a rival firm?" Clementine demanded suspiciously.

Amaryllis hesitated and then made a decision. "I discovered that on the day of his death Professor Landreth had an appointment with Gifford. I wanted to ask Gifford if Landreth had kept the appointment."

"What does Landreth have to do with any of this?"

"I'm not sure. Clementine, I know this is going to sound strange, but I've begun to wonder if Landreth's death was something more than an accident."

Clementine whistled softly. She sprawled in the nearest chair. "What makes you think that?" Her eyes narrowed. "Prism intuition?"

"Partially. But there are some other things that make me uneasy." Amaryllis told her about the phone call, the visit to Vivien, and the note about the three o'clock appointment with Gifford on Landreth's calendar. She decided not to explain just how she had come to see the appointment calendar.

When she was finished, Clementine stared at her, incredulous.

"You went to a syn-sex club?"

Amaryllis blushed. "Yes. I wanted to talk to Vivien of the Veils."

"Alone?" Clementine's voice rose. "You went to a syn-sex club all by yourself?"

"Not exactly. A friend accompanied me."

"What friend?"

Amaryllis pressed her lips together. "Lucas Trent."

"Trent? Five hells."

"He accompanied me because I invited him," Amaryllis said quickly. "It wasn't his idea."

"I wasn't talking about him, I was talking about you. I can't quite envision you in a syn-sex club."

Amaryllis felt herself turn a brighter shade of pink. "The synergistically generated sex was all an act."

"No kidding."

"The dancers didn't actually have sex on stage. They just simulated the motions. The talent and prism who worked in the show didn't focus any real sexual feelings, either. Lucas and I checked using his detector-talent."

Clementine's mouth kicked up at the corner. "You were expecting maybe the real thing? A focus-induced orgasm, courtesy of a bunch of syn-sex nightclub performers?"

"Clementine."

"Sorry. Didn't mean to embarrass you." Clementine laced her fingers together and raised her eyes toward the ceiling. "What I wouldn't have given to see Trent's reaction when you invited him to go to the club. He must have thought he'd fallen through the curtain and come out on some planet on the other side of the universe."

Amaryllis failed to see the humor in the situation. "I explained that it was a business matter."

"Sure." Clementine sat forward in her chair. "Okay, tell me what this Vivien of the Veils had to say about Landreth."

"Not much, unfortunately. Just that she had seen Professor Landreth the day before he died and he seemed a little more tense than usual."

Clementine's brows rose. "Tense?"

"Vivien claimed that Landreth was always tense."

"That's what Gracie said, too."

"Gracie?"

"She worked with him on a committee a couple of years ago. One of those town-and-gown things where academics and businesspeople get together to discuss matters of mutual interest. She said Landreth was a real pain in the ass. Very anal retentive."

Amaryllis decided to let that observation pass. "At any rate, after I spoke to Vivien, I decided to talk to Gifford. I wanted to ask him about the three o'clock appointment with Professor Landreth. He said he knew nothing about it."

"Hmm."

"Clementine, I'm beginning to wonder if Professor Landreth discovered that Gifford was operating a bit over the line, ethically speaking. I know Landreth would never have approved of Gifford's business practices. The question is, did he know about them?"

"You think maybe Landreth made the appointment in order to confront Osterley about his business ethics?"

"Or lack thereof," Amaryllis said.

"I think I know where this is going. You're wondering if Osterley got pissed when he realized that Landreth might soil the reputation of his operation. You think your friend Gifford croaked the old dude to keep him quiet?"

"No, of course not." Amaryllis was shocked. "Gifford would never kill anyone."

"From what Gracie says, Osterley is the kind of guy who has a price. Pay it and you get his services. A man like that might kill to protect his business interests."

"Gifford may be unethical but he is no murderer. Perhaps that note on Landreth's calendar wasn't a scheduled appointment. Maybe the professor simply intended to call Gifford at three o'clock to discuss matters."

"And never made the call?"

"Or Gifford refused to take the call," Amaryllis said. "Clementine, it's all getting so complicated. I don't know what's going on, but I feel that something is very wrong."

"Look, no one respects a prism's intuition more than I do," Clementine said. "But, frankly, I think you're going off the deep end here. I'll admit that Unique Prisms may be operating on the shady side of the street, but I doubt that Osterley is actually doing anything illegal."

"I agree."

"Got to admit, I wish we had Osterley's client list. From what Gracie says, it includes a nice selection of the movers and shakers in the city. We're lucky Trent didn't go to Unique Prisms in the first place."

"Lucas told me that he chose Psynergy, Inc. because he wanted to deal with a reputable agency," Amaryllis said.

"Good for him." Clementine grinned. "Wonder what he'll say when he finds out that you went to see your old flame today."

"What do you mean? Lucas knew I intended to speak to Gifford."

"Men are kind of weird about stuff like that."

"How would you know?"

"Because women are kind of weird about it, too."

"You're talking about jealousy," Amaryllis said quietly. "Trust me, Lucas is highly unlikely to feel that emotion."

"Yeah?" Clementine pushed herself to her feet. "What makes you think that?"

"He's not the type."

"Bat-snake shit."

Amaryllis composed herself. "Furthermore, he's in the middle of a marriage agency registration, just as I am. Neither one of us has any reason to become jealous in a relationship that we both know has no future."

"You're sure about the no future part?"

Amaryllis wrinkled her nose. "Believe me, even if we weren't high-class talent and full-spectrum prism, we still wouldn't be a good match. Lucas and I have almost nothing in common."

Clementine looked thoughtful. "Gracie and I said that the first time we met each other. Couldn't imagine why the agency had matched us."

He had no right to be feeling this way, Lucas thought as he climbed Amaryllis's front steps that evening. Jealousy was not a logical response to the situation. His relationship with Amaryllis was nothing more than a short-term affair. No strings attached. They were both just killing some time in a mutually pleasurable relationship until they were ready to meet their respective agency dates.

He had turned in the completed Synergistic Connections questionnaire this afternoon. Hobart Batt would be calling any day to schedule the next phase of the process.

Lucas determined to play it cool. He was the Iceman. He would not allow his emotions to get in the way of his common sense. He'd done that once before on the occasion of his first marriage, and the results had not been good.

He took a deep breath and knocked on the door.

Amaryllis's footsteps sounded on the tile floor of the hall as she hurried toward the door. Light, quick, eager. It sounded as if she was flying down the hall to throw herself into his arms.

Without warning, Lucas's mind conjured up an illusion that needed no prism to bring it into focus. It was all too painfully clear. As though he stood in a long gallery lined with endless mirrors, he looked into the future.

He saw a lifetime of greetings from a wife he did not yet know. Simultaneously, he saw Amaryllis hurling herself over and over again into the arms of the stranger who would be her husband. The icy pool inside him grew deeper and colder.

The door in front of him opened.

"Lucas? Is something wrong?"

He came back to the present with a jolt. Amaryllis was smiling at him, her eyes quizzical. The aroma of something delicious cooking on the stove wafted toward him from the kitchen. He would pretend that everything was normal. This was just a short-term thing. No future.

"You went to see Osterley today." So much for being the Iceman.

"Yes, I did." Amaryllis stood on tiptoe and brushed her mouth lightly against his. She stepped back before he could respond. "I told you that I had to speak to him about that appointment."

"So?" Lucas stalked into the hall. "What did he have to say?"

"He claims he knew nothing about it." Amaryllis took his jacket and hung it in a closet. "He said he would never have made an appointment with Landreth. He pointed out that he and Landreth had not parted on good terms."

"Why didn't you call me first?" *Think, Iceman*, Lucas told himself as he went down the hall toward the kitchen. Cold, calm. No emotion. No jealousy. No future. "I thought we were partners in this thing."

"Partners?" Amaryllis hurried after him. "I hadn't actually thought of our association as a partnership."

"Is that right? I figure that under the circumstances the least I deserve is partnership status." Lucas stalked into the kitchen and started to open cupboards in a methodical fashion. "We've been through a lot together during the past few days, you and I."

"That's very true." She frowned as he yanked open another cupboard door. "Lucas, what are you looking for?"

"Something drinkable." He got lucky on the fourth cupboard. "I thought I remembered seeing that bottle in here."

"Help yourself." Amaryllis came around the edge of the counter and lifted the lid of a pot that was sitting on the stove. "Are you always this moody and difficult when you're annoyed?"

"I am never moody and difficult." Lucas jerked open a drawer, scanned the contents, and seized a corkscrew. "But I do occasionally get irritated. And I am definitely irritated at the moment."

"I'm sorry if you feel that I slighted you today, but I honestly thought I could handle Gifford better if I talked to him alone."

A sinking feeling hit Lucas. "Handle him?"

"I thought I could get the truth from him."

"Because the two of you have a history?" Lucas snapped the opener into position and began to pull the cork with a rough, efficient twisting movement.

"We were friends once. Colleagues."

"Not lovers." Lucas jerked out the cork. "Never lovers."

"No." Amaryllis concentrated on stirring the contents of the pot. "He's changed."

"Is that a fact?"

"Clementine said you might be jealous," Amaryllis said softly. "I told her she was wrong."

Lucas stilled, one hand resting on the bottle. He met Amaryllis's eyes. "Jealousy has nothing to do with this."

"That's what I said."

"But speaking as your *partner*," Lucas said very carefully, "and as your lover, I feel that I have some cause for concern. If Gifford Osterley is connected to Landreth's death, he might be tempted to drag you into the mess."

"I understand," Amaryllis said in a subdued tone. "But as I told Clementine, I can't bring myself to believe that Gifford is a murderer."

"Don't rely too much on your prism intuition."

"Funny you should say that." She gave him a strangely shuttered look. "I keep giving myself the same advice."

The evening did not go well after that. Conversation was stilted. The atmosphere was uncomfortably tense. Amaryllis was very polite, but it was obvious, even to a nonintuitive talent, that she was not happy. Lucas had a hunch that she was going to throw him out before bedtime.

He knew that he had only himself to blame. Barring some miracle, he would sleep alone tonight. It no doubt served him right, but the prospect was, nonetheless, deeply depressing.

At ten o'clock, desperate for something to break the lengthening silence between himself and Amaryllis, he picked up the television remote and switched on the evening news.

Nelson Burlton's square-jawed, clear-eyed visage materialized on the screen. The sight did nothing to elevate Lucas's mood. Burlton was covering a political event. Behind him Madison Sheffield could be seen standing at a podium.

Sheffield was speaking to a large crowd of people seated at circular tables. Lucas recognized the setting. It was a meeting of the New Seattle Business Association. He rarely attended the monthly gatherings himself.

Burlton gazed lovingly into the camera. His hair was rakishly windblown, even though he was indoors. He was wearing his trademark Western Islands jacket, although everyone else in the picture wore suits and ties. His teeth were very straight and very white.

"Good evening." Burlton's expression was devoutly sincere. "Once again the race for the governorship of New Seattle City-state tops the news. This evening Senator Madison Sheffield addressed the New Seattle Business Association. His theme, as usual, was a return to founders' values."

The camera shifted from Burlton to Madison Sheffield, who was holding forth in front of the audience. Sheffield's teeth were just as white and even as Burlton's, Lucas noticed. His expression was even more sincere.

"We have come a long way in the past two hundred years," Sheffield intoned. "But even as we reach out to seize the future, we must not forget the bedrock values of our past. We need those values now, as we have always needed them. We face a world that is still largely unexplored. The recent discovery of the alien artifacts reminds us all of just how many unknowns await us. We must be prepared."

Amaryllis, perched on the sofa beside Lucas, studied the screen. "There's no way Sheffield could be focusing charisma to a whole crowd of people."

"No," Lucas agreed. "He could only use the focus in one-on-one situations. The rest of the time he has to make do with his natural political charm."

"He has his fair share of that, but I don't think I'm going to vote for him, after all."

Politics was never a safe topic, Lucas reminded himself. Still, any conversation was better than no conversation, and he was very anxious to keep Amaryllis talking. "Mr. Founders' Values? I would have thought he would have been your ideal candidate."

"He talks a lot about founders' values, but a real First Generation founder would never resort to such underhanded tactics as Sheffield is using to get money for his campaign."

"Don't kid yourself. I have a hunch that the founders didn't survive by being nice guys."

Amaryllis whirled to confront him. "What a cynical thing to say. It was the values of the founders that enabled them to survive. Integrity. Justice. Courage. Honor. Determination. Those are the qualities that got the First Generation through the difficult times."

"You left out expediency," Lucas said. "Something tells me that our exalted founders were very expedient when necessary."

"How can you say that?"

"What's more, I'll give you odds that there were just as many Madison Sheffields in politics back in First Generation days as there are today. Some things never change."

Amaryllis simmered with righteous indignation. "Are you deliberately trying to provoke me?"

"Yes."

She opened her mouth to utter something that would no doubt have scorched his skin, but at the last minute she apparently changed her mind.

"Why?" she asked.

Lucas punched the button on the remote, blanking the screen. "Because I'm trying to get your attention. I feel like you've been slipping away from me all evening."

"That's not true."

"Isn't it? We're supposed to be having an affair, but at the rate things are going, this will be one of the shortest relationships on record."

"Oh, Lucas." Amaryllis moved into his arms and leaned her head on his shoulder. "I'm sorry, but this has been a difficult day."

"You can say that again." Lucas wrapped her close.

"What we have can't last long. We both know that."

"I don't want to talk about the future. I just want to enjoy the present."

"Yes."

Silence fell. Lucas felt the tension slowly ebb away into the night. Amaryllis was warm and soft and safe in his arms. For now, at least. He wanted to take her to a place where they could be alone together, far away from the rules and conventions of society.

"Link," Lucas said into Amaryllis's hair.

She said nothing, but he felt the moment of disorientation, and then he became aware of the prism taking shape on the psychic plane. It was powerful, strong, and clear. He eased psychic energy through it and began to shape an illusion.

A grotto formed around the sofa. The television set, desk, and other furnishings disappeared behind banks of lush ferns. Curved stone walls framed a deep jungle pool. The water was a mirrored surface that revealed nothing.

"Is this a real place?" Amaryllis's voice was soft with wonder.

"Yes."

"A special place in the islands?"

"Yes." Lucas added moss to the grotto walls and piled large rocks around the pool. He carpeted the floor with thick grass and draped streamers of brilliant yellow rose-orchids at various locations. He would have used amaryllises, but he had no idea of what a real, Earth-grown amaryllis looked like.

Amaryllis gazed at the scene. "It's beautiful. So peaceful."

"I found it years ago when I was a kid. I never told anyone else about it, not even Icy Claxby. Sometimes I went into the grotto and sat on the rocks looking down into the pool for hours at a time."

"What did you do there?"

"Lots of things," Lucas said. "I practiced controlling my talent. Sometimes I wondered if there were others like me around. I wanted to talk to someone else who understood what it was like to have so much power and to know that you had to keep it a secret."

Amaryllis snuggled closer. "I had a place like this, too. Not a jungle grotto, naturally. We lived in farm country. My hiding place was located in the barn loft. I remember how the sunlight filtered through the boards in the side walls. I could hear the animals moving about in their stalls. I used to go up there to think and read and just to be by myself."

"What did you think about?"

"Lots of things." Amaryllis's smile was fleeting. "When I was very young, I wasted a good deal of time plotting revenge against my grandmother on my father's side, Elizabeth Bailey. As I got older, I put my energies into figuring out how to get out of Lower Bellevue forever."

"Yeah? I thought you were a small-town girl at heart."

"For as long as I can remember, I wanted to escape to the city. I wanted to find a place where no one knew about my past. A place where people wouldn't be secretly watching to see if I would grow up to humiliate my family the way my mother had done. A place where the kids didn't point their fingers at me and call me names. A place where I could use my prism abilities to the fullest extent possible."

Lucas tightened his arm around her. "Sounds like we both had secrets we wanted to keep." He deliberately strengthened the illusion until the grotto seemed solid and real. The stone walls shielded the occupants of the sofa from the past and the future. He knew he had it right when he looked into the pool and sensed that it was bottomless.

"Lucas?"

"Hmm?"

"It feels good to use our skills together, doesn't it?"

"Very good."

"Don't you think it's strange that no one has ever documented a connection between sexual attraction and the act of holding a focus?"

"I don't think there is any true paranormal connection." He raised her chin on the edge of his hand and looked down into her eyes. "I think that the two things happened to coincide in our case. Just being around you arouses me. It makes sense that linking with you has the same effect."

She smiled and put her arms around his neck.

Lucas bent his head to kiss her.

The shrill jangle of the telephone shattered the illusion as surely as a hurled stone shatters glass. Startled by the intrusive noise, Amaryllis broke the link.

"That's probably my aunt or uncle." She untangled herself from Lucas's arms and reached for the phone. "Hello? Yes, he's here. Just a second."

"Sorry about this." Lucas took the phone from her hand. "I left your number with my answering service." He spoke into the phone. "This is Trent."

"Lucas?" Dillon Rye's voice sounded strained. "Man, am I glad I finally located you. Listen, I'm in kind of a bind here. I hate to bother you, but I need some help. Fast."

"What's wrong?"

"It's a little hard to explain over the phone. The bottom line is that I sort of owe a guy some money and he, uh, wants to be paid right away. And I don't have the cash. I was sort of wondering if you could make me a loan."

"Five hells."

"Lucas?"

"Yeah?"

"I don't mean to push, but I need the money *right now*."

Chapter 11

"Are all prisms this stubborn?" Lucas deactivated the Icer's engine with an impatient twist of his hand. He studied the lights of the casino on the other side of the street. "Or is this just the result of a small-town upbringing?"

"I don't know about other prisms," Amaryllis said. "And I won't presume to speak for all small-town residents. I insisted on coming with you tonight because you might need me. We're partners, remember? You said it yourself."

Lucas turned his head briefly. Derision gleamed in his eyes. "I'm not likely to need a prism to get Dillon out of hock. All it will require is money. I wonder how much the young fool lost to Nick Chastain."

Amaryllis chose to rise above Lucas's obvious irritation. The argument had been running since Dillon Rye's phone call had interrupted Lucas's grotto illusion twenty minutes earlier. When she had discovered what was going on, Amaryllis had insisted on accompanying Lucas on his mission to rescue Dillon.

She leaned forward in the seat to peer at the brilliantly lit entrance of Chastain's Palace. The drizzling rain blurred the colors of the jelly-ice lights, converting them into gaudy liquid jewels. The casino was not the biggest gambling club on the strip, but even Amaryllis had heard of it. She knew it had a certain cachet with the city's swank set. It also had a reputation for big-stakes play that attracted high rollers from the other city-states.

"Do you know this Nick Chastain person?" asked Amaryllis.

"Let's just say that Chastain and I have a few things in common." Lucas opened the door and got out. He seemed oblivious to the light rain.

Amaryllis opened her own door before Lucas could circle the Icer to assist her. She jumped out, tugging at the hood of her raincoat. "Why did Dillon call you? Why didn't he call his father?"

"I'm not sure yet, but I suspect that Dillon doesn't want his parents to know that he got himself into this mess."

Amaryllis nodded. "They probably wouldn't approve of his gambling."

"That's one factor." Lucas took her arm and waited for a break in the clogged traffic. "The other is that they probably wouldn't approve of what he intended to do with his winnings."

"What did he plan to do with them?"

"Invest in some featherbrained scheme to locate fire crystal." Lucas tightened his grip on her arm and drew her swiftly across the busy street.

The revolving glass doors of Chastain's Palace were in constant motion. A steady stream of well-dressed people came and went. Some were laughing. Several were not. A few had the grim, glittering look of desperation in their eyes. Many appeared to be at least partially inebriated.

Two polite but hard-eyed looking individuals kept an eye on the crowd that milled around the entrance of the casino. One guard was male, the other female. Both wore formal evening clothes that did nothing to conceal their sturdy, muscled torsos.

Lucas and Amaryllis gained the sidewalk and started to make their way toward the casino doors. A gaunt, long-haired figure dressed in a long, flowing black tunic loomed in their path. He took one look at Lucas and appeared to come to the conclusion that there was no hope in that direction. He chose to thrust his sign directly in front of Amaryllis. The message was written in large, crude, hand-drawn letters. It was simple and direct.

WILL YOU BE READY WHEN
THE CURTAIN RISES AGAIN?

"Excuse me." Amaryllis made to step around the long-haired man.

"The curtain will rise sooner than you think, woman." There was a feverish excitement in the man's eyes. "Will you be ready for the return to Earth? Will you be clean enough in body and mind to return to the Utopia that awaits?"

"Please let me pass, I'm in a hurry." Most people were rude and impatient whenever they were confronted by a Return cult fanatic. Force of habit made Amaryllis more polite than many, but sometimes the persistence of the cult members tried even her patience.

"The curtain will be forever closed to those who fall into the five hells of sin. Think about your future, woman. Only the pure of heart shall return to Earth."

"I appreciate your point of view," Amaryllis said, "but there is no indication that the curtain had any religious or supernatural aspects. It was a natural phenomenon of some sort. An energy construct that appeared and then disappeared."

"It was designed by the superior beings of the home planet as a test for those of us sent to St. Helens," the fanatic screamed.

"If you would simply study the subject from a synergistically sci- entific viewpoint—" Amaryllis broke off as Lucas drew her firmly around the grimy, black-robed man.

"There's no point talking to those people." He pushed her gently through the casino doors. "It's a waste of breath."

"I know. But sometimes I just can't help myself. Those Return cults do a lot of harm. I have a friend whose brother got caught up in one for a while. He turned his back on his family and his education to walk the streets carrying one of those ridiculous signs. Fortunately, he eventually came to his senses but it was a very near thing."

"You can't save everyone, Amaryllis."

She glanced at him. "You should talk. What, exactly, are we doing here tonight?"

"Damned if I know," Lucas muttered.

"The Ryes are the closest thing you've got to family, aren't they?"

"I can promise you that they don't see it that way."

There was no bitterness in his words, Amaryllis realized. Just a bone-deep acceptance. Jackson Rye had once been Lucas's friend and partner. In spite of all that had happened, Lucas still honored the old ties. That was why he was here tonight.

The casino appeared to have been designed by an interior decorator who had been torn between decadence and outright garishness. Amaryllis noted a great deal of green velvet and a lot of gold tassels. The ceiling was mirrored and so were all of the walls. The effect was confusing to the eye.

"It's like walking into a fantasy," she muttered to Lucas.

"That's the whole point."

The subdued clang and clatter of various types of gambling machines created a background noise that infused the crowded room with a sense of frenetic energy. Beautifully dressed people hovered around card tables presided over by elegantly dressed croupiers. Gold-suited servers carrying trays of glasses circulated through the room.

"This way." Lucas guided Amaryllis around the perimeter of the gaming floor.

They walked past more large guards with polite smiles and cold eyes. At the end of a mirrored corridor, they found themselves in a quiet passageway. A man stepped forward.

"Mr. Trent?"

"Tell Chastain I'm here."

The guard glanced at Amaryllis. "We were told that you would come alone, sir."

"As you can see, I didn't. Miss Lark is a friend. If Chastain can't deal with that, you can tell him for me that it's time he visited a syn-shrink. He's definitely getting paranoid."

The guard hesitated. Then he nodded once. "This way, sir. Ma'am."

Lucas and Amaryllis were ushered into a chamber that was thickly suffused with crimson, gold, and black. A small group of people were clustered near a massive carved and gilded desk.

Amaryllis glanced around quickly and tried not to let her disapproval show. Taste was a personal thing, she reminded herself. But there was no getting around the fact that if the casino designer had been torn between decadence and garishness elsewhere, in this room he or she had definitely gone for full-blown tacky.

Heavy red velvet curtains covered the windows. Ornate pillars framed the walls. The furnishings were all gleaming black lacquer and crimson velvet. The red, gold, and black carpet was so thick, Amaryllis was afraid she would trip on it.

"Lucas." Dillon Rye leaped to his feet. He looked very relieved and not a little embarrassed. "I am really glad to see you. I'm sorry about this. I couldn't think of anything else to do."

"Hello, Dillon." Lucas met the eyes of the man seated in regal splendor behind the desk. "Chastain. It's been a while."

"Good evening, Trent." Nick Chastain's smile was cool. His emotionless eyes flickered toward Amaryllis. "You must be Miss Lark. A pleasure to make your acquaintance."

Amaryllis nodded brusquely. "Mr. Chastain."

She decided that she did not like Nick Chastain. He was a lean, cold-eyed man who looked to be about the same age as Lucas. He gave the impression that he was a good deal more dangerous than any of the hired muscle who worked for him.

"What do you think of my decor, Miss Lark?"

"It's unusual," Amaryllis said cautiously.

"Presumably that is a polite euphemism for tasteless, outrageous, and gaudy. Thank you. I supervised the interior design myself." Chastain's eyes gleamed. "You must admit that it's a step above Trent's monstrosity of a house."

"Lucas's home is virtually an historical landmark," Amaryllis retorted sharply. "It's a splendid example of the Early Explorations Period. It reflects the exuberant style and vitality of the era. There is no way it can be called tacky. It's beautiful."

Lucas raised one brow but said nothing.

Nick looked at him. "She's either in love with you or she has very bad taste."

Amaryllis blushed furiously. "You, Mr. Chastain, have exceptionally bad manners."

Nick smiled briefly. He kept his attention on Lucas. "I'm a little surprised to see you here, Trent. I expected young Dillon to call his father."

"Disappointed?" Lucas asked dryly.

"Somewhat," Nick admitted.

Amaryllis glowered at Nick. "Lucas is a friend of the family. He has every right to deal with this unpleasant situation."

Dillon's eyes flickered nervously from Lucas to Nick. "I don't get it. Why do you care who gives me the money to make good on my debt, Mr. Chastain?"

It was Lucas who answered. "Chastain prefers to take his money from people who consider themselves his social superiors. He gets a great deal of satisfaction from the fine art of putting very important people in his debt, don't you, Nick?"

Nick shrugged. "I'll admit it's a good deal more amusing than taking your money, Trent. You've never tried to pretend that you were anything but what you are, a man without family or background, just as I am. Everything you have today you earned the hard way. The Ryes, on the other hand, have always traded heavily on their family's position and connections. They prefer not to deal with our sort. Unless, of course, it's financially rewarding."

"Now wait just a damn minute here," Dillon said in heated tones. "I resent that comment. Lucas is my friend. He was my brother's partner. He's practically a member of the family."

"Whatever kinship your family felt toward Trent ended the day your brother died," Nick said flatly.

"That's not true," Dillon protested.

Nick ignored him. He looked at Lucas with a malevolent gleam in his cold eyes. "I must admit, it would have been rather pleasant to watch Calvin Rye stand in front of me and try to hold his nose while he wrote out a check."

"My money spends just as well as Rye's does," Lucas said.

"True. And I do have a great fondness for money, regardless of the source." Nick spread his hands. "I shall be happy to take yours. But tell me, why are you bothering with Dillon's small financial problem? We both know that you don't owe the Ryes a damn thing."

"Let's just say it's for old times' sake." Lucas glanced at Dillon. "How much?"

Dillon swallowed. "Uh, sixty-five thousand."

Amaryllis was aghast. She turned on Dillon. "Sixty-five thousand? You just gambled away sixty-five thousand dollars in this casino? How could you do such a foolish thing? No wonder you called Lucas. I can just imagine what your folks would say if they learned of this nonsense. Where's your sense of family honor and responsibility?"

Nick gave a crack of laughter.

Dillon turned red.

Lucas pulled his checkbook from an inside pocket of his jacket. "Amaryllis has strong opinions on some things."

"Yes, she does, doesn't she?" Nick's grin held a hint of genuine amusement. "A regular little paragon of founders' virtues. I heard you were shopping for a wife, Trent. Is Miss Lark a candidate from a marriage agency?"

"That isn't any of your business, Chastain." Lucas scrawled his name on the check. "Here's your money. Where are Dillon's vouchers?"

Nick nodded to one of the silent men who hovered nearby. "Give Trent the vouchers. The debt has been paid in full."

Without a word, the vouchers were handed to Lucas. He pocketed them without comment and turned to Dillon. "Let's go," Lucas said.

Dillon was already heading for the door. "You bet."

"A poor choice of words," Amaryllis said in a frosty tone.

Dillon winced. "Yeah, I guess so."

Lucas started to follow Amaryllis and Dillon through the door.

"Trent?" Nick called softly.

Lucas glanced back over his shoulders. "What now, Chastain?"

"Take my advice and marry Miss Lark. Something tells me she's a good match for you."

Amaryllis felt rather than saw Lucas grow very still. The dangerous tension in him flowed through the room.

"Since when did you take up marriage counseling, Chastain?" Lucas asked.

Nick gave him a smile that would have done credit to a fallen angel. "In my business you learn a great deal about synergistic psychology."

Lucas did not hang around to argue. He went through the door, caught hold of Amaryllis's arm, and escorted his small party out of the casino.

"Where on St. Helens did you meet that dreadful man?" Amaryllis demanded as they walked toward the car.

"Chastain's okay so long as you play straight with him. I met him in the islands. He set up his first casino in Port LeConner. He was there when the pirates made their move."

Dillon glanced at him with sudden interest. "Chastain was in the Western Islands Action?"

"Yes."

Dillon whistled softly. "I never heard his name mentioned on the news."

"He doesn't like publicity of that kind," Lucas said.

"He certainly has deplorable taste," Amaryllis observed. "It's almost too awful to be real. I think he actually enjoys offending people."

"I think you're right," Lucas said.

"Okay, so I panicked." Dillon slumped in the old-fashioned wire-root chair in Lucas's big kitchen. His hands were stuffed into the front pockets of his trousers. "I'm sorry, Lucas. I couldn't call Dad. You know how he feels about gambling. I didn't know what else to do except phone you."

Lucas poured coff-tea into two mugs. "You actually thought that you could win the stake you need to invest in your friend's fire crystal project?"

"After you refused to give me a loan, I figured it was the only way I could get my hands on that kind of money."

"Dillon, you know the odds are always in favor of the house."

"Chastain's place is supposed to be honest."

"It is. Why should Chastain bother running it in a dishonest manner when the odds are already on his side?"

Dillon's expression turned mutinous. "I was winning for a while."

"Everyone wins for a while. Too bad you didn't stop while you were ahead." Lucas carried the mugs to the table and put one down in front of Dillon.

It was well after midnight. Amaryllis was home, safely tucked up in her own bed. Lucas would have given a great deal to be there with her, but he had resigned himself to the task of dealing with Dillon's problems. Tonight it had become clear that Jackson's younger brother was determined to get himself into trouble. Someone had to do something.

"Go ahead and lecture me," Dillon muttered. "I deserve it."

"Then I won't waste my breath." Lucas sipped coff-tea.

"It's going to take me a long time to pay you back, you know. I haven't even got a job at the moment."

"I'll wait."

Dillon shoved his fingers through his hair in a gesture that reminded Lucas of Jackson. "Damn, what a mess. If Mom and Dad ever find out about what happened tonight, they'll never let me forget it. It will reinforce their conviction that I can't handle responsibility."

Lucas said nothing.

There was a long silence while Dillon reflected on his options. "I could pay you off if I went to work for you," he finally said tentatively.

"Yes."

"But we both know Mom and Dad would never go for it."

"Probably not."

Dillon met his eyes. "Are you going to tell Dad about the sixty-five grand I owe you?"

"No."

"How long will you give me to pay you back?"

"As long as it takes."

"You really mean that, don't you? Most guys in your position would go to my father and demand that he pay my debt."

"You're old enough to handle your own debts."

"My father wouldn't agree with you. And I sure didn't do a very good job handling them tonight, did I?" Dillon's mouth tightened with determination. "I will pay you back, you know. One way or another."

"Okay." Lucas smiled faintly. "But do me a favor. Keep it legal. And stay out of casinos."

Dillon groaned. "That doesn't leave me with a lot of choices."

―――――――――

Amaryllis regarded Irene Dunley across the width of the restaurant table. "Thanks for agreeing to meet me for lunch. I know it isn't easy for you to get away from the department."

"I took a short lunch hour earlier this week," Irene said. "Professor Yamamoto said it would be all right for me to take a long one today. She believes the rules of office behavior should be relaxed on Fridays, anyway. Professor Landreth would never have approved, but that's the way things are now."

"I appreciate it." Amaryllis glanced at the menu in front of her, not really seeing the selections. Her attention was on the questions she intended to ask Irene.

The restaurant was crowded with downtown shoppers and businesspeople. Amaryllis had deliberately chosen it because it was located a long way from the campus.

"What did you want to see me about, Miss Lark?" Irene looked apprehensive. "Is it something to do with Professor Landreth?"

"Yes." Amaryllis impulsively reached across the table to touch Irene's hand. "Please tell me the truth. Were you the one who called me the other night to tell me I should talk to Vivien of the Veils at the SynCity Club about Professor Landreth?"

Irene's eyes widened in stunned dismay. "You knew it was me?"

"Not at the time. But during the past several days I've had a lot of time to think about it." There was no point mentioning Gifford's name. That would only further upset Irene. "You knew Professor Landreth had a standing appointment with Vivien, didn't you?"

Tears glittered in Irene's eyes. She dabbed at them with her napkin. "He went to see her once a week. I still can't imagine why. He never associated with people of her sort. I sometimes wonder if she used some form of diabolical talent to hold him in thrall. Do you think that's possible, Miss Lark?"

Irene's pain was so evident that Amaryllis could not bring herself to deny such an improbable explanation. "Maybe," she hedged.

"It's the only reason that makes sense. Professor Landreth was such a fine man in other respects. A true gentleman."

"Oddly enough, that's just what Vivien said."

Irene appeared not to have heard her. "He was such an upright, upstanding man. He personified the best in founders' values."

"We seem to be hearing a lot about founders' values these days."

"Thanks to that wonderful Senator Sheffield." Irene put down her napkin. A resolute expression replaced the tears in her eyes. "We're so fortunate to have a candidate of his stature running for office. He's a man of purpose and vision. He'll put this city-state back on the right path. I only wish that Professor Landreth could have lived to see Sheffield take the governor's office and perhaps, in time, become president of the United City-States. I know the professor would have approved."

"Irene, why did you send me to talk to Vivien?"

Irene's gaze was clear and purposeful. "Because I have begun to wonder about the circumstances surrounding the professor's death. The more I think about it, the more questions arise. I knew the police had closed the case. I knew that no one else cared if there had been foul play. I didn't know what to do until you showed up at the office a few days ago. It was as if I had been given a sign."

"You knew that I would care if there was something suspicious about his death, didn't you?"

"You were the only other person besides myself who could be counted on to pursue the matter. I'm just an aging secretary. I didn't have the vaguest idea of how to approach the situation. But you are so clever, Miss Lark. Professor Landreth often talked about how intelligent you are. How determined and persistent. I thought that if anyone could get answers, it would be you."

"So you sent me to Vivien."

"Yes." Irene sighed. "I was too much of a coward to go see her myself. I wouldn't have known how to approach a woman of that sort. But I did think she might know something. Professor Landreth's acquaintance with her was obviously of a very intimate nature, after all. There's no telling what secrets he shared with her."

"Did you know that on the day he died, Professor Landreth had made an appointment to see Gifford Osterley?"

"Osterley? Irene's thin lips parted in brief astonishment. "Highly unlikely. Professor Landreth and Gifford Osterley were not on good terms."

"Did you check the last entries in the professor's calendar when you packed up his desk?"

"No. To tell you the truth, I was crying so hard that day, I could hardly see what I was doing. I couldn't bear to look at his calendar. All those perfectly normal, routine appointments that he would never again keep. It was too much."

"Can you think of any reason why Professor Landreth would have made an appointment with Gifford?"

"No." Irene's face crumpled. "But, then, I can't think of any reason why he would patronize a cheap syn-sex stripper, either." She blew her nose and then frowned at Amaryllis. "How did you discover that the professor had an appointment with Gifford Osterley?"

"I've got a confession to make." Amaryllis flushed and looked down at the table. She must not drag Lucas's name into this. "I went into your office the night before the boxes were to be taken away. I found the carton that had Landreth's desk calendar in it. I looked at the last entries. I know it wasn't right, but I couldn't think of anything else to do."

An odd silence fell on the table. When Amaryllis looked up, she saw that Irene was gazing at her with a strange expression on her face.

"Oh dear," Irene said.

"What is it? Have I shocked you? I didn't take anything. Honest."

"You swear it?"

Amaryllis lifted her chin. "On my honor as a Lark."

"I believe you. But it only makes things more confusing."

"What do you mean?"

"I have something to confess, too," Irene said slowly. "When I discovered that the files were to be removed, I got very uneasy. I'm a limited-spectrum prism, you know. Not much power, but a bit of intuition. Do you recall how Professor Landreth always kept a special file for his current projects?"

"I remember. He called it his hot file. What about it?"

"Just before the movers showed up to take away the boxes, I did something very impulsive. I searched the cartons for that file."

"Did you find it?"

"No." Irene's gaze was stark. "The file was missing from its box. Someone else had already taken it."

....

"A pleasure to meet you, Lucas." Gifford Osterley beamed with unctuous enthusiasm as he took the chair in front of Lucas's desk. "I've admired you for years. Your company's performance is a tribute to your intelligence, skill, and determination. A model for corporate success."

Lucas regarded Gifford with perverse curiosity. This was the man Amaryllis had once considered as a possible candidate for marriage, yet she had never made Osterley her lover. Picky, picky, picky.

"Why did you ask to see me?" Lucas asked.

Gifford cleared his throat with an important air. He opened a black leather briefcase that contrasted nicely with his silver gray suit. "It has recently come to my attention that you occasionally have the need for the services of a full-spectrum prism. My firm, Unique Prisms, specializes in providing highly trained prisms to talents in positions such as yours."

"I use another firm."

"Yes, I know. Psynergy, Inc. But I can assure you, sir, that Unique Prisms can offer all of the services Psynergy, Inc. offers and much more."

"What more is there to offer?"

"Discretion, Mr. Trent." Gifford gave him a knowing look. "Absolute discretion."

"Psynergy, Inc. offers discretion and confidentiality."

"Ah, but their services cannot begin to compare with ours. For example, we do not even require a talent certification from our clients.

No need to be tested first in order to use our services. Our prisms can all handle class-nine and even class-ten talents, so there is no danger of a mismatch."

"Psynergy, Inc. has provided me with a full-spectrum prism."

"That would be Amaryllis Lark." Gifford winked. "Forgive me, Mr. Trent, but I know Miss Lark very well. And while I would be the first to admit that she is a powerful, well-trained prism, I must point out that she is inclined to be a bit, shall we say, conventional."

"Your prisms aren't so conventional?"

"Mine are creative rather than conventional." Gifford chuckled. "I can assure you that none of my prisms are burdened with Miss Lark's somewhat limited concept of what constitutes proper, ethical focusing. My people understand that the client is always right."

"I see."

"We respect our clients' right to determine how, when, and where to use their talents. We do not attempt to impose someone else's standards on what is essentially a private decision. Do I make myself clear, Lucas?"

"Very clear. Now you can leave. I have a lot of untalented work to do today."

A small furrow appeared in Gifford's forehead. "Perhaps you don't understand just what I'm offering. Surely you want the freedom to use your own personal talent in any way you see fit without worrying about the restrictions of some prissy little ex-academic who thinks she has the right to determine ethical guidelines for you."

"I'll let you in on a little secret, Osterley. Lately I've begun to discover that virtue has its own rewards."

"Lucas, it's Amaryllis."

Lucas leaned back in his chair and grinned into the phone. "Strangely enough, I recognized your voice."

"Oh. Well, I've got some interesting news. Irene Dunley also went through those boxes containing Professor Landreth's things."

Lucas stopped grinning. "Landreth's secretary searched them?"

"Right. She also admitted that she's the one who sent me to Vivien."

"Five hells."

"Apparently she's been suspicious of the way Landreth died ever since the accident happened. But she didn't know what to do. Anyhow, when I showed up at the department and started asking questions about a case of unethical focusing, she got the idea of involving me in the questions surrounding the professor's death."

"Amaryllis, there aren't any questions."

"Then she decided to search those boxes in her office."

"Why?" Lucas demanded.

"She was looking for Landreth's special hot file."

"Hot file?"

"Yes. It was his habit to keep one, and she distinctly recalls packing it after he died. But get this. The file was missing, Lucas."

He did not like the excitement he heard in her voice. "Amaryllis—"

"Don't you think that the missing file is a strong indication that Professor Landreth might have been murdered because of something in that file?"

"No."

She ignored that in a headlong leap to her conclusions. "Maybe someone pushed him off that cliff and then searched his files to remove the evidence that could have linked the killer to his victim."

"Why would this so-called killer bother to search the boxes? The police considered Landreth's death an accident right from the start."

"Yes, but the killer may have wanted to play it safe. Maybe he took the file just to be certain that no one ever found it. It all makes sense."

Lucas groaned. "No, it doesn't. Amaryllis, think about it. You only have Irene Dunley's word that the file is missing. It could simply have been misplaced. From what you've told me, she was very upset by Landreth's death. She may not have been thinking clearly when she packed up his things."

There was a short pause while Amaryllis digested that. "She did say she was crying so hard that day that she didn't even notice Gifford's name on Landreth's desk calendar. I suppose she might not have a clear memory of where she put the hot file. But, Lucas—"

"Let's talk about it later." Lucas glanced at his watch. "I've got a few things to finish here. It's Friday and I feel like leaving the office early. I can pick you up around six. How does that sound?"

"Impossible, I'm afraid. My aunt and uncle are in town. Don't you remember? I told you that I'd be cooking dinner for them at my place tonight."

"I see." Lucas reminded himself that he had no reason to expect an invitation to a family dinner. He didn't even want one. After all, he wasn't a real matrimonial candidate, just Amaryllis's lover. Here in the city no one took much notice of an affair, but things were different in the country. A small-town farmer and his wife were hardly likely to approve of Lucas's relationship with their precious niece. Amaryllis would be well aware of that. She wouldn't want Lucas there, either. She was very keen on not embarrassing her family.

"Would you like to join us?" Amaryllis asked.

"What time?"

"Six?"

"I'll be there."

No doubt the evening was going to be a big mistake, Lucas thought as he hung up the phone. But he didn't really have much to lose. After all, the entire relationship was a mistake.

Chapter 12

"So, Lucas, I understand you're in the jelly-ice business," Oscar Lark said as he polished off his straw-peach pie.

"Yes, sir." Lucas eyed the last slice of straw-peach pie, which was sitting on a plate in the center of the table. He wondered if it would be rude to ask for it.

He glanced around surreptitiously. Everyone else seemed to be finished with dessert. No one appeared to be about to make a move on the one remaining slice of pie. It was practically staring Lucas in the face. It had been years since he'd had home-cooked straw-peach pie, and he could not recall ever having had any that tasted as good as this one had.

Amaryllis's aunt, the small-town doctor, smiled at him from across the table. Hannah Lark was an attractive, petite, irrepressibly cheerful woman with bird-bright blue eyes and a short bob of graying red-blond hair. There was an air of great competence about her in spite of her size. There was also an aura of power. Without even bothering to employ his own talent, Lucas could sense the invisible hum of Hannah's strong diagnostic talent. It simmered away inside her, a palpable force even without the aid of a prism's focus. There was also something about her that made him fret about his manners.

Oscar Lark sat at the opposite end of the small table. He was as big as Lucas, a rock-hard ag-talent whose years in the fields showed in the toughened planes of his face and in his large, calloused hands. It had taken Lucas only a moment to figure out why he looked vaguely familiar. Oscar could have stepped right out of a portrait of First Generation founders.

"How long have you been in jelly-ice?" Oscar probed.

"All of my life, Mr. Lark." Maybe he could get the slice of straw-peach pie later, Lucas thought. After everyone had left. Unless someone else ate it first.

"I told you that Lucas was with Lodestar Exploration, dear," Hannah said. "You've heard of Lodestar."

"Lodestar, eh?" Oscar gave Lucas a shrewd glance. "Big company. What do you do with the firm?"

"I own it, sir."

"Is that a fact?" Oscar looked skeptical. "Rather young to own a company that size. Are you sure it isn't your father who owns the firm?"

Lucas took his eyes off the pie to meet Oscar's gaze. "My parents were both killed when I was three. I built Lodestar from the ground up. The company is mine."

Oscar blinked owlishly. "I see." He cleared his throat. "What about the rest of your family? Are they all employed at Lodestar?"

A tense silence gripped the table.

"There are no other members of my family," Lucas said bluntly. "Or, at least no one close enough to count."

"No family?"

"No, sir." Lucas made up his mind. The lack of a proper family was no doubt the last nail in his coffin. He had nothing else to lose. He reached out and seized the pie pan. "But I intend to change that soon." He shoveled the last slice of straw-peach pie onto his plate.

"Lucas is registered at a marriage agency, Uncle Oscar." Amaryllis rose abruptly and started to clear the table. "He expects to go in for the final interview soon."

Oscar narrowed his eyes. "Same as you, eh, Amaryllis?"

"That's right." Amaryllis carried a stack of plates into the kitchen.

"Registration with a good agency is the only way to go," Oscar said. "A decision as important as marriage should never be made without proper guidance. Runaway marriages always end in disaster."

Lucas fell to the pie. He told himself it might be a long time, if ever, before he got a chance at another slice of homemade straw-peach pie.

"Anyone for coff-tea?" Amaryllis asked from behind the counter.

Hannah got to her feet. "I'll fix it, dear." She gave Oscar a meaningful look. "Why don't you two men go into the living room? Amaryllis and I will take care of these dishes."

"Whatever you say, dear." Oscar gave Lucas a stony stare. "You finished, Lucas?"

Lucas wolfed down the last bite and met Oscar's grim gaze. "Probably, but what the hell."

There was no avoiding the inevitable, so he got to his feet and followed Oscar into Amaryllis's tiny living room. His instincts warned him that the grilling was not yet over. He had a feeling the worst was yet to come.

Things hadn't been too bad until now. Hannah's graciousness had offset Oscar's ill-concealed scrutiny of his niece's new "friend." Lucas thought he had handled himself quite well in the circumstances. Everyone had been polite. The conversation had not flagged during the mouthwatering meal. He had even indulged himself in a harmless little fantasy in which he and Amaryllis were married and entertaining relatives for the evening.

But the illusion Lucas had woven for himself was about to be smashed to pieces. He could not blame Oscar Lark. If he were in the older man's boots, he would do the same thing. It was Oscar's duty to protect Amaryllis.

Oscar lowered himself into a fragile-looking chair near the miniature jelly-ice fire that blazed on the hearth. "Well, now. So, you're both registered with an agency."

"Yes, sir." Lucas sat down in the small chair on the other side of the fire.

"My niece tells me you're a strong talent."

"Yes, sir."

"She's a full-spectrum prism."

"I'm aware of that, Mr. Lark."

"Not much chance of a match between the two of you."

"No, sir."

Oscar gazed into the flames. "A man and a woman can get some strange notions when they first register with an agency. The business of getting serious about marriage makes some people a little skittish."

"Yes, sir."

"They start to wonder if the agency will really be able to find someone who's right. Someone they'll want to spend the rest of their lives with."

"It does make you think."

Oscar peered at him. "Some people even tell themselves that they can make better decisions than an agency counselor can."

Lucas said nothing.

"Other people figure they better have a few flings before they settle down," Oscar said. "Everyone knows that here in the city folks are more inclined to fool around both before and after marriage."

Lucas didn't see any smart response to that heavily loaded remark, so he maintained his silence.

"I don't want to see Amaryllis hurt, Trent."

Lucas met Oscar's determined eyes. "Yes, sir."

"Nor will I allow her to ruin her life the way her mother did. You know about that?"

"Amaryllis told me the story."

"Amaryllis's mother, Eugenia, was my sister." Oscar turned his attention back to the fire. "That sonofabitch who persuaded her to run off with him was from the richest family in Lower Bellevue. The Baileys. I suppose Amaryllis told you that he was married."

"Yes."

"It was one of those family-arranged marriages. No counseling, unfortunately. It was no secret that Elizabeth Bailey was more concerned with property and social standing than she was with her son's happiness. Young Matt didn't know how to stand up to her. He was only twenty-one when she bullied him into the marriage. Much too young."

"Yes."

"Still, that's no excuse for what happened. Matt was married and that was the bottom line. We don't approve of affairs in Lower Bellevue, but we all know they happen on occasion. It's sort of understood that married folk who fool around are supposed to do it with other married folk, and they're supposed to be discreet. Young Bailey broke all the rules when he involved Eugenia in an affair."

Lucas nodded in solemn understanding.

Oscar shook his head. "I don't know what Eugenia and Matt Bailey told themselves to justify the pain and humiliation they caused their families, but I will always put the bulk of the blame on Bailey. My sister was just a girl. Barely eighteen years old. She hadn't had her birth control shots because there had been a recent scare about the quality of the vaccine."

"I see."

"Bailey's vaccination had been temporarily neutralized because he and his wife were attempting to have a child of their own."

"So neither one of them was protected."

Oscar's hand curled into a meaty fist. "I wanted to murder Bailey when I found out what he had done to my sister. We all did. But there wasn't a damn thing we could do. And then they were both lost at sea. Poor little Amaryllis was left to bear the burden of being a bastard. A heavy load to carry, especially in a small town."

It didn't take a prism's intuition to sense the fires of old anguish and rage that still burned within Oscar. His guilt at having failed to protect his sister only made the volatile mix especially dangerous.

"I understand," Lucas said quietly.

Oscar turned his head once more to fix Lucas with piercing eyes. "Amaryllis is not eighteen. She's a mature adult. If she wants to have a romantic fling before she gets married, that's her choice. My wife assures me that her birth control shots are current, and I assume yours are, too."

"Yeah."

Oscar nodded brusquely. "Good. Because I warn you, Trent, I won't stand by and see Amaryllis put into the same situation her mother was. Do I make myself clear?"

"Yes, sir."

"I want Amaryllis to have a decent chance at happiness. We both know that means a proper agency marriage. It's the only way to provide some guarantee of contentment between two people. Short-term passion, no matter how powerful, is never a good substitute for long-term compatibility."

"No, sir." Lucas decided it would not be wise to assure Oscar that he had already learned his lesson about runaway marriages the hard way. Things were awkward enough as it was.

"Amaryllis is a fine young woman. Her aunt and I and the rest of the family saw to it that she was raised with a good, solid sense of responsibility."

Lucas morosely considered all the pithy little lectures he had heard Amaryllis give on the subject of family honor and responsibility. "I'm aware of her feelings on the subject."

"My wife worried for a time that we did our job a little too well. She was afraid that Amaryllis was a bit too prim and proper. Too rigid." Oscar shot Lucas a speculative glance and then cleared his throat again. "If you know what I mean."

"Yes, sir."

"Now you've come along. I can't say I approve of you having an affair with her, but the most important thing is that she doesn't get pregnant out of wedlock the way her mother did. I will not stand by and see my niece ruined and left with an illegitimate child to raise. Do you hear me, Trent?"

"Yes, sir."

Oscar gripped the arms of his chair. He leaned forward, his expression as grimly determined as that of any stalwart founder. "Then you best make damn sure Amaryllis doesn't get pregnant because if she does, I'll haul you into court so fast, you'll never know what hit you."

Lucas raised his brows but said nothing.

"I don't care who you are or how much money you have, Trent. Keep your shots current. If you get my niece in trouble, I'll follow you all the way to the Western Islands, if necessary. And we both know I'll win in the courts. You won't be able to hide behind a wife. You'll be forced to marry my niece."

"I know that, sir." Lucas met Oscar's stony gaze. "I give you my word of honor that I won't disgrace Amaryllis or her family."

Oscar continued to eye him closely for another moment, and then he visibly relaxed. "That's all right, then. You may not have a family of your own, but I have a feeling you know what family means."

"I know exactly what family means."

Lucas wondered if the extra slice of straw-peach pie had been laced with a little straw-peach brandy. He was feeling light-headed. *Forced to marry Amaryllis.* For some reason Oscar's threat did not send any chills of dread down his spine.

In the next instant, however, the knowledge that the notion of a nonagency marriage would horrify Amaryllis rendered him stone-cold sober.

"Elizabeth Bailey came to the office two days ago." Hannah dried a glass and set it in a cupboard. "First time she's been to see me since Matt and Eugenia died. She always drives into the city for her medical care."

Amaryllis scrubbed industriously on a pot. "Was she ill?"

"No. She wanted to talk to me."

"About what?"

Hannah reached for another wet glass. "She told me that she wants to see you."

Amaryllis looked up quickly. "Why?"

"I don't know. She just said that she needed to speak to you."

"What do you think she wants?"

Hannah smiled sadly. "I expect she's feeling the weight of the years. Something tells me she's begun to realize just how much she lost when she refused to acknowledge you."

"I don't believe that for a minute." Amaryllis hoisted the clean pot out of the sink and set it on the drain board. "Elizabeth Bailey doesn't care about me. She's got plenty of legitimate grandchildren. Matt Bailey was not an only child. His brothers and sisters have married."

"But Matt was her eldest son."

"So?"

Hannah paused in her drying. "Aunt Sophy says that Elizabeth probably feels guilty because she pushed Matt into an early marriage with the wrong woman."

"I doubt that Elizabeth Bailey knows the meaning of guilt. The only reason she might want to see me is to tell me how my mother ruined her son's life and got him killed. I can do without that kind of scene."

"It's your choice, of course, but I think you should see her, Amaryllis."

Amaryllis recalled the day of the ice cream incident. *I'm not your grandmother. You have no grandmother. You're a bastard.*

"I choose not to see her," Amaryllis said.

―――――――

Amaryllis could hardly wait to talk to Lucas the next day. She dove for the phone before she had finished her morning coff-tea.

"I think that last night went rather well, don't you?" she said as coolly as possible when Lucas answered.

"Great pie."

"My uncle is a wonderful cook."

Lucas paused. "Oscar made the pie?"

"Yes. He has a magic touch with pastry."

"Figures."

"If you like, I'll ask him to give you the recipe."

"Never mind," Lucas muttered. "I don't do any fancy cooking."

"Well, I wasn't talking about the food, anyway. I meant that I thought Aunt Hannah and Uncle Oscar took to you."

"Could have fooled me. I had the distinct impression that your uncle would have liked to rip my guts out."

"That's not true." Amaryllis was shocked by the bitterness in his words. "They liked you, Lucas. I know they did."

"It doesn't really matter what they thought of me, does it? After all, our relationship is temporary."

Amaryllis's spirits plummeted beneath the weight of that incontestable statement. "But we're friends, Lucas. Actually, we're more than friends. I think it's important that they liked you."

"Speaking of important, I'm a little busy here, Amaryllis. Was there something you wanted?"

The Iceman was back in control, Amaryllis thought. She forced herself to remain calm and composed. She would not let him know how unhappy his chilling words had made her. "As a matter of fact, yes, there is something I wanted. We didn't get much of a chance to talk last night."

"That was because it became obvious that your aunt and uncle were not going to leave until I did," Lucas said dryly.

That was true, Amaryllis reflected. Hannah and Oscar had made it clear that they were prepared to sit in Amaryllis's living room all night, if necessary. They had accepted the affair that was going on between Amaryllis and Lucas, but that did not mean they intended to facilitate it.

"I think they've guessed that we're involved," Amaryllis said delicately.

"Yeah, you could say that. I got a long lecture from Oscar last night, and it was not about how to make a straw-peach pie."

"The thing is, Lucas, they worry about me. They can't bring themselves to actually approve of our relationship. You know how the older generation is. In their day folks were very discreet about this kind of thing. They still are in places like Lower Bellevue."

"Yeah, I know."

He was definitely getting surly now. Amaryllis made herself move on to a more neutral topic. "Lucas, I've been thinking about what Irene Dunley told me at lunch."

"Ah, yes, the case of the missing secret file."

Surly and sarcastic. Amaryllis began to get annoyed. "This is serious. The more I think about it, the more I think Irene may be right. It's perfectly possible that someone did kill Professor Landreth. And that missing file may hold the clue. Why else would anyone bother to steal it?"

"You have absolutely no proof that it was stolen. Try this scenario instead—Irene Dunley has concocted a fantasy for herself because she can't let go of Landreth."

"I think you're wrong."

"All right, let's say that a file was stolen from one of the boxes. How do you propose to convince the police of that?"

"I don't know yet." Amaryllis lowered her voice. "But I'm getting worried because Gifford's name keeps coming up in this mess."

"Yes, it does, doesn't it? Noticed that myself."

"It concerns me."

"Me, too," Lucas said, "but I suspect for different reasons. Did I mention that Osterley paid a call on me yesterday?"

Amaryllis nearly dropped the phone. "No, you didn't. What did he want?"

"Tried to sell me on the superior services of Unique Prisms. He made a pitch for my business with a strong emphasis on how very discreet his employees are. He made it plain that his prisms don't try to impose any pesky code of ethics on their clients."

"Oh, dear. I was afraid of something like this. Professor Landreth would have been incensed by Gifford's business practices. I can't help wondering if he knew what Gifford was doing."

"You think Osterley killed Landreth because the professor threatened an investigation of Unique Prisms?" Lucas sounded only mildly concerned by the possibility. "I guess an inquiry into his business operations could have been potentially embarrassing."

"No, I don't think Gifford murdered him." Amaryllis's fingers tightened reflexively on the phone. First Clementine and now Lucas had suggested quite casually that Gifford could be a murderer. "Absolutely not. I can't envision Gifford as a killer."

"You envisioned him as a potential husband at one time."

Amaryllis was outraged. "That's different. My intuition isn't perfect. Nobody's is." She thought quickly. "The big unknown here is just how far over the line Unique Prisms is operating."

"You mean is Osterley merely running a less than ethical business or is he actually aiding and abetting criminal talents?"

Amaryllis swallowed uncomfortably. "That's putting it in very blunt terms."

"I'm not the subtle type. Ask anyone. The question is an interesting one, but probably purely academic."

"Why do you say that?"

"I doubt if there's any way to get an answer," Lucas said. "It would be damn tough to prove that any of Osterley's clients were committing crimes using the focus services of Unique Prisms."

"A strong detector-talent might be able to catch someone in the act."

"Don't get any ideas. I've got better things to do with my time than trail around after Osterley's clients waiting to see how they're using his services. Besides, even if I did catch one of them focusing for criminal purposes, the police would still need some hard evidence before anyone could bring charges. Something tells me Osterley's not stupid enough to allow his prisms to get into such awkward situations."

Amaryllis considered that for a moment. "I need to know more about how Unique Prisms works," she said finally.

"Damn it, Amaryllis, I just told you—"

"I want to find out just how far Gifford has gone. I need to know if what he's doing is beyond unethical. I want to find out if he's doing anything that's actually illegal."

"How do you intend to find out?" Lucas sounded grimly amused. "Go undercover? Infiltrate his operation?"

"I could do that. He offered me a job. But I think I'll start by observing one of his clients in action," Amaryllis said thoughtfully.

"You only know the name of one of his clients. Senator Sheffield."

"Precisely."

"Five hells." Lucas sounded genuinely alarmed now. "Amaryllis, what are you planning to do?"

"Take an active interest in politics. Didn't you tell me that your secretary is always throwing away invitations to political fund-raisers?"

"I get an endless stream of them. So what?"

"When's Sheffield's next fund-raising event?"

"I don't know. I'd have to check with my secretary. She has instructions to toss all of the junk mail into the trash before it gets to my desk."

"See if you can find an invitation to one of Sheffield's receptions, will you? I'd really like to observe him in the act of using his talent for an extended period of time."

"You'd need a detector for that," Lucas said.

"Luckily I know one."

"Now listen here, Amaryllis, if you think that I'm going to waste an evening eating tough turk-chick that tastes as if it's been fried in jelly-ice, you can think again. Furthermore—"

"Sorry, I've got to run." Amaryllis hung up the phone before Lucas could explode in her ear.

". . . And it is those values, ladies and gentlemen, the values of our founders, to which we must return." Madison Sheffield braced both hands on the podium and gazed out at the audience with the expression of a man of vision. "We must reject those who would weaken the very fiber of our moral structure. We must protect our young people from the influence of sleazy syn-sex clubs. To that end, I wish to announce that I have launched an investigation into those unsavory businesses. That is only one small example of what I plan to do. With your help, I am prepared to lead us forward into the future."

Thundering applause filled the room. Amaryllis, seated next to Lucas at a table near the front, clapped politely. She had been waiting impatiently for three days for this event. She glanced around at the faces of those sitting nearby.

"He doesn't need to focus charisma," she whispered to Lucas. "Just look at these people. He's saying exactly what they want to hear."

"I have a hunch he saves the charisma punch for the one-on-one hard sell situations." Lucas did not bother to join in the applause.

Amaryllis watched Sheffield leave the podium to join a strikingly beautiful young woman at the head table. "I'll bet that's his prism for the evening."

"She's new. That's not the one he burned out at the museum reception," Lucas said. "But there's some similarity."

"Same color hair and same bra size," Amaryllis muttered.

"Now that you mention it—"

"He's pretending that they're all agency dates. Very clever."

The announcer returned to the podium. He smiled triumphantly at the crowd as the clapping slowly subsided. When the room was again silent, he leaned toward the microphone.

"Ladies and gentlemen, thank you all for coming here tonight. The gubernatorial elections are less than three months away. We must not lose the momentum we have going for us. We must hold true to our course. Remember, voting the Founders' Values ticket is the only way to secure our future."

Another round of vigorous applause heralded the end of the event. People began to leave the hall. Amaryllis glanced around uneasily.

"I thought you said we would have a chance to see Sheffield in action," she said to Lucas.

"We will." Lucas rose from his chair and reached down to take her arm. "I've got an invitation to a private reception that's scheduled to follow this speech. Only those who look like good targets for hard-core arm-twisting were asked to attend. I think it's safe to assume that Sheffield will be working that room."

Amaryllis smiled with satisfaction. "Great work, Lucas. I knew I could count on you, partner."

"Stop me if I look like I'm about to reach for my checkbook."

Half an hour later Amaryllis found herself standing next to Lucas in a chamber filled with a small, select crowd of the city's more prosperous denizens. She held a glass of fizzy green wine in her hand and created a prism for Lucas with her mind.

A few seconds of seeking. Brief sense of vulnerability.

Link.

Energy poured through the prism.

Sheffield was definitely working the room. With the aid of Lucas's talent and a steady focus, it was easy to "see" the waves of energy Sheffield was directing. Every time he stopped to shake hands and chat with one of the guests, he focused.

An aura of unlimited strength, great trustworthiness, and resolute determination flowed from Sheffield in tangible energy fields. The unwitting victim of the focus responded as if by magic. He or she suddenly glowed with enthusiasm and excitement. People nearly tripped over their own feet in their hurry to write out checks to the campaign fund.

There was no doubt but that the lovely woman on Sheffield's arm was working as his prism. Amaryllis could feel the familiar undercurrents of Landreth's style filtered through Gifford's technique.

"Get ready," Lucas murmured as Sheffield moved across the room. "I think we're the next targets."

Amaryllis readied a polite smile as Sheffield and his companion came to a halt in front of them. She was still holding the focus for Lucas when Sheffield turned the full force of his talent on him.

The impact was stunning. The Senator's charisma was breathtaking at close quarters. In spite of the fact that she had been expecting it and knew exactly how he was doing it, Amaryllis was shaken by Sheffield's power.

No question about it, Sheffield was a born leader. Exactly the sort of man that the city-state of New Seattle needed at this time in history. He was a man of extraordinary vision.

"Nice to see you here tonight, Trent." Sheffield's eyes conveyed his extraordinary pleasure in Lucas's presence. The senator was both humble and proud to have drawn such an important businessman to this gathering. "Lodestar Exploration has done a lot for New Seattle, and I want you to know that if the people of this city-state put me in the governor's chair, companies such as Lodestar will have a strong voice in my administration."

Sheffield continued to chat. Companies such as Lodestar would flourish with Sheffield in office. Men such as Lucas Trent would receive the respect they deserved. They would be able to influence the decisions that impacted their operations. Taxes and regulations would be rolled back. Government would work to help business, not restrain it.

Amaryllis realized that Lucas, as the main target of the focus, was getting an even heftier dose of the powerful, quasi-hypnotic charm than she was.

Without warning, the flow of Lucas's detector-talent through the prism altered slightly. Amaryllis wondered what was happening. She watched the crisp, clear patterns of light soften and diffuse into a jumbled wall of meaningless energy.

Sheffield continued to talk about his plans for New Seattle, but his voice no longer sounded so wonderfully warm. His charm faded. Amaryllis realized that she was not quite so ready to believe everything he said. His hair, which had looked so right a moment ago, appeared too slick for her taste now. His eyes held a cool, calculating quality and his smile looked artificial.

Out on the psychic plane, Amaryllis watched Lucas's wall of energy shimmer and pulse in a random fashion. She suddenly realized that he was using his talent to block Sheffield's energy.

Sheffield leaned closer, as if confiding in Lucas. "I want you to know that as the next governor of this city-state, I intend to form a business advisory council. I'd be honored if you would accept a position as the head of that council, Trent. You would have my full attention whenever you felt it necessary."

"I appreciate your confidence," Lucas said.

Sheffield's smile remained in place, but his gaze grew more intense. The woman with him began to look uneasy.

"I can't think of anyone better suited to the job than you, Trent."

"I'm a little busy at the moment."

Sheffield appeared to realize that he was not having his customary effect. Amaryllis saw Lucas's energy barrier shimmer beneath a renewed onslaught of focused charm. Sheffield was strong. Very, very strong.

The woman standing next to Sheffield put her fingertips to her forehead, as though she had developed a splitting headache.

Lucas fought Sheffield's psychic power by easing more energy through the prism that Amaryllis had created. She held the focus for him. The waves of hypnotic charisma receded.

A battle was being waged on the psychic plane. It was a silent skirmish between two very powerful talents. This sort of thing was supposed to be impossible. It was like something out of one of Orchid Adams's novels.

Sheffield's jaw clenched visibly. He took a step closer to Lucas. The attractive woman at his side looked haunted now. Perspiration dampened the hair at her temples. Amaryllis knew she was struggling to hold Sheffield's focus.

There was a surge of energy and then, with astonishing sudden-ness, it was all over. The silent warfare ceased. The last remnants of Sheffield's enthralling charm vanished in a heartbeat.

Sheffield, sweat glistening on his brow, nodded abruptly to Lucas and moved off to talk to someone else. The woman with him trailed unhappily in his wake.

"He burned out his prism," Amaryllis whispered.

"No wonder he's never submitted to testing and certification. He's strong."

"Stronger than you are, do you think?"

"Maybe. Who knows?" Lucas smiled faintly. "All the power in the world won't do him any good unless he finds himself a prism who can handle his talent."

Chapter 13

———————

Lucas awoke very suddenly right after midnight, the dream still vivid in his mind. In the nightmarish images he had been running through the wild, thick jungles of the Western Islands, searching desperately for Amaryllis. She was lost somewhere in the impenetrable foliage. He had to find her.

He opened his eyes and gazed into the dark shadows of Amaryllis's bedroom. Adrenaline still pounded through his veins. He was damp with perspiration.

He reached for Amaryllis, found her, cradled her close against him. Even now, wide awake as he was, a part of him was still afraid that she would disappear, just as she had in his dream.

Amaryllis stirred in his arms.

"Lucas? Is something wrong?"

"Hobart Batt, my counselor at Synergistic Connections, called today. He gave me an appointment for the personal interview. Two days from now. At four in the afternoon."

"What a coincidence." Amaryllis sat up slowly and wrapped her arms around her knees. Her eyes were dark and mysterious in the moonlight. "I got a call from my counselor, too. Mrs. Reeton made my interview appointment for Friday also. Clementine said I could take the afternoon off from work."

It was all happening too fast, Lucas thought. In the beginning he had signed on with Synergistic Connections because the company had a reputation for efficiency as well as for working with high-class talents. But the matchmaking firm was proving to be too efficient for his taste.

"It will take the agency a while to find some suitable candidates for us," Lucas said. "Everyone knows class-nine talents and full-spectrum prisms are difficult to match."

"It might take weeks or even months," Amaryllis said on a hopeful note.

But eventually the agencies would find a man for her, Lucas thought. He had another painful vision of Amaryllis's future. In this one she lay in bed, waiting for the faceless stranger who was her husband. It was worse than any nightmare.

"Lucas?"

Desperation gripped him. He was cold. Ice cold. He needed Amaryllis's warmth or he would surely freeze to death.

Lucas reached for her, pulling her down beside him, easing her onto her back. Wordlessly she raised her arms to enfold him. He sprawled on top of her with rough urgency. He sought her mouth, found it, claimed it.

His hand went to her soft breast. He felt the nipple tighten at his touch. She gripped his shoulders as though she would never let him go. Her legs parted for him, wrapped around his waist.

He moved his hand lower and splayed his fingers across her belly. The tensed muscles beneath the silken skin signaled her readiness, as did the warm dampness between her legs. He drove himself slowly into her, hungry for the welcoming heat.

She was tight and hot and slick. She seemed as desperate for him as he was for her. The response should have banished the ghosts of his dream, but it did not. It only served to make them all the more vivid.

He was going to lose her.

In a last, despairing effort to drive the visions from his head, Lucas silently groped for the mind link. She was waiting for him there on the psychic plane.

There was a flicker of vertigo and then he saw the prism. It was a strong, brilliant crystal construct created from Amaryllis's psychic energy. Lucas poured energy through it in a torrent. He made no effort to focus the bands of light. Instead, he allowed them to dance and shimmer in endless, rippling waves.

The ebb and flow of energy pulsed with the rhythm of the love-making, building swiftly in intensity. Lucas could feel Amaryllis in every part of himself, mind and body. For this moment in time they knew each other in every sense of the word.

The startling intimacy of the link meshed with the physical inti-macy of their passionate embrace. The combined power of both psy-chic and sensual energy succeeded at last in driving out the icy chill that had invaded Lucas's bones.

But even as he gave himself over to his shuddering climax, Lucas knew the joy was very temporary.

The jungle waited.

"Lucas?"

"Yeah?" Lucas roused himself just enough to tighten his grasp on Amaryllis.

"I've been thinking about what happened at the Sheffield recep-tion tonight." Amaryllis propped herself up on one elbow. "We haven't talked much about it."

"What's to discuss? Sheffield's a very strong talent, and he's got the ability to project charm and charisma. He's chosen a career path well suited to his psychic skills. His high school counselor would be proud of him."

"Lucas, this is not a joke."

He exhaled heavily. "You still don't have any proof that he or Unique Prisms is operating illegally."

"Sheffield wasn't just radiating charisma tonight, he actually tried to manipulate us with it."

"I hate to be the one to tell you this, but there's no law against that."

"Because the issue has never arisen," Amaryllis retorted. "It's sup-posed to be impossible to use psychic energy the way Sheffield used it tonight." She frowned. "Although Professor Landreth was always reminding us that there was still a lot we did not yet understand about the whole phenomenon. He said psychic powers were evolving so quickly in humans that there was no way to predict what directions the trend would take."

"Amaryllis—"

"Professor Landreth said that the volatile evolutionary situation is just one more reason why the Code of Focus Ethics is important. The code is the only way to govern the effect of psychic powers in society."

"Yeah, yeah, I've heard that rationalization before."

"It's a justification, not a rationalization," Amaryllis said. "And I'll tell you something else, the prism who worked with Sheffield tonight must have known that what she was doing was wrong."

"True. But don't be too hard on her. Sheffield burned her out within a minute or two once he started pushing her limits. You see? Nature took care of the problem. You don't need to put Sheffield or Osterley in jail to deal with the situation. Furthermore, they're both smart enough to know that."

"It's hard to believe."

"What is?"

"That Sheffield burned out a full-spectrum prism trying to get through the wall of energy you created. How did you do it?"

"You want the truth?"

Her eyes widened. "Yes, of course."

"I haven't got the foggiest idea how I did it," Lucas said. "It was an experiment."

"What do you mean? You deliberately created some kind of barrier by scrambling the talent you put through the prism. I felt it. Saw it happen on the psychic plane. It was very effective."

"I guess you could say that it was all done with mirrors."

"What are you talking about?"

"I'm an illusion-talent, remember?"

"So?"

"In the old days illusionists worked a lot with mirrors," Lucas said. "Tonight I created a psychic mirror in an attempt to reflect Sheffield's own energy straight back at him."

220

"What a concept." Amaryllis was genuinely awed. "Sheffield went down under a concentrated dose of his own charm. Talk about having an inflated opinion of himself."

"I think he sensed what was happening." Lucas folded his arms behind his head. "That's why he tried to rev up his own output to break through my mirror. But he lost his prism when he went too far."

Amaryllis frowned. "You've never done anything like that before?"

"Never." He took a handful of her long hair and made a fist in it. He savored the silken feel of the stuff against his skin. "But, then, I've never encountered a psychic attack of that nature."

"Psychic attack. What a scary thought." A shudder went through Amaryllis. "That's something else that's supposed to be impossible, except in psychic vampire romance novels."

"You know what they say about truth being stranger than fiction. But I'm not so sure it's as impossible as you assume. A very strong hypno-talent might be able to pull off something similar to what Sheffield did tonight."

"Whatever it was, Sheffield's talent is not a form of hypnosis," Amaryllis said with great certainty. "I've worked with hypno-talents. Trust me, I recognize the effects when I see them in action. Remember when you insisted that Miranda Locking must have been under the influence of a strong hypno-talent?"

"Don't remind me."

"I told you then that even the most powerful talent couldn't get her to act against her will or against her own strongly rooted principles."

"So?"

"Neither you nor I is a strong Sheffield supporter, yet tonight both of us responded to the effects of Sheffield's charisma. We had to actively resist him in order to keep him from overwhelming us with his wonderfulness. Psychic hypnosis just doesn't work like that."

"You're sure?"

"I'm sure. Furthermore, in the hands of a good hypno-talent, the subject either goes under completely or he doesn't go under at all. When it's successfully handled, the subject doesn't recall anything about the experience. You and I, on the other hand, were fully aware of everything that was happening."

"Probably because we were prepared for it."

"That was part of the reason, but it doesn't change the fact that Sheffield's power is different from ordinary psychic hypnosis. His talent is more in the nature of a blunt weapon. It's scary when you think about it."

"We fought back," Lucas reminded her.

"Only because you're such a strong talent and because we understood what was going on. I suspect that most people who get a full dose of the Sheffield charm are oblivious to the fact that they're being manipulated."

"They start out liking the guy, and by the time he's finished with them, they think he's terrific."

"Something like that."

From out of nowhere an uneasy thought crept into Lucas's awareness. It squatted insectlike in the corner of his mind. "I wonder why he pushed me so hard tonight."

"Good question. He must have realized very quickly that you were a talent and that you knew what he was doing because you deliberately erected a barrier to his focus." Amaryllis drummed her fingers on Lucas's chest. "One would think that under the circumstances he would have backed off fast. He's not stupid. Instead he turned the whole thing into a battle."

"Maybe he was just curious."

"About your power?"

"He's probably never encountered anyone as strong as he is."

"If Professor Landreth knew that Gifford was supplying prisms for a man of Sheffield's nature and strong talent, he would have been horrified."

Lucas groaned. "We're back to Osterley again. I was afraid of that. Amaryllis, I don't like this any better than you do, but I think it's time you got out of the prism detective business."

"I have to do something."

"No, you don't. What would you tell the cops? That Sheffield tried to overwhelm you with charm? They'd laugh themselves silly. Tonight we witnessed something that a court of law would consider impossible but not illegal."

"But if Sheffield is focusing with intent to defraud—"

"You'd have to prove it. Hell, Sheffield didn't even get around to asking me for a campaign donation. All he did was try to convince me that he would make a heck of a governor."

Amaryllis straightened her elegant spine in a gracefully resolute movement. "I still think there's a possibility that Professor Landreth's death may be connected to all this."

"It's not your job to clean up city-state politics. How many times do I have to tell you that, technically speaking, there is no crime involved here?"

"The missing file."

Lucas did not like the new note in her voice. "What about it?"

"If only I could figure out how to go about locating that missing file that Irene Dunley mentioned. There must be a clue in it."

Lucas sat up fast. "Oh, no, you don't." He closed his hands around her upper arms. "This has gone far enough. Listen to me, Amaryllis, you are not to pursue this investigation any further."

She regarded him with wide, troubled eyes. "I have to do what I feel is right."

"Even if it's stupid?"

"There is nothing stupid about trying to determine the truth," she said with frosty hauteur. "I'll understand, naturally, if you'd rather not be involved. After all, you've got your position as one of the foremost business leaders in this city-state to consider. You wouldn't want to jeopardize your reputation and standing in the community."

"That's enough," Lucas said through his teeth. "If you're going to insult me, do it fair and square. Don't try to manipulate me with your self-righteous founders' values blather."

"Then stop calling me stupid just because I feel I have to find out what happened to Professor Landreth," she said fiercely. "I'll bet you would do the same if you were in my shoes."

"You just don't know when to back off, do you? Use some common sense. There is no crime here, just a little dirty city-state politics. Business as usual. Stay out of it."

"I can't do that," she said with passionate intensity. "I feel a responsibility to get to the bottom of this situation. There are questions that must be answered."

"Responsibility, hell. You're just being stubborn."

"It's no different from the way you felt when you rescued Dillon Rye from the clutches of that dreadful casino owner. We both know that you don't owe the Ryes anything, but you had to help Dillon anyway, didn't you?"

"That was different."

"No, it was not. Professor Landreth was my friend and my mentor. He taught me everything I know about my craft. I owe it to his memory to find out if his death was an accident."

"It *was* an accident." Lucas forced himself to release his grip on her shoulders. "Can't you get that through your head? The only person who had even half a reason to want him removed from the scene is Gifford Osterley and you told me yourself that Osterley isn't the kind to commit murder."

"He isn't. At least, I don't think he is. But what about Sheffield?"

"Any politico who wants the governor's chair as badly as Sheffield does might be willing to kill for it, I'll grant you that much. But there was no need to murder anyone in this case. Landreth was not a threat to Sheffield."

"He could have exposed Sheffield's connection to Unique Prisms."

"How many times do I have to tell you that there is nothing illegal going on between Sheffield and Unique Prisms."

"There is a question of ethics," Amaryllis insisted.

"I can't see Sheffield risking a murder charge simply to avoid an investigation into his use of some very discreet prisms. Any such inquiry would be bound to find him innocent."

"Some of the prisms might be willing to testify against him."

"Then he would be far more likely to murder a few of them, wouldn't he? Come on, Amaryllis, think about it. Sheffield isn't killing prisms for the same reason that he didn't kill Landreth. He's got no reason to commit murder. You saw him in action tonight. He's headed straight for the governor's office."

"This whole situation feels wrong, Lucas."

"Damn. I can't believe I'm arguing with you about something so obvious." Lucas flexed his hands. "I suppose this is one of the reasons why the conventional wisdom holds that full-spectrum prisms and strong talents don't make good marriage partners. They'd likely spend all their time quarreling with each other."

The second the words were out of his mouth, he wanted to recall them, but it was too late.

There was a very long silence before Amaryllis answered.

"Yes," she said. "It would be a pretty miserable existence, wouldn't it? Thank heavens for the marriage agencies and all of their tests and interviews."

Lucas felt as if he had just fallen into a bottomless well of jelly-ice. The cold was endless. "Yeah. Right. Lucky us."

———

"Mr. Trent, you have a visitor."

Lucas glared morosely at the intercom. "Who is it, Maddie?"

"Mr. Calvin Rye."

Just what he needed, Lucas thought. As if things weren't bad enough today. He was still feeling bruised and battered from the midnight quarrel with Amaryllis. Now Dillon's father wanted to see him. "Send him in, please."

Maddie ushered Calvin into the inner office and then quietly closed the door behind him.

Lucas rose. The old habits of politeness died hard. "Have a seat, Rye. What brings you here today?"

"I think you can guess the answer to that." Calvin settled into a chair with statesmanlike composure. The outward assurance was belied by the expression in his eyes. "Dillon told me everything."

"Everything?"

"About his losses at that damned casino. About the way you came to his rescue and covered his debts. The whole sordid tale."

"I see." Lucas sat down, unable to think of anything else to say. "I had a feeling he might do that."

Calvin's mouth thinned with disgust. "Yes, I'm sure you did."

"Rye, what is this all about?"

"I'll be blunt. What do you want from me?"

"I don't want anything from you."

Calvin narrowed his eyes. "We both know you didn't rush to Dillon's aid out of the kindness of your heart. You took advantage of the situation for your own purposes. I would like to know what those purposes are."

"I don't want anything from you, Rye." Lucas was aware of a great weight of weariness descending on him. Absently, he rubbed the back of his neck. He wished he could lose himself in an illusion of the hidden grotto in the islands. But he would need a capable prism for that sort of talent project, he reminded himself. A full-spectrum prism. Hell, he needed Amaryllis.

"There is something you should know," Calvin said quietly. "Shortly after the conclusion of the Western Islands Action, a reporter came to see me at my office."

Lucas stopped massaging his neck. He folded both hands on his desk. "Nelson Burlton?"

"Yes." Calvin's mouth twisted. "Burlton said he had some information about Jackson's death. He wanted to discuss the matter."

"I hope you threw him out the door."

Calvin's gaze was unblinking. "I did. Eventually. But I made the mistake of listening to what he had to say first. It was . . . upsetting."

"Forget Burlton. I dealt with him in the islands. The man is an opportunist. He'll say or do anything to get a story."

Calvin got to his feet and went to the window. He stood there looking down at the street below. "He certainly told me a pack of outrageous and insulting falsehoods."

"I'm not surprised."

"He claimed that during the period in which he covered the Western Islands Action he heard talk of an affair that had supposedly gone on between Jackson and your wife, Dora."

"You should know better than to listen to a reporter's lies, Rye. Burlton was just trying to goad you. He hoped you'd become emotional and blurt out some tantalizing tidbit he could have used on the ten o'clock news."

Calvin's shoulders stiffened. "He also informed me that he had heard rumors that Jackson actively conspired with the pirates. He said that there was a strong possibility that my son had betrayed you not just with Dora but in a business sense as well. Burlton said Jackson may have sold you out in exchange for the promise of becoming the sole owner of Lodestar Exploration."

"I'm glad you didn't give any credence to Burlton's lies."

Calvin fell quiet again for a long moment. Then he turned slowly to face Lucas. "I didn't believe a word of what he had to say, of course."

"Of course not."

"But I have always wondered if he approached you with the same disgusting gossip."

"He did. But I reminded him that I was the one who found Jackson's body. And I was the one who searched the records and files of the pirates' leader after it was all over. I know the truth."

"Yes. Yes, I suppose you do."

"Nelson Burlton hasn't bothered you again since that one visit, has he?"

"No."

"I didn't think so. When he came to see me, I warned him that if he attempted to go public with his lies, he would answer to me. It all happened three years ago, Calvin. I know Burlton's kind. There's no profit for him now in resurrecting ancient gossip. He'd only lose ratings if he went on the air with unfounded, three-year-old rumors."

Calvin watched Lucas intently. "It occurred to me at the time that the only person who had the clout to refute Burlton's accusations was you."

"You're right. As the president of Lodestar and the one in charge of the defense of the islands, my account of events is unassailable. Burlton could do nothing without my cooperation."

"And you refused to give it to him?"

"Why would I bother to help him put together a story filled with lies and innuendoes?" Lucas leaned back in his chair and braced his hands on the arms. "There was certainly nothing in it for me. Lodestar didn't need that kind of publicity."

"You're telling me that you forced Burlton to drop the story because you feared it would be bad for business?"

Lucas smiled humorlessly. "You know me as well as anyone, Rye. Can you think of any other reason why I would have bothered to kill Burlton's story?"

A deep flush suffused Calvin's patrician cheekbones. He held Lucas's gaze for a long moment, but eventually his eyes slid away. He began to pace the office. "You have acknowledged that your actions are grounded in reasons of expediency. Can you blame me for wondering why you chose to rescue Dillon the other night?"

"No. But you'll have to take my word for it that I had no ulterior motive. If Dillon had not chosen to tell you the truth about his situation, you would never have heard it from me. I promised him that I wouldn't discuss the subject with anyone. Whatever else you may think of me, I'm a man of my word."

Calvin paused to study a photograph of Port LeConner that hung on one wall. "Dillon tells me that he wants to go to work for Lodestar."

"I know."

"His mother is opposed to the idea."

"I'm not surprised."

"She blames Lodestar for Jackson's death."

"You mean she blames me."

Calvin did not respond. He stared at the photo.

"She can't protect Dillon forever," Lucas said quietly. "He's twenty-three years old. You and I both know he needs a chance to become a man. He can't do that if you and Beatrice keep him tied to home and hearth. I realize you don't want him to work for me, but there are worse alternatives."

"You refer to that damned huckster who's trying to get him to invest in a fire crystal exploration project?"

"Yes. One way or another, Dillon will seek his own path. He's got spirit and ambition, and he hungers for adventure. Don't kill those qualities, Calvin. He'll resent you for the rest of his life if you try."

"I don't need your advice on how to rear my son."

Lucas said nothing.

Calvin put his hand on the knob. "I owe you sixty-five thousand dollars."

"No. You don't owe me a damn thing. I won't accept your check. Dillon owes me the sixty-five grand. Someday he'll repay it."

"It's a huge debt for a boy his age."

"If he's as ambitious as I think he is, he can pay it off in three years working for Lodestar."

Calvin's jaw tightened. "I tried to make him take money from me to pay you off. He refused."

"That and the fact that he confessed the truth about the debt should tell you something important about him."

Calvin drew himself up. "And just what would that be?"

"That you've done a fine job raising him," Lucas said softly. "It's time to show him that you have some faith in him. Let him become the man he wants to be."

"My wife is terrified that he'll come to the same end that his brother did. We don't need another dead hero in the family."

"There are no more pirates in the Western Islands," Lucas pointed out dryly. "And I can assure you that, as president of Lodestar, I've taken measures to protect the islands and the people who work there."

Calvin's hand clenched around the knob. "I wish I could be certain that you didn't believe anything Nelson Burlton had to say about Jackson."

Lucas met Calvin's eyes across the width of the office. "I know the truth about Jackson."

"So you say. Still, I can't help but wonder if you've got your hooks into Dillon in order to exact revenge for what you may think happened in the islands three years ago."

"I'll be honest with you, Rye. Even if I believed all of Burlton's innuendoes and lies concerning Jackson, I wouldn't take my revenge out on Dillon."

Calvin searched his face. "Why not?"

"Dillon is not Jackson. I don't believe in the old adage about making the family pay for the sins of the children."

"How do I know that?"

Lucas smiled bleakly. "I guess you'll just have to have a little faith in an old friend of the family."

Shortly before five, Amaryllis left the offices of her last client for the day, a gem-talent who had needed her services in order to ascertain the quality of the stones in a recent shipment.

A long white limousine with ink-dark windows waited at the curb. She glanced at it curiously as she turned to walk toward the bus stop.

The rear door of the big car opened. Gifford stepped out of the limo. He was dressed in his trademark silver gray suit and red bow tie. He gave Amaryllis a wry, diffident smile.

"You're certainly traveling in style these days, Gifford." Amaryllis came to a halt on the sidewalk.

"Amaryllis, I have to talk to you."

"I'm on my way back to the office."

"I'll give you a lift." Gifford took a step closer. "Please. This won't take long."

"I'd rather walk."

"Wait." Gifford put out a hand to catch hold of her arm. "I've got a problem. A big one. I need your help."

She saw the desperate, beseeching urgency in his eyes and knew intuitively that it was genuine. "What's wrong?"

"I'll explain everything in the car. Amaryllis, if I ever meant anything at all to you, please say you'll at least listen to me."

"I don't have much time." Amaryllis reluctantly allowed herself to be drawn toward the sleek limo. "If you promise this won't take long—"

"It won't. I swear it."

She didn't see the other occupant of the car until she got into the rear seat. By then it was too late.

"Good afternoon, Ms. Lark," Madison Sheffield said. "I can't tell you how much Osterley and I appreciate your willingness to help the cause."

Chapter 14

"What is going on here?" Amaryllis glowered furiously at Madison Sheffield. "I haven't volunteered for anything. Furthermore—"

She broke off as the limo door closed with a soft, solid *kachunk*. She whirled in the seat to confront Gifford. "Open that door this instant, do you hear me? I do not intend to go anywhere in this vehicle."

Gifford grimaced but said nothing as the car slithered into motion.

"Did you hear me, Gifford?"

"Please calm down, Ms. Lark." Madison's voice was soothing. Very soothing. He reclined on the opposite seat, a picture of sober, conservative elegance in his dark suit and discreet tie. "I am only asking for a few minutes of your time. I assure you it's in the interests of our beloved city-state."

"This is kidnapping, which happens to be illegal in our beloved city-state," Amaryllis snapped. "Stop this car and open that door at once or I'll notify the police."

"Take it easy, Amaryllis," Gifford pleaded. "Give Sheffield a chance to explain, will you?"

"Please, hear me out." Sheffield's eyes were eloquent with humble need. "I must have your help. Gifford here has done his best, but it has become obvious that he is out of his league."

"You burned out another one of his prisms last night, didn't you?" Amaryllis did not wait for a response. She turned back to Gifford. "Just what league are you playing in, Gifford Osterley?"

"I can't supply Sheffield with a prism strong enough to work with the upper ranges of his talent," Gifford muttered. "You're the only one I know who might be able to handle him. He's a class ten." Gifford gave Madison an uneasy glance. "Maybe higher."

"Considerably higher, I suspect," Amaryllis said. "Gifford, how could you get involved in this situation?"

"I haven't done anything wrong." Gifford tugged at his red bow tie as if it was too snug around his neck. "It's not a crime to provide focus services for a high-class talent."

Amaryllis did not bother to conceal her disgust. "You must know how Sheffield is using his talent."

"I am attempting to use my God-given talent for the good of my city-state, Ms. Lark." Madison appeared to be deeply hurt by her implied accusations. "I will admit that I have trouble controlling it at times, but that is hardly my fault. I'm sure you are well aware that there are few if any mentors for class-ten-plus talents."

"How would you know?" Amaryllis retorted. "You've never bothered to get yourself tested."

"I consider it an invasion of privacy," Madison said. "The founders would never have submitted to having perfectly natural, normal human abilities tested, certified, and ranked. But that is not the point."

"What is the point?"

"I need you, Ms. Lark." Madison's mellifluous voice reverberated in the confines of the big car.

"You want me to help you use your talent to raise campaign funds? Forget it. I do not consider that an ethical use of talent."

Gifford shot Madison a shuttered glance. "I told you this wasn't going to be easy."

"I would have been deeply disappointed if it had been." Madison's gaze warmed with admiration as he studied Amaryllis. "I have great respect for your reservations and ethical concerns, Ms. Lark. Gifford here tried to dissuade me from seeking your assistance, but the more I heard about you, the more I knew that you were the prism for me."

Amaryllis glared at Gifford. "Just what did you tell him?"

"That you were a prissy, straitlaced, self-righteous full-spectrum prism who seemed to think it was her job in life to act as a goddamned conscience for everyone else."

Amaryllis felt the heat rise in her face. "I see."

"A conscience is precisely what I want, Ms. Lark," Madison said gently.

Amaryllis blinked. "I beg your pardon?"

"It's not that I lack one of my own." Madison chuckled ruefully. "I assure you my parents saw to it that I was raised to uphold the strictest set of principles. My family believed in the basic tenets of our founders' values before the term became part of our common parlance."

"How nice for you."

"But there are few guidelines for off-the-scale talents, as you well know, Ms. Lark."

"Such talents don't require special rules," Amaryllis said. "The nature of right and wrong does not alter as one rises higher on the psychic energy scale."

Gifford rolled his eyes and tugged at his bow tie again.

"You don't understand, Ms. Lark," Madison said gently. "I still fumble with my great talent from time to time. As I said, it is not always easy to control it, let alone to apply it appropriately."

Amaryllis tapped one finger on the plush car seat. "Is that right?"

"Yes. But I am determined to use my gifts for the betterment of our city-state. To accomplish my goals I require the focus services of a strong-minded, highly principled full-spectrum prism. Someone who can guide me when my talent surges to the fore. Someone who can control and focus my psychic gifts so that they may be used to help others."

It occurred to Amaryllis that the compelling power of Madison's voice had grown stronger during the past few minutes. She realized it was getting easier to believe that he meant every word he said.

Too easy.

She glanced suspiciously at Gifford. He did not look at her. He sat silently in his corner, gazing out the tinted windows.

"There are those who would consider a prism with your high moral standards as something of a nuisance, Ms. Lark." Madison leaned forward slightly. His eyes gleamed with an almost overpowering sincerity. "But I consider you to be a godsend. You are the prism for whom I have been searching all my life. I seek a helpmate and a soulmate, someone whose own psychic powers match my own and whose sense of values is in harmony with mine."

He had been looking for her all of his life. Unlike everyone else, he didn't consider her ethical standards to be irritating and naïve. He valued her skills and her integrity. Madison Sheffield needed her to help him fight the good fight.

A sense of glowing pride unfurled within Amaryllis. At last she had found a high-class talent who appreciated her. It would be so immensely satisfying, both professionally and personally, to work with such a powerful, influential man. How deeply rewarding it would be to focus for a man who sought her guidance and direction. Madison Sheffield offered the culmination of her dreams.

It would be a perfect psychic match.

"I don't know what to say." Amaryllis shot another glance at Gifford, who was still staring out the window. "You've taken me by surprise, Senator."

"I realize that." Madison smiled wryly. "And after what happened last night, you have every right to be suspicious of my intentions."

Amaryllis shook off a seductive urge to brush the matter aside. "That brings up a very important issue. What you did last night was wrong, Senator. Using your talent to try to coerce people into supporting you is very unethical. I'm sure the founders would never have approved."

"You're quite right, of course." Madison looked into her eyes. "But in my own defense, I must tell you that I was not really interested in acquiring Trent's support last night. It was all something of a smoke screen."

"Smoke screen?"

"In my own clumsy fashion, I was trying to test your psychic capabilities." Madison shook his head with admiration. "Gifford had told me that you were a very powerful prism and that you were currently focusing for Trent. Frankly, I doubted the extent of your abilities. When I saw you at the reception, I decided to conduct a quick test."

"I see."

"Forgive me. But allow me to tell you that I was extremely impressed. I envy Trent. I have never had the pleasure of working with a prism as strong as yourself."

Amaryllis considered her sudden wish to let bygones be bygones. It was very strong. Too strong.

She glared at Gifford's averted face.

"Stop it," she said.

Gifford glanced at her. "Stop what?"

"You're focusing for him. Stop it right now. We both know you aren't strong enough to handle much more of his talent, anyway. You're close to your limits. You may as well quit."

Gifford sighed, glanced at Madison, and then shrugged in resignation.

Madison's compelling sincerity faded back into the normal range. It was still palpable, but now it had a practiced, superficial quality. It was the sort of sincerity one associated with politicians. Easy to discount.

"Think about my offer, Ms. Lark." Madison's smile had not altered, but it no longer held the warmth it once had. "Both of us know that it is unsatisfying not to be able to use one's psychic gifts to the fullest extent. Rather like wearing blinders to prevent oneself from seeing properly. One chafes under the restriction. Surely nature never intended for people like you and me to allow our powers to languish from lack of use."

"I'm not sure what nature's intentions are, but I won't help you use your talent in an unethical manner," Amaryllis vowed.

"I would not dream of asking you to do so. If you come to work for me, I guarantee that you will have every opportunity to use your ability to focus in ways that are completely acceptable to you. Think of it, Ms. Lark. You can devote yourself to serving your city-state. You will act as my guide and my mentor."

Amaryllis looked at him very steadily. "I don't have a great interest in politics. Please take me home, Senator."

Madison's fine mouth tightened. But he inclined his head politely.

"As you wish, Ms. Lark. I trust you will consider my offer. We would make a great team. Together we can make a difference."

"You should be ashamed of yourself, Senator. You say you hold to the traditions of the founders, but a true founder would be appalled at how low you're willing to stoop in order to get to the governor's office."

Sheffield's gaze hardened. "My dear, you are painfully naïve. The truth is that the founders believed in doing whatever was necessary to protect the city-state. I am proud to follow in their footsteps."

Amaryllis did not respond. She sat silently in her seat until the limousine glided to a halt in front of her home. Her cozy little house had never appeared so warm and safe and welcoming.

When the door of the limo opened, she saw that Lucas's Icer was parked at the curb. He was leaning against the fender, arms folded across his chest.

"Ms. Lark?" Sheffield put his hand on her arm. "Remember what I said. I offer you a future of selfless public service. The governor's chair is only a stop along the way. One day I shall be president of the United City-states. You can be at my side when that day comes. Not only as my prism but as my wife."

"Your *wife*. "Amaryllis stopped half in and half out of the car.

"Why not?" Sheffield smiled coolly. "Think about it. You were born a bastard, Ms. Lark. I can make you the wife of the president. I offer you the opportunity to rise above all the shame and humiliation your family suffered because of your birth."

Amaryllis flew out of the limo. She ran to Lucas, who opened his arms and folded her close.

She buried her face against his shoulder as the long, pale limousine snaked off into the distance.

———

"That does it. Sheffield has gone too far." Lucas stood in front of the jelly-ice fire and gazed into the flames. He had to work hard to conceal the depths of his anger from Amaryllis. He was afraid it would alarm her to know just how furious he was.

Sheffield had tried his own perverted brand of seduction on Amaryllis, and he had been unforgivably shrewd about it. He had been clever enough to appeal to the core of indomitable virtue that was so much a part of her.

"It's all right, Lucas." Amaryllis was curled in the corner of the sofa, her feet tucked under her. "I told him that I had no intention of going to work for him."

"I should have guessed that sooner or later Sheffield would come after you. There aren't that many prisms who can handle a class-nine or ten talent, let alone one who is off the scale."

"Gifford told him about me."

"Osterley has probably run through every full-spectrum prism on his own staff trying to satisfy Sheffield."

"Yes. Lucas, this is growing more difficult at every turn. Sheffield is obviously bound and determined to use his talent to get to the governor's chair and eventually to the presidency. He gave me a pious speech about wanting to employ his gifts with the ethical guidance of a trained prism. But if he actually had any ethics of his own, he would never have used his talent the way we've seen him use it."

"I don't give a damn about his ethics," Lucas said. "He's a politician. But he sure as hell had better not scoop you up in the back of that white limousine again."

"He won't. Forget his designs on me. I can deal with him. The real question is, do you think he might have murdered Professor Landreth?"

"What?" Lucas swung swiftly around to face her.

"When you think about it, Sheffield had as strong a motive for killing the professor as Gifford did. Stronger, in a way. If Landreth had discovered what Sheffield was doing with his talent, he might have threatened to expose him. Sheffield might have feared the damage to his campaign."

"Stop obsessing on Landreth's death. We've got other problems."

"I told you, Sheffield is not a problem." Amaryllis looked past him into the flames. "Unless he killed Professor Landreth. Lucas, we need to find that missing file."

"You haven't got the foggiest idea of how to go about finding a missing file," Lucas exploded. "And I don't want you trying to dream one up. Every time you try to play prism detective, you get yourself into trouble."

"I can't quit now. Lucas, I have to know what's going on. Try to understand. I need answers."

He studied her face in the firelight and knew that there was nothing he could do to change her mind. Her stubborn nature was as much a part of her as her fierce integrity. He knew when he was beaten.

"You want to find a missing file?" he said. "Hire a real private investigator."

Amaryllis's eyes lit with fresh enthusiasm. "Do you know one?"

"Yeah," he said. "As a matter of fact, I do."

―――――――――

The following morning Lucas strode past the desks of two assistant secretaries and a clerk. He entered a small, tastefully paneled antechamber. The refined, conservatively dressed woman seated behind the large desk bore a striking resemblence to the prisms Lucas had seen focusing for Sheffield. Same hair color. Same bra size.

"Can I help you?"

"I'm here to see Madison Sheffield."

"I'm afraid Senator Sheffield is busy at the moment." The secretary gave him a polite, inquiring look. "Did you have an appointment?"

"No. But don't worry about it. I don't need one." He moved across the chamber to the closed door of the inner office and reached for the knob.

"Sir, I cannot allow you to just barge in on the senator." The secretary leaped to her feet and hurried around the corner of the desk with a surprising turn of speed. "I told you, he's a busy man. If you have an issue you wish to discuss with him, you'll have to make an appointment."

Lucas glanced at his watch. It was five minutes to ten. "Put me down for ten o'clock. I'm a little early." He opened the door and walked into the inner office.

He shut the door in the secretary's face and activated the lock.

Madison Sheffield was deep in conversation on the phone. He frowned when he saw who had invaded his sanctum. "Excuse me, Bob, something's come up. I'll call you back later to discuss those changes in the bill." He slowly replaced the phone.

A series of muffled thuds sounded on the heavy door. Lucas ignored them.

"This won't take long, Sheffield."

"What do you want?"

"Five minutes to explain the facts of life." Lucas crossed the thick carpet and halted in front of the broad desk. "You're smart enough to have gotten all the way to this fancy office, but if you expect to make it to the governor's chair, you had better be smart enough to keep your hands off Amaryllis Lark."

"What the hell are you talking about, Trent?"

Lucas planted both hands on the wide desk. "She's off limits, Sheffield. Touch her and you can kiss good-bye to your hopes of becoming the next governor of our fair city-state. Do I make myself clear?"

"You can't threaten me."

"Normally I don't get involved in politics," Lucas said softly. "It's not a great interest of mine. But for you I will make an exception."

"What's that supposed to mean?"

"For you, I will call Nelson Burlton personally to give him the inside story of how you use your off-the-scale talent to raise campaign contributions."

"No one will believe you."

"The public loves Nelson Burlton. They also love a scandal. But just to make certain, I will also call the biggest donors on your list of contributors and warn them privately that they were manipulated into giving money to the Founders' Values Party."

"You have no proof."

"That's the beauty of it, Sheffield. I won't need proof. I'm the Iceman, remember? The guy who ran the pirates out of the islands. The man who discovered the alien artifacts. I even turned down the chance to run for your seat in the city-state senate. Important people, the kind who give you money, will believe me."

"How dare you!" Sheffield shot to his feet, his face working with rage. "Get out of my office before I have you thrown out."

"Stay away from Amaryllis. If the rumors about you start with me and flow through Nelson Burlton, you'll never be able to shake them. Every major contributor you've got will get nervous. People will talk, Sheffield. Ever hear the term *psychic vampire*? That's what they call off-the-scale talents like you."

"Damn you, Trent, you're one yourself, aren't you? That's the only explanation for what happened when I leaned on you last night. And you've found yourself a prism who can handle something more than class-ten talent."

Lucas smiled faintly. "You're mistaken. I'm only a class nine. And I've got the certification papers to prove it."

"You're a hell of a lot higher than a class ten. You must have rigged the test."

"Impossible. Everyone knows the tests are infallible."

A feverish excitement flashed in Sheffield's eyes. "How did you do it?"

"I didn't do a damn thing, Sheffield. I just took the test and got myself certified a class nine."

"Tell me how you did it."

Lucas shrugged. "Unlike some people, I have nothing to hide."

"Listen to me, Trent, there's no need for us to be on opposite sides. I could take you with me to the president's office. I could name you as my vice president."

"No thanks."

"I'm offering you power, Trent. Real power."

"I've got all the power I need."

"It's Amaryllis Lark, isn't it? You don't want to give her up. I don't blame you. But there's no need to worry. Prisms can work for any talent. We can share her, Trent."

It took every ounce of self-control Lucas possessed to keep his hands from Sheffield's throat. "Touch her and I'll destroy you."

Sheffield made a visible effort to regain control of himself. His composure settled over him, a slightly tattered cloak. "The most you can do is accuse me of focusing a personality trait, and everyone knows personality traits don't count as true talents."

"People don't like to feel that they've been manipulated, Sheffield. And the sort of contributor who gives big bucks to a campaign doesn't like to feel that he or she has been made to look like a fool."

"Get out of my office. I don't have to listen to this."

"Your power is limited by the strength of the prism who works with you. So long as you're getting your focus from a normal full-spectrum prism, I figure you're not much more of a threat than any other smart politician. But if you try to link with Amaryllis, your career is finished. Count on it."

Lucas turned and walked out of the office.

————————

Amaryllis wrapped her coat more securely around herself and surveyed the night-darkened street with grave misgivings. "Are you certain that this Stonebraker person is a qualified private investigator?"

"Rafe Stonebraker is fully qualified." Lucas locked the Icer's door before he joined Amaryllis on the cracked, uneven sidewalk. "The trick is to convince him to take the case."

"I thought all investigators needed work. In mystery novels they're always hard up for clients."

"Stonebraker only takes cases that interest him. He's a little eccentric."

"You can say that again. Lucas, I don't like the look of this neighborhood."

"What's wrong with it?"

"You have to ask? It looks like a cemetery."

"Your imagination is running away with you." Lucas took her arm. "Come on, let's go see Stonebraker."

Amaryllis glanced up and down the silent, empty street. It was not her imagination, she thought. The neighborhood did look like the sort of place where one might encounter a few specters.

The address of Stonebraker Investigations was located on a hillside overlooking the city. The district was an old one dotted with huge mansions built by the wealthy during the Later Expansion Period. Fifty years ago the heavy, somber architecture had been all the rage, an overreaction to the ebullience of the Early Explorations Period.

The style had quickly fallen out of favor. Most of the great, dark houses were empty these days. They crouched on the hill like so many brooding gargoyles frozen in time. Their windows were shuttered, and their doors had been nailed closed. Realtors threw up their hands whenever one came on the market. There were very few buyers for the old, decaying mansions. Even the Historical Preservation Society was not very interested in them.

Amaryllis shivered when Lucas brought her to a halt in front of a massive iron gate. "I don't like this, Lucas."

He grinned for the first time all day, his teeth white and dangerous in the shadows. "If you think the neighborhood is spooky, wait until you see Stonebraker's home."

"Why did we have to come here at night? Why couldn't we have made an appointment during regular business hours?"

"These are Stonebraker's regular hours. He only works nights."

Lucas's warning about the house proved correct. Rafe Stonebraker's mansion was an eerie mausoleum lit by old-fashioned jellyice flare candles that cast long, flickering shadows on the stone walls. Amaryllis had little opportunity to examine the interior closely, but what little she saw as she and Lucas were shown into a fire-lit library was enough to make her shudder. It was a house filled with darkness in more ways than one.

"You're really going to have to see about getting an interior designer in here, Stonebraker," Lucas said as the library door closed. "You may have pushed the atmosphere bit a little too far."

"I'll take your advice under consideration, Trent." The voice, as dark as the shadowed halls of the mansion, emanated from the depths of a deep chair that faced the fire. "What brings you here tonight?"

"Business."

"Naturally." There was a laconic, soul-weary sigh buried in the single word.

"My friend Amaryllis here has a small job for you, if you're interested." Lucas strolled over to a side table and picked up a crystal decanter filled with a clear, sparkling liquid. "Might help you shake off a little of that pesky ennui for a while."

"What sort of job?"

Amaryllis cleared her throat. "I want you to find a missing file, Mr. Stonebraker."

"Are you certain that it's missing?" Stonebraker asked.

Amaryllis scowled. "Of course I'm certain. Why would I be here if it weren't? The contents relate to an investigation I'm conducting into the matter of the death of a very fine man."

There was a long silence from the vicinity of the chair.

"It has been my experience that such investigations generally reveal more than anyone really wants to know about the victim."

"Are you or are you not interested in my offer of employment?" Amaryllis snapped.

"Tell me about it," Stonebraker said at last.

She did, as succinctly as possible. It only took a few minutes during which time Lucas lounged against the side table and sipped the bright, clear brew that he had poured from the decanter.

Amaryllis finally got to the end of her tale. Braced for a rejection, she was surprised when Stonebraker gave her his answer.

"I'll look into it," he said softly.

Amaryllis glanced at Lucas, who shrugged and put down his glass.

"You've got your investigator," he said. "Let's let him get on with his work."

Amaryllis did not hesitate when Lucas started toward the door. With one last, uneasy glance at the back of the chair, she hurried after him.

A few minutes later she breathed a sigh of relief as they walked back through the iron gates. "You said he was a little eccentric. You didn't tell me that he was downright weird."

"Stonebraker is kind of difficult to explain."

"He's impossible to explain. Lucas, I don't like him, I don't trust him, and I don't think he'll find the missing file. Hiring him is a complete waste of time."

Lucas unlocked the car door. "You're just saying that because you don't approve of him."

"Who could possibly approve of a man who keeps bizarre hours, has no discernible work ethic, and who doesn't even use modern light fixtures?" Amaryllis glowered at Lucas as she slid into the passenger seat. "I never even got a good look at him. The only illumination in that creepy old house was from the fire and a couple of old-fashioned jelly-ice candles."

"Stonebraker has excellent night vision." Lucas got behind the steering bar. "It came in handy when we went pirate hunting in the islands."

Amaryllis groaned. "I should have guessed. He's another one of your acquaintances from the Western Islands Action, isn't he?"

"Yeah." Lucas activated the ignition system. "He may be weird, but if anyone can find your missing file, he can."

Amaryllis shuddered. "Are all of your friends off-the-scale talents?"

Lucas gave her a strange sidelong glance as he pulled away from the curb. "What makes you think Stonebraker is a talent?"

"I could feel the power in him." Amaryllis paused. "The same way I could feel it in Nick Chastain. They're both as strong as you, aren't they?"

"Probably." Lucas shrugged. "But neither of them has any interest in getting tested, and neither has ever met a prism who could work with them at the full range of their power."

"I'm not surprised. No reputable prism would work with an untested talent."

"Picky, picky, picky."

Chapter 15

"Amaryllis, my dear, I hear today is the big day." Gracie Proud paused in the doorway of Amaryllis's office. "Clementine tells me you've got an appointment at four for your marriage agency interview."

Amaryllis looked up from the notes she was making for a client's final bill. She managed a wan smile. She liked Gracie, but so did everyone. Gracie was one of those warm and charming individuals people gravitated toward instinctively.

She was Clementine's opposite in many ways, tastefully fashionable where Clementine was defiantly outrageous in her choice of clothes and hairstyle; soft-spoken where Clementine was loud and brusque; even-tempered where Clementine was inclined to jump to conclusions or fly off the handle.

Today Gracie was dressed in one of her trademark pastel business suits that fit her elegant figure like a glove. Her dainty high-heeled shoes and stockings were carefully toned to match the pale blue jacket and skirt. Clementine had once told Amaryllis that Gracie had all her suits made by a tailor in New Portland.

"Hi, Gracie." Amaryllis put down her pen. "Yes, this is the day."

Gracie raised her finely drawn brows. "You don't appear to be too thrilled about the whole thing."

"To tell you the truth, I'm a little nervous."

"Don't worry, everyone is. I practically had an anxiety attack right there in the counselor's office on the day of my interview." Gracie smiled reminiscently. "Of course, that was nothing compared to my reaction when the agency introduced me to Clementine and told me it would be a perfect match. I very nearly had heart failure on that occasion."

"What's this?" Clementine loomed in the doorway behind Gracie. "For crying out loud, don't terrorize her, Gracie. She's already a nervous wreck."

"I was about to point out that the agencies generally do an excellent job," Gracie said smoothly. "Certainly much better than most people could manage on their own. Just look at you and me."

Clementine grinned. "Yep, here we are, about to celebrate fifteen years of happy camping. It's a sure bet that you and I would never have gotten together without the aid of a good matchmaking agency. Left to my own devices, I would have run a mile the first time I saw you. I'll never forget that ridiculous little pink suit you wore that day."

Gracie gave Amaryllis a reassuring look. "Clementine and I are walking testimonials to the fact that occasionally opposites do attract, and the syn-shrinks at the agencies are shrewd enough to figure it out. When's your appointment?"

"In half an hour." Amaryllis glanced at Clementine and then switched her attention back to Gracie. "Any last words of advice?"

"Yes, as a matter of fact, I have," Gracie said. "Don't try to fake it. The counselors are all trained syn-psych talents working with strong prisms. They'll be able to tell immediately if you're trying to make yourself look like something other than what you really are."

"There's a time and a place for cheating," Clementine said cheerfully, "but this interview ain't it, kid. Your whole future is at stake."

The bottom fell out of Amaryllis's stomach. She jumped to her feet and headed for the door. "Excuse me, I have to get to the restroom. I think I'm going to be sick."

———

"Well, now, Mr. Trent, that takes care of the portion of the interview that covers your attitudes toward vacations and hobbies." Hobart Batt glanced up briefly as he turned the page. His eyes sparkled behind the lenses of his round glasses. Hobart obviously loved his work.

The counselor was a small, dapper man who apparently had a penchant for vividly patterned vests and heavy gold jewelry. The prism who was focusing for him this afternoon was an older woman who sat quietly nearby.

During the grueling interview, Lucas occasionally felt the erratic twinges of awareness which told him that Hobart was focusing his syn-psych talent.

Without Amaryllis to construct a prism and hold the focus for him, there was no way for Lucas to tell just how much Hobart was relying on his psychic skills. Lucas didn't care. He was not in a good mood. He felt trapped. He could almost see the door of a large cage slowly closing on him.

"Let's go on to the section that details your feelings about sex, shall we?" Hobart asked brightly.

"Sex?" Lucas stared at Hobart. "What about it?"

"Do you enjoy extensive foreplay or do you prefer to engage in the sexual act with a minimal amount of the preliminaries? In other words, would you call yourself a touchy-feely sort of person?"

Lucas glanced at the prism. "Do we have to discuss this in great detail?"

"Don't mind Mrs. Drake," Hobart said. "She's been through hundreds of these interviews. Now, about foreplay."

Lucas thought about the indescribable intimacy of the focus link that he experienced with Amaryllis. Sex would never be as good again without it.

"Foreplay's okay," Lucas said.

Amaryllis watched with morbid fascination as the syn-psych counselor turned the page.

"Now, that takes care of vacations and hobbies." Mrs. Reeton, a pleasant, competent woman in her early forties, looked at Amaryllis. "Let's proceed to the section on sexual attitudes."

Amaryllis blushed and glanced at the prism seated next to Mrs. Reeton. "Is this part necessary?"

"Don't be shy, Amaryllis, we're all professionals here." Mrs. Reeton gave her a reassuring smile. "And I assure you that sex is a very important part of marriage. Do you enjoy extensive foreplay?"

"Foreplay?" Amaryllis thought about the deeply sensual feelings that flowed through her whenever she was with Lucas. She cleared her throat and avoided the prism's serene gaze. "Yes, I think foreplay is very important."

Hobart Batt turned to the next page with a crisp movement of his beringed hand. "Do you agree or disagree with the following statement, 'Marriage is forever but the occasional affair is an acceptable diversion, so long as it is handled discreetly and does not embarrass the family.'"

Lucas remembered the cold emptiness he had felt when he had realized that Dora had gone to another man. "Disagree. Strongly disagree."

Mrs. Reeton waited, pen poised, for Amaryllis's response to the question she had just asked.

Amaryllis thought about the parents she had never known. She recalled a photo she had once seen of a laughing, green-eyed man named Matthew Bailey. He had gotten her mother pregnant although he was not free to marry. Another image followed on the heels of the first, a picture of her mother, Eugenia, carefree and careless at eighteen. They were both locked in Amaryllis's memory, the two people whose affair had produced repercussions that had haunted two families for years.

Are you really my grandmother?

You have no grandmother. You're a bastard.

A sudden sharp pain made Amaryllis glance down. She saw that she had made a fist with one hand. She was sinking her nails into her palm.

"I strongly disagree with that statement," she said softly.

Lucas glared at Hobart Batt. "What the hell do you mean, how do I deal with anger? I get angry, that's how I deal with it. Damn it, how much longer is the stupid interview going to take?"

"I feel that people should communicate their emotions freely in a relationship," Amaryllis said. Then she thought of all the taunts and name-calling she had endured as a child. "But they should exercise self-control and restraint so as to avoid hurting the other person's feelings."

"Food?" Lucas thought about it for approximately three seconds. "I like home cooking best." Home cooking presupposed a real home. "I don't care what it is, just so it's cooked at home."

"Food?" Amaryllis frowned in thought. "It's all right to eat out in restaurants once in a while, but most of the family's meals should be prepared at home. The food we eat directly affects the various syner-gistically aligned systems of the body. The only way to assure a proper balance of fresh, nourishing fruits and vegetables in the diet is to do most of the cooking in the home."

Mrs. Reeton smiled. "How would you describe your attitude to-ward money, Amaryllis?"

Amaryllis heaved a small sigh of relief. This was an easy one. "I believe that a household should have a disciplined, comprehensive budget. Every source of income and expense should be carefully mon-itored and recorded. A certain percent of the income should be put into savings every month. All the bills should be paid on time. There is no excuse for receiving past-due notices. Credit is to be avoided except for very rare, extremely large, and important purchases such as a house."

"Let's move on to the topic of money." Hobart chuckled. "I'm sure that's an important subject for you, Mr. Trent. Any man who's made as much money as you have will no doubt have some definite opinions on the matter."

Lucas thought about it. He had never set out to get rich. He had searched for jelly-ice because he was good at it and because it gave him an excuse to lose himself for days or weeks at a time in the jungle, where he could be alone with his maddening flashes of talent.

At first, the money had simply been a way to keep score. It paid for the next exploration trip. But somewhere along the line it had taken on a life of its own. He needed it to support the rapidly increasing number of people who depended on him. Icemen and their families looked to him for a livelihood. Contracts had to be filled. Young, enthusiastic syngineers kept asking for more research and exploration funding.

One day Lucas had looked around and realized that the entire economy of the Western Islands had become completely dependent on Lodestar Exploration. He had obligations.

The money had come with the package, but in and of itself, it had never meant very much. No amount of it would ever fill the void in his life after Amaryllis married another man.

"Easy come, easy go," Lucas said.

Amaryllis felt utterly drained when she walked through her front door shortly before six. The interview had been an ordeal she hoped she never had to repeat. Every question had been an excruciatingly painful reminder that her affair with Lucas was doomed to be short-lived.

She kicked off her shoes and hung her jacket in the closet. With some vague notion of making a salad for dinner, she trailed listlessly down the short hall and went into the kitchen.

The first thing she saw when she opened the icerator was the bottle of green wine that she had put there that morning. It looked considerably more therapeutic than the lettuce beside it.

She removed the bottle and set it on the counter. It took a while to find the corkscrew. Lucas had stored it in the wrong drawer. It figured. He did not have her organized approach to housekeeping.

Well, she wouldn't have to worry about that sort of thing much longer, she thought as she went to work on the cork.

She poured a glass of wine and hoisted it in a silent toast to the scientific wonders of modern matchmaking techniques. *The only way to go*, she reminded herself as she took a swallow of the green wine.

She heard the front door open just as she prepared to take a second sip.

"Amaryllis?" Lucas sounded as if he had just come home from a very bad day at the office.

But he had not just come from the office.

Amaryllis poured a second glass of wine and carried it out of the kitchen. She stopped when she saw Lucas.

He closed the door of the hall closet and turned to look at her. The bleak expression in his eyes tore at her heart. Wordlessly, she held out the glass of wine.

He came toward her, took the glass from her hand, and downed half the contents in a single swallow.

"No need to look so forlorn." Amaryllis summoned a shaky smile. "As my boss said earlier today, it's just your whole future at stake."

"Yeah. Right. My whole future." Lucas put the glass down on a nearby shelf and reached for Amaryllis.

His arms closed around her with a fierce gentleness. She pressed her face against his shoulder and hugged him with all of her strength.

After a moment she opened her mind to a focus link and found him there, waiting for her on the psychic plane. She created a prism and Lucas poured energy through it in a glittering, chaotic pattern.

They stood there in the hall, holding each other for a very long time.

Monday afternoon Lucas had no sooner hung up the phone when his private line warbled again. He eyed the instrument with impatience. Perhaps it was time to get a new private number. Too many people seemed to have his present one.

"Trent here," he growled into the phone.

"Lucas?" Amaryllis sounded startled. "Is that you? Are you all right?"

"Sorry. I was just going to call you."

"With a report from Mr. Stonebraker, I hope?"

"I haven't heard from Stonebraker."

"Hah. I knew it. I thought he was supposed to be a real hotshot investigator. You said he could find just about anything."

"Amaryllis, we just asked Stonebraker to find that damn file. It's only Monday. Give him a chance."

"He could probably work a good deal more efficiently if he didn't keep weird hours."

"I'll pass along your advice." Lucas lounged back in his chair and gazed out the window. "That's not what I was going to talk to you about."

"So? What's up?"

"Dillon just called. He asked if he could have dinner with me tonight."

"Maybe his folks have decided to let him go to work for Lodestar, after all," Amaryllis suggested.

"I doubt it. Dillon probably wants some advice, and I don't know what the hell to tell him."

"Just let him talk. From what you've told me, he views you as a substitute for his older brother."

"You don't mind?"

"If you have dinner with Dillon? Of course not. I've got some things to catch up on at home, and I've been looking for an opportunity to start reading a new book I bought. Don't worry, I can entertain myself for one evening."

"I'll call you when Dillon and I are finished. If it's not too late, maybe I could drop by your place." Lucas rubbed the bridge of his nose. There were going to be so few nights together. He could not bear the thought of missing a single one.

"That will be fine," Amaryllis said gently.

Something was wrong. The link was intensely personal, incredibly intimate. The essence of his masculinity was ines-

capable. It excited all her senses. It enveloped her, a flowing cape made of midnight colors.

His desire for her blazed through the prism in a near-blinding pattern of light. It was disturbing, erotic, and, Samantha suspected, probably quite dangerous.

It was not supposed to be this way, she thought as his mouth came down on hers. She had focused many times for many people. It had always been an impersonal connection, no different than shaking hands.

"Do not be afraid," he whispered against her mouth. "You create the prism. Without you I can do nothing. You control the link between us."

But Samantha was no longer so certain that she was in command of the mind link. She felt his power coiling around her. He was so strong, she thought. She had never met any talent as strong as Justin.

What if the legends were right? she wondered as he deepened the kiss. They said a psychic vampire could chain a powerful prism with mental bonds and use her for his own dark purposes.

If she did not burn out beneath the fierce flames of his psychic energy—and she showed no signs of doing so—then she might be in very grave danger.

The power in him surged through the prism. She knew in that moment that Justin St. Clair could take control of her mind the way he took control of her senses.

"It is desire that links us," Justin said. "Surely you do not fear it?"

But she did fear it. Samantha knew that she had to act before it was too late.

The ringing of the telephone interrupted Amaryllis before she discovered just how the heroine of Orchid Adams's latest novel intended to deal with Justin, the psychic vampire.

She marked her place, closed the book, and reached for the phone.

"Hello?"

"Is this Amaryllis Lark?" The voice on the other end of the line was vaguely familiar, although it was barely above a whisper.

"Yes. Who is this?"

"It's me, Vivien Huggleston."

"Vivien Huggleston? I don't know anyone named—"

"Vivien of the Veils," Vivien muttered. "You came to see me after one of my shows. You asked me some questions about Jonny Landreth."

Amaryllis sat up swiftly on the sofa. "Yes, of course, Vivien. What is it? Did you remember something important?"

"It's a little more complicated than that. I never actually forgot anything. I just didn't see any reason to tell you everything I knew that first time. I had my reasons, y'know? But now I think I'd better explain about me and Jonny."

"I'm listening."

"Jonny gave me something to keep. He said he didn't want it to fall into the wrong hands."

Amaryllis gripped the phone more securely. "Was it a file?"

"How did you know?"

"Never mind. Have you still got it?"

"Yeah, that's what I want to talk to you about. It's in a safe place, but I think I better get rid of it. Things are getting a little out of hand. Look, can you come and pick it up? I don't feel right about just burnin' it. It was real important to Jonny."

Amaryllis glanced at her watch. "I can be there in fifteen minutes."

"Come alone. I didn't much like the looks of that guy you had with you the last time. He made me nervous."

"He sometimes has that effect on people. Don't worry, I'll come alone. Where are you?"

"In my dressing room. I'm between performances. I don't go on for another hour and a half. Take a cab. That way you won't have to park on the side streets. Gets a little dangerous around here after dark, y'know. But you'll be safe enough so long as you stay on the main strip."

"I'll be there as soon as I can get a taxi."

Amaryllis cut the connection and then dialed the number of a cab company.

She was on her way out the door a few minutes later when she remembered that Lucas would be calling to tell her that his dinner with Dillon was finished. He would worry if she failed to answer the phone.

She dashed back into the living room, grabbed the phone, and re-corded a new message into her answering machine.

When she was done, she ran back to the door and opened it. The cab was waiting at the curb.

The strip that marked the heart of Founders Square was thronged, as usual. Although it was nearly ten o'clock, the gaudy jelly-ice lights of the clubs and casinos blazed brighter than the sun at high noon.

Amaryllis got out of the taxi in front of the SynCity Club. She glanced at the long line of cruising cabs that clogged the street. There would be no problem getting one to take her home when she had fin-ished talking to Vivien.

"Thank you," she said as she handed the driver his fare and what she considered a reasonable tip. "No need to wait."

The driver scowled at the money she had thrust into his hand. "Don't worry, I won't."

Amaryllis chose to ignore the rudeness. She had more important things on her mind. Shoving her hands into the pockets of her coat, she made her way through the crowd to the narrow alley that led to the stage door entrance of the SynCity Club.

The massive guard who had blocked the door last time was not at his post. At least she was to be spared an unpleasant discussion about a bribe. That was fortunate. She only had a few dollars in her purse. She needed to save some cash for the cab fare home.

Amaryllis opened the stage door and stepped into the cramped cor-ridor.

The outer door closed behind her. She paused, allowing her eyes to adjust to the dim light. A dull rumble reverberated down the ugly green hallway. The floor trembled beneath Amaryllis's feet. It took her a moment to realize that what she heard and felt was the rumble of the music being played on stage in the club.

She turned and went down the corridor, mentally counting off the doors. The thunder of the music grew louder as she moved deeper into the bowels of the SynCity's backstage environs.

The door with the glowing purple star on it was closed. Amaryllis knocked once. There was no response.

"Ms. Huggleston?" Amaryllis put one ear to the door. "Vivien? It's me. Amaryllis Lark."

There was still no response. The muffled roar of the music rose and fell in a throbbing wave of sound and vibration. Amaryllis wrapped her hands around the doorknob and twisted cautiously.

The door opened without protest. Amaryllis caught a faint whiff of smoke, as if someone had just lit a jelly candle.

"Vivien? I'm here." She peered around the corner of the door.

There was an untidy bundle of purple veils lying in the middle of the threadbare carpet. It looked as if Vivien had discarded her stage costume in a hurry and left it on the floor.

Then she saw the feathery, high-heeled slippers sticking out from beneath a cascade of gossamer purple fabric. Vivien's feet were in the shoes.

"Vivien." Amaryllis started forward. Her first thought was that the stripper had fallen and knocked herself unconscious.

The dressing room door swung shut behind her as she crouched beside the fallen woman. "Vivien?"

Amaryllis heard a faint squelching sound. The carpet was wet. She glanced down and saw the dark stain.

A scream rose in her throat

Blood soaked the thin carpet and several layers of veils. The puddle had its origin in the terrible black hole in the center of Vivien's forehead.

Amaryllis snatched back the hand she had been about to place on the dead woman's shoulder. She managed to stagger to her feet. Her stomach churned. The room started to spin gently. The noise of the pounding stage music shook the walls.

She turned and ran for the door. She had to get help.

But when she opened the door she found only darkness in the hallway. Someone had turned out the weak overhead lights that had illuminated the narrow corridor.

Then she felt a faint, not unfamiliar, trickle of awareness on the psychic plane.

It was gone in an instant but not before Amaryllis recognized it. What she had sensed was the brush of a strong but unfocused talent instinctively seeking a link. It was the sort of spiking surge of energy that often occurred when a talent was tense or anxious or under stress.

Someone waited for her out there in the shadowed corridor.

Chapter 16

In the endless heartbeat of time that it took Amaryllis to realize that there was someone lying in wait for her, she realized something else. She made a juicy target silhouetted in the dressing room doorway.

She leaped back into the tiny room and slammed the door shut. Her fingers were trembling so violently that it required two or three tries to activate the lock.

Not that it would do much good, she thought when she finally heard the bolt slide into place. The door of the dressing room was so flimsy that she could have put her own fist through it. Anyone bent on kicking his way into the room would have little trouble.

She whirled around and braced her back against the thin door, trying not to look at Vivien's body as she searched the tiny cubicle for a way out.

Her gaze fell on the bathroom door. She remembered what Vivien had said about having to share the facilities with Yolanda. There had to be a another entrance to the bathroom from the adjoining dressing room.

Amaryllis took a deep breath and made her way cautiously around the blood-soaked puddle of purple veils. She reached the narrow bathroom door and unlatched it. The smell of smoke was stronger inside the tiny cubicle.

There was another entrance on the far side of the small functional room.

Amaryllis turned off the lights behind her and stepped into the bathroom. She shut the door to Vivien's dressing room and fumbled for the latch on the opposite door. When she opened it she found herself in darkness.

She stepped carefully into the deep shadows of the adjoining dressing room and promptly struck her foot against the leg of a table. The pounding rhythms of the music muffled both the thud and her gasp of pain.

Not daring to search for a light for fear that it would show beneath the door that opened onto the hallway, Amaryllis groped her way across the room.

Her searching fingers brushed against a knob just as a wisp of powerful talent flickered somewhere nearby. The unnerving sensation reminded Amaryllis of a film she had once seen that depicted a bat-snake using its tongue to taste the air for the scent of prey.

She wondered if the killer was deliberately using his unfocused psychic energy to try to locate her in the darkness. That fear elicited another. If she could sense his power, he might well be able to sense hers. She was a prism, not a talent, but psychic energy was psychic energy, and she produced a great deal of it when she was working. Her mind no doubt gave off whispers of power under stress, too, just as the minds of strong talents did.

She could not dither here in Yolanda's dressing room much longer. All her instincts warned her that she was being hunted. The terror of being trapped in the small chamber threatened to swamp her. She had to make her move.

She crouched low, gripped the knob, and waited until the music reached another thunderous crescendo. When the wall shuddered, she held her breath and cautiously opened the dressing room door.

Dense darkness spilled into the dressing room, mingling with the shadows that already swirled around her. The corridor lights were still off. Whoever was out there wanted the cover of night.

The urge to jump to her feet and run was a compelling one, but Amaryllis resisted it for another few seconds. She had to move slowly and she had to stay low. The killer would be as blinded as she was by the darkness, but if he sensed that she was running away down the narrow passageway, he might well try a blind shot with the gun that he had used to murder Vivien. He would most likely aim at chest height.

Trusting to the noise of the music to cover any sound she might make, Amaryllis moved out into the corridor on her hands and knees. The killer was no doubt blocking escape via the alley stage door. That left only one choice.

Amaryllis turned left and started to crawl along the dark passageway. She had no idea of where she was headed, but she knew that sooner or later the corridor had to end.

Another whisper of psychic energy slithered across her nerve endings. The killer was on the move behind her. Fear snaked through Amaryllis. She told herself she must not let it turn into panic. She had to get to safety.

The floor of the hallway pulsated with the beat of the music. The grit on the shabby carpet ground into her palms. Her knees began to burn.

Another snakelike tongue of talent flickered. Amaryllis sensed that the power was weaker this time. Different somehow. A sputtering candle compared to what she had felt earlier. She reminded herself that the ability of a talent and a prism to seek each other out for a link diminished rapidly with distance.

Amaryllis crawled faster. She willed every trace of her own power to the farthest depths of her mind.

Dillon smiled ruefully at Lucas from the other side of the restaurant table. "I told Dad the whole story."

"I know." Lucas cut into the slab of copper-colored fish on his plate. "Your father came to see me."

"I was afraid of that." Dillon's smile faded. "What did he say?"

"Tried to pay off your debt. I told him that the arrangement was between you and me and that he wasn't involved."

Dillon straightened in his chair. "Same thing I told him. He was pissed."

"You want my opinion?"

"What's that?"

Lucas forked up a bite of the fish. "I think he was also impressed. Don't get me wrong, he was still furious about the debt. But he seemed to accept the fact that you had gotten yourself into the mess and intended to get yourself out."

A gleam of hope appeared in Dillon's eyes. "You think maybe he's coming around?"

"I don't know."

Dillon's jaw tightened. "Lucas, I want to ask you something."

"I was afraid of that." Lucas put down his fork. "Before you get too carried away, you should know that I'm not known for the depths of my intuition and understanding of other people. If you want to ask me about the best way to deal with your parents, be advised that I have zero experience in that kind of thing."

"My parents are my problem. I want to ask you for a job."

Lucas eyed him for a long, considering moment. "You're sure?"

"I'm sure. I've got to pay off my debt, and going to work for Lodestar is the best way to do it. I really want to do this, Lucas."

"What about your parents?"

"This is something I have to do. I'll tell them my plans and hope for the best. If I wait for their approval, I'll wait forever. Dad might eventually understand, but I don't think Mom ever will. She'll always blame Lodestar Exploration for Jackson's death."

Lucas hesitated. "Your mother will probably hate my guts if I give you a job."

"So what else is new?" Dillon asked softly. "Let's face it, she's hated you since the day she got word that Jackson was dead."

The bluntness of the words hit Lucas with the impact of a cold wave. "She hates Lodestar."

"You *are* Lodestar Exploration. You always were. It was your company before Jackson met you, and it was your company after he died. She will never be able to separate the two."

"Yeah, I know." Why should he care, Lucas wondered. He had never really been a member of the Rye family. Just an acquaintance and business partner. Beatrice Rye's superficial kindnesses to him in the past had been acts of expediency, nothing more.

"I'm sorry, Lucas."

"Forget it."

"Try not to take it too personally. You know how mothers are."

Lucas let that slide. "All right, if you want a job and you're prepared to take the heat from your folks, you've got it. Check in with Lodestar employment tomorrow."

"Thanks." Dillon grinned. "Hot synergy, this is great. I can't wait to get out to the islands."

"Just one small helpful hint before you go."

"What's that?"

Lucas surveyed Dillon's stylish Western Islands attire. "Don't take those clothes with you. Nobody dresses like that in the islands. You'll get laughed out of Port LeConner. Wait until you get there and buy local."

Dillon laughed. It was the exuberant laugh of a young man looking forward to an exciting future. It made Lucas feel good for some reason.

An hour later Lucas paused by a public phone on the way out of the restaurant. He dialed Amaryllis's number, hoping that she would still be awake. He wanted to talk to her. More and more he found himself wanting to share things with her. Tonight he wanted to tell her about Dillon.

Instead, he got a message on her answering machine: "This is Amaryllis Lark. I am not able to come to the phone right now. If this is Lucas, I'm in Founders Square. Vivien called and told me she wanted to talk. Don't worry, I took a cab. I'll call and tell you all about it when I get home."

"Damn." Lucas slammed down the phone.

Dillon glanced at him. "What's wrong?"

"I have to go to Founders Square." Lucas headed for the front door. "Don't forget. Report to employment tomorrow."

"Don't worry," Dillon called after him. "I won't forget."

Without warning, a fresh surge of fierce, questing talent swept out of the darkness behind Amaryllis.

This was a new talent, not the one that had been hunting her.

Strong power searched for a prism and *demanded* a mind link. The shock of stunning intimacy that accompanied the whip of psychic energy identified the source immediately.

Lucas. He was somewhere in the building.

Amaryllis crouched between what seemed to be two large wooden crates and almost sobbed with relief. The brief flare of hot talent winked out of existence before she could unlock her own damped-down power.

Frustrated by having missed the opportunity to link with Lucas, she fought the compulsion to rise to her feet and scream his name aloud. Even as the dangerous thought occurred to her, she experienced another brush from a slimy tongue of talent.

The killer was still here with her in the darkness.

Amaryllis forced herself to think. She had to let Lucas know that she was nearby. She readied herself so that she would be able to link with him the next time he sought her out.

It occurred to her that there might be some risk involved in using her prism capabilities to identify herself to Lucas.

She had no fear that the murderer would seize the link during those first few seconds of disoriented vulnerability. In spite of her affection for psychic vampire romances, she was too well schooled in the focus sciences to believe that a rogue talent could actually take control of her.

The real hazard in linking with Lucas right now was that the killer might be able to get an approximate fix on her location during those few seconds when her mind was open.

But she had to do something, Amaryllis thought. If Lucas did not find her with his psychic search, he might conclude that she had left the building. He would never know about the danger that was closing in on her.

Lucas's dark whisper of power unfurled through the shadows once more. Amaryllis mentally leaped for it, caught it as if it were a swinging trapeze, and formed the link. Talent surged through a prism in a display of chaotic light. Amaryllis wondered if this was the psychic color of relief or anger or frustration. There was no way to tell. But at least Lucas now knew she was nearby.

It was unfortunate that there was no such thing as telepathy, she thought. It would have been very useful to be able to have a quick chat with Lucas at that particular moment.

She was trying to think of a way to use the psychic connection to warn him of danger when the scent of a man's cologne wafted toward her through the shadows. It shattered her concentration so completely that she dropped the link.

The booming music masked sound but not smell. The masculine fragrance drifted past her nose again. It was vaguely familiar. Definitely not Lucas. He did not use any cologne.

The killer was close. Much too close. She wondered if he could smell the fear she knew she must be exuding like some dreadful perfume of her own.

She put out a hand, groping cautiously for something that she could use as a weapon. There was nothing on the floor beside her. With the music as a cover for any sound she might make, she rose slowly to her feet and felt for one of the crates.

The lid on the nearest one was open. There were objects inside. Hard objects.

Amaryllis selected one at random. She had no idea what it was, only that it seemed to be made of metal and it fit her grasp.

She sensed rather than saw something move in front of her. The smell of the expensive cologne was very strong in her nostrils.

She swung wildly with the long, heavy object that she had taken from the crate. Her makeshift weapon thudded against flesh.

"Uuumph."

Amaryllis did not wait to see the results of her handiwork. She dropped the metal object and bounded forward into the shadows. Her toe caught on something, a foot, perhaps. There was a muffled curse. She leaped aside and nearly fell.

She was totally disoriented in the darkness. The roar of the music was her only guide. She went toward it, hands outstretched to ward off any collisions with crates, stage props, or killers. She came to a jarring halt when one palm touched stone.

A wall.

Using her sense of touch, she made her way along the stone barrier. The music grew louder. She turned a corner and saw a sliver of light beneath a heavy blue stage curtain. The music was thundering in her ears now.

At that moment Lucas attempted another mind link. She knew from the strength of his energy thrust that he was very, very close. Amaryllis responded as she fumbled to find an opening in the curtain.

She felt a hemmed edge and yanked it aside.

Intense white light blinded her. The music was deafening.

Amaryllis blundered out onto the stage, blinking furiously against the brilliant light. The drummer saw her first. He shouted something at her, but she could not hear a word he said.

Two couples, one garbed in matching black leather and hoods, the other nattily attired in a few strategically placed silver sequins, simulated some very energetic sexual gymnastics at the front of the stage. Moans of excitement emanated from the audience.

Two handsome young men in red tights and flowing blond hair stood in one corner of the stage. Their faces were contorted with grimaces as they did an excellent impression of focusing the sexual energy that was being expended on stage.

It was obvious from the feverish sounds produced by the audience and the rising throb of the music that a climax, both literal and figurative, was close at hand.

Amaryllis ran to the front of the stage. The performers ignored her as she came to a halt in their midst. She frantically waved her arms to get their attention.

"Stop. Stop. There's been a murder. A killer is loose in the building." She realized that no one could hear her above the relentless music. *"Stop."*

The audience, apparently concluding that she was part of the act, went into a frenzy. The performers rose to the occasion in several senses of the word. Sequins and portions of black leather underwear fell to the stage at Amaryllis's feet. The musicians redoubled their efforts.

Out of the corner of her eye, Amaryllis saw a figure stagger through the dark blue curtain and emerge onto the stage. He stood there, dazed and blinking in the unrelenting glare. He clutched his shoulder with one hand. His hair was standing on end, and his elegant suit was rumpled, but there was no mistaking his identity.

Madison Sheffield.

He spotted Amaryllis at the same instant that she recognized him. Rage replaced the confusion in his eyes. He took one step toward her and then apparently realized that he was standing in front of an audience. He swung around and tried to flee back through the stage curtain.

Lucas came through the heavy velvet drapes in a long, low rush. He plowed straight into Sheffield. The two men crashed to the floor and rolled toward the front of the stage.

The musicians went wild. The overworked sound system shrieked in protest. Amaryllis could smell the performers' sweat.

Lucas managed to straddle Sheffield. He slammed a fist into the senator's jaw.

The audience went orgasmic.

"Vivien was obviously blackmailing Sheffield with the contents of the file that Professor Landreth left with her." Amaryllis, seated on the sofa in front of Lucas's exotic fireplace, pulled up her knees and hugged them. She still shivered from time to time, even though the room was warm. "It's hard to believe."

"I'm sure Sheffield's hoping the cops will find it hard to believe, too." Lucas picked up the two glasses of moontree brandy that he had just poured and walked toward Amaryllis. "He told the police that the reason he happened to be backstage at the SynCity tonight was because he was investigating the club's activities. Fulfilling a campaign promise, as it were."

Amaryllis gave a ladylike snort. "Likely story. He can hardly deny his motive for murder now that they've found what's left of the file."

Lucas nodded as he sat down beside her. "It was in the restroom sink. That was the source of the smoke you smelled. Sheffield apparently tried to burn the file after he shot Vivien, but he must have had trouble keeping the fire going. It was a charred mess, but his name was all over what remained, together with a lot of observations about his lack of ethics. All neatly typed and annotated, I might add. Nothing illegal, but the accusations of unethical behavior could have ruined him."

"Professor Landreth was always very thorough. Well, so much for the expertise of Mr. Stonebraker. He never did find the file. I had to do it myself."

Lucas raised his brows. "That's one way of looking at it."

"I trust he'll give you a refund."

"I'll be sure to ask for it."

Amaryllis frowned. "Professor Landreth realized that Senator Sheffield was focusing in an unethical manner. He documented it in that file. But why did he give the file to Vivien?"

"Landreth was probably afraid that Sheffield would try to snatch the file before he was ready to go public with his accusations." Lucas cradled the brandy glass in both hands. He gazed thoughtfully into the fire. "He must have figured that no one would think of searching for the evidence in the dressing room of a syn-sex stripper."

"He was right. Poor Vivien. She must have realized that she was in danger tonight. That's why she phoned me. But I got there too late to save her. I wonder if she called the guard?"

"Wouldn't have done any good. The cops found the guard a block away getting drunk in a bar. Said some guy gave him a hundred bucks to get lost for a couple of hours."

"Sheffield was safe. With the music pounding away, there was no way anyone would have heard the shot."

"No." Lucas put down his brandy glass and reached out to catch Amaryllis's chin on the edge of his hand. His eyes were more intense than the jelly-ice flames on the hearth. "You should never have gone to that club tonight. Do you know what I've been through?"

"Now, Lucas, I had to do something when Vivien called. There was no time to track you down at the restaurant."

"Damn it, I went through all five hells when I got that message on your answering machine. And that was nothing compared to what I endured when I realized that you were somewhere in the darkness behind the stage. The alley door was locked. I had to find and break a window to get into the back of the club. You should have called the cops if you couldn't find me."

"In retrospect, I can see that you have a point."

"A point? I've got more than a point. I've got the whole damn argument."

"Lucas, be reasonable. I didn't know that Vivien was in imminent danger. She didn't tell me that. All she said was that things were getting a little out of hand. One would think that if she had felt she was in real jeopardy, she would have called the police herself." Amaryllis paused. "Come to think of it, why didn't she do just that?"

"Because, as you just pointed out, she was a blackmailer. At any rate, that's not what I want to discuss here."

The phone rang.

Amaryllis smiled brightly. "Better get that. It might be the police. They may have a few more questions to ask you."

"I've already answered more than enough questions tonight." But Lucas released her to grab the phone. "This is Trent. Oh, hello, Stonebraker. We were just talking about you. Amaryllis tells me I should get a refund."

Lucas fell silent as he listened to whatever Stonebraker was saying on the other end of the line. Amaryllis sipped her moontree brandy and stared into the fire. It was nearly three in the morning, but she still did not feel normal. Her pulse no longer pounded, and she was able to breathe properly, but she felt strange. Exhausted, yet unnaturally, painfully alert. She was practically tingling with an overstimulated sense of awareness. Memories of the evil, questing tongue of talent flickered at the edge of her mind.

"Interesting," Lucas murmured. "Possible. Yeah, don't worry, Amaryllis gave the cops a stern lecture about the necessity of reopening an investigation into the circumstances of Landreth's death. I think they'll do it." He paused again. "Right. Talk to you later."

Amaryllis looked at him as he hung up the phone. "Well? What did your brilliant private investigator have to say?"

Lucas's mouth curved faintly. "He said he'll consider the refund when he gets around to billing me."

"I should think so. What else did he have to say?"

Lucas stopped smiling. "He said he just learned that the New Portland city police picked up Merrick Beech late this afternoon. Miranda Locking was with him. They were boarding a plane to the Western Islands."

"Beech and Locking? Did they have anything to do with tonight's events?"

"Doesn't look like it. But they apparently admitted that they paid those thugs who attacked us that first night in Founders Square." Lucas stretched his legs out in front of him. His face was grim. "Said something about wanting to teach me a lesson."

Amaryllis shivered. "That's the last of the answers then. For both of us."

"Yeah."

Amaryllis turned her attention back to the fire. "It feels weird somehow."

"What does?"

"Knowing that it's over."

Over. The single word hung in the air between them. It was over. Everything was over.

Amaryllis realized then that her self-imposed mission to discover the truth about Professor Landreth's death had been inextricably bound up with her relationship with Lucas. The two were not really connected, she told herself. Yet in a way, they were.

Her mission had ended. The end of the affair was inevitable, too. In fact, it was already in sight. She thought about all the forms she and Lucas had filled out for Synergistic Connections. She recalled the interview. It would not be long now.

"Yeah." Lucas rested his head against the back of the sofa and watched the fire through slitted eyes. "It feels weird."

Amaryllis didn't need telepathy to tell her that he was thinking the same thing that she was thinking. A great sense of loss welled up inside her.

From out of nowhere Amaryllis felt the tendril of psychic energy seeking a link. Lucas was reaching for her with his mind. This was not the fierce, white-hot demand he had sent out earlier when he had been searching for her in the darkness backstage at SynCity. This was a tender, gentle brush of talent questing for synergistic wholeness.

"Lucas." Amaryllis wrapped her arms more tightly around her knees. She tried to blink away the dampness she could feel in her eyes. "It would probably be better if we didn't do this anymore."

"Probably."

"According to every syn-psych theory in the book, we're all wrong for each other."

"Yeah."

"It would be stupid to take this relationship any further," Amaryllis insisted. "Neither of us wants to risk repeating the mistakes of the past."

"You think we're both afraid of the past?"

The perception in his words startled her. She stared into the flames. "I've been telling myself that doing the proper thing was a matter of responsibility and duty. But maybe you're right. Maybe in the end it just comes down to a fear of the past. We both have reasons to be afraid."

"Are you going to spend your whole life being afraid?"

Amaryllis was stunned. An entire life spent living with a fear of the past stretched out before her. Every action guided by fear. A marriage based on avoiding fear. It was a dreadful vision.

"I don't know," she said. "Are you?"

"I hate to think of myself as a complete and total coward."

She frowned. "You're no coward."

"Neither are you."

"Where does that leave us?" she asked.

"Marry me."

Amaryllis whirled around on the sofa to stare at Lucas. Shock

waves went through her. At first she thought she had not heard him,
that she had conjured the words in her own mind.

He hadn't moved. His head still rested against the back of the sofa.
His eyes were still narrowed as he gazed into the flames. The Iceman.

"It's okay," he said without any trace of emotion. "I know the answer. Just thought I'd give it a try."

"Oh, God, Lucas, I thought you'd never ask." Amaryllis threw herself into his arms. "What took you so long?"

He caught hold of her mentally and physically. Brilliant beams of
psychic energy poured through a crystal-clear prism. Power crashed in
glorious waves.

When Amaryllis opened her eyes, she discovered that she and
Lucas were safe inside his secret island grotto.

Chapter 17

He made love to her there in the hidden grotto, just as he had dreamed of doing. He undressed her slowly beside the fathomless green pool, peeling away blouse and slacks and layers of neat, serious underwear. Her skin glowed pale gold in the firelight that passed easily through the illusory stone walls of the cave. He cupped one graceful, elegant breast in his hand, marveling at the perfect shape and texture of it.

Amaryllis fumbled with the buttons of his shirt and the fastenings of his trousers until he grew impatient with the slow torture.

"Wait." He sat up beside her and yanked off his clothes with a few brusque movements. Then he stretched out slowly above her.

She reached up to splay her fingers across his bare chest. "I love the feel of you."

Lucas longed to ask if she loved him as well as the feel of him, but he told himself he would not push his luck. She had agreed to marry him. It was enough for now. Everyone said that when the match was right, love came after marriage.

When the match was right.

This has to be right, Lucas thought. If it wasn't, he was doomed.

"I'm a beat-up iceman." He watched her eyes as he caught one of her hands and pressed it to the spider-frog scar on his shoulder. "I spent too many years in the islands to ever be anything else."

"No, you're gorgeous. Spectacular. Unbelievably sexy."

"I'm covered with scars and calluses. My manners are rough and so is my accent."

She dismissed that with a wave of her hand. "Who cares? You've got gray eyes. I was very particular about wanting gray eyes on the Synergistic questionnaire, you know."

For some reason he had to keep going. He had to make certain she knew everything. "I cheated on my talent certification test. I don't have your high standards when it comes to that kind of thing."

"You have your own code and you stick to it. That's all that matters."

"If I could have figured out how to fool the syn-shrinks at Synergistic Connections into thinking that I would be a perfect match for a full-spectrum prism such as yourself, I would have done it in a heartbeat."

Amaryllis's smile was brilliant. "It occurs to me that the counselors at the agency aren't qualified to find a match for either of us because they've had no experience matching off-the-scale talents and prisms."

"We're opposites in a lot of ways, Amaryllis."

"I'm not so sure about that. I feel closer to you than I've ever felt to anyone else in my whole life."

A great sense of exhilaration drove out the last of his fears. "That pretty much sums up how I feel about you. It's as if I've been waiting for you forever."

"And I've been waiting for you." She wound her arms around his neck. Her eyes gleamed. "Do you think I could interest you in using your psychic vampire talent to turn me into a love slave?"

"Actually, I was sort of hoping that you would use your amazing prism powers to turn *me* into a helpless victim of your relentless desire."

"Hmm." She drew a fingertip down to his bare stomach and then moved her hand lower. She cradled his heavy shaft in her palm. "The notion is fraught with possibilities."

"Yeah." Lucas sucked in his breath. The grotto walls shimmered and dimmed for a few seconds as he diverted psychic energy into old-fashioned self-control. "It is, isn't it?"

"Oh, Lucas, I want you so much." The teasing light in her eyes was replaced with unabashed need. She brought his mouth down to hers and arched herself against him.

The passion sparked between them, hotter than raw, unfocused psychic energy.

He reveled in the feel of her body. He worked his way downward, tasting the small valley between her breasts, the gentle curve of her belly, the inside of her thigh. When he touched the hot, moist flesh between her legs, she shuddered in his hands.

"Lucas."

On the psychic plane, the crystal prism winked out of existence. The grotto walls disappeared. Lucas felt a surge of triumph. This time Amaryllis was the one who had lost control of the link.

"You're so beautiful," he whispered.

"You make me feel beautiful." She shivered again and sank her nails into his shoulders.

Together they found the focus link again. Lucas did not bother to rebuild the grotto. He simply let the power flow in a shimmering river. The sense of deep intimacy enveloped him. He was a part of Amaryllis and she was part of him.

He moved back up along the length of her trembling body. He used one hand to guide himself to the entrance of her snug passage. Slowly he eased himself inside. She closed around him.

When Amaryllis cried out and convulsed in Lucas's arms, he thought that he would lose the mind link again, but to his surprise, it held steady and clear. Unfocused talent flashed through the prism and ricocheted around the psychic plane.

Power and passion flowed together.

A long while later, Amaryllis felt Lucas disengage himself carefully from her arms. He slid his leg from between her thighs. She opened her eyes as he sat up on the edge of the sofa.

"Lucas? Where are you going?"

"To check the fire. Don't worry, I'll be right back."

"I'll be waiting." She turned onto her side, stretched, and propped her head on the arm of the sofa. She watched Lucas as he crossed the room to the hearth.

He was magnificent. Big and sleek and utterly masculine. The firelight gleamed on his strongly muscled flanks and broad shoulders. Just the sight of him sent little frissons of excitement through her thoroughly sated body.

She felt a brush of energy on the psychic plane and silently responded. Lucas held the intimate link with her for a few minutes while he crouched to adjust the supply of jelly-ice.

He finished his small task, rose to his feet, and braced one hand on the mantel. Instead of returning to the sofa, he stood gazing down into the flames.

"You're brooding," Amaryllis said.

In the flaring firelight, the fierce planes and angles of his face appeared harder edged and more grim than usual. "It won't be easy, you know."

As if she could read his mind, she understood. "I know. If you come with me to Lower Bellevue to celebrate my aunt's birthday the day after tomorrow, we can tell my family together."

He turned slowly to face her. With his back to the fire, it was impossible to see his expression. "What will you do if your aunt and uncle refuse to give you their blessing?"

"Marry you anyway. They'll come around in time. They love me. All they want is for me to be happy."

"Will you be happy with me?"

"I don't see how I could be happy with anyone else," she said simply.

"We'll argue."

"Everyone argues at times, even people who are matched through an agency."

"You'll probably pull that virtuous little founder act on me from time to time, and I'll tell you that you're prissy and straitlaced and too damn picky."

She smiled. "And then you'll remember that I picked you."

Lucas came toward her. "Yeah." His voice roughened. "Then I'll remember that you picked me."

He lowered himself onto the sofa and pulled her into his arms. His eyes reflected the flames on the hearth as he bent his head to take her mouth.

"Incredible." Clementine whistled softly as she refolded the newspaper. "Who would have believed it. Senator Madison Sheffield, Mr. Founders' Values man himself. Blackmail victim and murderer. We came too damn close to losing you, Amaryllis. This is one scary story."

"You're telling me." Amaryllis poured herself a cup of coff-tea from the office pot. "I tried to tell everyone that Sheffield was unethical and very likely dishonest, but no one would listen to me."

"I know, I know." Clementine held up her hand. "Amaryllis, hasn't anyone ever told you that no one likes a person who keeps saying I told you so?"

"The boss is right," Byron said. "That sort of person is very irritating."

"Hah. Better get used to it." Amaryllis smiled blandly. "I intend to say it a lot around here. And I'll tell you something else, when the police reopen their investigation of Professor Landreth's death, they're going to discover that he was murdered, too."

Clementine's brows rose. "By Sheffield?"

"Who else?" Amaryllis said. "He must have learned about the file that Professor Landreth had made on him. He couldn't risk the possibility that Landreth would go public with his accusations."

"I wonder if they'll be able to prove it," Clementine mused.

"Even if they can't tie Sheffield to Landreth's death, they should be able to nail him for killing that stripper," Byron said.

"Don't count on it," Clementine said dryly. "He's a city-state senator, after all, and he's denying everything. When was the last time a high-ranking politician did any serious prison time?"

"One way or another, I'm sure justice will be done," Amaryllis said. "That reminds me, I must phone Irene Dunley. She'll be anxious to hear the details of what happened last night. She's the only one who supported me when I started looking into the matter of Professor Landreth's death."

"Let me see that paper." Byron leaned over his desk to snatch the newspaper out of Clementine's hands. He studied the headlines with something that might have been pride. "Wow. Like totally synergistic. Interesting shot of you, Amaryllis."

"Really?" Amaryllis went around the reception desk to look at the news photo. For an instant she didn't recognize the scene, let alone herself. Then her face went red. "Oh, my God. I hope my family doesn't see this."

The picture had obviously been taken by someone in the SynCity Club audience. A patron had smuggled in a camera in spite of the rules, Amaryllis thought grimly. The photo showed her, center stage, hands raised in her frantic attempt to get someone's attention.

Clementine leaned over the desk. "Sort of looks like you're conducting the activities on stage, Amaryllis."

"This is so embarrassing," Amaryllis muttered. "I wonder if the *Lower Bellevue Journal* will run the same shot."

In the photo she appeared to be orchestrating the erotic actions of the outrageously attired syn-sex performers on either side of her. Discreet portions of the dancers' anatomies had been covered with small, black squares. The *New Seattle Times* was a family newspaper, after all.

In the background of the picture, one could just make out Lucas and Sheffield on the floor. They looked as if they were locked in each other's arms.

"Great advertising for Psynergy, Inc.," Byron declared. "The phone's going to be ringing all day. Every talent in town will want to hire Amaryllis."

"They can't have me," Amaryllis said. "At least not for a couple of days. Clementine said I'm not to accept any assignments today, remember? And I'll be out of town tomorrow and most of the following day."

"Oh, yeah." Byron frowned as he scanned the story of Amaryllis's adventures. "You're going to your great-aunt's birthday party, aren't you? Bet your family will be excited when they hear what you've been up to in the big city."

"Not as excited as they're going to be when I tell them that I'm getting married," Amaryllis murmured.

Byron's head snapped up abruptly. "You've been matched already?"

Clementine looked thoughtful. "Not likely. There hasn't been enough time for the agency to find a good selection of candidates for you. What are you up to, Amaryllis?"

Amaryllis braced herself. This was only the beginning, she thought. It would get worse before it got better. No one approved of runaway marriages. "I'm going to marry Lucas."

"Trent?" Clementine's jaw dropped. "Are you crazy? He's a class nine."

Byron's eyes widened. "Holy synergy. What will your family say?"

"I'll find out tomorrow," Amaryllis said.

Clementine propped one hip on Byron's desk and crossed her arms. She regarded Amaryllis with troubled eyes. "Are you sure you know what you're doing?"

"Yes."

Clementine cleared her throat. "Passion is a tricky thing. I hope you're not making the mistake of thinking that it's always linked to love. Marriage is forever, you know. You don't want to take any risks—"

The office door opened before Clementine could finish her lecture. Grateful for the interruption, Amaryllis turned to see who had entered. She stifled a small sigh when she saw Gifford.

"Good morning." Gifford was dressed in his customary silver gray suit, but his red bow tie appeared a little wilted. He nodded stiffly to Clementine, ignored Byron, and turned immediately to Amaryllis. "I've got to talk to you."

Amaryllis took a sip of coff-tea. "The last time you said that, you stuck me in the back of a limousine with a murderer."

"What's this?" Clementine gave Gifford a sharp look.

"Never mind," Amaryllis said. "It's a long story. Come into my office, Gifford."

Clementine glowered ferociously at Gifford. "Touch her and you're a dead man."

Gifford tugged slightly at his drooping bow tie. "I just want to talk to her, Clementine. It's personal. Not business. Don't worry, I won't steal her away from you."

"He knows I would never go to work for Unique Prisms," Amaryllis said.

Clementine favored Gifford with a steely smile. "Damn right, she wouldn't. Amaryllis has standards, unlike some people we could mention. She prefers to be employed by a reputable agency."

Gifford flushed and hurried past the reception desk. He followed Amaryllis into her office and closed the door with a groan of relief.

"Synergistic hell, Amaryllis, how can you stand working for an eccentric character like Clementine Malone? I can see you at Proud Focus, maybe, or even True Focus, but not this place. Malone has all the social graces of an alley cat-dog. And her taste in clothes is abominable. Worse than yours."

"I'm quite content here, Gifford. As Clementine said, I prefer a reputable agency."

"Reputable. Give me a break." Gifford rolled his eyes as he sat down in the nearest chair. "Clementine Malone can be difficult, but she is a businesswoman, I'll say that much for her. If Madison Sheffield had walked into this office looking for a prism, I have a strong hunch Malone would have found one for him."

"I disagree," Amaryllis said firmly. "Clementine runs an ethical business." She went behind her desk, sat down, and folded her hands on the neat, polished surface in front of her. "Now, what was it you wanted, Gifford?"

"The cops were waiting for me when I got to my office this morning."

"I'm not surprised. They probably wanted to ask you a few questions about your association with Sheffield."

"That's putting it mildly. They grilled me." Gifford's mouth tightened. "I had to do a lot of explaining. I hope you realize that this mess could really hurt me. I've got my reputation to consider. Unique Prisms has found a very special market niche. We guarantee discretion. This kind of publicity is not good for business."

Amaryllis felt a pang of guilt. "I'm sorry you got dragged into it."

"So am I," Gifford said with great depth of feeling. "Why the hell did you have to get involved in an investigation of Landreth's death?"

"I did what I felt I had to do. Questions arose and had to be answered."

"Only you would give a damn about the answers. Landreth was an obnoxious old busybody. Nobody liked him."

"I liked him. And so did his secretary, Irene Dunley."

"Well, let me tell you, the two of you are probably the only people on St. Helens who cared about the old bastard."

"Gifford, the man died under mysterious circumstances. Last night a woman was murdered. You can't just ignore these things because the publicity might be bad for business."

"We pay the police to look into this kind of stuff, not nosy little prisms who think they have to personally see to matters of truth, justice, and the St. Helens way."

Amaryllis sighed. "If you came here to argue synergistic ethics with me, I'm afraid you've wasted your time."

"That's not why I came here." Gifford got to his feet and began to move restlessly around the small office. "I want to ask a favor."

"What sort of favor?"

"I told the cops the basic truth about my connection with Sheffield. I said I provided him with prisms. I told them that Sheffield had not provided a certification of talent, but that I only hired full-spectrum prisms, so I assumed there would be no risk to any of my employees. How was I to know that he would start burning them out?"

"Indeed."

"Hell, that's not the point. The police aren't particularly interested in whether or not Sheffield was properly matched with the prisms he hired. It's not a crime to burn out a prism."

"True. But it's not very pleasant for the prism."

"But no permanent damage is done," Gifford insisted. "And no one is sure just what Sheffield was focusing, anyway. Even the prisms he worked with have a hard time describing his talent. Personality traits aren't psychic powers."

"I don't know about that," Amaryllis mused. "Do you recall how Professor Landreth once theorized that strong personality traits might be manifestations of psychic energy?"

"Please." Gifford held up a palm. "Don't mention Landreth's name to me. The point is, I'm an innocent victim in this situation."

"Innocent?"

"Not only innocent but a damn good citizen. I was trying to help the Founders' Values candidate. The man who would have been the people's choice for governor. Sheffield was a city-state senator who had refused testing on principle. Why should I doubt his word when he told me that he estimated his own strength at around a class nine?"

"Gifford, I don't think there's much point in this conversation. Perhaps you had better leave. I've got work to do and I'm sure you do, too."

"No, wait, I'm not finished." Gifford jerked at the knot of the red bow tie. "Look, Amaryllis, I'll level with you. I told the cops the truth this morning, I swear it. I provided Sheffield with qualified prisms. That was my only connection to him. I'm asking you as my friend and former professional colleague not to drag me any deeper into this thing."

For some reason, perhaps because she truly did bear some responsibility for involving him in the situation, Amaryllis felt another twinge of guilt. "I have no intention of doing that."

Gifford spun around, hope in his eyes. "What about Landreth's calendar? You said that the last entry indicated he had made an appointment with me. Remember? That was how you got me into this mess in the first place."

"Oh, yes, the calendar entry." Amaryllis frowned. "Well, I think that's neither here nor there now."

"The police said it looks like Sheffield murdered the stripper because she tried to blackmail him using the information in Landreth's file," Gifford said impatiently. "But they're also going to look into the report on Landreth's accident. I'd just as soon not have the cops find out that my name was the last entry in the old coot's calendar."

"Why are you so worried?"

"I'm just asking you not to bring up the subject, okay? I'd like to keep my name out of the investigation as much as possible. Damn it, is that too much to ask?"

"Stop whining, Gifford. If it makes you feel any better, I have no intention of mentioning Professor Landreth's calendar to the police." There was no reason to do so. Gifford was not the murderer.

"Thanks." Gifford's relief transformed his features. Even his red bow tie appeared a little perkier. He crossed the office in three strides, came around behind the desk, and hoisted Amaryllis to her feet. "I'll owe you for this. If you ever need a job, come see me. Got that?"

"I don't expect that will be necessary."

"And I'm sorry about the way you found me with that little blond talent that day in the lab. She meant nothing. Absolutely nothing."

"Yes, well, that's in the past now, Gifford. I don't—"

"You were too good for me, darling. Don't you understand? That's why our relationship fell apart. I felt I couldn't live up to your high standards. The pressure was just too much."

Amaryllis reflected briefly on all that had happened during the past couple of weeks. She had broken into the offices of her former employer, gone to a syn-sex nightclub, visited a stripper, begun an affair with an unsuitable talent, nearly gotten herself killed, and now she was preparing for a runaway marriage. Life had certainly changed recently.

"Actually, my standards aren't quite what they used to be," Amaryllis said.

Lucas spoke from the doorway. "They're still way too high for you, Osterley, so don't get any ideas."

Gifford released Amaryllis as if she had suddenly turned red hot under his hands. "Trent. What are you doing here?"

"I came to see my fiancée."

"Fiancée?" Gifford looked thunderstruck.

"Yeah. I know you can't wait to congratulate us."

"But you're a talent. A big one. She's a full-spectrum prism. There's no way any marriage agency would match the two of you."

"Who said anything about going through an agency?" Lucas asked.

Gifford's mouth opened and closed several times. He stared at Amaryllis. "I don't believe it. A nonagency marriage? You?"

Amaryllis smiled very sweetly. "Sort of makes synergistic hash out of everything you've ever taken for granted about me, doesn't it, Gifford? I'm afraid I'm not the woman I used to be."

"Comes from hanging out with bad company," Lucas explained. "I, on the other hand, have become extremely narrow-minded in recent days. One might even call me a straitlaced prude. For example, I don't like finding my fiancée in another man's arms."

"I was just having a little chat."

"Get out of here, Osterley, before I get really annoyed."

Gifford did not hesitate. He walked quickly toward the door. "Amaryllis and I were simply discussing some private business," he muttered as he went past Lucas. "Nothing of an intimate nature occurred, I assure you."

Lucas did not bother to respond. He folded his arms across his chest and regarded Amaryllis with grave interest. "I wonder if you'd care to demonstrate a few of your newly lowered standards."

"What did you have in mind?"

Lucas straightened, closed the door, and locked it. "We once discussed the propriety of making love on a desk."

Amaryllis's mouth went dry. "Did we?"

"Yeah. My memory is real clear on the subject." Lucas walked toward her.

"Clementine will wonder what's happening in here."

"Your boss and I had a short conversation a few minutes ago. She said you had the day off in order to recover from your traumatic experiences last night."

"Yes, I do." Amaryllis watched, fascinated, as Lucas's hands went to the buckle of his belt. "What about your newfound streak of prudery?"

"It only applies to some things." Lucas came around the desk and gently pinned Amaryllis against it. He reached down and eased her legs apart.

"That's odd." Amaryllis put her arms around his neck. "My standards have only been lowered in some areas."

"There you are." Lucas's smile held the devil's own satisfaction. "Our relationship has made interesting changes in both of us. A perfect example of synergy in action."

Amaryllis pulled his mouth down to hers before he could get carried away with a boring lecture on synergistic principles.

————————

Much later, after Lucas had gone back to his own office, Amaryllis tidied her desk and picked up several items that had fallen to the floor. Then she reached for the phone and dialed the Department of Focus Studies. Irene Dunley answered on the second ring.

"Miss Lark." Irene sounded anxious. "Are you all right? I saw the morning papers. I could hardly believe what I read. Imagine, Senator Sheffield a murderer."

"I know. What's more, it's likely that he killed Professor Landreth, too. The police are going to reopen the investigation."

"Is that a fact? Perhaps justice will be done at last."

"I think so, although, as my boss pointed out, Sheffield is a city-state senator and he's denying everything. He may walk."

"At the very least, his career in politics will be ruined," Irene said. "He probably won't be able to recover from this scandal."

"I shouldn't think so, but I wouldn't count on it."

"This is not a happy day. I wish the criminal had been anyone other than Senator Sheffield. This city-state needed his vision and leadership."

"I expect we'll all get along just fine without him," Amaryllis assured her. "Irene, I have to go away for a couple of days. Family stuff. But I'll be back the day after tomorrow. Probably quite late. Would you like to get together for coff-tea the day after that? I think we should talk. After all, you and I sort of solved this case together."

"I would enjoy seeing you again, Miss Lark."

"Great. Irene, I want to thank you for supporting me during this whole thing. You were the only one who believed in me and who tried to be helpful."

"Professor Landreth was very special," Irene said softly. "In spite of that unfortunate relationship with the syn-sex stripper. There will never be anyone else quite like him here at the Department of Focus Studies."

"He was one of a kind," Amaryllis agreed. "It's people such as Professor Landreth who truly embody the best virtues of the founders."

"Well said, Miss Lark. Well said. Good-bye. I'll look forward to having coff-tea with you when you return."

"Good-bye, Irene."

After she hung up the phone, Amaryllis sat gazing at the instrument for a long time. Not every question had been answered with Sheffield's arrest, she thought. One small one remained. She wondered if she would ever learn the answer to it.

Chapter 18

"What do you mean, how did Madison Sheffield discover that Landreth had put together a file that could embarrass him and hurt his election chances?" Lucas took his eyes off the highway long enough to give Amaryllis a wry glance. "If you're looking for the person who leaked the information to him, you've got a long list of candidates. I'd say that there are as many possibilities as there are people in the Department of Focus Studies."

Although she had been thinking the same thing, it jolted Amaryllis to hear her fears put into words. "I don't want to believe that someone in the department, someone Professor Landreth trusted, did such a thing."

Lucas lifted one shoulder in a negligent shrug. "Hell, it could have been a janitor or a guard or one of the lab techs who stumbled onto some of Landreth's notes. Who knows?"

"It must have been someone who felt strongly about supporting Sheffield's candidacy. Whoever did it must have thought that he or she was doing the right thing by warning Sheffield about the existence of the file."

"Amaryllis, I know that this will come as a great shock to you, but not everyone is motivated by a driving need to do the right thing. Lots of people are motivated by other stuff."

"Such as?"

"Money."

She stared at him. "You think someone sold that information to Sheffield?"

"Why not? Someone tried to blackmail him with it later. The world is full of people who do things for cold, hard cash. Come on, you're not that innocent."

"Someone leaked the information about the file to Sheffield. Sheffield opted for a direct method of dealing with the threat. He murdered poor Professor Landreth, not realizing until too late that the professor had taken the precaution of giving the file to Vivien of the Veils."

"Yeah," Lucas said softly. "Simple. Most things are at the core."

Just like her feelings about Lower Bellevue, Amaryllis thought. She hated the place. Pure and simple.

She lapsed into silence and gazed at the cultivated farmland slipping past the car window. By any measure, it was a beautiful sight. The carpets of verdant green fields stretched into the distance, prosperous, rich, and full of new promise. The founders would have been proud. The knowledge did nothing to lessen Amaryllis's dislike of Lower Bellevue and the surrounding environs.

"You okay?" Lucas asked after a while.

Amaryllis crossed her arms beneath her breasts. "Yes."

Lucas slanted her another sidelong glance. "You sure?"

"Yes."

"What's wrong?"

"Nothing."

Lucas's hands tightened on the steering bar. "Don't lie to me. Please, don't do that."

"Lucas, for heaven's sake." Stunned by the harshness of his voice, Amaryllis turned abruptly in her seat. "I never meant—"

"Look, we've established that I'm not real good at second-guessing other people. Just give me the truth, that's all I ask. If you've changed your mind about marrying me, tell me now. Get it over with."

"But I wasn't even thinking about our marriage," she said gently. "I was thinking about how much I detest Lower Bellevue."

He looked disconcerted by her response. "The town?"

"I love my family, but I hate the place where I grew up. Do you think that's so strange, under the circumstances?"

"No." Lucas's hand relaxed slightly. "No, I guess not. Your uncle said you had it rough here when you were a kid."

"My family tried, but they couldn't always protect me from the other kids. Or from the Baileys. Funny how you can't shake old memories of your childhood. You'd think that once you're an adult, you could just close the door on the past. But it doesn't work like that, does it?"

"No. It doesn't. Sometimes you just have to learn to be stronger than your own past." Lucas took one hand off the bar and reached across the seat to wrap Amaryllis's fingers in his.

She was amazed at the depth of the comfort she took from the simple gesture. After a moment she raised his hand to her mouth and brushed her lips across his bold knuckles.

"I've been thinking," Lucas said after a moment.

"About what?"

"About the fact that your uncle will be the tough one. If I can convince Oscar that it's all right for you to marry me, I have a hunch that the rest of the family will go along with his judgment. Am I right?"

She glanced at him in surprise. "Well, yes, I suppose so. But I think you're worrying about this far too much, Lucas. My family will come around once they get used to the idea of a nonagency marriage. And Uncle Oscar is really just a big softy at heart."

Lucas gave her his humorless smile. "Your uncle is going to try to rip my head off my shoulders."

"Don't be ridiculous."

"Amaryllis, I may not be the most intuitive man who ever lived, but I think I've got a pretty good fix on your uncle. He's going to try to rip my head off my shoulders."

Oscar tried to rip Lucas's head off his shoulders.

Lucas gave him credit for waiting until they were closeted together in Oscar's study.

"What the hell do you think you're doing, Trent?" Oscar stalked back and forth in front of his desk, hands clasped behind his back, chin outthrust. "We're still recovering from the news that Amaryllis was nearly murdered a couple of nights ago by a city-state senator, no less, and now you land on my doorstep and tell me you're planning to run off with her in a nonagency marriage."

"We're not exactly going to run off." Lucas stayed seated in the chair near the window. His instincts told him that he looked less threatening in that position. "You'll all be invited to the wedding."

"There isn't going to be a wedding." Oscar's bushy brows bristled. "At least, not to you. Not if I can help it." He paused, clearly struck by a horrifying thought. "By the five hells, she'd better not be pregnant. If you got her pregnant thinking that would force the issue, I swear I'll beat you to death with my own hands right here and now."

"Amaryllis is not pregnant. Sir, I think there are some things you should take into consideration before you make any hasty decisions."

"Such as?"

Lucas met his eyes. "Amaryllis is more important to me than anything or anyone else on the planet. If she'll have me, and she's said that she will, I'm going to marry her. I will do so, regardless of her family's opinions on the matter. But both of us would prefer to have your blessing."

"My blessing?" Oscar's voice rose to a roar. "For a nonagency marriage?"

"I know you would have preferred a proper agency-matched arrangement."

"You're damned right. And it's what she's going to have. Do you hear me, Trent?"

Lucas winced. "I hear you. Hell, the whole house probably hears you."

Oscar curled one thick hand into a fist and slammed it down on the desk. "I will not stand for this, Trent. I will not allow Amaryllis to risk her happiness on a nonagency marriage, and that's final."

Lucas felt his determination to remain calm, polite, and nonthreatening start to slip away. He got to his feet. "Sir, I respect your desire to protect your niece."

"Good. Because that's exactly what I'm going to do, damn you."

"I think you should remember that Amaryllis is an adult, however. In the end, this is not your decision. It's hers."

Oscar took his massive fist off the desk and launched a solid punch at Lucas.

Lucas ducked. The blow struck the lamp beside the chair. It crashed to the floor. With a growl of rage, Oscar charged.

The wall that divided the kitchen from the study shuddered. Amaryllis, seated at the table with Hannah and her great-aunt, Sophy, jumped. "My God, what are they doing in there?"

Hannah, interrupted in the middle of an earnest lecture on the pitfalls of nonagency marriages, frowned in concern. "It sounds as if something fell."

Amaryllis shot to her feet. "They're fighting. Good heavens, Lucas was right. Uncle Oscar is trying to rip his head off his shoulders."

"Beating each other's brains out, no doubt." Sophy helped herself to a cherry-grape from the bowl in the center of the table. "Typical approach of the male of the species to any problem involving interpersonal relationships. They find it so much simpler to just pound away on each other than to actually sit down and discuss the situation."

Amaryllis whirled toward the door. "We've got to stop them."

Hannah pushed back her chair. "Perhaps we'd better call Cousin Charles."

"Sit down," Sophy ordered sharply. "Both of you."

Amaryllis and Hannah exchanged uneasy glances and then looked at the older woman. Sophy regarded them with unruffled aplomb.

"I said sit."

Amaryllis and Hannah sat.

Sophy's eyes gleamed with satisfaction. She was eighty-two years old, and she rarely exerted her authority as the unofficial matriarch of the family, but when she chose to do so, people generally responded briskly.

"Now, then," Sophy said smoothly. "Let's leave the gentlemen to their discussion. We were having our own little chat, as I recall.

Hannah, I believe you were saying something about the wisdom of waiting until the right man came along."

"Lucas is the right man for me," Amaryllis said. "I know you don't understand how I can be so certain, but I am certain." Another thud from the vicinity of the study made her flinch. "We can't just sit here and pretend nothing is happening in there."

"Don't see why not," Sophy said. "Trust me, young lady, I've been around a lot longer than you have and I've learned a few things about men." She paused. "I also know something about situations such as this one."

"What are you talking about?" Amaryllis demanded.

Hannah looked at Sophy in surprise. "Yes, what do you mean by that?"

"I refer to my own colorful past." Sophy smiled beatifically and reached for the bottle of cooking brandy that she had been using earlier to flavor the stew. "Amaryllis isn't the first female in this family to make a nonagency marriage, you know."

Amaryllis stared. She had to swallow twice before she could form words in a proper sequence. "Aunt Sophy, are you telling us that you ran off with Great-Uncle Harold?"

"Indeed," Sophy murmured. "Caused quite a stir in the family, I don't mind telling you. Thought my father would murder Harold before it was all over. But they eventually came to terms."

"Uncle Harold?" Hannah's eyes widened. "I don't believe it."

"It's the truth. Word of honor." Sophy poured a measure of cooking brandy into a glass and took a healthy swallow. Her eyes snapped with mischief. "It was all hushed up, of course. Everyone pretended that Harold and I had been properly matched by a big agency in the city. But that was nothing more than a social lie. Harold and I never went to any agency. We went to bed. As often as we could."

Amaryllis gazed at her, astonished. "That's amazing."

"Not nearly as amazing as the fact that you're planning to do the same thing I did, my dear. Congratulations." Sophy toasted her with the brandy glass. "Nice to see that there's a bit of the rebel in you after all. I must say, I'd begun to worry that you were doomed to turn into a prissy little straitlaced prude."

Amaryllis winced.

Hannah was outraged. "Aunt Sophy, how can you say such a thing?"

"Because it's true." Sophy aimed an accusing finger at Amaryllis. "You've spent your whole life trying to make up for what your mother did. About time you went out and caused a little excitement for yourself. No guts, no glory."

Hannah's mouth tightened with anger. "Sophy, we are talking about Amaryllis's marriage here. It's one thing to cause some excitement. It's quite another to risk making a mistake she'll have to live with for the rest of her life."

A crash from the adjoining room made all three women glance toward the wall. The pots on the stove trembled.

"I'm not so sure that she's making a mistake." Sophy sounded thoughtful. "Mr. Trent appears to be the sort of man who's willing to fight for what he wants. If Oscar has an ounce of sense, he'll negotiate a truce."

Hannah made a disgusted sound. "How can there be any truce between them? Oscar will never accept a nonagency marriage for Amaryllis."

The thuds and crashes from the study ceased abruptly. A great silence descended.

When the study door opened a long time later, Amaryllis dropped the knife she had been using to chop vegetables. It clattered on the drain board. She hastily wiped her hands on her apron and rushed out into the hall.

Hannah and Sophy followed.

Lucas emerged first from the study. He had a cut lip, his shirt was torn, and his hair was mussed, but he looked amazingly pleased with himself. He grinned wryly at Amaryllis.

"After extensive discussion of the situation, your uncle and I have reached an agreement that is suitable to both parties," Lucas said.

"What agreement?" Amaryllis asked, suspicious.

Oscar strolled out of the study. He looked as battered as Lucas. He cradled one hand gingerly in the other and gave Amaryllis a satisfied smile.

"Long engagement," Oscar said succinctly.

Amaryllis glanced from her uncle to Lucas. "How long?"

"A year," Oscar said forcefully.

"Six months," Lucas said quietly. "At the outside."

Oscar glowered at him. Then he sighed. "What the hell. She's smart. She'll come to her senses in six months."

"In the meantime, we will follow an old family tradition," Sophy said imperiously.

Oscar scowled. "What old family tradition?"

"As far as everyone outside the family is concerned, this is an agency match." Sophy eyed each of the people standing in front of her in turn. "All of our friends, neighbors, business associates, and enemies will be told the same thing. Amaryllis and Lucas were brought together by a proper marriage agency in the city. Is that clear?"

"Quite clear," Hannah said.

Oscar grimaced. "I hear you, Sophy. Don't worry, I sure don't plan to discuss it."

"This is family business," Amaryllis murmured. She looked at Sophy. "I take it the old family tradition Lucas and I will be following is the one you and Great-Uncle Harold established?"

"It is," Sophy said grandly. "We will look everyone right in the eye and we will lie through our teeth." She switched her attention to Lucas. "Well, Lucas? Do you have a problem with that?"

Lucas grinned. "It works for me. Lying through my teeth is something I do real well."

⸻

That evening after dinner Lucas left the large crowd cleaning up in the kitchen and went outside onto the wide veranda. Sophy reclined in a lounger at the far end. The porch light turned her hair into a silver cloud around her strong face. She was keeping an eye on the host of youngsters who were playing beneath the porch lights in the large yard.

The children were the sons and daughters of the adults who were gathered in the kitchen. There seemed to be an endless number of them. It struck Lucas that the youngsters, as well as the cluster of youths and adults inside the big house, were all related in one way or another to Amaryllis. After the wedding, they would all be connected to him.

After so many years of being on his own, he was going to have a family. A very large family.

He paused for a moment, wrapped his hands around the veranda railing, and allowed himself to absorb the prospect of being related to so many people. He would have obligations, responsibilities, and duties. There would be christenings, birthday parties, engagement parties, weddings, and funerals to attend. Given his position as the owner of a large corporation, he would no doubt be expected to find jobs for some of the members of the younger generation.

The children ran, shrieking and laughing, through the warm night. The twin moons combined with the lights from the big house gave them all the illumination they needed to pursue their games. In a few years, Lucas thought, the kids that he and Amaryllis would have together would be playing out here in the night with their cousins. It was all part of an endless web that reached into the future even as it stretched back into the past.

A family of his own.

Lucas released the railing and continued on to the far end of the veranda. He sat down in the chair next to Sophy and stretched out his legs.

Sophy smiled with satisfaction. Her request for him to join her had been civil enough, but Lucas was not fooled. He had recognized an order when he had heard one.

They sat quietly, side by side, for a while, watching the children.

"So you're the one she's chosen," Sophy said after a time. "Took her long enough. But, then, it's not easy for an off-the-scale prism."

"You know the full extent of Amaryllis's psychic abilities?"

"Recognized them when she was in her teens," Sophy said. "It was like watching myself mature all over again."

Lucas exhaled slowly. "You, too?"

"It's in the blood. Runs through the women on my side of the family. Getting stronger with each generation, I think."

"I see."

"It's not easy for prisms like us. Officially, our level of psychic power doesn't even exist because there's simply no way to test it beyond assessing our ability to handle a class-ten talent. The fact that we don't burn out doing so doesn't really tell the researchers anything except that we are full spectrum." Sophy shrugged. "We go through life aware that we're different but never really understanding just how different."

Lucas was silent for a moment. Then he decided to tell Sophy the truth. She was family, after all.

"I know the feeling," Lucas said.

"Yes, I expect you do. Just how far off the talent scale are you?"

"I have no idea."

"Of course not. Stupid question. There's no way to test you, either, is there?"

"No." Lucas settled deeper into his chair. "But I've got my papers. Class nine. Faked the talent certification exam. Lied through my teeth."

"As you now know, that's an old family tradition. Ever burn out Amaryllis?"

"No."

"I knew she was strong." Sophy watched two of the children chase the ball into the shadows at the edge of the garden. "Talent or prism, it's all psychic energy. A very volatile component of our being. We all have to wage our own private struggles to learn to cope with our sixth sense."

Lucas thought about the long hours he had spent in his secret grotto. "Yeah."

"I have a hunch that the stronger it is, the harder it is to manage. Personally, I went a little wild during my younger days. Gave my family fits. Amaryllis chose the opposite approach. She tried to control her world, herself, and her psychic powers with lots of personal rules."

"She didn't invent all those rules just to control her psychic abilities," Lucas said. "She needed them for other reasons, too."

"Yes," Sophy said. "She did. Growing up in this town as Matt Bailey's illegitimate daughter was the kind of experience that was bound to make or break her character. She came through it with flying colors, I'm pleased to say."

"But she paid a price," Lucas said.

Sophy shrugged. "We all do, one way or another. I asked you to come out here tonight because I wanted to make certain you understood that. I can see that you do."

Lucas contemplated the shape of Amaryllis's derriere as she climbed up the barn loft ladder ahead of him. It was a pleasant sight, one he would have been content to enjoy for an extended period of time. Unfortunately, there were not many rungs on the ladder.

"This is it," she announced as she scrambled off the ladder and tumbled into the straw. "No beautiful green pool and no dripping rock walls for atmosphere, but on a farm you take what you can get."

Lucas reached the top rung of the ladder and looked around the shadowy loft with great interest. This was Amaryllis's secret place. Sunlight seeped through the small cracks in the wooden walls. The scent of the stored feed and straw was rich in his nostrils. Down below, a big ox-mule shifted on its six legs.

"It's a good place," Lucas said.

"Yes, it is, isn't it? But it seems smaller now than it did when I was a kid."

Lucas eased himself off the ladder and sat down beside her. "I guess things in the past often seem smaller when we go back and face them as adults."

Amaryllis rested her chin on her knees. "I'm going to test that theory this afternoon."

"What do you mean?"

"I'm going to call on Elizabeth Bailey."

Lucas nodded. "What changed your mind?"

"You did."

"*Me?*"

"What you did for Dillon, even though his parents had shunned you for three years. It was the right thing. The kind of thing one does for family. It made me think."

"Fancy that," Lucas murmured. "Me, a model of family values."

Amaryllis smiled. "A regular paragon of founders' virtues. But, then, I always knew you were a hero."

Elizabeth Bailey was, indeed, smaller than Amaryllis had remembered. No taller than Amaryllis, herself, to be exact. But she was no less formidable than she had seemed that day all those years ago when Amaryllis had run up to her on the street and asked her the question that defined their relationship. *Are you really my grandmother?*

Elizabeth was still every bit as striking as Amaryllis recalled. Her aristocratic features were firm and strong. Her eyes were a sharp, vivid green, the same shade of green that Amaryllis saw in the mirror every morning.

"I suppose you are wondering why I asked you to visit me." Elizabeth put down her delicate porcelain coff-tea cup. She regarded Amaryllis and Lucas with the cool, contained expression of a woman who had encountered many obstacles over the years and who had surmounted them all.

"Yes," Amaryllis said. "I am."

Elizabeth flicked an assessing glance at Lucas. Then she looked at Amaryllis. "I understand that the two of you are engaged."

"Yes," Amaryllis said.

"Congratulations."

"Thank you." Amaryllis waited.

Other than the soft hum of the mantel clock, there was no sound in the vast, elaborately draped and carpeted living room. The atmosphere was heavy and oppressive. Amaryllis had to resist a strong urge to open a window. It felt as if there had been no fresh air in this house for years.

"I requested this meeting so that I could give you something," Elizabeth said after a moment.

Amaryllis barely managed to conceal her surprise. "That's not necessary. I don't want anything from you."

"Yes, I know." Elizabeth's smile was bitter. "Your mother's family has given you everything you've needed."

"Yes, they did." Amaryllis put down her untouched cup of coff-tea. She glanced at Lucas. "I've been very lucky."

"I have not been lucky at all," Elizabeth said. "But it is only now that I see the woman you have become that I realize the true extent of my misfortune."

Amaryllis stilled. "I don't understand."

"No, I don't suppose you do. Well, that is not important any longer. I am responsible for most of my own ill luck, and I have no one to blame but myself."

Amaryllis thought of what Sophy had said about Elizabeth assuming the guilt for what had happened in the past. She smiled in spite of herself. "My great-aunt once said that you had a talent for drama. She thinks it's a shame that you didn't go into the theater."

Elizabeth looked briefly disconcerted. "Am I being melodramatic?"

"A little, but that's all right." Amaryllis felt herself begin to relax for some inexplicable reason. "It's a somewhat melodramatic occasion, isn't it?"

"It certainly strikes me that way." Elizabeth picked up a small box that had been sitting on the table beside her chair. "Well, I mustn't keep you. This is for you."

Warily, Amaryllis took the box from Elizabeth's hand. She opened it slowly and looked inside. A heavy, masculine ring set with a large, brilliant fire crystal rested on a small, white satin pillow. Amaryllis knew little about jewelry, but everyone knew the value of fire crystal. She hurriedly closed the lid.

"I can't possibly accept this." She held the box out to Elizabeth. "It's much too valuable."

Pain flared in Elizabeth's eyes. "It belonged to my son Matthew. Your father. I want you to have it."

"My father." Amaryllis clutched at the small box. "This was his ring?"

"Yes. He would have been very proud of you, Amaryllis. Any parent would have been proud of such a fine daughter."

Amaryllis stared at the ring box. "I don't know what to say."

"Many years ago you asked me a question."

Amaryllis raised her gaze from the ring box to Elizabeth's face. The anger and the pain still stood there between them, an impossible wall that could never be climbed.

But there are other ways to get past a wall, Amaryllis realized. If one felt strong enough, one could walk around the far end of it and find oneself on the other side. It didn't mean that the wall suddenly ceased to exist. It simply meant that there were methods of dealing with walls.

"Are you really my grandmother?" Amaryllis asked.

The gleam of hope in Elizabeth's eyes warmed the cold room.

"Yes," she said. "I am."

Chapter 19

"I've been dreading that visit to Elizabeth Bailey." Amaryllis watched the scenery flash past the Icer's window. "But in the end, after all was said and done, I realized that, although I'm never going to actually learn to like the woman, mostly I just felt sorry for her."

Lucas flexed his hands on the steering bar. "She screwed up a lot of lives."

"She believed that she was doing the right thing. But she was rigid, inflexible, and proud."

Lucas said nothing.

Amaryllis grimaced. "I know, I know. I have a lot in common with her. What can I say? She's my grandmother."

"She's your grandmother, all right, but you don't have very much in common with her. Elizabeth Bailey is one cold eel-fish. Five seconds after meeting her this afternoon, I could have told you that she's spent a lifetime coercing others into doing what she thought they should do."

"I'm sure she had her motives."

"Yeah, right. Motives like trying to control everyone and everything around her."

"Is that a fact?" Amaryllis smiled blandly. "What about me? What would you say motivates my actions?"

Lucas did not hesitate. "Loyalty. A sense of justice. Family."

"Elizabeth Bailey could claim that her actions were based on those same three principles."

"I have a hunch that for Elizabeth, her principles stand alone in a vacuum. There is no place in her rigid little world for friendship, compassion, and love. Your values, on the other hand, are sunk deep in that kind of bedrock."

"Hmm. Well, in that case, I guess you and I have a few things in common, after all, don't we?"

Lucas shot her a derisive glance. "Oh, no, you don't. I'm no modern-day version of one of your idealized founders. Don't you dare try to pin a halo and some wings on me."

"Nobody ever said the founders were angels. But I do think that you work much too hard at concealing your own virtues."

"Amaryllis, I'm warning you."

"Just look at all the fine, altruistic things you've done since we met." Amaryllis held up one hand and ticked her points off on her fingers. "You let that thieving vice president, Miranda Locking, get away with her crimes because you felt sorry for her. You helped Dillon Rye out of the mess he got himself into because he was your disloyal ex-partner's kid brother. You helped me track down a murderer because you wanted to protect me."

"Funny how hard it is to distinguish between my virtues and my weaknesses," Lucas muttered.

"Oh, I don't know. Most of the time the distinction is as clear as prism crystal to me."

"Yeah?" Lucas glanced at her. "What about those occasions when it's not quite that clear?"

"I'm learning not to worry too much about the vague stuff." Amaryllis grew thoughtful. "But there are a couple of things I'd like to see cleared up."

"About me?"

"No. About Professor Landreth's death."

"Damn. You never give up, do you? Now what?"

"I'd still like to know how Madison Sheffield discovered that he was the subject of Professor Landreth's hot file."

Lucas exhaled deeply. "Just so you'll know in the future, tenacity is one of those vague virtues you mentioned a minute ago. It's not always a good thing."

An hour and a half later, Lucas drove into the night-darkened city. It was raining. The light from the streetlamps glimmered on the wet pavement and reflected in the shop windows.

Amaryllis roused herself from thoughts of the meeting with Elizabeth Bailey just as Lucas turned a corner and drove slowly down the quiet street to her house. The answer to the problem that she had been mulling over during the long drive suddenly crystallized.

"Irene Dunley," Amaryllis said.

"Huh?"

"I've been thinking about my grandmother."

"What's Elizabeth Bailey got to do with Irene Dunley?" Lucas asked as he brought the Icer to a stop at the curb.

"There's something about my grandmother that reminds me of Irene."

"What?"

"It's hard to explain." The excitement of intuitive discovery hummed through Amaryllis. She was suddenly seething with impatience. "They've both spent a lifetime controlling everything around them."

"I'll go along with that conclusion." Lucas deactivated the ignition and turned slightly in the seat. He rested one arm on the steering bar and watched Amaryllis from the shadows. "Where does it lead?"

"I'm not sure." Amaryllis tapped one finger on the seat. "To tell you the truth, I'm almost afraid to think about it. Irene was one of Madison Sheffield's staunchest supporters. She believed in him. Lucas, what if Irene was the person who told Madison Sheffield about Professor Landreth's file?"

Lucas thought that over. "Okay, it's a possibility. But so what? We've already decided that the person who told Sheffield about the file was probably connected to the Department of Focus Studies."

"Of all the people in the department, Irene would have been the one most likely to know about the contents of the file. She had worked with Professor Landreth forever, and he trusted her more than anyone else. She was fiercely loyal to him. I think she even loved him. But what if she learned about the file and was torn between what she felt was her duty to the future of New Seattle city-state and her loyalty to Professor Landreth?"

"Hard to tell what she would do."

Amaryllis shook her head. "No. I think I know Irene Dunley well enough to believe that in a situation like that, she might very easily have concluded that she had a responsibility to inform Sheffield about the threat to his campaign."

"And then what?"

"Why, she would have felt guilty for having betrayed Professor Landreth, of course. Just as Elizabeth Bailey felt guilty for having ruined her son's chance of happiness. That kind of guilt would have eaten at Irene. Tormented her. Even though she knew she had done what she felt was the right thing."

"You think that's why she tried to help you when you decided to solve the mystery of Landreth's death?"

"Yes." Amaryllis watched the rain fall on the Icer's windshield. "I think she must have begun to wonder if she had inadvertently signed Professor Landreth's death warrant when she told Sheffield about the file."

"She did sign it. But it's over now. She'll have to live with it." Lucas opened his door. "Come on, let's get the luggage inside."

Amaryllis tugged the hood of her raincoat up over her head and got out of the car. Lucas hauled the suitcases out of the trunk and joined her on the sidewalk.

Together, they hurried to the shelter of the small overhang above the front steps. Amaryllis unsealed the lock, pushed open the front door, and stepped inside the darkened hall.

The whisper of talent brushed against her senses and raised the fine hairs on the back of her neck.

Someone was inside the house.

"Lucas."

"I felt it." He dropped the suitcases and clamped a hand around her arm. "Let's get out of here." He started to pull her back out onto the steps.

Amaryllis did not resist. She swung around, ready to run. There was a familiar tingling on the psychic plane. Lucas was reaching for a focus link even as he drew her to safety. He no doubt wanted to use his detector-talent to try to learn something about the intruder.

Amaryllis opened herself to the link. Felt the instant of disorientation, the jarring seconds of complete vulnerability as her mind constructed a prism . . .

. . . And then she staggered and nearly fell as an impossible surge of talent seized her in an iron fist. Alien, powerful, and brutal.

This was not Lucas. Amaryllis panicked. *Not Lucas.*

She tried to pull back but she was trapped. To her horror, the prism took shape on the psychic plane.

Someone or something else took control of the energy construct. Power poured through it. Torrents of dark power.

Amaryllis screamed. She clutched her head with both hands and tried to cut off her own flow of psychic energy. "*No.* Stop it. *Stop it.*"

Nothing happened. She could not shut down the link. Lucas had her outside on the steps. Rain whipped at her coat. Frantically she tried to blank her mind. The link held strong.

"What is it?" Lucas pulled her to him. "What the hell is going on?"

"Another talent." Amaryllis collapsed against him.

"Five hells." He caught her. "I can feel the bastard."

"Strong. So strong." If she did not get free, she would go insane, Amaryllis thought. A fresh wave of panic crashed through her.

Lucas picked her up in his arms. "Break the link. Destroy the prism."

"I can't. Lucas, I can't release the focus. I'm trapped." Distance would help, Amaryllis knew. The strength of any talent was directly affected by proximity. "Get me away from here."

"As fast as I can," Lucas vowed. He started toward the car with Amaryllis in his arms.

Talent slammed through the prism. Amaryllis looked fearfully back over Lucas's shoulder toward the open doorway of her house. She expected to see a monster lumber into view.

Instead, a familiar figure emerged from the shadows of the hall and moved out onto the front step.

The weak light from the jelly-lamp above the door gleamed on the gun in Irene Dunley's hand.

"Come back inside at once," Irene said in the same tone of voice that she used to give instructions to student assistants. "Really, some people don't know enough to come in out of the rain."

"Lucas, she's got a gun."

"Stop right where you are, Mr. Trent, or I shall be forced to shoot."

Lucas halted halfway down the walk. He turned slowly to face Irene. Amaryllis sensed that he was weighing the odds of getting her to safety before Irene could pull the trigger. She felt the precise instant when he accepted the fact that he could not outrun a bullet.

"Come here," Irene said.

Lucas carried Amaryllis slowly back up the steps and into the house. Irene rewarded him with a smile of cold approval.

"That's better. Now, kindly sit down." Irene trained the nose of the gun on Amaryllis as she gave the order. "Over there on the sofa will do."

Lucas said nothing. He carried Amaryllis into the living room and set her carefully on her feet. He searched her face.

"Are you all right?" he asked.

There was no trace of emotion in his voice, but the bleak chill in his eyes frightened Amaryllis almost as much as the assault on her sanity that was taking place on the psychic plane.

"No." Amaryllis reached for the arm of the sofa to steady herself. "I'm not all right. I can't get free." She lowered herself gingerly down onto the cushions. "Lucas, I'm going crazy."

Lucas looked at Irene. "Let her go."

"I don't think that would be wise." Irene moved slowly toward them. "She would be free to link with you, then, Mr. Trent and I suspect that you are a very strong talent. As I am uncertain about the exact nature of your psychic abilities, however, I would prefer to keep them neutralized by restricting your access to a powerful prism."

Lucas shrugged as if the matter were not all that important, but he never took his eyes off Irene's face as he lowered himself to the arm of the sofa.

"Don't worry," Irene said pleasantly. "I expect she'll burn out any second. No prism is strong enough to handle my full range of power. Even Jonathan burned out when I used the complete spectrum of my talent."

Amaryllis sagged on the sofa cushion. She held her head in her hands and fought for her sanity. She'd never been trained for anything like this. What Irene was doing was supposed to be impossible.

Nothing she did seemed to alter the flow of talent that roared through the prism. As far as she could tell, Irene was not using the thundering flow of energy for any purpose other than to chain the focus so that Lucas could not seize it. She wondered fleetingly what sort of talent Irene possessed.

"You murdered Landreth, didn't you?" Lucas said casually to Irene.

Amaryllis felt the whisper of a cold, motionless wind. She lifted her head, fighting back waves of psychic pain to stare at Lucas. Then she turned toward Irene. "You killed Professor Landreth?"

"I had to kill him." Irene sounded vaguely regretful. "In the end, I realized that it had to be done. There was no choice."

"Was it because Landreth had figured out that you were capable of doing this to a prism?" Lucas touched Amaryllis's shoulder.

Pain exploded through her confused senses. Her seared nerve endings did not know how to interpret the feel of Lucas's hand. He withdrew his fingers instantly when Amaryllis cried out. She huddled on the edge of the sofa.

"Oh, no, you don't understand." Irene's expression was one of modest pride. "Jonathan was very respectful of my power. He worked with me for many years, teaching me to control it. We were always testing, training, and exploring the possibilities of my talent together. He said he'd never encountered anything like it. Those were glorious hours. I shall treasure them forever."

"He served as your prism, didn't he?" Amaryllis managed to ask.

"Yes, indeed. He was my only prism after my husband died. Jonathan did not want to use anyone else to provide a focus for me because he said it was too dangerous."

"For the prism?" Lucas asked.

"No, no. For me." Irene chuckled. "Jonathan felt that for my own safety, no one should know the extent of my talent. It was our little secret, he said. It bound us together more surely than any wedding license."

"So why did you kill him?" Lucas asked. "Because you didn't want him to know about your little secret any longer?"

"Oh, no, that wasn't the reason."

"Why?" Amaryllis got out hoarsely. "Why did you murder him?"

"Because he was not the man I had believed him to be." Irene's mouth tightened. "I thought he was made of the very stuff of our founders. Instead, I discovered that he was perverted and corrupt. He betrayed me."

"Oh lord," Amaryllis whispered. "This had nothing to do with politics or Gifford. You killed Professor Landreth because of those standing appointments with Vivien, didn't you?"

"Jonathan proved to be just as weak as my husband had been. No moral fiber at all. It was very disappointing."

Pain flared on the psychic plane. Amaryllis flinched and tried not to move. "He left that Friday to go to his mountain cabin. You met him there and pushed him off the cliff."

"We often went to the mountains together," Irene said. "No one else knew of our weekend rendezvous at his cabin, naturally."

"Another one of your little secrets," Lucas said.

Another eddy of cold wind moved in the room. Amaryllis took heart. She probed cautiously, trying to dampen the clarity of the prism. It stayed sharp and precise, providing a focus for Irene's raging talent.

"Jonathan and I were always very discreet." Irene sighed. "But on that last occasion, I was obliged to end our relationship. We took a walk along the cliff path after dinner as usual. Formed a last prism link. I took him to his psychic limits and then, just as he was about to burn out, pushed him over the edge. I don't think he even knew what had happened."

"Dear God." Amaryllis sank deeper into the sofa.

"Afterward I tidied up and came home alone," Irene said. "It was the saddest day of my life, but I felt good about it. I knew I had done the right thing."

"And the authorities never questioned Landreth's accident," Lucas said.

"It all went very smoothly," Irene assured him. "Most things do if one organizes them properly."

"You mean it went smoothly until Amaryllis started asking questions," Lucas said.

Irene glared at Amaryllis with accusing eyes. "A most unfortunate turn of events. A bit of bad luck that I could not have anticipated. Your encounter with Sheffield while he was focusing in what you considered an unethical manner led you back to the Department of Focus Studies."

"You knew that questions about a Landreth-trained prism focusing in an unethical manner for a powerful politician could lead to questions and speculation," Amaryllis whispered.

Irene sighed. "Eventually that speculation would have led to questions about the professor's death. It was inevitable because you were bound to realize that you had uncovered a possible murder motive. It was the wrong motive and the wrong suspect, of course, but your persistence could have led you to me."

"Why did you send me to Vivien?"

"I tried to nip the whole thing in the bud by demonstrating to you that Jonathan Landreth was not worthy of your loyalty. I thought perhaps you'd let the entire matter drop once you realized what he was."

"You sent me to talk to Vivien of the Veils thinking that I would be shocked and disgusted when I learned about her relationship with Professor Landreth." Amaryllis gritted her teeth as power spiked on the psychic plane. "You thought I'd drop my investigation into his death because he was seeing a syn-sex stripper?"

"If you had possessed a proper sense of values, you would have done so. You'd have understood that Jonathan's death was nothing less than what he deserved. He had consorted with a creature of low morals. Justice had been done."

Rage flashed through Amaryllis. "You have no right to condemn poor Vivien for her morals. Yours are a lot lower than hers ever were. You're a murderer."

The rush of talent energy dimmed. Hope sparked in Amaryllis. But as her own red-hot anger receded, Irene's crude power surged once more.

Irene shook her head. "I thought you and I had a great deal in common, Miss Lark. I believed your standards to be as high as my own. You seemed like such a nice young lady. Obviously I was mistaken."

Lucas shifted slightly on the sofa. "When you realized that Amaryllis intended to continue pushing for answers, you took another step. You tried to point the finger at Gifford Osterley. He had a motive, after all. Everyone knew that he and Landreth had quarreled."

"When Miss Lark inquired about the appointments Jonathan had made on the last day of his life, it occurred to me that it might be useful to bring that dreadful Gifford Osterley into the picture," Irene agreed.

Fury erupted like a geyser inside Amaryllis. And again she thought she detected a slight weakening of Irene's energy flow. "You set out to frame Gifford. You wrote down that three o'clock appointment in Professor Landreth's calendar."

"After all these years, it was a simple matter to imitate his handwriting," Irene said.

Lucas watched her intently. "But you changed your mind about framing Osterley. You set Madison Sheffield up for the fall, instead. Why the switch? I thought you were a big fan of his."

Irene's eyes blazed. "I discovered that Madison Sheffield was no better than Jonathan."

"How?" Lucas asked.

"Natalie Elwick," Amaryllis said.

"Indeed." Irene's mouth tightened. "Gifford Osterley's secretary is an old acquaintance of mine. We worked together for years before she left the department to manage Unique Prisms' new office. She confided to me that Sheffield demanded only beautiful, young, female prisms who were willing to sleep with him as part of their services. He got some sort of perverted sexual thrill out of it, Natalie said."

"No wonder Gifford was worried about having his firm dragged any deeper into the investigation," Lucas said softly. "He's running a full-spectrum call girl operation."

"Can you believe it?" Irene's voice rose. "Madison Sheffield was the Founders' Values candidate. The next governor of this city-state. He would have been president if I hadn't stopped him."

"So you decided to destroy his career by framing him for Vivien's death," Lucas said.

"I had already planned to punish the syn-sex stripper. She was the one who led Jonathan astray, after all. I could not allow her to live. But I had not yet finished organizing the arrangements for her death when everything started to fall apart."

"Because Amaryllis started asking questions," Lucas said.

"She was a threat to all of my plans." Irene tightened both hands on the grip of the gun.

"Professor Landreth had no file on Sheffield, did he?" Amaryllis managed tightly. "You created it as part of your plan to dispose of Vivien, me, and Sheffield in one neat package."

Lucas looked at Irene. "You left that phony file, half-burned, in Vivien's dressing room after you killed her."

"I singed it just enough to make it appear that Sheffield had tried to destroy blackmail evidence," Irene said. "I thought it was a nice touch."

"What did you tell Sheffield to get him to Vivien's dressing room that night?"

"I was with Vivien when she placed the calls to both you and Sheffield. I held a gun on her and forced her to read the script I had prepared before I killed her."

"The guard," Amaryllis said. "How did you get rid of the stage door guard?"

"I paid a street person to offer the man a bribe to leave his post for an hour. Really, one simply cannot get reliable help these days."

"You planned to kill me after I discovered Vivien's body. You waited for me in the hall outside her dressing room, didn't you? You wanted it to appear that Madison Sheffield had shot both me and Vivien."

"That was the way I had organized it, but you ruined that plan, too."

"How dare you?" Amaryllis's anger soared above the psychic pain. The energy gushing through the prism slowed discernibly.

Out of the corner of her eye she saw Lucas glance at her. She knew that he had sensed that Irene's grip had wavered for a instant. He was a detector, after all. And he was very powerful. He had demonstrated before that he had enough control of his own talent to marshal it for brief flashes of energy.

Irene frowned. "Why did you go back into Vivien's dressing room that night? Why didn't you run for the stage door entrance after you discovered her body? I was sure you would dash for help. I had turned out the corridor lights so that you wouldn't see me. I knew that you would be silhouetted against the light from the dressing room. A clear target. But you leaped back and slammed the door before I could pull the trigger. Why? *Why?*"

"I felt you." Amaryllis sat very still on the edge of the sofa. "I sensed your talent sputtering like oil in a frying pan. You were not in full control of it."

"That's not true," Irene hissed. "I am in full control of my talent at all times."

"You must have been nervous that night," Amaryllis whispered. "Not surprising, given the fact that you had just committed murder and intended to kill again."

"You're wrong. My talent is always under my complete control." Irene's voice rose. "But you upset all my plans when you didn't come out into the hall. I was trying to decide what to do next when Madison Sheffield arrived. He was the one who was nervous. It was his talent you felt leaping about like . . . like hot oil."

"Later, yes, when I was hiding from him in the backstage tunnels. But not at first." Amaryllis forced a derisive smile. "At first, it was you, and you were definitely out of control."

"No, it was Sheffield," Irene shouted. "It must have been him. He's weak."

The energy pouring through the prism shimmered and slowed. A human being had only so much power of any kind on which to draw, Amaryllis reminded herself. Irene's rage had briefly siphoned off energy from her psychic efforts. Not enough to allow Amaryllis to break free, but enough to give her hope.

Somewhere in the distance, at the very edge of her awareness, she sensed Lucas's talent stirring. It prowled there in the shadows, a psychic beast of prey watching for an opening.

"Sheffield never even noticed me in the darkness." Irene calmed herself with a visible effort. "For a terrible moment I thought everything had gone wrong. I was afraid that when he was unable to find the hall lights, he would turn and run back out into the alley. Instead, he used the glow of that ridiculous star on Vivien's door to guide him. Foolish man. He was too scared to turn back. Vivien had told him on the phone that she had information that could damage his campaign, you see."

"When he went into the dressing room and turned on the light, you went out through the stage door entrance," Lucas concluded. "And then you locked the alley door so that Sheffield would be forced to wander blindly around the backstage tunnels looking for another way out."

"I knew that sooner or later he would blunder into someone who would recognize him," Irene said. "And then the body and the file would be found, and everything would be neat and orderly again. It was true that Amaryllis would not be dead as I had intended, but I thought that surely she would stop asking questions once Sheffield was arrested for murder. Surely that would satisfy her."

Amaryllis stared at Irene while she fought the psychic pain. "But the day before I left the city to visit my family, I told you I wasn't satisfied and I had a few more questions."

"You had become obsessive," Irene raged. "It was obvious that you were never going to quit. I understood then that nothing would stop you. You would continue to poke and pry until eventually you stumbled onto the truth. It has become clear to me that both you and Mr. Trent must die. Then things will be tidied up at last. Everything will be back under control."

"It's too late for everything to be made neat and orderly." Amaryllis summoned every ounce of emotion she could find: righteous anger at the grave injustices that Irene had perpetrated; fear for Lucas's life and her own; and love. The love she had for Lucas was more powerful than the other emotions combined. She would not let him die. She had to save him.

For some reason, she suddenly recalled the visit to Elizabeth Bailey. Some walls were too high to climb. But there were other ways around them.

Irene must be distracted so that Lucas could act. The easiest way to divert the attention of a high-class talent was to force her to use more power. Extreme power required extreme concentration.

Amaryllis consciously tore down the civilized barriers of self-control that had been built up over a lifetime. A flood of emotion and passion poured through her. She fed the fierce feelings of the moment with all the stored anger, righteous indignation, and sheer determination she had ever known. And then she threw in the will to survive and to save Lucas.

A witch's brew boiled through her bloodstream, a heady, intoxicating drug that affected everything, even events on the psychic plane.

The focus shifted and dimmed.

Irene fought back, using more energy to hold the link. Amaryllis screamed silently as the bands of talent brightened visibly. Then she forced Irene to use more power.

"Stop it." The gun trembled in Irene's hands. "Stop it this instant, do you hear me? You'll only burn yourself out if you keep it up."

Burning out would be a blessing, but Amaryllis sensed that might not happen, at least not in time. She braced herself against the mounting fear of being driven insane and concentrated on what she had to do.

"What's the matter, Irene?" she said. "Afraid you'll be the one to burn out first? Professor Landreth had a theory that it was possible to actually destroy a talent this way. Did he ever tell you about it?"

"That's a lie. You can't destroy my talent." Irene took a step closer. "I'm too strong for you. Jonathan said I was too strong for him. I was too strong for my husband. I'm stronger than any talent who ever lived. That's why everything must be organized, don't you see? That's why I must be in control."

"But you're not in control, are you, Irene? You're crazy."

"*No.*"

Lucas moved slightly again. But Amaryllis knew that as long as Irene had the gun aimed at her, he would feel pinned down. Irene could not miss at this close distance.

Amaryllis closed her eyes against the rising tide of pain. And then she deliberately fed the pain into the fiery river that flowed through every vein and artery in her body.

Her muscles went rigid. There was a prickling sensation on her skin. Her mouth was as dry as dust. But she knew that Irene was finally beginning to realize how great the price of control over the focus link would be.

She wondered when Irene would lose it altogether and pull the trigger.

The icy wind howled across the psychic plane. It was as strong as the violent talent that had seized control of the link. A dark fog gathered.

Amaryllis was astonished to see Professor Landreth in the mist. His head was a gory horror. He was covered in blood. She opened her mouth to ask him what he was doing in her living room.

Irene screamed. "No, you're dead. *You're dead.*"

There was a roar of sound in Amaryllis's ears. More screaming. High, shrill, it seemed to go on forever.

At the edge of her fading vision Amaryllis saw Lucas come up off the sofa in a fluid, lethal movement.

The talent that had surged so steadily and so painfully through the prism was cut off abruptly. Amaryllis was suddenly free. The abrupt release was too much for her overloaded system. An endless wave of unconsciousness rolled toward her.

She slipped headfirst into the waiting darkness. The last thing she saw was a river of blood coursing across the carpet. She wondered vaguely whose it was.

Chapter 20

"Irene Dunley, psychic vampire." Clementine propped one hip on the edge of Amaryllis's hospital bed and shook her head in wonder. "Who would have believed it?"

"Sort of takes the romance out of the whole psychic vampire thing, doesn't it?" Byron said. "Irene Dunley doesn't quite fit the image. Not exactly the lethally elegant, sophisticated, world-weary type. I wonder if Orchid Adams will change genres when she learns about this. Maybe she'll decide to write mysteries or Western Islands adventure tales instead of psychic vampire romance."

"She's not going to hear the truth about Irene Dunley from us." Amaryllis lounged against a mountain of pristine, white pillows and glowered at both of her visitors. "And neither is anyone else. We all agreed that the fewer people who know about this, the better. The police are satisfied that Irene was a nutcase who murdered her lover when she discovered that he had a relationship with a syn-sex stripper."

"Hey, sure, no problem," Byron said quickly. "Staid secretary murders lover and then kills syn-sex stripper. Big-time politician gets caught up in the mess and campaign falls apart. End of story."

"Exactly," Amaryllis said. "We certainly don't need Nelson Burlton doing a lot of cheap, tabloid-style stories about psychic vampires on the ten o'clock news. It would only make people nervous about high-class talents."

Clementine grinned. "Kind of a shame not to let Burlton have the story. Just think what he could do with it."

"The first person who calls Burlton answers to me," Lucas growled from the doorway.

Amaryllis turned her head to look at him. It was the first time she had seen him since the police had hustled both of them off to the emergency room the previous night.

Lucas smiled at her. He had a fistful of yellow rose-orchids in one hand. His other arm was in a sling.

"Whatever you say, Trent." Clementine held up a copy of the *New Seattle Times* to display the headline. "Local Prism Solves Murder." "This is the best press Psynergy, Inc. has had in years. It's going to do amazing things for the bottom line."

"I wonder what would have happened if Amaryllis had not gone to that reception with you that night, Mr. Trent." Byron looked thoughtful. "If the two of you hadn't accidentally detected Sheffield while he was working the room with his focused charm and charisma, none of the rest would have come to light."

Amaryllis shook her head. "No, the truth would have eventually surfaced, one way or another. Irene was getting crazier by the day. When she killed Professor Landreth, she murdered the only person who could help her control her talent. She had already planned to murder Vivien, and when she learned about Sheffield's penchant for sleeping with his prism, she was determined to take him down, too. Eventually she would have gone too far."

"Yeah, but how many more people would have died before she committed a mistake and finally got caught?" Byron said.

"Hmm." Clementine propped her square jaw on her hand. "I wonder if Psynergy, Inc. should put more of an emphasis on security work. I'd hate to lose the momentum here."

"If Psynergy, Inc. goes into the security business in a big way, I can guarantee that you'll have one less employee," Lucas said grimly. "Amaryllis will be looking for another job. My nerves can't take any more of her investigations."

"Now, Lucas, don't get excited," Amaryllis murmured.

"I'm not the one lying in a hospital bed." Lucas crossed the room, bent down, and kissed her. "You're the one who's supposed to be resting." He handed her the flowers. "How are you feeling?"

"Fine." She sniffed the yellow rose-orchids. "In fact, I'm going to get sprung from this joint today."

"You're sure you're ready to come home?"

"More than ready. I was just suffering from temporary shock and exhaustion. You were the one who took the bullet."

"Yeah, well, you may not want to rush home," Lucas said. "Your uncle called an hour ago. He said that he and your aunt are driving into the city today to find out, and I quote, just what in the five hells is going on."

Amaryllis grimaced. "I was afraid of that."

Byron glanced at Lucas with interest. "What will happen to Irene Dunley?"

Lucas looked down at Amaryllis. "The doctor says they're processing paperwork to commit her to a mental institution."

"No trial?" Clementine was obviously disappointed.

"I doubt it." Lucas closed his big hand around Amaryllis's fingers. "Apparently when she realized that her talent had been destroyed, she lost whatever small grasp she still had on her sanity. The emergency room syn-shrink says he's never seen a case quite like it."

"Because no one's ever heard of a talent being destroyed," Clementine said. "All the research indicates that while prisms can burn out temporarily, talents simply lose strength if they get too close to their personal limits. All a talent has to do in order to regain full power is drop back down into his or her working range."

"I guess Irene proved that there are some hazards for very high-class talents," Byron said.

Clementine nodded. "Yep. There's just one thing I'd like to know."

"What's that?" Lucas asked.

"What kind of talent was Irene Dunley? None of the news accounts mentioned it."

"I wondered the same thing." Amaryllis hesitated. "I know this is going to sound strange, but I have a feeling that Professor Landreth

may have told me the truth the day he said that Irene Dunley had a
superior talent for organization."

"We did it together, didn't we?" Amaryllis asked very soberly as Lucas
carried her up the waterfall steps and into the airy hall of his big house.
"We destroyed Irene's talent and her sanity."

"I think it's safe to say that her sanity was almost gone. Don't start
blaming yourself for that." Lucas carried her into the spacious living
room and settled her carefully on the sofa. "But, yes, we did burn out
her talent together. You forced her to her limits. I put her over the edge."

"She was screaming at the end." Amaryllis shivered. "I found a
way to dampen the flow of her energy. She must have feared that I
might be strong enough to sever the link after all. So she kept increasing her own power. When she understood that I wasn't going to burn
out, I think that she tried to cut the link herself."

"But it was too late," Lucas said. "She had lost control of her mind
and her talent. She aimed that gun straight at your heart. There was no
way she could miss you."

"But you did something, didn't you? What was it?"

"I only needed to hold a focus for a couple of seconds. I can do
that on my own."

"You created an illusion to distract Irene." Amaryllis searched his
face. "But what was it?"

"I knew I'd only have one chance. I had to come up with something that would really jolt her. Remember the photo of Landreth that
hung in Irene's office?"

"You didn't—"

"Yeah." Lucas sat down on the edge of the sofa and rested his elbows on his thighs. "I did. I knew what he looked like because of that
photo. I created an illusion of him standing next to you, bleeding from
a crushed skull."

"The blood." Amaryllis shuddered again. "I saw a river of blood."

"I probably went a little overboard on the blood. I didn't have time
to fine-tune the image. Irene freaked. She aimed the gun at the illusion

of Landreth instead of at you. Pulled the trigger. By then, I was on her." Lucas glanced at his injured arm. "Unfortunately, the gun went off once more before I got it away from her."

"No wonder she wouldn't stop screaming. Irene must have thought she'd seen Professor Landreth's ghost."

"I talked to Rafe Stonebraker last night after the medics finished working on my arm. Told him the whole story. He said to tell you that he's going to bill me for time and expenses."

Amaryllis was outraged. "That's ridiculous. There was no missing file for him to discover. Irene created a fake."

"Stonebraker says that only proves just how good he is at what he does. He couldn't find a missing file because there was no missing file."

The doorbell chimed, interrupting Amaryllis before she could think of a suitable rebuttal to Rafe Stonebraker's argument.

"The last thing either of us needs is a visitor," Lucas muttered as he got to his feet. "I'll get rid of whoever it is."

Amaryllis listened as he went down the hall to answer the door. The low rumble of masculine voices a moment later aroused her curiosity. She pushed herself off the sofa and trailed after Lucas.

She saw Calvin Rye standing in the open doorway. He nodded politely when he noticed her.

"Miss Lark."

"Hello, Mr. Rye."

"I understand you're not feeling well," Calvin said stiffly. "I don't intend to stay long."

Lucas braced one hand against the doorjamb. "What do you want, Rye?"

Calvin looked at him. "Dillon tells me he's going to work for Lodestar."

"Yes."

"I wanted you to know that I told him he had my approval and my blessing. Beatrice is anxious, naturally, but I've had a long talk with her. I think she understands."

"That Dillon needs to go off into the world on his own?" Lucas asked.

"That we can trust you to look after him," Calvin said deliberately. Without waiting for a response, he nodded to Amaryllis again and walked back down the steps.

Lucas closed the door very carefully and turned to look at Amaryllis.

"He knows the truth," Amaryllis said. "I could see it in his eyes."

"The truth about Jackson?"

"Yes. He's probably known it all along deep inside. He was Jackson's father, after all. He would have understood his son's weaknesses better than anyone. But he also knows that he can trust you to keep the family secret."

Amaryllis awoke sometime after midnight. She felt the familiar, intimate brush of awareness. Lucas was seeking a link. She opened her mind. Out on the psychic plane a prism shimmered into existence.

Glowing, exquisitely controlled power flowed gently through the sparkling crystal. Amaryllis savored the sensation.

"Am I hurting you?" Lucas asked. "If you're not ready for this, tell me."

"You're not hurting me." Amaryllis smiled into the darkness. "I love you, Lucas."

Power surged through the prism in a glorious rush of light. Lucas turned on his side and gathered Amaryllis into his arms. "I wish I had the words to tell you how much I love you."

"You just said it." She touched his cheek.

He bent his head to kiss her. Talent flowed, brilliant and beautiful and so powerful that it took Amaryllis's breath.

Lucas raised his head. "Are you sure you're up to this?"

She pulled his mouth back down to hers. "I won't break."

"Just one thing you and I need to straighten out here, Trent." Oscar studied the grove of giant hybrid fern-trees that surrounded the rear terrace of the old mansion. "You'll have to do a better job of keeping

Amaryllis out of trouble if you're going to marry her. She's been in one scrape after another since she met you."

Lucas handed Oscar a cold bottle of Five Hells beer. "Don't worry, I'm going to insist that she accept only routine focus assignments from here on."

"You do that." Oscar took a swallow of beer and wandered closer to the nearest fern-tree. "If you can."

The phone rang somewhere inside the house. Lucas ignored it. Hannah and Amaryllis were in the kitchen. One of them could answer it.

"Hell of a garden you've got here." Oscar pulled down a massive frond to examine it with professional interest.

"Place used to belong to a horti-talent."

"Horti-talents always go in for the fancy stuff. We ag-talents prefer to concentrate on crops that have some practical use."

Lucas hid a grin. "Is that a fact?"

"It is." Oscar released the huge frond. He looked at Lucas. "I won't pretend that I'm entirely satisfied with this marriage you're planning. I'd feel a hell of a lot better about it if you two had met through an agency. But I can see that Amaryllis has her heart set on marrying you. Just remember what I once told you. Hurt her and I'll—"

"Lucas?" Amaryllis appeared in the doorway. "Phone call for you. Shall I take a message?"

"No, that's all right. I need a good excuse to get away from Oscar here. He's lecturing me again."

Amaryllis frowned at Oscar. "I told you to stop that, Uncle Oscar."

"Can't help myself," Oscar said.

"The hell he can't." Lucas brushed Amaryllis's arm and her mind in a light, fleeting caress as he went past her to take the phone call. "He plans to spend the next six months trying to scare me off."

"Aunt Hannah will handle him," Amaryllis assured Lucas.

"Somebody better or I'll have to do it myself." Lucas picked up the phone. "This is Trent."

"Mr. Trent. Hobart Batt here. As we marriage counselors like to say at times like this, have I got a girl for you."

"Forget it, Batt. I've decided to cancel my registration with Synergistic Connections."

"What?" Hobart sucked in air. "But, Mr. Trent, you don't want to do that. I've got a wonderful match for you."

"I'm no longer in the market."

"Just let me tell you about this one. It's a bit unusual. However, I can assure you that I've already spoken to Miss Lark's counselor. Mrs. Reeton and I have double-checked our results. We are convinced that this is an excellent match."

Lucas held the phone away from his ear and stared at it in stunned amazement. Then he repeated the only two words he had heard clearly.

"Miss Lark? Miss Amaryllis Lark?"

"Why, yes. You once asked me if I had ever matched a high-class talent and a full-spectrum prism. I told you at the time that such matches were rare, but they did occur occasionally."

Lucas started to laugh.

"Mr. Trent? Are you listening?"

Lucas laughed harder.

"The thing is," Hobart Batt continued in a determined tone, "we feel that your strengths and those of Miss Lark nicely complement each other. Definitely a synergistic balance between the two of you. Certainly there will be areas of slight disagreement. There's no such thing as an exact match. We are dealing with human beings here, after all, but on the whole . . . Mr. Trent, is something wrong?"

Lucas did not respond. He was laughing so hard that he dropped the phone.

"Lucas?" Amaryllis smiled quizzically from the doorway. "What's so funny?"

"You aren't going to believe this." He strode toward her, caught her up in his arms, and swung her around in a circle. Then he pulled her close and cupped her face between his hands. "We're a perfect match."

Hobart Batt's tinny voice continued to babble somewhere in the distance. Lucas ignored it. All he cared about was the love that shone more brilliant than a thousand massed jelly-lamps in Amaryllis's eyes.

"For some odd reason," Amaryllis said, "that doesn't come as any great surprise."

Lucas grinned. "No, it doesn't."

He bent his head to kiss her. Out on the psychic plane a crystal clear prism formed. Energy poured through it in a rainbow of color that seemed to stretch out into the future.

The focus was perfect.

Just like the woman in his arms, Lucas thought.